Sucking Ben and Joey into my scheme was easy. They didn't suspect a thing when I pulled a cute poochie act and dragged my leash into the living room . . .

How much cozier can a couple get than to take a walk in the park with a cute, frolicking dog—me, in other words? For the cause, I could lower myself to being downright adorable, though it did turn my stomach.

As we walked, I pranced around in typical dog fashion, managing to wrap the leash around their legs. My victims couldn't possibly have suspected ulterior motives. One of the few advantages of being a dog is that no one ever suspects you. Humans think that dogs aren't smart enough to plot. They are so wrong!

I got Ben and Joey into such a tangle they nearly went down one on top of the other. They were as close as two people can be without being welded, and I didn't miss the spark that flew between them. If the voltage had been any higher, their hair would have stood on end. Am I good or what?

Bantam Books by Emily Carmichael

Finding Mr. Right

A Ghost for Maggie

DIAMOND
IN
THE RUFF

Emily Carmichael

BANTAM BOOKS

DIAMOND IN THE RUFF

A Bantam Book/November 2001

ISBN 0-553-58283-6

Published simultaneously in the United States and Canada

Bantam Books are published by Bantam Books, a division of Random
House, Inc. Its trademark, consisting of the words "Bantam Books" and the
portrayal of a rooster, is Registered in U.S. Patent and Trademark Office and
in other countries. Marca Registrada. Bantam Books, 1540 Broadway, New
York, New York 10036.

PRINTED IN THE UNITED STATES OF AMERICA

OPM   10 9 8 7 6 5 4 3 2

I would like to express a special, heartfelt thanks to three special Welsh corgis—Teri, Jack, and Bobbie, who spent many wonderful hours acquainting me with the inner workings of the corgi mind.

PROLOGUE

◆

I, LYDIA KEANE, am proof that the universe is unjust. Really, really unjust. During my life, I made one or two mistakes. Well, maybe I made more than one or two, but nothing truly huge. Misjudgments, really. Small lapses of character from time to time. But these weren't my fault. In trying to walk the straight and narrow—and I did try, occasionally—I labored under a great disadvantage: I was gorgeous. Drop-dead, magnificently, deliciously gorgeous. I was also high-spirited, fun-loving, clever, witty, and unfailingly stylish. An absolute fox, if I do say so myself.

How is that a disadvantage, you ask? Don't all of us girls want to be beautiful? Of course. Absolutely. But do you know how many sinful opportunities plague a beautiful girl with a fun-loving temperament? Legion, I tell you. I should have gotten a medal for resisting at least half the propositions that came my way. But did I get a medal? No, I didn't get a medal. I got murdered.

My untimely demise was in an alley behind a restaurant in Denver, Colorado. A lowlife who had just broken into my date's car took offense when we chased him into an alley.

Actually, my stupid macho date chased him into an alley. I'm not quite that stupid. Stupid enough to follow, though. Big mistake. It got me killed.

Now, some would have us believe that death can be a downright cheerful experience: the recently deceased floating toward a heavenly light, maybe a little singing, peace, joy, and all that garbage. Maybe for some, but not for me. All I got was an unpleasant interview in a place I can only describe as limbo. It certainly wasn't Heaven. And the fellow who interviewed me, a being with the improbable name of Stanley, was nobody's idea of an angel. He looked rather like Mr. Collins, the high school principal who used to automatically give me detention whenever he saw me. Mr. Collins was short, scrawny, and middle-aged, with a bad haircut and a perpetually pinched expression. So is Stanley. You'll notice that I refer to him in the present tense, because the troublesome fellow is still around. Forever, unfortunately. It was my bad luck that Stan is very starchy about rules of the Sunday-school sort.

To make a long story short, I wasn't exactly on the A list in the afterlife. The Powers That Be weren't pleased with my casual attitude toward a lot of things, morality being one of them. The big-ticket item seemed to be that I'd been getting it on with my best friend Amy's husband, who just happened to be my date and co-victim the night I met the Grim Reaper. Stanley gave me a lecture blistering enough to qualify as the first level of hell—except that he assured me there was no hell à la fire and brimstone. What he had in mind for me was much worse. He assigned me a task as atonement for my sins—to travel back to Earth to find a perfect new husband for my friend Amy.

The job should have been easy, even though Amy is a bit of a dork. There's no one better than me at reeling in men, and I thought it would be a snap to throw one Amy's way. At least, that's what I thought until I woke up in the same stinking alley where I'd met my end, and a glance into a rain puddle showed me the reflection of a mangy, flea-bitten, sausage-shaped dog with big pointy ears and no tail.

Now you realize the extent of Stanley's twisted sense of humor. I, a bright, terrific-looking woman, had been transformed into a pudgy little Welsh corgi, a weasely dog that looks like a stumpy-legged fox on steroids—one who's lost its tail. You can imagine my dismay. I'd never cared much for dogs; they're smelly, noisy creatures who leave hair on the furniture and nose prints on the windows. Let's not even mention their appalling sanitary habits. My friend Amy was the one who was dog crazy—dog shows, dog classes, dog trials, dog clubs. The list of her doggy activities was endless, and Stanley had it all planned that I would join her furry four-legged household. His goal was to make things as difficult and embarrassing for me as possible, I'm sure.

But in spite of the difficulties, the obstacles, the utter humiliation of being a dog, I performed my mission to the utmost. I swallowed my bitter pill with just the tiniest bit of complaint and covered myself with glory, not only finding Amy the perfect husband but saving her life as well. I did everything Stan expected of me. Everything and more. And if there were a couple of missteps and detours along the way, no one has the right to complain. I was trying to work in a stupid dog suit, for heaven's sake. You can't expect perfection.

But enough about my adventures with Amy; I've already told that story in another volume, and if you want the details, you'll have to read it. Just take my word that I performed miracles, with absolutely no heavenly help. And did I get my just reward? Did I get to spend the rest of eternity strumming a *harp and admiring my wings? Hardly! Stan dished out more injustice. The twerpy bureaucrat gave me a choice: promotion to a position involving even more work and more responsibility, or the dubious privilege of living out the dog's life—as a dog, of course.*

Now, I've never been big on work and responsibility, so the prospect of promotion didn't appeal. On the other hand, being a dog involved a host of disadvantages. No phone or refrigerator privileges, a monotonous diet, and the only powder room is the backyard, where everyone who cares to look can watch you take care of very personal business. Embarrassing.

Being one of Amy's spoiled pooches wasn't as bad as it could have been, however. I got to sleep on the bed, and if I was very clever, I ended up with all the pillows. Lying around the house all day isn't bad duty, and by that point, the other household dogs, Molly and Drover, had learned to give me the respect I deserve.

So I chose the life of a dog. It would be a vacation of sorts, I told myself, and this little angel in a dog suit deserved a vacation. If only Stanley would leave me alone.

And that was the greatest injustice: He didn't.

CHAPTER 1

◆

"I THINK THERE'S a natural law," Josephine DeMato grumbled to Samantha Cole, whose sturdy frame barely fit into the passenger seat of Joey's classic Triumph TR-6. "Freeway traffic increases in direct proportion to a person's need to get somewhere in a hurry."

Samantha glanced at her watch. "We have twenty-five minutes if you want to be there by ten."

Joey made a face. "You'd think that would be enough time to get from north Denver to Boulder, wouldn't you? Really, wouldn't you? But look at this!" She waved a hand toward the clogged highway. "I can understand Interstate 25 being a parking lot on weekdays, but this is Saturday, for cripes' sake."

"Twenty-three minutes."

Joey sent her passenger a sharp look. "What are you, Mission Control?"

Samantha grinned. "Houston, we have a problem."

"Funny."

"I was teasing, boss lady. It's the duty of a good

assistant to keep the boss apprised of schedule difficulties. And also to help the boss to lighten up. Don't worry. It's the bride and groom who are supposed to be nervous, not the wedding consultant. Marcia and Donald are not going to panic because you're fifteen minutes late. It's their wedding day. They're both numb."

"I hate it when things don't go as planned."

"In your six years of doing this, when has anything gone exactly as planned?"

Joey rolled her eyes. "Pretty much never."

"So stop worrying. You always manage to make things look perfect, no matter what goes wrong."

"Sometimes things stay closer to the plan than other times. This is going to be one of those times when miracles are called for. I feel it in my bones. I can't believe the photographer double-booked. It's a good thing I called him before we left."

"So that was the ear-blistering I heard you delivering."

"You bet. I give that man over fifteen thousand dollars of business every year in referrals. I told him if he made a scheduling mistake, he'd better find a way to be in two places at the same time, or his business was going to dry up faster than a puddle in Death Valley. I wish Amy Cameron was available. She's a better photographer."

"You mean Amy Berenger."

"Berenger, right. She married that hunky veterinarian in one of the weirdest weddings I've ever seen. Oh good!" She punched the accelerator and darted into an almost imaginary space between traffic in the next lane.

The pickup truck behind her honked. She flashed him an apologetic smile in her rearview mirror, but his responding gesture was anything but forgiving. Joey shrugged. "Usually the smile works."

Ten long minutes passed between the I-70 interchange and the exit to the Boulder Turnpike, but once on the turnpike, they cruised along on a much more open road. "This is more like it," Joey declared as the scenery began to fly by.

Samantha continued the countdown. "Twelve minutes."

"We'll be late, but not that late."

They were just past Sheridan Boulevard when blue lights started flashing in the rearview mirror.

"Uh-oh," Samantha said. "Denver's finest."

"Damn! What else can go wrong?" Joey glanced down at the speedometer and grimaced. "The sneaky so-and-so. Where do these guys hide, anyway?" She pulled to a stop on the shoulder and endured the smirks of passing motorists. This was really, really not turning out to be a good day.

The officer who peered down at her as she lowered her window looked as if he didn't give a damn what kind of day she was having. The obligatory sunglasses hid his eyes, but his face was set in grim lines of constabulary displeasure. It was a face neither old nor young, but it might have passed for handsome if its expression hadn't been reminiscent of a grizzly bear on the prowl. The square jaw was set and downright combative, the mouth a grim line etched from granite. In defiance of police dress code, he wore no hat, and short black hair ruffled in the February breeze. The thin line of a scar nicked his chin—probably the legacy of a teed-off motorist, Joey thought peevishly.

"Good morning, Officer." She smiled and did her best to look charming. Sometimes it worked.

He didn't sound at all charmed. "Ma'am, do you know how fast you were driving?"

"Sixty?"

"Eighty."

"Oh dear," she said innocently. "My speedometer must be wrong."

The grim mouth slanted upward. "Like I haven't heard that one before, Flash."

Joey's eyes narrowed. Not only grim, but sarcastic as well. "Aren't you people supposed to be at least polite?"

"I am being polite. May I *please* see your registration, driver's license, and insurance card?"

"Just a minute." Opening the glove compartment without bruising Samantha's knees was a feat, but finally they managed it. Then Joey began digging through the confetti of gas receipts, owner's manual, stereo manual, a jumble of tape cassettes, a sewing kit, maps, and a hairbrush in search of the required documents.

"Today would be good," the cop commented.

"Just hold your horses," Joey snapped, bent over Samantha's lap to paw through the glove box. "They're here somewhere."

"Joey!" Samantha whispered a warning. "Be polite to the cop!"

"This is a very cheeky cop!" she hissed back.

"Just don't be cheeky back!"

"That would take the fun out of getting a ticket," Joey growled sotto voce. "Here it is," she said finally, struggling back upright and shoving the documents out the window. "There! Anything else?"

The officer raised a brow at her driver's license.

"Yes, that *is* me," Joey assured him. "Contact lenses and a haircut," she said coldly, reaching out to take the license from his hand. He held it firmly, not letting it go while he peered down at her.

"Hair color change?"

She sighed impatiently. "Yes. Officer, women change their hair all the time without criminal intentions."

He gave her a look. She gritted her teeth. "Could we hurry this along, please? I'm late for an appointment."

"Is that so?"

The Neanderthal was enjoying this. Joey could tell from the beginnings of his smirky smile. "Yes," she snapped. "That's so. If I'm late, I might lose business. And if I lose business, maybe I can't pay my taxes. The taxes that pay *your* salary."

Above the mask of his shades, one brow arched upward. "If I miss my next paycheck, I'll know who to blame." He looked from the license to the registration. "This car isn't registered to you, Ms. DeMato. The owner is Harvey Jordan?"

"No. It's my car. I bought it a couple of weeks ago, but I haven't had time to change over the registration."

"I need to see the bill of sale, then."

Joey's heart dropped. "Bill of sale?"

"Yes, the bill of sale."

"Well, I have the bill of sale, of course, and the title certificate as well, but they're back at my house."

He sighed. "Step out of the car, please."

"Why?" she demanded.

"You are a very difficult woman. Do you know that?"

"I'm not difficult. I'm busy. And I'm late."

"Well, Flash, you're going to be later. Just get out of the car, would you? You too." He flashed a look at Samantha.

Samantha nudged Joey, who heaved a sigh and extricated herself from the car as gracefully as she could; it was a very small car and she was a fairly lanky woman. Her long legs were not made for graceful exits from sports cars, and the straight, knee-length skirt of her tailored suit didn't make the task any easier. The cop kept a straight face when she pulled her skirt back down to her knees, but the lines around his eyes deepened, bearing witness that behind those dark glasses, the eyes were laughing. She was in no mood to be laughed at.

"You're a difficult man. Do you know that?"

He actually grinned as she threw his words back at him. "That's my job, ma'am."

She sniffed. "You do it very well."

"We aim to please."

"Right," she replied, nettled. "What now? Hands on the car and spread 'em?"

"That might be entertaining, but not necessary. I do think a brief search is called for, though, considering the lack of title or bill of sale."

"Lay a hand on me and I'll—"

"The car, Flash. A car search."

"Oh." Her face heated. "Search away, then."

As he bent down to conduct his absurd search, Joey contemplated the effect her rather pointy-toed shoes might have on his backside if driven by the indignant power of her foot. How she wished she had the nerve. It was a nicely tight backside, she observed as an aside.

Samantha came to stand beside her and watched anxiously. She looked at her watch. "We have five minutes to get to the church."

"Thanks to Mr. 'Serve and Protect' here, we're not going to make it."

"We have plenty of time before the ceremony, though. I know you like to get there way early to fix any last-minute problems, but maybe there won't be any problems."

"If the day continues as it has been, the church will have blown up."

"Oh, I hope he doesn't find that little box of tampons I put behind the seat. I would be so embarrassed."

He did, but it was the only thing of note he found besides two ballpoint pens, a lint remover, an iron, and a box of tissues. Joey hoped he was mortally embarrassed, but he didn't look it.

"You ladies can get back in the car now."

"What?" Joey gibed. "No cocaine or marijuana? No bodies in the trunk?"

He had the nerve to look amused. "You could be arrested for that mouth of yours, Flash."

She glared.

"Okay. *Please* get back into the car."

"Are we done?"

"No, we're not done. Stay put."

"I don't believe this," Joey muttered as the officer marched back to his car and spoke to his partner, who no doubt had been running their plates on the patrol car's computer. "This could take all day."

"This always happens when a person can least afford the time," Samantha agreed, wedging herself back into the Triumph.

"I feel a case of road rage coming on. What's taking him so long?"

"You might as well get in the car, dear."

"The way my luck is running today, the guy I bought this car from will have Grand Theft Auto stamped across his records."

An eternity seemed to pass before the patrolman sauntered once more to the car window and handed her a speeding ticket. "Here you go, Flash. Try to drive the speed limit from now on, okay?"

"Can I go now?" Joey asked through clenched teeth.

"Be my guest." He gave her an infuriating smile. "You have a nice day now."

"Right back at you, Officer." As she pulled out, the rueful shake of his head showed he knew exactly what she meant.

They arrived at the church nearly a half hour after Joey had planned to be there. Predictably, things were in an uproar. The bride paced the ladies' dressing room in her petticoat. Her bridesmaids and maid of honor hovered about her looking like a flock of taffeta-clad pumpkins. The color scheme of the wedding was white and gold, but the material the bride had selected looked remarkably orange once made up into the bridesmaids' gowns.

"Where have you been?" the bride crossly demanded of Joey when she walked into the dressing room. "Donald isn't here yet, the ushers aren't here yet, and you weren't anywhere to be found. You promised you would be here by—"

"I know, I know. Traffic held me up. I'm sorry."

"I've been frantic! This isn't the kind of service I expected of a top wedding consultant! And Donald! Where the hell is he?"

"Marcia, relax." Joey pushed aside the problems of the morning and donned her serene everything-is-going-to-be-perfect face for the nervous girl. "Grooms are always late for the wedding. It's tradition. You wouldn't want to break tradition, would you?"

Marcia's face crumpled. "If that's tradition, it's bullshit! How could he be late to his own wedding?"

"Is that wad of lace over there your veil? Tch, tch! Robyn"—she looked at the maid of honor—"would you find Samantha and ask her to fetch the iron from my car, please? The sleeves of Marcia's gown need a bit of a touch-up as well. Thank you, dear," she said as the girl left. "Sit down, Marcia. You're going to overwhelm your deodorant. Dollie"—she commandeered another attendant—"how about going to the church kitchen and getting all of us something cold to drink from the fridge? Sound good?"

While the bride and her ladies were chilling out, Joey headed for the sanctuary to make sure everything there was as it should be. It wasn't. The flowers had been delivered, but they were white roses, not the

yellow Marcia had selected. Out came Joey's cell
phone, and a chagrined florist confessed to confusion.
The yellow roses had been delivered to the reception
hall, where the white roses were supposed to be. Joey
demanded a truck be dispatched posthaste to do the
exchange. The florist quibbled, but Joey won. She
usually did. When Samantha hurried in with the iron,
Joey gave her the keys to the Triumph with instructions to drive to the reception hall and make sure the
exchange was done properly.

Meanwhile, the groom and best man arrived. The
groom looked anxious, as befitted a groom. The best
man looked solemn, as befitted a man delivering a best
friend into the thrall of matrimony. And they both
looked hungover from the bachelor party the night before. At least they'd remembered to bring their tuxedos. Joey dispatched them to the men's dressing room
with instructions to use a cold cloth on their faces and
to send the tuxedos over to the ladies' dressing room to
get a last minute touch-up from the iron.

Joey had said hello to the minister, soothed the
ruffled feathers of the photographer, who was still
smarting from the tongue-lashing she'd given him earlier, and was headed back to the ladies' dressing room
when her cell phone tweedled. It was the carriage
rental—yes, carriage rental. Marcia had wanted to be
conveyed from her wedding in a fancy carriage ever
since she'd seen pictures of the Prince and Princess of
Wales's wedding. The ill fate of that union hadn't di-
minished her longing, and Joey had managed to find a
stable in Boulder that actually rented such a thing, not
of royal vintage, but good enough. Bad luck, the rather

crusty old stable manager told her on the cell phone. Just that morning, not an hour ago, the carriage had broken a wheel.

"Fix it," Joey suggested gently, clenching her teeth.

She listened to explanations of why that was impossible in such a short time. One couldn't just use some piece of scrap wood to replace a broken spoke. It had to be crafted, turned, fitted.

"Certainly not scrap wood," Joey agreed. "How about whittling down a nice table leg, or a chair leg. Just as a stopgap. The route from church to reception is less than a mile. And there'll be practically no weight in the carriage. The bride is a tiny thing. Size six at the largest. And the groom's a scarecrow. The wheel would probably do very well without a spoke at all."

She listened, grimacing, to his outrage. She was the first to admit that she knew nothing about carriage wheels or what was required to keep them in order. But she did know that she would have one very disappointed bride if that carriage didn't show up.

"I sympathize with your concerns, Mr. Redfern. I truly do. And if it just isn't possible, then it isn't possible. It's a shame, though, because at least two other people expressed an interest in such an unusual wedding conveyance, and they're attending this wedding. They both have weddings in the near future. I know you haven't used the carriage for this purpose before, and you might have found a blossoming business in this sort of thing. But if it doesn't work, then . . ."

She listened and nodded as he backpedaled at bit, speculated on solutions, and then gave his promise that the carriage would be there on time. Thanking him profusely, Joey rolled her eyes as Samantha walked up. She punched the "end" button with a satisfied flourish.

"The flowers are done. Who was that?"

"The stable. It's a miracle what the mention of money can do. The carriage wheel broke, but they'll fix it in time."

Samantha smiled sentimentally. "It brings back to mind one of my weddings—the second one. An antique Model A Ford was supposed to carry us to the reception, but halfway there the thing died. Deader than a brick. My new husband took off his coat and got under the hood with the driver. They had a great time getting greasy and banging on this and that with a wrench and screwdriver. I'm sure Henry would have rather stayed with that stupid car than go to the reception. We ended up calling a taxi." Samantha sighed. "It was a sign, sure thing. I should have known right then how things were going to end up."

"Well, I hope the carriage is the last crisis."

"It isn't. The bride is in the dressing room in tears."

"I'd be in tears too if I were marrying Donald."

Samantha grinned. "That's not it, fortunately. She's gained a pound or five since the last dress fitting, that's all."

Joey found Marcia sniveling in the midst of her attendants. Her wedding dress—a confection of lace and satin whose cost nearly equaled that of the entire reception—hung off her shoulders and gaped open in back.

"Now, Marcia," Joey said firmly. "No tears on your wedding day. There's no problem that can't be solved."

"My dress won't fasten," Marcia choked out. "I knew I shouldn't have had that pie last night."

"One piece of pie?"

"Practically the whole pie," the maid of honor informed them. "With ice cream."

Marcia gave a liquid sniff. "I was nervous."

"Don't worry," Joey told the distraught bride. "A tiny thing like you, with your metabolism, will take it off in no time." She pulled the dress into its proper position and observed the ugly pucker of the precisely fitted bodice. "Suck it in," she advised.

"I can't suck it in any more than it's sucked," Marcia wailed.

"Don't start crying again, sweetie. It's not a tragedy. Mama Joey is going to fix it."

"You are?"

"I am."

Joey always carried a sewing kit in her oversized handbag. That and the half dozen other emergency items were why the bag was oversized. Whipping out tiny scissors and white thread, she set to work moving buttons over the amount required to compensate for last night's pie.

"What you need to remember," she advised her charge, "is that today isn't about the dress, the flowers, the carriage, the band, the tuxedos, and the champagne. Today is about you starting a life with Donald, the man you love. Even without all the wedding trappings, this would be the happiest day of your life, right?"

Marcia's eyes met Joey's in the mirror as Joey fastened the last button of the now smoothly fitting gown. "Right." Her voice was a bit tremulous, but her eyes had begun to glow with something other than tears. "You're the best, Joey."

"I'll put that on my resumé," Joey said with a smile. "Let's get this veil on your head. Judy certainly did a wonderful job on your hair. All these curls!"

Finally, the bride looked suitably beautiful. The pumpkin bridesmaids were all zipped, primped, and ready to go, including the seven-year-old flower girl, who had required the services of "Mama Joey" to properly tie her pumpkin-colored hair ribbon. Marcia and her attendants all laughed about the sobriquet. Indeed Joey did step into the mothering role with many of her clients, acting as confidante and adviser, sometimes as a defender or go-between for the bride.

"You all look beautiful," Joey told the group. "Let's head for the foyer to line up, just like in the rehearsal. And Marcia—don't breathe too deeply, sweetie. Remember the buttons. But do try to breathe."

As the bride and her ladies filed out, Joey spared a moment to check herself in the full-length mirror. She always took great care about her appearance at her weddings, dressing elegantly, professionally, but in a manner that allowed her to fade into the background. Joey was the director of the grand event, but the bride was the star. The measure of a wedding consultant's success, Joey believed, was how little she was noticed.

In spite of the harrowing morning, she looked cool and collected. Her tailored beige suit was elegantly understated. The French braid that she'd labored over had just a few rich brown tendrils making a bid for freedom, just enough to keep her from looking too severe.

A quick brush of powder across her nose defeated the beginnings of a shine.

Joey counted herself fortunate in her looks. No one would ever call her beautiful. But she wore clothes well, having a tall, athletic figure with long legs and slim hips. And if her shoulders might have done a linebacker proud, they were easily toned down by wearing the right clothes. Other flaws were legion: Her mouth was too wide, her teeth too big, and her brows—her own mother had frequently noted—were fit only for a gorilla. She could have tweezed them, but that was too much bother. Taken as a whole, though, her face was striking, even if it wasn't exactly pretty.

"Such an honest face," she told the image in the mirror. How could that wiseacre cop have given a ticket to someone with such an innocent, honest face? He obviously was a very poor judge of character. She smiled wryly, half amused, half annoyed. Be cool, she reminded herself. Cool and calm. It was just too bad that she couldn't get an intravenous slug of aspirin.

By some miracle, the rest of the wedding and reception went off without a hitch. The groom managed to pull himself together enough to say his vows, Marcia's dress held together, the photographer didn't run out of film or videotape, and the carriage pulled up just in time to carry the bridal couple to the reception, where everyone enjoyed mystery chicken—or was it pork?—and vanilla cake iced with enough sugar rosettes to kill an elephant. Joey was on her feet more than she was in her seat, checking on the band, the photographer, the caterer, and making sure the little pack of preteen cousins didn't stage a second raid on the champagne.

She was endlessly grateful that Marcia had engaged someone else to cater the affair, for often she did that as well.

As the reception wound down and Joey wound down as well, Samantha pulled up the chair next to her. "Another couple dispatched to happily ever after," the older woman said, stretching her tired back.

"We can only hope."

Samantha smiled mistily. "It's always so romantic at the beginning."

"You should know," Joey said with a chuckle. "This last husband was which number?"

"Three. But he lasted only six months, so he scarcely counts."

"At least it's made you a real expert on weddings."

"On-the-job training, you might say."

They both laughed. "We're getting punchy," Joey warned, stretching.

"Or champagney."

"Time to go home. I have company coming over tonight. Amy Berenger, in fact."

"Ooooh! Is she bringing the hunky husband?"

"I don't know, but she is bringing a couple of her dogs. I'm keeping them while she and Jeff take a month's trip to Hawaii."

Samantha snickered. "It would be more fun to keep Jeff while Amy takes the dogs to Hawaii."

"Like I have time for a man." Joey sighed. "After so many weddings—some for repeat clients, coming back with different partners after the first wedding didn't stick—I don't have an ounce of romance left in my brain. I not only don't need a man, I don't even want a man."

Samantha shook her head sympathetically. "What you need is a vacation."

"What I need," Joey said emphatically, "is a thirty-six-hour day and a full bottle of aspirin."

Joey liked Amy Berenger. She was a nice person, a talented photographer, and very pretty in a down-home, unpretentious fashion, with snappy blue eyes and a mop of curly hair that owed its style more to nature than design. Amy's only odd quirk was the dogs. She was totally gone to the dogs. Before she'd married, her house had been ruled by corgis—short-legged, foxy little dogs who thought they were created to boss the universe. When she married Jeff Berenger, her husband's two border collies had joined the pack, and her best friend's collie visited so often that the odds were a fairly steady three dogs to every person.

Joey didn't quite understand the lifestyle. Amy was constantly vacuuming dog hair from the floor or picking up you-know-what from the backyard. Her dishwasher had more dog dishes in it than people dishes, and her bookshelves overflowed with pet supply catalogs, training manuals, and old dog-show judging programs.

When Amy wasn't photographing weddings—frequently Joey DeMato's weddings—she was hopping from dog show to dog show, her decrepit motor home filled with corgis, border collies, and, occasionally, her husband, who was a veterinarian. Joey didn't understand it, but Amy didn't seem to expect her to. It wasn't that Joey didn't like dogs. She did, especially dogs who were affectionate and obedient, cuddly and entertaining. She'd had a dog when she was growing up, a golden retriever, so she knew the basics of canine care. The offer to keep two of Amy's while Amy and Jeff were in Hawaii, however—that probably had been a moment of insanity.

She wasn't going to back out, though. With Joey, a promise given was a promise kept. After all, corgis were small and cute. How much trouble could they be?

So when Joey opened the front door that night to Amy's smiling face, Joey had only the slightest bit of trepidation.

"Amy! Hi!"

"Hi, Joey!" Amy gave her an affectionate hug. "This is such a nice thing for you to do. Are you sure? You can back out, you know."

"No, I don't want to back out." Joey bent to greet the corgi who sat politely beside his mistress. "Who is this handsome fellow?"

"This is Drover. You've met Drover lots of times."

"Sure. I remember. Such a sweet face!"

"He's a sweet boy. Goofy, but sweet."

"And here's Jeff," Joey noted as Jeff Berenger, six feet plus and boyishly handsome, walked up the steps to her front porch.

Amy smiled. "He's sweet, too."

"But not nearly as handsome as Drover," Jeff said with a grin.

They all laughed. The second corgi, the one bringing up the rear on the end of Jeff's leash, looked annoyed. She plunked her fat little tailless butt onto the porch and regarded them with indignant brown eyes.

"This must be Piggy," Joey said.

"This is Piggy," Amy confirmed with a sigh.

"Are you sweet as well?"

Jeff laughed. "No. Piggy isn't sweet."

Amy shot him a look. "She's sweet in her own unique way. But Joey, she is a bit peculiar. Are you sure you want to put up with her?"

"Come on, Amy! She's a little dog, and didn't you say her favorite pastime is sleeping on the couch? How much trouble could she be?"

Jeff laughed again.

"Come in, you guys. Let's have a glass of wine to celebrate your leaving for Hawaii tomorrow. You're going to have such a good time!"

Joey brought a chilled bottle of cabernet and three glasses into the living room, where Amy, Jeff, and Drover had settled onto the couch. Amy grinned as she accepted her glass. "I see you're prepared for our coming."

"The throws on the couch and chairs? Yes indeed. You did warn me that corgis consider all furniture to be theirs, and I know how spoiled your dogs are. Don't deny it."

"I can't."

"But look at poor Piggy." Joey squatted down beside the pudgy little sausage shape that sat stoically in the middle of the living room rug. "She looks very put out. Poor dear isn't exactly an affectionate, cuddly sort, I can tell."

"I've known her for almost a year," Jeff said, "and I haven't seen an ounce of cuddly anywhere."

Amy leaped to the little dog's defense. "She's unique."

"Well, at least she doesn't push me into creeks and poop in my shoes anymore," Jeff admitted.

Joey scratched Piggy's ears. "But isn't this the dog who saved Amy's life when that awful newsman tried to do her in?"

"It certainly is!" Amy said with a mock glare at her husband. "You should remember that when you say such uncomplimentary things about her."

"I remember it. How could anyone forget? She milks that one good deed for all it's worth."

Amy gave him a playful push. "Ungrateful lout!"

"Why should I be grateful?" he said, chuckling. "It wasn't me she saved."

"Well, at least she won't be any trouble," Joey concluded, "if all she does is sit around the house and look put-upon."

Amy and Jeff didn't stay long, because their flight left Denver International very early the next morning. Amy left a typewritten page of instructions for feeding, grooming, and disciplining, along with the number of her friend Selma, who was caring for Amy's third corgi and Jeff's border collies. Joey was sure she didn't need an instruction manual to care for two small dogs, but she assured Amy she would read every word, then gave her friend a hug before closing the door behind them. Finally alone with her two charges, she regarded the dogs with a measuring stare. They stared right back. Drover still sat on the couch. Piggy hadn't moved from the center of the rug. Both regarded her with critically questioning expressions on their foxy little faces.

"We'll get along just fine," Joey assured them. "As long as you follow the rules."

Drover grinned. Joey guessed that the good-natured boy seldom wore anything but that happy, accepting smile. Piggy, on the other hand, looked at her with narrowed eyes and a remarkably human expression.

"Rule one," Joey lectured. "No peeing on the floor. Or doing anything else on the floor, either. Understand?"

No response.

"Rule two: Wipe your little feet—all four of them—when you come in from the backyard. No muddy paw prints on my oak floors."

Drover cocked his head as if he understood.

"And here's the most important thing, so listen carefully. I've had a bad day, I am very tired, and tomorrow is Sunday. Wake me before eight, and I won't be responsible for what happens."

CHAPTER 2

◆

I CONTEMPLATED MY ill luck as I lay curled on the rug beside Joey DeMato's bed. This was going to be a very trying month. Not that I held it against Joey that she wasn't dog crazy like Amy. At one time I would have heartily agreed with her. I've never cared much for dogs either, but since becoming a dog, I've had a shift of attitude. Life as a dog is hard enough without putting up with people who don't show you the proper respect. And a month is a long time in dog years. For the fiftieth time since Amy had dropped me at Joey's house, I reflected that I should have accepted Stanley's offer of promotion. Being a hardworking middle-management angel wasn't my idea of a great afterlife, but it beat being a heroic but underappreciated dog.

As if my thoughts had conjured him from wherever he spends his time, Stanley himself popped into the room. Dressed in jeans and a Denver Broncos sweatshirt, he perched on the window seat and regarded me with the characteristic smugness that always made me grit my teeth.

"Yo, Piggy."

Stanley trying to be cool is as ridiculous as Barry Manilow trying to be hip. It doesn't work.

"Yo, Stan," I returned. He hates the shortened version of his name as much as I hate the unflattering name Amy hung on me. "It's about time you turned up. Do you see what's happened here?"

Stanley smiled, my first hint that I might be in trouble. As I said earlier, he doesn't have much humor in his pinched soul, and what there is of it is unpleasant.

"Don't smile, Stanley. This isn't fair. I'm supposed to be the apple of Amy's eye, rolling in soft dog beds and liver cookies. And she's flown off to Hawaii with Dr. Dumb while I'm stuck here with a bitch who thinks dogs should sleep on the floor and eat only dog food."

Don't get me wrong. I didn't call Joey a bitch out of spite. The word was simply recognition that we shared a certain temperament. Becoming a dog taught me that there can be glory attached to being a bitch. I pride myself in it. But I wouldn't want to live with me, and I didn't want to live with Joey, either.

Stanley looked surprised. "You don't like Josephine De-Mato?"

"I'd rather be in Hawaii with Amy."

"If you were in Hawaii, you'd be quarantined in a stuffy kennel. They're particular about who they let in, you know."

Details, details. "Then send me there with two legs and opposable thumbs. A little vacation. I deserve it."

"You don't want to discuss what you deserve, young lady. You've had one minor success in atonement. That scarcely makes up for all those years of venial behavior when you were a woman."

Venial behavior. Do you see why I call him uptight?

I spent a few minutes reminding him that my success had been anything but minor—spectacular was a more likely description—and how I really deserved a better deal, but I knew it was hopeless from the start. Once Stanley sets his mind, he never listens to reason.

"Stop your whining, Lydia."

At least now he was calling me by my real name.

"If you're so bored, you might try your hand at a little project I have in mind."

"Project?" I asked suspiciously. Stan's last project almost got me killed for a second time.

"Nothing in Heaven or Earth happens without purpose, my dear. You are with Josephine for a reason. She's about to join a crew sailing into turbulent waters."

Like I cared?

"This project involves both romance and a bit of danger—both your specialties. You showed definite promise in extricating Amy from her problems and neutralizing a very real threat to her life. It would be a waste of talent not to develop that promise."

When Stan starts throwing out the compliments, you know things are going to be rough. I didn't like that hint about danger. "Suppose I say no?"

"Now, Lydia—do you really think you're in a position to say no?"

I should have seen it coming. Blackmail, pure and simple. Commit a few minor sins in your life and you hear about it forever. And I do mean forever.

I heaved a great sigh, surrendering, but not with good grace. "All right. Tell me about it."

He literally rubbed his hands together with satisfaction, and I wished I had been satisfied with just being bored.

The hour was nowhere near eight the next morning when Joey opened her eyes to see another set of eyes—big brown ones set below perky pointed ears—regarding her with unwavering, hopeful attention. She could just barely see, because the room was a dull morning gray, but Drover was very close—on top of her, in fact, flat on his stomach, the length of him stretched out from her chest to mid-thigh.

She groaned. "Too early."

He didn't even blink.

"Eight o'clock. I told you eight o'clock, you little monster."

Drover wuffed softly.

"Get off me and go back to sleep." Corgis might be small, Joey discovered, but they were not lightweights. Breathing had become hard labor. "Get off!" Disgruntled, she pushed herself upward. The dog stayed just long enough to let her know that he really didn't have to go, then nonchalantly hopped off of her. But he didn't go far. With another patient woof he settled near Joey's pillow like a furry sphinx, watching her expectantly.

Joey grunted sleepily. "Where's your friend? Ah, there you are, Piggy."

Piggy was curled at the foot of the bed, looking on with queenly condescension.

"Didn't we start out the night with you two on the floor?"

Neither of the dogs looked in the least ashamed.

"Never mind." Joey sighed and wilted back into her pillows. "Sleep where you want. Just sleep. Or let yourself into the yard. Make your own breakfast. Just be quiet about it." She closed her eyes and drifted, luxuriating in the knowledge that no one was getting married today, at least no one she knew. She didn't have to answer her cell phone; it could stay firmly turned off. Her part-time office manager wouldn't be in today, and neither would Samantha. She could close the door to her home office and pretend it wasn't even there. Blessed, blessed Sunday.

Drover whined.

"Quiet! Sleep."

He was quiet, but he didn't go to sleep. He belly-crawled across the bed until his nose was inches from Joey's face. Hot dog breath steamed her cheek; soft panting puffed against her ear. For a few minutes Joey kept her eyes tightly, determinedly shut. Finally, she grumbled, "I don't believe it. What time is it?" She squinted at the bedside clock radio. "Six A.M., and you're going to make me get up." Tossing back the covers, she skewered them both with reproachful looks. "Amy owes me big time. I hope you furry little freeloaders learn the meaning of 'sleep in' really soon." She pulled on a terry-cloth robe. "I had a golden retriever once," she informed her little guests as they jumped off the bed and bounced around her feet. "Her name was Blondie. Golden retrievers are smart, you know. She let me sleep in any time I wanted. She lived a long, happy life and didn't die until she was very old. You could learn something from that."

The kitchen windows were on fire with a glorious Colorado sunrise, but Joey didn't appreciate the splendor. She saw entirely too many sunrises during the week and on the many weekends when she had to rise early to prepare for someone's big day. This particular sunrise she could have done without. To make the morning even more irritating, as she poured herself a cup of coffee she spied her traffic ticket still lying where she'd chucked it onto the kitchen table the day before. The sight of it inspired a sigh.

"I should write to the police department and complain about that smart-mouth cop. Really I should. It would be a public service."

Drover bounced up and down on stubby front legs, seemingly in complete agreement.

"Unfortunately, a person who's gotten two speeding tickets in the last six months isn't in much of a position to complain to the police. They just don't understand that busy people are sometimes on a tight schedule, and that fifty-five miles per hour on an expressway is totally ridiculous."

Piggy strolled into the kitchen, stretched, yawned, then lay down and stared at the pantry door.

"How do you know the dog food is in there?"

Piggy spared her a not too tolerant glance before staring once again at the pantry.

"All right. Geez! You two have the manners of piranhas." She opened the pantry door and dragged out the travel bag that Amy had brought with the dog's toys, rawhide chews, brushes, vitamins, and a nail clipper. "You dogs travel with more baggage than I do. Let's see . . . what do we have here? No dishes." She ducked back into the pantry to look in the forty-pound bag of dog food. There were no dishes there, either.

"Well, your mom forgot to bring your dog dishes. Guess you don't eat."

Piggy shot her an incredulous look—almost as if she understood English.

"All right, all right. I'll pull out some cereal bowls."

The enthusiasm with which Piggy and Drover attacked their food only just left the finish on Joey's expensive pottery. She gingerly rescued the bowls and put them in the dishwasher under baleful glares from both corgis.

"They're empty. If you didn't inhale your food, you might remember that you've eaten it. And that's the last time you little hyenas eat off civilized dishes. I think some cheap doggy tinware is in order."

A quick trip to the dog supply superstore up the road could be an adventure, Joey decided. Besides, it would allow her to delay turning on her cell phone and opening the door to her office, which had plenty of work to fill up her day. Every Sunday that she didn't have a wedding she woke up and wallowed in the beautiful concept of actually not working, and every Sunday she ended up sitting at her desk most of the day. It never failed.

She chose Piggy as company on the adventure. One couldn't show up in these pet places without a dog to prove you were part of the animal in-crowd. Piggy was the quieter of the two dogs, so Joey figured she would be easier to manage. Joey was wrong.

The people who manage pet supply stores are not novices at marketing to the canine set. Joey thought that letting the dogs actually go into the store with their owners was simply a cute public relations gimmick until she realized, too late, the marketing value of the aromatic dog treats placed temptingly at dog nose level, not to mention cannily placed toys that simply begged for dogs to reach out and help themselves. Everywhere Joey looked there were basted rawhides, bones, dog cookies, and fuzzy stuffed toys just the size to fit into an eager dog's mouth. And to get to the dog dish section, she and Piggy had to run the gauntlet of all these enticing prizes.

Like a miniature Clydesdale, Piggy pulled Joey down the nearest aisle, straining at the end of the leash, checking out merchandise on both sides. When Joey tugged her away from the rawhide chews, she scrambled over to the doggy version of pork rinds. Then there were the knuckle bones, the rubber balls, the stuffed toys, and the gummy bones. Everything deserved a nudge or a sniff.

"Piggy, stop that!"

Joey's admonition fell on deaf ears. Piggy was focused.

"Behave yourself, young lady, or I'll—now drop that!"

With a deft snatch, Piggy had grabbed a good-sized dog cookie shaped like a bone. She stood with her prize in her mouth, stubbornly defiant as Joey worked her way up the leash, hand over hand, refusing to give the dog enough slack to trot out of reach. "You little shoplifter! Give me that cookie!"

Every bit as stubborn as the dog, Joey grabbed the end of the cookie. A tug-of-war ensued. The cookie wasn't up to the strain. It broke, leaving the smaller part in Joey's hand. Piggy chomped happily on the larger section.

"You little toad! See if you get dinner tonight."

Piggy didn't seem concerned. She turned her attention to a bin of beef-basted rawhide sticks.

By the time Joey reached the checkout counter, the dog dishes were only a minor portion of her purchases, or more accurately, their purchases, for most of the shopping had been accomplished by Piggy. On the counter Joey piled two rawhide chews, partially chewed, a small stuffed hedgehog rather damp from Piggy's mouth, a box of Doggie Cheez-its, caved in on one corner where Piggy had knocked it off the shelf, and two amazingly disgusting dried pig ears.

"I can't believe dogs like those things," Joey said, grimacing at the ears.

The clerk snorted. "They're really gross, aren't they?"

"I wouldn't buy something like that, but she jumped right onto the display and grabbed them."

The girl leaned over the counter to grin at Piggy. "You're a live wire, aren't you, you cute thing." And to Joey, "I saw her taking off like a steam locomotive with you trailing behind. You know, we offer obedience training classes here. There's information over there on the bulletin board."

"Oh, this isn't my dog!" Joey denied quickly. "No, no. I would never have a dog this unruly. She's truly a menace."

As if to show Joey up for a liar, Piggy sat at her side politely, looking like a canine model of good manners.

Until the skittering of little claws on the floor made her ears perk up. A cat the color of a lush mink coat came around the corner of the Frisbee display, paused to look around with kingly dignity, then trotted into the toy aisle.

"Puddin! You come back here, you naughty cat!" came a feminine cry from the unseen owner. "Where did you go?"

"Oops!" the clerk said with a smile. "Sounds like kitty made a break for it."

Piggy gave an indignant bark and launched herself in the direction of the cat. Her leash dragged uselessly behind her.

Joey was caught totally off guard. "Oh no! Piggy! Come back."

Her call had the expected effect—nothing. The cat was busy sorting through the contents of the fuzzy-mouse bin and didn't notice Piggy's approach until the dog announced her presence with an ear-splitting bark. Then Puddin took up the challenge with an angry hiss.

Hurrying down the aisle to the site of the confrontation, Joey reached for the end of Piggy's leash just as the dog pulled it out of her reach. The cat backed away, an oversized orange-tailed fuzzy gray mouse held firmly in his mouth. Piggy relentlessly herded him down the aisle and away from the toy mouse display.

At this point in the little drama, the cat's owner appeared at the end of the aisle. "Oh no!" she cried.

"Piggy! Come back this instant! You are a very bad dog."

"My poor cat!"

Piggy didn't spare either of them a glance. The cat, seeing his escape route blocked, flattened his ears, sprang forward with claws extended, and whapped Piggy across the nose in a quick one-two of retribution. Then he dashed for the safety of his owner.

Piggy yelped, but her furious pursuit was slowed by Joey, who finally was able to grab hold of the leash. Piggy was in locomotive mode, however, and dragged Joey forward until both cat and cat owner were flattened up against the display of flea remedies.

"I'm so sorry!" Joey gasped, using all her strength to pull Piggy backwards. Piggy yapped indignantly, and the cat launched straight upward and landed on the woman's shoulder.

"Oh!" the woman gasped. Then she laughed. "You wascally puddytat! Look at the trouble you caused."

Seeing her prey so humiliated, Piggy sat down with a satisfied woof.

"I am soooo sorry," Joey apologized. "This isn't my dog, and I had no idea she was such a monster."

"Don't blame her! If my silly cat hadn't decided to go shopping on his own—Joey? Josephine DeMato? Is that you?"

Joey took her first good look at the cat lady. She was a petite porcelain doll with perfect blonde hair tousled into artful curls. Designer jeans hugged willowy hips and toned thighs, and her cashmere sweater, casually baggy though it was, couldn't have cost less than a couple of hundred dollars. "Alicia Somers?"

"Yes! My God! Joey! I haven't seen you since college!"

"Good old Mills!"

Alicia laughed. "Good old Mills. It feels like forever ago."

"Yes, it does."

"And here you are, still in Colorado. Believe it or not, I sent a note to your old address a few weeks ago, but it bounced back Recipient Unknown."

"I haven't been at the old house for three years. Dad moved into a retirement place, so we sold it."

"How is your dad?"

"He's good. He'll be happy to hear that I ran into you."

The two college chums stood in the aisle catching up while the animals regarded each other warily. Piggy glared, and Puddin responded with that haughty superiority that only cats can manage. He balanced deftly on Alicia's shoulder, the orange-tailed fuzzy mouse still in his mouth.

"Sooo . . ." Alicia said. "Do you have a husband and three kids like everyone else we went to school with?"

"No. I'm too busy trying to make a go of my business."

"You have your own business? I'm green with envy. I should have majored in business, like you. English literature gets you absolutely nowhere."

As Joey remembered it, Alicia Somers, whose father was of one of Denver's oil barons of the seventies, didn't need to get anywhere. Financially, she was already there. But her excitement for Joey seemed genuine. "It's just a small business, Alicia."

"But small business is all the rage now. Are you one of those Internet companies that made a mil their first day on the stock exchange?"

Joey laughed. "My company isn't exactly stock exchange material. I'm a wedding consultant and caterer. Three people and a bunch of part-timers who come in for the big parties. I call it A Perfect Wedding."

Alicia's eyes glowed. "A Perfect Wedding. Perfect! Oh, how perfect! It's fate!"

"Fate?" Joey smiled, reminded of Alicia's habit of being overdramatic.

"Yes! Fate! You, me, lunch, today. Right now, in fact. Do I have a deal for you!"

Now you understand what I mean about injustice. I didn't get to do lunch with the girls. No indeed. I got stuffed into my kennel in Joey's minivan while they had lunch without me. I was left behind without a thought, just as Amy had left me behind to go Hawaii. Let my case be a lesson to you. Anyone who tells you that life after death is fun and games is blowing smoke out his caboose.

The Hawaii thing really was a slap in the face, especially after all I'd done for Amy and Jackass Jeff. I turn myself practically inside out fixing those two up for a lifetime of wedded bliss, not to mention risking my hide to save Amy, and what thanks do I get? Two bowls of kibble a day and a lousy pat on the head. All right, maybe Amy and Jeff did get together in spite of me instead of because of me, but I did genuinely and courageously—surprising even myself—challenge a murderer for Amy's sake. Very, very scary. Don't you think that Amy, who prides herself on being such a dog lover, would have stopped to consider that the heroic, self-sacrificing dog might need a vacation? Couldn't she and Dr. Dull, DVM, have gone someplace that welcomes pets? Like maybe a nice warm California beach? California has just as many palm trees as Hawaii. Why did they have to go clear across the ocean?

Fame and celebrity fade more quickly than the buzz you get from light beer, and gratitude fizzles just as fast. One day I had my pointy-eared face all over the human interest section of the Denver Post, and the next I was just another dog to be left behind while the "important people" went gallivanting off to have fun.

I told you the universe was unjust.

As you might have guessed by now, I was not in a good mood, and as I sat in my kennel in Joey's car, my spirits sank even lower. Being a dog was getting me down. More and more I was losing the stylish, sexy, clever persona that was the real me and becoming comfortable in this bag of fur. I was no longer a fox, just a dog—Piggy, with her overstuffed sausage of a body and a personality that made a weasel seem cuddly. What's more, not only had I been left behind while Amy and Jeff had fun, I was stuck with goofy Drover, who is the only suitor I've actually had to bite to discourage. And we were both in the clutches of this unsympathetic Joey person.

I had nothing against Ms. DeMato, generally speaking. If I had been still walking around as Lydia Keane, I would have admired her, sort of. Her nose-to-the-grindstone attitude was dull, but she knew how to use makeup to her best advantage—very important in a woman—and she did have a sense of style. In exploring her house, which is a very classic old Victorian in an "in" section of northwest Denver, I stuck my nose in her closet. Nothing but designer stuff. Very expensive, if a bit conservative for my taste. If clothes don't exactly make the woman, they at least tell something about where her head is *at, and I thought Joey was going to be a big improvement over Amy, whose closet is stuffed with sweatsuits and jeans.*

But Joey wasn't an improvement at all. After just one night at her place, I could tell that the woman truly did not like dogs. She claimed to like dogs, but all the evidence pointed to the contrary. She put her used dishes straight into the dishwasher without letting the dogs lick them clean. She had swept the dog hair from her kitchen floor twice just that very morning. And she had the nerve to object to my innocent bit of window-shopping in the pet supply store. Not only that, but the woman totally misinterpreted my attempt at being a good citizen. That cheeky cat was decimating the fuzzy-mouse display, and do you think the stuck-up furball intended to pay for the damage? Ha! Cats are like that. Dogs can be dull, but at least they're honest. Cats, on the other hand, specialize in sneaky. Unpleasant creatures who think they own the world.

Stanley may be an officious, sadistic creature, but at least he didn't send me back to Earth as a cat.

Joey figured that Pizza Hut wasn't the sort of place people in Alicia's social stratum went for lunch, but it was handy, being just around the corner from the pet supply store. Not only was it handy, but it fit her budget. Business had been good, but cash outflow had a habit of keeping pace with cash inflow.

"Mmmm!" Alicia was enthusiastic. "Doesn't that smell wonderful? I do love pizza."

Joey smiled. Trust Alicia to not be haughty about it. For a rich kid, she was remarkably sane. They'd met at Mills, an upscale women's college in California where Joey had won a scholarship and Alicia's father had endowed a chair in English literature. Both from Colorado, both homesick, they had become fast friends, standing as a solid front against what they termed "California weirdness." Whether or not there was truly weirdness to defend against was inconsequential. The notion gave them an excuse to stick together. But they'd lost touch after graduation. The common ground of school was removed, and they moved in different circles.

They ordered pepperoni and mushroom, then settled down for a session of catch-up.

"So what's going on?" Joey asked. "You look positively like the cat who ate the canary."

"I am! I am! But you have to hear the whole story. My life has become a Humphrey Bogart romance, or maybe Tommy Lee Jones or Mel Gibson."

"There's a big difference there. And I think at least a couple of those fellows would take exception to being called romantic."

"Well, yes, but you get my meaning."

"And you're playing the Katharine Hepburn part?"

"Yes! Except red hair just doesn't go with my coloring."

Joey took a sip of her Diet Pepsi and chuckled. "And color coordination is so important when we're taking about romance."

"Don't laugh at me!"

"Would I laugh?"

"Yes, you would! You were always laughing at me!"

They easily fell back into the bantering, companionable friendship they'd known in school. Alicia had always been the romantic—a passionate idealist who wanted to love everyone and have everyone love her in return. Joey had been the one with her feet planted firmly in reality, practical, hardheaded, and a bit skeptical. They'd been the perfect match. Alicia had sweetened Joey's life with a bit of whimsy, and Joey had kept Alicia from flying completely into the clouds.

Over hot pizza Alicia told a tale that was both harrowing and, even Joey had to admit, romantic. She'd been the target of a stalker, a man she'd dated briefly and had dumped because he made her nervous.

"He was totally intense," she said, rolling her eyes. "Taking things way too fast, and he went postal if I so much as talked to another guy. You know the type."

Joey didn't, but she nodded sagely.

"He started showing up unexpectedly wherever I was, trying to talk to me, be with me—whatever. And the more I said no, the crazier he became. Finally he started sending letters. The first couple were love letters, or at least I guess that's what you would call them. Then they got nasty and threatening. That's when Daddy called the police. No one could find Jason—that's what this creep's name was, so the police sent out this sergeant detective as protection until they could bring Jason in." She laughed. "Oh, he was mad."

"Jason?"

"No. The detective. I guess watching out for a spoiled little rich girl—he actually called me that!—wasn't his idea of a plum assignment, but he and his boss were on the outs. He and his boss are generally on the outs, it turns out."

"And . . . ?" Joey prompted.

"And we were like your Piggy and my Puddin."

"She's not *my* Piggy."

"Whatever. We were all claws and teeth. He didn't want to trail after me, and I didn't want some ape with a shoulder holster telling me what I could do and not do."

"Kevin Costner and Whitney Houston. *The Bodyguard.*"

"Exactly! Only Ben is much handsomer than Costner. He saved my life. We fell in love. And now we're getting married."

"And Jason?"

Alicia's face clouded. "Dead. And I would have died with him if Ben hadn't been so brave."

Joey sensed that her friend didn't want to talk about the grisly details. "You don't like this Ben or anything, do you?"

Alicia brightened. She laughed like a delighted child. "You can tell?"

"I can tell you're very happy. I think it's great."

"And you're going to do my wedding for me."

"I am?"

"Please say you have time. Please, please." Alicia donned her "pretty please with sugar on it" face, which she must have perfected at the age of five, and which was so ludicrously appealing that no one could refuse her anything. "I do want this to be a perfect wedding. Not a big or flashy wedding. Just a perfect wedding."

"And this wedding is when?" Joey asked.

"Oh, you have plenty of time. The end of March. A whole month from now."

Joey laughed and buried her face in her hands. The
next month was slow, as it happened, but she had deliberately planned her schedule that way. She needed a
vacation. She really, really did. But Alicia was a friend,
and like everyone else in Alicia's life, Joey couldn't turn
down the face. Besides, Alicia had given Joey friendship and kindness at a time in her life when she badly
needed those things. The least Joey could do was help
Alicia with her wedding—her perfect wedding.

She'd no sooner said yes than the bride-to-be was
on her cell phone, calling her stalwart detective to tell
him the "good news."

"Ben?" she chortled into the phone. "Guess what?
The best thing! I just ran into . . . yes, I remember
what you said about not bugging you when you're on
duty, but this is important! This old friend of mine is a
wedding consultant. Can you believe? A wedding consultant! And she's going to do our wedding. What do
you mean 'what wedding?' " Her blue eyes sparkled.
"You are such an old poop. It's a good thing I love
you. . . . Yes, I know you have to get back to work.
We're taking my friend to dinner tomorrow night."
She angled a look toward Joey to get her consent. Joey
surrendered with a shrug. "Yes, we are. She's a famous
wedding consultant, and we're lucky she's going to
help. So toe the line, Officer." She laughed. "That's
better."

Alicia punched the "end" button and smiled impishly. "I hope you don't mind, but I thought dinner
would be a nice place to talk about details. And you'll
get to meet Ben. He is so sweet, though he can be a
fuddy-duddy when he's working."

Joey's head was spinning. She'd forgotten how much of a bulldozer Alicia could be when she set her sights on a goal.

Alicia smiled sweetly. "You're going to love Ben. I just know you will."

CHAPTER 3

◆

A DENVER POLICE Department patrol car lay in wait behind a screen of skimpy trees on the verge of Interstate 25 between Santa Fe Avenue and Federal. Inside the car sat Ben Ramsay and Abel Verdeen. Abel sipped from a Styrofoam cup of steaming coffee while Ben munched a Fig Newton and washed it down with Coke.

"I don't know what you're so cranky about," Abel complained. "Not that you were a barrel of laughs before Case got on your case. Ha! Hear that? Case got on your case."

Ben shot him a lethal glance.

Abel shrugged it off. "So you get to be an ordinary cop for a few weeks instead of a high and mighty detective. That's not the worst that's happened to some poor slob who's run off at the mouth with the captain. Joe Maslawsky got smart with Case and ended up pounding a beat. Can you believe that? Actually pounding a beat. No car. No nothin'. I'll bet he wore the soles of his shoes clear through to his socks. And did you ever see that guy's socks? Or smell them? I swear that guy wouldn't buy a new pair of socks if he won the lottery."

Ben brushed cookie crumbs from his blue uniform shirt. "Verdeen, you've got diarrhea of the mouth."

"Well, somebody has to relieve the silence. Sheesh! Going out with you is like riding with a zombie."

"We're not on a date."

"Now there's a thought that makes me shudder."

Ben held up the radar gun and shot a red Porsche in the northbound lane. "Sixty. What the hell is a Porsche doing sixty for? Why would you buy a car like that if you only want to do sixty goddamn miles per hour?"

"The guy probably knows that every motorist's nightmare is sitting behind these trees."

"Give it a rest, Abel. I'm not in the mood."

"You're never in the mood. Or rather, you're always in a mood lately. A black one."

"You want me to celebrate a demotion from detective to squad car jockey?"

Abel laughed sourly. "Oh yeah. Get out the violins. You get stuck back in a patrol car for a few weeks, which, by the way, is your own frigging fault for telling Case he had his head up his ass in the Somers deal. On the other hand—let's see—what would Ben Ramsay possibly have going for him that might put an ordinary, sane guy in a good mood? He knows he'll be back at his hotshot detective desk as soon as Case simmers down—nope, not enough. He's marrying a society broad who has more money than she knows how to spend—nope, still not enough. What else? Oh yeah, the society broad has the body of a porn star and a face that's not going to stop a clock, either. That was her on your cell phone, wasn't it? I could tell from the sappy smile on your face."

Ben gave his partner a cold look. "Number one: Don't call Alicia a broad."

"No offense intended."

"Number two: Don't even mention her in the same sentence with the words 'porn star.' "

"Picky, picky. She's a great-looking lady."

"She's got class."

"I won't argue that, man. If someone like her offered to make me a kept man, I'd jump at the chance."

Ben crushed the Fig Newton wrapper with more force than necessary and threw it on the floor of the car. "I am *not* going to be a kept man."

"Whatever you say, Ben."

"And Alicia's money has nothing to do with why I'm marrying her. Tess needs a mom, and I need a wife. Alicia is a hell of a girl. Generous. Gutsy. Smart. She has a good heart."

"Don't forget the great body. Oops. There I go again."

Ben glared.

"Hey, man! I don't mean any disrespect to the lady. Having a great body is a good thing, isn't it? If it were me marrying a gal like that, I'd hang up my badge and start doing some serious living. Know what I mean?"

Ben tried to ignore him. Abel Verdeen was a good cop and a good man, but he couldn't resist needling. The whole force was needling Ben, especially since he'd shot off his mouth at Case—a bad habit of his, saying exactly what he thought—and got swatted down a couple of ranks. The whole force was jealous. That's what the problem was. They couldn't understand what a sensational lady like Alicia Somers could see in a plain, hardworking detective. At least he had been a detective up until a week ago. He wasn't exactly a jet-setter, nor was he a sensitive, enlightened, politically correct kind of twenty-first-century guy.

As he remembered it, in fact, his last girlfriend, a high school teacher from Golden, had accused him of being on a par with her students. When they'd finally broken up, she'd said he made Dirty Harry look civilized.

In a mood to wreak mayhem on someone, and Abel being off-limits, Ben radared a black semi pulling a double trailer. "Fifty-five. Right on perfect. Let's go."

"What do you mean let's go? He wasn't speeding."

Ben peeled the squad car out of their hiding spot and sped down the on ramp. "It's been a while since I read the regs, but I do believe we can stop any commercial vehicle without cause, just for a spot inspection." He switched on the flashing lights. "I said to myself when I woke up this morning—this is a black truck day. And that ahead of us is a black truck. Besides, none of those guys do the speed limit unless they have something to hide."

"Oh yeah," Abel said, shaking his head. "That driver's gonna love us. Ben, you are one mean son of a bitch."

Ben grinned wickedly.

"I hope for the sake of the poor Denver drivers that you get back in your detective suit real fast."

Indeed, the trucker was not at all happy as he hopped down from the cab onto the shoulder of the freeway. He was young, with scraggly blond hair, wary eyes, and a quid of tobacco in his cheek. "What can I do for you today, guys? I wasn't speedin' or anything."

Ben copied down the license plate number of the truck. "A routine check, sir. I need to see your paperwork. Logbook too."

"I wasn't doing nothin', man! Why'd you stop me?"

"We don't have to have a reason. You know as well as I do that a commercial vehicle is subject to random inspections by state troopers and local police. If I could see your paperwork, please."

"Just what I need," the driver muttered as he climbed back into his cab. "Of all the fucking trucks on the road, he picks mine."

Ben checked the paperwork while Abel plugged the license number into their squad car computer. All seemed to be in order, but Ben didn't like the way the driver jittered up and down, his eyes in constant movement. "I'll just take a look in the truck."

"Man, I'm on a tight schedule, and I get fined for late delivery. There's nothing in the truck."

"Then this should go fast, shouldn't it?" Ben whistled a little tune as he pulled himself into the cab. Seeing someone have a worse day than his truly did give his mood a lift.

The cab smelled of the driver's lunch—a hamburger heavy on the onions, Ben guessed. The seats were grimy, but that was no crime. All the usual hidey-holes contained nothing more damning than old packets of mustard and taco sauce. If the driver was high on some substance, he hadn't left it around for a diligent cop to find. But behind the door to the sleeping compartment Ben hit pay dirt.

"Bingo!" he said softly. "Hello there."

A girl who couldn't have been more than thirteen tried to make herself as small as possible. Long toothpick legs drew up to her chest and long toothpick arms wrapped tightly around them.

"That's my cousin!" the driver shouted into the cab.

"What's your name, kid?" The cutting edge left Ben's voice at the same time his mood approached murderous. He drew the line at taking his temper out on scared children.

The girl chewed on a thumbnail. "Uh . . ."

"Tell me your name, girl. Nothing's going to happen to you." Nothing, at least, compared to what was going to happen to this truck-driving Romeo for transporting an underage girl across state lines for presumably lascivious purposes.

"Susan Morley."

"Okay, Susan Morley. Step down here with me."

"She's my cousin!" The driver was beginning to sound frantic.

They ran the girl's name on the computer and found that she was a reported runaway from Iowa who'd been gone a month.

"You're not his cousin, are you?" Ben asked her with a smile.

"Nah. Even I know better than to screw my own cousin."

"You been with him the whole time since you ran?" Ben asked her.

"Pretty much. He's not bad. He said we were going to Disneyland, but I'm beginning to wonder."

"Right." He turned diamond-hard eyes to the driver and said for his ears alone, "Like them a little young, do you?"

The man scowled.

Abel put the girl in the squad car while Ben called for a tow for the semi and a backup car to take the driver in. He didn't want the snake riding in the same car with the child he'd taken advantage of. He tried not to think of his own daughter when he looked at the girl. Just nine years old, Tess was a long way from being bait for a lowlife who liked his ladies young. All the same, he could feel the spark of murderous rage that would consume him if anyone like this slime bag ever so much as looked at her. He wondered what Susan Morley's father would feel when he learned where his daughter had been.

The driver was belligerent when they stuffed him into the second squad car. "I didn't do nothin' wrong, goddamn it! She's my fuckin' cousin, I tell you. I didn't touch her, no matter what she says. I've got your badge number, man, and I'm gonna raise a fuckin' stink that'll make you wish you'd never seen my face."

Abel grinned at Ben. "Aren't you the popular one today?"

"Hell, I've been popular all week." Unbidden came the picture of the sassy lady he'd stopped the day before on the Boulder Turnpike. She'd been every bit as mad as the semi driver, in a much more ladylike way, of course. In that case, she'd had the right to be hot under the collar, because he'd been an ass. Lately, he'd been an ass entirely too much.

Still, that particular stop had been a lot more fun than this one.

Samantha hummed as she arranged the antipasto plates with just the artistic flair that Joey had taught her. Two spears of fresh asparagus, lightly steamed and then chilled. A jalapeño pepper stuffed with home-made mozzarella cheese, two kinds of salami, sliced thin, and a chilled swirl of aged balsamic vinegar. "These must be very fancy friends coming to dinner tonight," she commented to Joey. "Last time you fixed dinner for a friend—and that was me—you ordered out pizza and popped a couple of cans of Coors. And you were wearing that yucky green sweatsuit whose knees are thin enough to see through."

"That sweatsuit is very comfortable." Joey was busy at the blender making her special vinaigrette. "And the pizza was great."

"It was. But it wasn't steamed bluenose bass in piccata sauce."

"Well . . . This old friend we're having dinner with is sort of special. What's more, she's getting married, and she wants us to handle the wedding. Believe me, it'll be very high profile. Very good for business. So I guess maybe I want to impress her just a little bit. She actually invited me out to dinner with her and her fiancé, but I turned the invitation around and in-sisted she come here. If she sees the gardens and the sunroom, she may decide to have the ceremony here. You can never tell. Even this time of year that's a nice room with a beautiful view."

"I should have guessed this had something to do with work. Otherwise you wouldn't be wearing those Ralph Lauren slacks and that gorgeous sweater. Whose is the sweater, by the way?"

"My sister made it."

"It's beautiful. She should be a designer."

"She is. In New York. And very successful, too."

"I should have known. You DeMatos are all busy little bees in your successful, busy little hives. How do you do it?"

"We DeMatos don't let ourselves get distracted by little things like three husbands," she said, one brow raised.

Samantha laughed. "Touché. But distractions can be such fun." She tossed a tidbit of cheese to Piggy, who caught it with the practiced ease of a Denver Broncos pass receiver. Drover promptly moved forward with an anxious whine.

"Ah–ah!" Joey admonished. "No snacking for those two. Amy left strict instructions about their diet. Especially Piggy. She's too chubby."

"Oh, but look at those pathetic little faces."

"Con artists, both of them. They get plenty to eat in their own dog dishes."

Samantha pouted. "I feel your pain, Piggy. From one pudgy girl to another." She darted a quick glance at Joey before slipping a piece of salami to each dog and whispering, "We can't all be fashionably skinny."

"Samantha!"

"They're just tiny pieces. It's not going to hurt them."

"You are such a sucker!"

"It's fun being a sucker. You know, dear, you need to lighten up. Break some rules. Get a life outside of business. Sometimes I worry about you."

Joey grinned. "Sam, you're sweet, but not to worry. I have fun."

"What about romance? You're not getting any younger, you know."

"Ouch! Thanks for the reminder. But pushing thirty isn't anything to panic about."

"Not panic. Just . . . well . . . sit up and take notice. The hunks go for the young honeys, and don't I just know it. Thirty might not be the time to panic, but forty-five definitely is."

"Time. Cripes, look at the time! I'd better check the table, and—oh no!—I got mustard on my sweater. God! What a klutz! I swear my whole week has gone like this. It's a good thing you could come over to help."

"I expect a lot of brownie points. I gave up a date tonight, you know."

"A date?"

"Ron the tax accountant. He was taking me to the Wynkoop Brewing Company for bratwurst and beer."

"You'd rather have brats than bluenose bass?"

"Joey, dear, a hotdog eaten on a date is better than caviar eaten alone."

Joey shook her head. "Well, I'm glad you came, anyway."

She dashed upstairs to her bedroom for a change of clothes. Hastily pulling off her sweater, she looked through her neatly organized closet for something to replace it. "How did dog hair get on my shirts?" she grumbled. She scowled at Piggy and Drover, who had followed her up the stairs. "You're here two days, and already I have clothing decorated in corgi fur? Look at this!"

She chose a silk blouse and brushed a few stray brown hairs—then noticed the coating on her slacks. "Cripes! What would Martha Stewart do in a case like this?"

Piggy belched. If Joey hadn't known better, she might have thought it was deliberate. "Very funny," she told the dog.

Joey got downstairs just in time to hear the doorbell chime. Alicia greeted her with a huge hug that left Joey smiling. The girl's spontaneity had always been endearing. Looking embarrassed, her fiancé—a tall, broad-shouldered fellow—lingered in the shadows of the porch.

"Oh wow!" Alicia exclaimed. "This place you have is absolutely great! When was it built?"

"1905."

"And right on Sloan Lake, too. I've always loved this part of town with the huge trees and old Victorians. Ben lives in an apartment that's so modern it positively turns your soul to stainless steel. Look at this! You have two dogs, not just one! A matched set!"

"The fat one is Piggy; the pretty one is Drover. Neither one is mine. I take no responsibility for their behavior."

Joey took Alicia's coat—an exquisite faux fox creation. Alicia would never stoop to wearing real fur, even though she could well afford it.

"They are sooooo cute. Aren't they darling, Ben?"

Joey turned to take the man's jacket and froze. Alicia's fiancé stopped in his tracks, his amiable, rugged face rigid with surprise, dark eyes widening almost imperceptibly as they locked gazes.

"You!" Joey breathed.

"Uh . . ." He smiled sheepishly. "Hi."

Alicia brightened. "You've met before?"

They both answered at the same time, a quick "no" from Ben Ramsay, a rueful "yes" from Joey. Flustered, Joey changed her answer to no at the same time Ben switched his to yes.

Alicia looked from one to the other. "Make up your mind, you two."

"Yes," Joey said more firmly. "We . . . it was business."

Ben smiled wryly. "I . . . uh . . . gave her a speeding ticket the other day."

Alicia's eyes widened. "Oh, you didn't! You are awful, Ben Ramsay. He's awful, Joey, he really is. Give the man a badge and a gun, and he just becomes a tyrant."

"I'm not a tyrant."

"You are too. But he does have his good points," she said with a smile. "Believe me, Joey, he does. And he'll make it up to you." She frowned at her husband-to-be with mock severity. "I promise he will."

Joey smiled, but when Alicia turned to exclaim over the beautifully set dining room table, she slid Ben a triumphant look. Entertaining the man who had caught her speeding was embarrassing enough. She wasn't going to let him know how awkward she felt.

A quick tour of the house—with Alicia ecstatic over the carved banister, the upstairs bath with its claw-foot tub, and the big bay window in the master suite—ended with predinner cocktails in the sunroom that overlooked the gardens. In late spring and summer the place came alive with cherry blossoms, roses, nasturtiums, daffodils, and marigolds. Now, in late February, the trees were naked and the flowers slept, but the fountain and rock garden—now more rock than garden—showed to good advantage. Enough sunlight remained in the day to make the place look very inviting.

Alicia made suitably delighted comments about the large arched windows, the gleaming oak floors, and the photos of wedding scenes framed on the walls—weddings that had taken place in the sunroom and gardens. "This is charming!" she declared. "This house is so quaint, Ben, isn't it? Doesn't it just make you feel like you've stepped back in time a hundred years?"

Ben smiled fondly but didn't interrupt Alicia's stream of chatter. When Alicia turned to Samantha and started to relate the great adventure that led to their engagement, he raised his glass—a whiskey on the rocks—to Joey and said with a wry smile, "Nice place here."

"Thanks." She grinned wickedly. "Caught you by surprise, eh? Didn't remember my name from the ticket?"

"Allie didn't mention your name." His eyes twinkled with a hint of the devil. "Believe me, I would have remembered. You make a certain impression."

"I'm not even going to ask what kind."

He merely smiled.

Joey cocked a brow in his direction. "Does Alicia know she's marrying an officious wiseacre?"

He seemed to consider seriously, but his eyes showed a gleam of mischief. His eyes, Joey noted, were almost black, and they could scrunch up and smile without any help from his mouth. "Seems Alicia said something to that effect when we first met, but she grew to like me."

Joey almost smiled, but not quite. She was still a bit miffed about that ticket. It was bad enough getting caught red-handed doing the speed limit plus twenty-five without having to fix dinner for the guy who wrote the ticket. "Lucky for you, Alicia's a tolerant sort."

"She is that, Flash, if she can tolerate both of us."

"Call me Flash one more time and I'm going to 'accidentally' knock that glass of whiskey down the front of your sweater, ice and all."

He smiled. "A name well deserved."

"You're flirting with danger, Officer Ramsay."

"I'm an engaged man," he said with a grin. "I don't flirt."

Joey was momentarily taken aback. Was that what they were doing? Mortified at the thought, Joey felt her face heat with embarrassment. Alicia appeared in time to save her from framing an answer.

"Take us on a tour of the gardens, Joey. It's not too cold to spend a few minutes outside. Ben, I hope you're apologizing to Joey for giving her that ticket. You know that nobody pays any attention to that silly speed limit on the turnpike. Did he apologize, Joey?"

Ben spoke first. "Joey and I were just talking about my deficiencies as a public servant. She and Captain Case would have a lot of fun comparing notes."

Alicia smiled indulgently. "Oh pooh! Captain Case just doesn't recognize hero material when he sees it. Come on, Joey. I really want to see the garden."

The dogs crowded ahead of them when Samantha opened the French doors that led to the deck and thence down to the gardens. With a great churning of stubby legs and scrabbling of little feet on the redwood deck, Piggy and Drover dashed into the grassy area below, Piggy leading the way. For two circuits Piggy led Drover a merry chase, dashing through the grass, swinging around the fountain, and then dodging through the rock garden with surprising agility.

"See," Ben said with a note of satisfaction. "Her dogs speed, too."

"You are incorrigible," Alicia told him. "It really is a good thing you saved my life. Otherwise I might never have realized what a wonderful fellow you are. Oh, look at those darling dogs. I swear Piggy flashes her butt in Drover's face whenever he slows down. What a little temptress!"

The dogs had become two speeding brown streaks when Piggy veered toward the green-striped hammock slung between the apple and cherry trees. Up she hopped, landing in the hammock and setting it swinging wildly. Unprepared for her abrupt change of tactics, poor Drover shot beneath the hammock. His momentum carried him into the bed of just awakening crocuses to do a nose plant in the dirt.

Everyone—even Ben Ramsay—laughed at the chagrin on Drover's face and the smug satisfaction on Piggy's.

"She is wicked!" Alicia declared. "Positively wicked."

"Clever girl," Joey noted.

"Definitely a female." This from Ben.

Alicia poked him in the ribs. "Watch it, mister. You are definitely outnumbered here."

"That, my love, is the way I like it."

Alicia giggled like a high school girl being teased by the class jock. She stood on tiptoe to give him a peck on the cheek.

"What has Drover found?" Samantha went to investigate. "Uck. It's a tennis ball, dead and buried for lo these many years. Did you know there was a dead ball buried in among the crocuses, Joey?"

"I do now."

"Smart boy!" Alicia picked up the ball, unmindful of the dirt clinging to the ancient toy, and started a game of fetch with Drover. Drover joyfully cooperated while Piggy stayed in her hammock and observed his frantic chasing with contemptuous eyes. Joey was left standing with Ben on the deck.

"So what is a 'heroic detective' doing harassing motorists on the Boulder Turnpike? I thought detectives had a higher calling."

"Demoted," Ben confessed.

"Bad attitude?" Joey guessed.

"Something like that."

"What a surprise!"

"But it's only temporary."

"Which? The demotion, or the attitude?"

He chuckled. "You always treat clients to this?"

"To what?"

"The sharp edge of your tongue."

"You should talk about sharp. Aren't our valiant men in blue supposed to be courteous and respectful to the good citizens whose taxes pay their salaries?"

"I was having a bad day. Actually, a bad week."

"So you take it out on poor innocent drivers."

"Hardly innocent, Flash. You were going eighty in a fifty-five-mile-per-hour zone."

"There's that attitude again. And you accuse me of having a sharp tongue."

He grinned wickedly. "A little police brutality doesn't surprise anyone. But wedding consultants are supposed to be all hearts and flowers, aren't they?"

"Usually I'm the soul of tact. But some things are just too tempting to resist. Besides, it's not necessary to treat a groom as if he's anything more than chopped liver. If you haven't learned this already, Officer Ramsay—"

"Ben."

"All right. Ben. If you haven't learned this already, you soon will. The person who gets all the attention, all the tact, and all the hearts and flowers in the wedding is the bride. Alicia calls the shots."

He sighed. "You got that one right."

I always enjoy dinner parties. Back when I was able to date, I preferred restaurants, or even better, a swinging club with a good band, good food, dancing, maybe a few recreational drugs floating around, and a sexy guy to pick up the bill. But restaurants and clubs, just like sexy guys, are a thing of the past for me. Dogs have to settle for dinner parties at home, and very seldom does a dog get his or her own seat at the table. Generally we have to sneak around between chair legs and people legs, practicing looks of pathetic starvation to wheedle a few lousy morsels from the diners. Unjust, I know, but we've already discussed the state of justice in the universe. With good old Amy, the pathetic starvation act works pretty well. Guests at her place are usually dog lovers who can't resist the on-slaught of soft brown eyes. Those that aren't dog lovers give over just to get rid of the dog drooling on their legs. Either way, the result is the same for the dog.

This was my first social event at Joey's place, and I was un-certain that anyone at her table was truly a dog lover. Even Alicia, who gushed over how cute I was and threw that dis-gusting ball for Drover—he'll chase anything that moves, the moron—might draw the line at sharing her plate. I knew first-hand that the woman had a cat, and cat people, like their pets, are unpredictable. Still, I was willing to try. The dog suit that Stanley stuck me in came complete with instinct and appetite, and food of any kind is right at the top of a corgi's priorities.

I at least had the sense to be subtle about my participation at the table. No one has ever accused Drover of subtlety, though, and it was his fault that we got shooed away to the kitchen with Joey apologizing to Alicia for the paw prints on her cashmere slacks. Banishment to the kitchen wasn't truly punishment, though. Since Joey hadn't had time to clean as she cooked, the counters and worktable had wonderful poten-tial. I'd just about figured out how to reach the pan in which the fish had been cooked—it would have involved pushing a step stool to the counter and climbing up two steps, but I could have managed it—when Joey came to her senses and realized that corgis in the kitchen was not a good idea. We were banished to the backyard with a couple of rawhide chews and a stuffed rabbit that squeaked when chomped upon, as if those things substituted for bluenose bass, grilled portobello salad, and cheesecake with fresh strawberry sauce.

Drover, being the slavish little conformist soul that he is, stayed on the deck and entertained himself by squeaking the rabbit. I, on the other hand, was not about to take banishment lying down. The planter under the dining room window was just high enough to let me peek in at what was going on if I trampled my way through the shrubbery. I had an excuse for my nosiness—not that I've ever needed an excuse. Stanley had given me a task, but he had left me on my own to find out exactly what needed doing. The infuriating twerp had gone on and on about how I should learn how to recognize need in others. I could have told him about a need he has, and it would have involved a button on his officious mouth. But that's neither here nor there. If I was to recognize where I was needed, then I had to be in the know about events around me. I was just doing my job.

The foursome at the dining room table were so intent on their conversation that no one noticed the pointy ears and alert brown eyes rise above the level of the windowsill. I had no trouble hearing every word they said. Dog ears, you know, are very keen. It's one of the advantages of being a dog. There aren't many.

Of course they talked about the wedding. Alicia had very ambitious plans. No mere church affair for her. She intended to be married in true Colorado style—at a ski lodge. And of course she planned on spending money as if it were wedding confetti. It's hard not to like someone who's rolling in money *and doesn't hesitate to share. Especially since she was willing to include us dogs in the fun.*

Samantha looked ecstatic as she outlined the details. Joey allowed that it could be a spectacular wedding. Alicia's lover boy just looked like all men do when women start talking weddings—blank.

Looking at bright Alicia and blank Ben, I suddenly understood what Stanley had meant about seeing a need without being told specifically what it was. Alicia, a fox and a very classy rich lady, needed rescuing from the mump she was about to marry. I don't know why Stan had moaned about Joey heading for turbulent waters. Alicia was the one who was hell-bent on tying herself to a man who didn't deserve her. She needed a winner, a star-quality stud who deserved her good looks and money.

Not that I have anything against cops—other than the obvious, like where were the cops when I was murdered in that Denver alleyway? They were all out eating doughnuts, that's where. Or giving a hard time to someone who just wanted to have some innocent fun smoking a little weed. Cops have their uses, I admit. But a fox like Alicia needed something more than a starched-up detective. The woman's judgment was obviously impaired by her recent traumatic experience.

I was very pleased with myself for making real progress, and I contemplated the crow old Stan would have to eat when I showed him once again that I was much smarter than he gave me credit for. This job was going to be a snap. Alicia was a lady I could relate to—beautiful, fun-loving, and rich. Putting her on the right path would be a pleasure, and I was an old hand at splitting couples apart. Look what I did for my friend Amy—split her off from that loser husband of hers and snagged her Jeff Berenger, and all that in spite of getting murdered, shipped back to Earth as a dog, and having every obstacle in the universe thrown in my path.

This job would be too simple, I thought. What could possibly go wrong?

CHAPTER 4

◆

BEN HIT THE dashboard of his ten-year-old Ford Taurus. Sometimes a businesslike fist to the dashboard made the fan work, and sometimes it didn't. Tonight it didn't. The heater wasn't much use without the fan, and the air that came in around the windows as they sped south on Interstate 25 was cold. The Taurus was a faithful old car, but it was a long way from airtight.

Alicia snuggled more deeply into her faux fox and pouted. "We could have come in the Mercedes," she reminded him. "At least the heater works in my car."

Ben chuckled. "I'll bet everything works in your car. But I don't think cops are allowed in Mercedes. Especially the sports models. It's an oil-and-water thing."

"Oil and water both would be frozen if they were in this jalopy. I'll bet it's twenty below tonight."

Ben glanced at the thermometer he'd installed outside the left window. "Twenty-five above."

"That's still freezing cold. Not that this car doesn't have ambiance." She gave him the beginnings of a smile. Alicia never could hold a pout for long—it was one of the things Ben liked about her. "What is this?" She held up a naked Barbie doll that sat in the cup holder.

"I believe she was once Businesswoman Barbie, or something like that. But she's fallen on hard times."

"Lost her business suit, I see."

"Among other things."

"And this?"

"A book. Don't you have eyes, woman?"

"On hamsters?"

"Tess's latest phase. She was drinking grapeade when she read it. That accounts for the purple wrinkled page."

"Mystery solved. Are you getting her a hamster?"

"She's begging me. I haven't decided if I'm going to give in."

"Oh come on, hardass. Give the kid a hamster."

"They bite, you know."

"What a weenie. I had a hamster once, and it never bit anybody."

He grinned. "They have big teeth."

"You are such a fraidy cat. I'll bet you're afraid of mice, too."

"Big teeth. Beady eyes."

"Guess I just lucked out that you aren't afraid of psychopathic stalkers who like to carve up women with a knife."

"Scared to death of those," he admitted.

She picked up his hand from where it rested on her knee and planted a kiss on his knuckles. "You are so full of shit."

He shot her a crooked smile.

"And speaking of full of shit . . ." Alicia pinched his arm. "What's this about you giving poor Joey a ticket?"

"She was doing eighty on the Boulder Turnpike."

"So?"

"So she was speeding."

"Joey and about ninety percent of the other drivers on the turnpike, I'll bet."

"She was doing twenty-five above the speed limit."

"Well, horrors! Send her straight to hell!"

Ben smiled dryly. "I believe that one can get there all on her own. She gave me a lot of lip."

"Good for her, you big bully!"

"Alicia, I'm not a bully, I'm a cop."

"And I'll bet you were a cop in a rotten mood."

"I probably could have been nicer."

"You've been in a very bad mood for the whole month. And I don't blame you, Ben. Really I don't. That Captain Case is such a tyrant. Really, you'd think you were in the Marines the way he expects everyone to say 'Yes, sir!' and 'No, sir!' I wish you would consider telling him to just go jump off the nearest mountain. You don't have to be a cop, do you?"

"It's what I am. And I'm a good cop—most of the time."

She interlaced her fingers with his. "That's a nice thing to be, Ben. A really great thing to be. But now that you're going to get married and maybe have a family, you shouldn't be in such a dangerous profession. We don't need the money, in case you hadn't noticed."

"I'd noticed," he said dryly.

"Don't act as if money's poisonous, you snob. You might as well take advantage of my being rich. You'll have to put up with me being spoiled, so you should take the good along with the bad."

He squeezed her hand and took his eyes from the highway long enough to wink at her. "The bad isn't all that bad, kiddo."

"Oh, stuff!" She laughed.

"And speaking of getting married."

"Here it comes!" she said with a mock pout. "You're going to dump me."

"Not today, gorgeous. I just thought we might talk about the wedding."

"The wedding," she reminded him loftily, "is the bride's affair."

"So your friend Joey told me."

"Good for her."

"But don't you think it would be easier to rent a church and a hall—maybe a really nice hotel, if you want it fancy—and have the ceremony there?"

"But this is the ultimate in romantic!" She batted him on the arm with the naked Barbie doll. "We'll combine a vacation with the wedding. Bear Run is the most wonderful place! And I'll get to show you off to my friends, and Daddy's too. Some of his business associates have been invited, because he wants to impress them with what a family man he is. Overall, I think I'm being very creative."

"I won't argue with your creativity, kiddo. But the whole thing seems really complicated, and in my experience, when things get complicated is when things get screwed up."

She tsked. "You have no sense of adventure. No possible way would Joey let anything go wrong. In school she always had to get everything perfect. It was almost annoying. Trust me, everything will go smooth as silk."

Ben sighed.

"Lighten up, Detective Ramsay. This isn't a crime we're committing, it's a wedding."

He managed to smile, even though the reminder that Joey DeMato would be in charge was less than reassuring. That woman had a way of getting under a man's skin and breaking his focus. Ben wasn't sure what it was about her. Maybe the clear, direct, "don't mess with me" gaze of those green eyes. Maybe the in-your-face challenge of her smart mouth. Or maybe it was the sensuous curves of that mouth. He had to admit this Joey was one terrific-looking woman. Different from Alicia in almost every way, but sexy as hell just the same.

Whatever it was about Joey, Ben didn't like having his focus diverted.

They exited the freeway onto Highway 285, heading them west to the foothills town of Evergreen, where Alicia lived with her father and grandmother. Evergreen was a lovely town, and many of its homes were fit for the cover of *Better Homes and Gardens*. Alicia wanted to live there after they were married— not with her family, of course, but somewhere nearby. On a policeman's salary—even a detective's salary, assuming Case cooled down after a week or two and reinstated him—Ben couldn't afford so much as a tool-shed on the property Alicia wanted to buy, but he didn't have the heart to deprive her of the luxury she'd lived in all her life. It would feel strange, living off a woman. Still, he could enjoy polished oak floors, a native-rock fireplace, and the theater-sized television as much as the next man. Not to mention season tickets to the Denver Broncos. If he tried hard enough, he could probably get used to having a rich wife.

"Turn here," Alicia told him, breaking in on a vi-sion of himself sitting in a skybox watching a playoff game.

"Here? Why here?"

"There's something I want to see." She gave him the sparkly-eyed, mischievous look he'd learned to beware.

"What?"

"You sound distrustful, Officer."

"With good reason. Where are we going?"

The pavement ended a hundred feet from where they had turned. The road was dirt, graded and pass-able for a low-slung car, but just barely. The Taurus bounced along gamely.

Alicia laughed. "They've improved the road since I was here last."

"What did you take up here last time you were here? A mule?"

"It's just a little way farther."

A mile of rough going brought them to a parking area overlooking the picturesque lake in the town of Evergreen. She directed him to a parking spot that had an unobstructed view of Colorado splendor. Above them, the stars swept the across the sky like so much silvery glitter, and the moon poured milky radiance onto a scene almost too beautiful to be real, rippling white across the lake, icing the tall pines with pearly frosting.

"Isn't it beautiful?" Alicia asked in an almost reverent tone.

"It is indeed." Sometimes in the nitty-gritty realism of his job, he forgot the world could be so beautiful. Yet here he was sitting beside a gorgeous woman who was as lovely on the inside as she was on the outside, looking down on a scene as far removed from the grime and turmoil of the city as anything could possibly be.

"I used to come here all the time when I was in high school." She slid him a glittery look beneath the challenge of a raised brow.

"Just to take in the view, huh?"

"No," she laughed musically. Walking her fingers up his arm, she gave him a smile that did more than the defunct heater could have done to warm him up. "We parked."

"You parked." He chose to be obtuse, knowing it drove her crazy.

"We made out," she explained, as if to a five-year-old.

"You did?"

"You are so dense," she said, laughing.

"Was there something you wanted to see up here?"

She punched his arm. "You drive me crazy! Kiss me!"

"I thought you were cold," he said with a grin.

"I am. I want you to keep me warm. When you take a girl out in an unheated car, it's your duty to keep her warm."

"You want to make out like a couple of teenagers?"

"You got it!"

"Maybe you want us to get in the back seat?"

"We could do that." She laughed, then happily tugged at his sweater. "You wear way too many clothes, Ben Ramsay."

Throwing his sweater into the back, Alicia worked on the buttons of his shirt. Her playful fingers teased and caressed, igniting fires as they touched. Ben began to feel warm in spite of the cold February air.

"Alicia, this is ridiculous." Still, he didn't push her away.

"This is not ridiculous." She pulled his undershirt free and skimmed her seeking little hands over bare chest. "We could do this better in the back seat. Oh, you're very warm."

Ben groaned when she pressed a kiss to his collarbone. He was too old to be playing adolescent games. A man reached a certain stage in life when once the pilot light was lit, the furnace exploded in expectation that things would progress to their natural conclusion. But that wasn't going to happen—not right then.

"Alicia, you don't know what you're doing to me."

"Yes I do." Her breath fanned warmth across his chest, and her hand slid between his legs, where he saluted her exploring skill in a very unmistakable way. She giggled. "Ben Ramsay, you're hard as a rock."

"Yeah. I noticed."

Without a bit of shyness, she wriggled herself into

the contortions necessary to sit astride his lap, facing him. The steering wheel pressed her tightly to him.

"Jesus!" Ben groaned.

"Nice, huh?" She settled herself more firmly, then "mmmmmm"ed in satisfaction when he instinctively surged against her. "I know we agreed not to sleep together until we're married, but that doesn't mean we can't play around a bit, hm?"

"Alicia . . ."

"If you won't kiss me, then I'll kiss you."

She did, and thoroughly, wriggling against him in a way that almost made him discard all his honorable intentions.

"I wish the wedding were tomorrow," she whispered against his mouth.

"God! So do I." Her scent was intoxicating. As was her soft skin, sweet, warm breath, and the firm, sensual insistence of the slender thighs gripping his hips. "So do I." If it weren't for the clothing between them, he would be inside her. A man could take only so much.

She kissed him again, pressing her fox-clad breasts against his bare chest. "Why did we decide to wait?" she groaned.

His mind was slow to respond, as every awareness was close to switching over to the upstanding and eager command center between his legs. He raided beneath her coat, beneath her silk shell and her camisole, where her breasts waited for his eager hands. He groaned in satisfaction when he finally found them.

"Let's change our minds," Alicia murmured, pressing herself into his hands. "Let's not wait."

The last brain cell still firing gave Ben a name. Tess.

"No," he said into her soft, beautiful mouth. "Honey, we can wait."

Impatiently she pushed away, creating a motion against his already overheated lap that nearly made him pull her back. But her scowl lasted only an instant. She shook her head with a wry smile. "You're such a prude."

With his hands still full of her breasts and his lap just full of her, he admitted it. "When you have a nosy kid who asks too many questions, you've got to be a prude."

"Ah, yes." She leaned back against the steering wheel. "That was the reason. 'Fathers can't play around if they expect their daughters to toe the line.' " Covering his hands with hers, pressing his palms more firmly to her breasts, she gave him a mischievous grin. "Of course, Tess is a long way from caring about the birds and bees."

"You'd be surprised what that kid cares about." Tess had been very up and down since Annie died. One minute she acted like a normal kid, bratty but lovable. The next she turned inside herself, quiet and downright strange. The thought of his vulnerable daughter immediately cooled Ben's ardor.

Alicia sighed, leaned forward and kissed him—much more chastely than before—and climbed off his lap. "I suppose I can't complain about your being such a good father. Someday you'll be a good father to our children."

Ben's eyes were just starting to unglaze when she tried to fasten his buttons. He pushed her hands away. "Have mercy, woman. Keep playing with my clothes and I'll never recover enough to drive us out of here."

She giggled. "You're buttoning your shirt crooked."

He merely grunted.

Alicia brushed back the lock of hair that had fallen over his forehead. "Poor Ben. I'm sorry. I shouldn't torture you. You are such a good man. The best I've ever known. And you make me feel so safe."

"You keep plunking yourself down in my lap like that and neither one of us will be safe."

She shivered. "Well, now I'm cold again, thanks to you being a prude. Since you won't let me seduce you, I might as well go home."

They said good night sitting in the long curved driveway of the Somers home. Ben declined Alicia's invitation to come in for a drink. He wasn't in the mood to greet her father and grandmother still mussed from nearly screwing their daughter between a bucket seat and a steering wheel. He wasn't all that comfortable with her family, and the lingering effects of a testosterone high weren't going to make things any less awkward.

"Coward," Alicia accused him with a grin.

"Guilty."

"I don't know why I put up with you."

"Because I'm the best man you know, remember?"

"Oh yeah. Now I remember. Just don't forget that we have an appointment with Señora Ramon on Saturday. I was lucky that Joey could talk her into seeing me so soon."

"Señora Ramon?"

"The dress designer, you cluck."

"Dress designer?" Ben had the feeling that he was caught in a flood without a life jacket.

"Wedding gown? Wedding? Remember?"

"Oh, that."

"Yes, that."

"You want me to be there when you talk about wedding dresses?"

"Yes."

He saw the wall of water coming straight for him. "Isn't that . . . uh . . . you know . . . women's business?"

"I want you to like the design I choose. It's your wedding too."

"I'll like anything you wear."

"Ben . . ." She gave him the face, imploring eyes impossibly wide.

"Oh God! She pulls out the heavy artillery."

"Please . . ."

"I don't have anyone to watch Tess."

"Bring her. She's a girl. All girls like to shop for clothes. It's in the X-chromosome."

"Tess is only nine. The X-chromosome hasn't kicked in yet."

"That's what you think. She'll have fun." She ran a finger down his chest and gave him a winning smile. "Please."

He sighed as the flood engulfed him. "What time?"

Alicia hugged him. "Thank you. You are the best man in the world. Ten A.M."

He watched her until she was safely in the house. Then he shook his head. "I am in such trouble," he told himself. "Dress designers, for crissake. Dress designers."

◆

Alicia peeked from the front atrium window as Ben drove away. She smiled to herself. In a month she would be his wife. Then she would buy him a decent car and call it a wedding present. Maybe that '67 Austin Healy she saw for sale in the Sunday *Denver Post*. That car would suit him well. It was a classic, just as he was. He could pooh-pooh fancy sports cars all he wanted, but Alicia didn't intend to ride in the Taurus any longer than she had to. Tess could play with her naked Barbie doll and her hamster book just as well in a car that had some class. And Ben would love it. He would just have to complain for a while to satisfy his male pride.

"Alicia!" came a call from her father's study. "Is that you?"

"Yes, Daddy!"

"Did you have a good time?"

"Yes, Daddy!"

"Teri Schaefer called. She wanted to know if you've chosen the bridesmaids' dresses yet."

"I'll call her tomorrow. I'm going to bed now."

Alicia's bedroom was her sanctuary, the one part of the house that she had all to herself. Not that she minded living with her father and grandmother. But she did need a place where she could be totally herself with no need to please anyone, follow anyone else's rules, or meet anyone else's standards. That was her bedroom, a big, sunny, mellow place with a little sitting room overlooking the valley. The only other being allowed through the door was Puddin. Even the maid didn't intrude into this private space. Alicia herself dusted and vacuumed once a week, or whenever the dust got bad enough to write herself a message on the dressing table.

Puddin slipped in before she closed the door behind her. The cat chastised Alicia with a sour meow before jumping onto the bed and curling into a sable ball. He glared accusingly. Puddin did not like Alicia to go out without him.

"Don't give me that look, mister. You aren't the only man in my life. And pretty soon you'll be putting up with your competition twenty-four hours a day. What's more, something tells me Ben Ramsay isn't the sort of guy who sleeps with a cat in his bed."

A grating meow showed what Puddin thought of that.

"Just get used to it." Alicia stripped off her blouse and tossed it into the corner where a pile of clothes awaited a trip to the dry cleaners. Her cashmere slacks followed. Clad in just bra and lace bikini panties, she stood in front of the full-length mirror and examined her appearance.

"Look at that," she told her reflection. "Almost thirty, and I'm still a dish. Ben's a lucky man."

Alicia knew very well she was gorgeous, but to her way of thinking, her looks were no big deal. Just like her family's money, her appearance was a gift. She was grateful. It made life easier. Her father would have been disappointed if she'd turned out plain. Plain just didn't cut it in Society, and her popularity in Denver society was very important to him. And what was important to him was important to Alicia. Her father had given her everything, and in return, she wanted to make him proud.

Besides, Alicia didn't think she had the strength of character to survive ugly. She just barely managed to survive being great-looking and rich, conditions which had their own disadvantages.

She turned around and posed for the cat, who regarded her with catlike condescension. "Do you believe what Ben resisted tonight, Puddin? He's a man of iron."

Slipping on a nightgown, Alicia couldn't decide if she was sorry or glad about Ben's restraint. She'd never before met a man—at least a man of the heterosexual variety—who wouldn't gladly jump her bones at the least encouragement. And sometimes without encouragement. She admired how Ben stuck to his principles. Being a tomcat was one thing when a man was young and stupid, he'd told her, but things were different when you were raising a kid. Curious eyes and curious ears invaded every part of his life, and awkward questions were kid specialties.

Having Tess in the picture was a bit awkward, Alicia admitted. She wasn't accustomed to dealing with a child. But for Ben she would get used to it. Wonderful Ben.

She shouldn't have made the mistake of telling him that she was still cursed with virginity at the ripe old age of twenty-nine. When he'd heard that, Mr. Fuddy-Duddy had become really adamant about putting the wedding first. She was obviously waiting for something special, and she deserved better than a stolen night in a motel. Alicia thought a stolen night in his car might have been plenty special.

Alicia's persistent virginity really hadn't been a conscious choice, and if she'd known that Ben would make such a big deal of it, she would never have told him. No rarified puritan standards had kept her from the beds of the men who had clamored after her—and there had been a lot of clamoring. It simply boiled down to distrust. Would her lovers have been making love to her or to her money? Probably the men themselves could not have said with any certainty.

But with Ben she knew. Knew without a doubt. The first days they had spent together he had despised her. She was sure of it, even though he'd never put it into words. And she had hated him, regarded him as a cramp in her style and a chain on her freedom. Things hadn't changed until she had proved she was more than a spoiled rich broad and he had revealed the caring man beneath his crusty exterior. But still he hadn't wanted any part of her money. Alicia had proposed to him, not the other way around. And now she wanted that final commitment that he was hers, that he saw her as a woman, not just someone he'd gotten into the habit of protecting. He didn't need to protect her anymore, much less from him.

She really did wish they had gone all the way there in his dark, cold car, Alicia decided. The act would have made her feel more secure about him, and about herself. Some tiny, lingering uneasiness about their future would have been laid to rest.

"Why are you males so hard to control?" she asked Puddin with a grimace. "Ben's just like you, puss. He mostly does what I ask him to do, but he's just indulging me. It's not like I have any true powers of persuasion with him."

Puddin flicked his tail and looked smug. She sat down on the bed beside him and took a photo album from the bedside table. The album displayed no photos. Instead, articles clipped from the *Denver Post* and *Rocky Mountain News* filled the plastic pages. Almost every night before going to bed Alicia leafed through the newsprint stories and pictures that told the harrowing tale of the stalker who had almost taken her life and the man who had had the courage and iron nerve to save her. Ben.

Her nightly ritual of scanning the old news stories reminded Alicia of what a hero lay at the core of the man she was going to marry. It assured her of his love more than any words that could come out of his mouth. He would have given his own life to save hers, had it been necessary. And in fact, he'd bought himself a load of trouble by calling his boss on the carpet for risking her life unnecessarily. All because he loved her.

"What a man, huh?" she asked the cat.

The cat seemed unimpressed.

"You're just jealous."

The hour was growing late, but Alicia wasn't yet ready to sleep—still keyed up from the evening with Joey and the aftermath with Ben. Her recent close encounter with death had left her with an uneasiness that sometimes made sleep impossible. Tonight it was in full bloom. So instead of turning out her light and trying to court elusive slumber from the dark, she donned a robe and stole downstairs to the music room. At the piano she could pour out emotions that could find no expression in words. Behind closed doors, she played softly, not wanting to disturb her family, but needing a release that nothing but music could bring.

Halfway through a Beethoven sonata her father came through the door and sat in one of the plush wingback chairs to listen. Her grandmother Irene wasn't far behind. Under watching eyes and listening ears, Alicia's fingers no longer flowed over the keys. The music became a thing to be recited instead of a sweep of feeling. So she finished the movement she was playing and stopped.

"That was beautiful, dear," her father said.

"Thank you, Daddy. I'm sorry if I disturbed you."

"You didn't disturb me at all. I wasn't sleeping."

Her grandmother sighed. "I seldom get to sleep before three in the morning, and then I wake up at six. But you should be getting some beauty rest, young lady. What with all you have coming up . . ."

And all she'd had going on before. No one mentioned the dark circles that hadn't quite disappeared from beneath Alicia's eyes.

"I was restless. That's all. I felt like playing."

"You have real talent, dear."

"Because I've made her practice every day since she was six," Irene said.

"I hope you'll take the piano with you after you're married."

"If you can get that policeman to buy a house big enough for a baby grand."

"Oh, Nana, don't start, please."

"Start what? All I said was . . ."

Alicia turned on the piano stool until she faced her family. "Don't start knocking poor Ben. He's the best man in the world. Isn't he, Daddy?"

"Ben Ramsay is a fine man. None better. And I said that even before you decided to marry him. A man with old-fashioned courage and honor is hard to find, but my baby found him."

Irene sniffed regally. "I'm sure Mr. Ramsay is all that. And we owe him much. After all, he saved Alicia's life. But still . . ."

"There is no but!" Alicia interjected. "I love him, and not just because he pulled me out of Jason Denny's car before I drowned. Or because he faced down the man when he threatened to cut my throat open."

"There's no need to be so graphic, dear. I know Sergeant Ramsay is a good policeman."

"None better," her father reiterated heartily.

"But a young woman in your position should give some consideration to suitability."

"My position?"

"Your social position, Alicia. You won't be doing Sergeant Ramsay a favor by pulling him into a world where he's not comfortable."

Alicia rolled her eyes. "We've been over this, Nana. And over it, and over it."

"And perhaps one of the times we discuss it you'll start to listen."

"Mother," Richard Somers intervened. "Stop giving the girl a bad time. Ben's a fine man, and Alicia loves him. It's a good, solid match."

Irene sighed dramatically.

"Besides, Nana, you were a secretary when you married Grandpa."

"And Grandpa—God rest his fine soul—was a mere plodding geologist at the time. Only five years after we were married did his little company discover that oil field in Wyoming. But you, my child, are third-generation wealthy. You're an established member of the best society Denver has to offer. You need to choose a husband wisely."

"Now, Mother. Give our girl the benefit of the doubt. She's a good judge of character."

"She's naive as a schoolgirl."

"Schoolgirls aren't really all that naive anymore."

"That's beside the point, Richard. . . ."

They bickered on for a few minutes more with Alicia becoming more a spectator than a participant. It was difficult to watch them disagree—almost as difficult as it was to disagree herself. Her father was proud that she'd chosen a "man's man," as he put it. Her grandmother—who'd stood in as mother since Alicia was five—would have preferred someone with an Ivy League accent and a Harvard degree. All her life Alicia had tried to please both of them. In this case, the task was impossible.

When they finally left and gave her back her privacy, she banged a discordant chord on the keyboard. Somewhere in the city, people concerned themselves with real problems, fretted about real challenges, lost sleep over things that made a difference in the world. And the most challenging things in her life were an overly gentlemanly fiancé and a buttinski grandmother.

She listened to the fading sound of strident notes and rolled her eyes. Someday, somehow, she would find the courage to do what she wanted, not what others wanted her to do.

CHAPTER 5

◆

DOLORES RAMON'S CLOTHING design shop was just off Speer Boulevard close to the fashionable Cherry Creek shopping district. It didn't look like a shop—that would have been much too tacky for Señora Ramon. A discreet plaque beside the front entrance announced the business. But for that, anyone passing by would have taken the place for a well-to-do home in a rather well-to-do neighborhood. Indeed, the señora herself lived right next door, and she was every bit as well-to-do as the exclusive clientele who paid her so handsomely for her services. Some of those clients were sent her way by Josephine DeMato, so it was with a welcoming smile that Dolores greeted Joey on the big covered porch that fronted the shop.

"Josephine, my dear, how are you?"

"I'm good, señora. And you look wonderful."

It was true. The señora's age was impossible to guess. Thick black hair piled upon her erect head in a conservative yet sophisticated arrangement, the tall, slender matron was the very picture of an indomitable aristocrat of Spain or Mexico, steeped in tradition and discipline. The sleek business suit that she wore—one of her own design, of course—did nothing to detract from the Old World aura of her presence.

"It is being a good year for me," she told Joey. "Partly because of you. Do you remember the young Mrs. Riley you sent to me for her trousseau?"

"Yes, of course."

"A woman of excellent taste. She decided to have me redo her entire wardrobe, and of course, she could afford it."

Joey smiled. "Of course." She didn't send anyone to the señora who couldn't afford her prices. But for those who could, the quality of her designs equaled anything in New York.

"And what of this lady who is coming this morning?" Dolores asked.

"Alicia Somers. An old college friend of mine who is in a great hurry for her wedding."

"Ah, yes. I know of her. Her family was in the oil business, I believe, and now funds entrepreneurs in a variety of technologies."

Trust the señora to have checked the pedigree of anyone seeking her services.

"Alicia is a wonderful person, and she was very enthused when I suggested that you design her wedding dress."

"Of course she was. But she is late." The señora glanced at her watch.

"Hm. Yes, well, I remember she was frequently late in college as well."

Ben Ramsay was not late, however. He pulled up to

the curb at a speed that Joey thought might deserve a citizen's arrest, if she'd had the nerve. But she put aside all thought of snarky remarks when a little girl in coveralls and pigtails got out of the passenger side of the car. Joey would have needed a very hard heart not to smile at the sight. This sweet-looking child simply couldn't belong to macho cop Ben Ramsay, she thought.

Apparently she did, however, for when the big cop squatted in front of the little girl and zipped her jacket, even from the front porch Joey could see the affection on his face. She'd thought it a harsh, arrogant face when he stopped her on the turnpike, but right then, with that little girl, he looked like a different man. Agreeably human. Almost attractively human.

"And who is that?" the señora asked with marked interest.

"That's Alicia's fiancé. I think Alicia twisted his arm to help her decide on a dress. His name is Ben Ramsay."

Dolores raised one brow. "Now it comes to me. I read the newspapers about them, Miss Somers and Mr. Ramsay. He is a policeman?"

"Yes," Joey confirmed somewhat ruefully.

The señora shot her a canny glance. "You sound disapproving."

"It's not up to me to approve or disapprove. Alicia likes him. That's the important thing."

"He was a hero and saved her life?"

"So I understand."

"And the child must be his little girl?"

"She must be."

"Ah."

Joey looked at her suspiciously. Dolores Ramon's "ahs" could carry a wealth of meaning. "What 'ah'?"

"I like him."

Ben had taken the girl's hand as they walked toward the house together.

"Dolores, you haven't even met him."

"I am very good with knowing about men. This one carries himself like a man who is comfortable in his own skin. I like that."

"Oh." He did have a certain refreshing lack of pretentiousness, Joey admitted. No macho posturing, no false charm. But for a man "comfortable in his own skin," he seemed a bit discomfited coming up to the porch where Joey and the intimidating Señora Ramon waited.

"Uh . . . hi," was his opener.

"Hi," Joey returned. She thought about letting him stew under the señora's frankly assessing regard, but didn't. "Señora Dolores Ramon, meet Sergeant Detective Ben Ramsay of the Denver PD. Or are you still on traffic detail?" She couldn't resist at least one little jab.

He lobbed it back without hesitation. "Someone's got to defend the world from all those speeders."

"I am happy to meet you, Sergeant Ramsay," Dolores intervened. "You are to marry Miss Somers, eh?"

"Yes, ma'am. I'm the lucky man."

"She is late."

"I'm sorry to tell you that Alicia is almost always late."

"But you are on time. Perhaps when you marry you will teach her punctuality, eh? And this is your daughter?"

"Yes, ma'am. This is Tess."

"Hello, ma'am," Tess said quietly.

"Hello, my dear. You are a very well-mannered young lady, I see."

"Thank you, ma'am."

"And very pretty."

"Thank you."

Tess was indeed pretty, with big brown eyes, brown hair pulled neatly back into pigtails, and a dimple indenting each cheek. She had a quiet stillness about her that was most unchildlike—none of the usual fidgeting or restlessness under adult scrutiny.

"You are soon to have a new mother, eh?" Dolores did not believe in verbal restraint.

"Yes, ma'am. Alicia is really rich. My father says that rich people can be a pain in the ass, but Alicia isn't. She's nice."

Color climbed up Ben's throat, and he grimaced. But Dolores smiled. "The honesty of children is so refreshing. Come with me, child. Do you like to look at clothes? But of course you do, such a pretty little thing as you."

As Dolores ushered Tess into the display room, Joey lingered behind with Ben in the reception area. "So refreshing, the honesty of children," she reprised tartly. "Just like little tape recorders, aren't they?"

Ben gave her a tolerant look. "You don't have children, do you?"

"No." She smiled, deciding Ben Ramsay was more likable when he was embarrassed.

The corner of his mouth crooked up sheepishly. "You've got to watch every damned thing you say.

Even if they're two rooms away. Kids have ears like satellite dishes. Anything that's said within a mile they can hear, especially if it's something you don't want repeated."

"She's really beautiful, you know."

"Yeah. She is. She's the image of her mother, beautiful and smart. Though sometimes I think she lives half in another world."

"Don't all kids?"

"I don't know. I only have the one."

"Her mother . . . ?" Joey knew she was being nosy, but she asked anyway.

"Dead," he said harshly.

She instantly regretted the pain in his voice. "I'm sorry. I guess I just assumed you were divorced."

He was silent.

"It seems as if positively everyone is divorced these days," she said weakly.

His mouth lifted wryly. "That's a strange attitude for someone in the wedding business. You're quite the cynic."

"I'm a realist," she said with a shrug. "When you start getting repeat customers who come back for another wedding after discarding the first bride or groom, it takes some of the meaning from 'till death us do part.' Oh damn! I'm sorry. My mouth is really running away with me today."

"It's okay." Still, his expression focused somewhere in the painful past. "Annie died five years ago in a riding accident. She loved horses. Really loved them. Tess likes to ride, too." He hesitated, then sighed. "Tess was very close to her mom."

On such an obviously painful subject, Joey didn't know what to say.

"Why the hell am I telling you this?"

"I don't know." The silence grew awkward. "I didn't mean to be nosy."

The awkwardness drew out, but then he ended it with a wry smile. "Yes you did."

"Well, okay, I did. Nosiness is one of my great failings."

"Nosiness is every woman's failing. It's in the genes."

"That's probably true. Some just keep it more under control than others."

"And you aren't one of them."

"Obviously. I really didn't mean to dredge up painful memories, though."

"Don't worry about it. I'm one of the world's luckier guys. What I need is someone to kick me in the pants when I forget it."

"I'm sure Alicia will be glad to perform that service. And speak of the little devil, here she is."

Ben looked out the window to see a sapphire Mercedes CL 600 pull jauntily to the curb behind his Ford. Alicia didn't look at all concerned that she was nearly thirty minutes late for her appointment, but Ben wasn't surprised. Alicia never meant for people to have to wait for her. Unlike Ben, though, she had no clock in her head, and it would never occur to her to wear a watch. She led a life unfettered by time.

"Hey, you two!" Her perfect blonde curls bounced with energy as she breezed through the door. Alicia managed to make jeans and an Irish wool sweater look sexy. "Are you getting better acquainted? Uh-oh. From the look on Joey's face, I'd guess that I'm late."

"You're late," Joey confirmed.

"Am I in trouble?" She gave Ben a kiss on the cheek, but she was talking to Joey. Trust her to know that Ben would forgive her, Joey thought.

"You'll have to charm Señora Ramon," Joey advised her.

"I can do that. Did Tess come with you?"

"I'm here." Tess came through the door from the back room, followed by the señora.

"So you are." Rather gingerly, Alicia gave the child a hug. Tess tolerated it, Ben noticed. Just tolerated it. She didn't dislike Alicia, never said a cross word about her or their plans to marry, but she didn't show much warmth, either. Give it time he told himself. "Are you excited?" Alicia asked the girl.

"I guess so."

"Of course you are. You'll be getting a dress too, you know. You're going to be in the wedding."

"I know," was Tess's polite reply.

"No one will be getting a dress unless you come in," Dolores warned. "I am a very busy woman, and I cannot take all day at this. Come in. Come in."

Ben felt very much an unnecessary player as the feminine game of discussing fashion, cut, fabric, and accessories got under way. Fortunately, nothing was expected of him other than adding token male approval to the proceedings, so he took the opportunity to watch Alicia, something that he'd found entertaining ever since their paths had first crossed. No red-blooded man could get bored watching Alicia. Not only was she gorgeous, but she was an absolute artist at manipulation. And one of the amazing things about Alicia was that none of her manipulation was calculated. She could have charmed the fangs off a rattler by pure instinct—perhaps a compliment to the exquisite diamonds on the snake's back or the quality sound of its rattles—all with perfect sincerity.

By the time Alicia had gone ten steps with the señora, the designer was in her back pocket. She had long admired Señora Ramon's designs, Alicia told the woman with genuine warmth. How honored she would be to wear one of her designs on the most important occasion of her life.

With any other woman, her compliments would have been a line of hooey. But Alicia pulled it off because she meant every word. The woman was a true-blue artless wonder. She always knew the right thing to say, and Ben had never known her not to mean it one hundred percent. People sensed it, and they loved her for it.

Look how she had wrapped him around her finger, Ben thought. He was no different than anyone else. Big tough cynical cop. Right. And why shouldn't he fall for Alicia? She was the goddamnedest most perfect woman he'd ever met.

It was just that sometimes he wished she came without the attachment of all that money. He'd been a self-reliant guy nearly all his life, supporting himself since the age of fifteen, more or less. How did a man get used to having a wife who would consider his entire annual salary small change?

"Ben? Are you listening?" Alicia was regarding him with tolerant affection. The other females in the room, including Tess, didn't look as patient.

"Uh . . . listening to what?"

"To my question." She held up two drawings of the sort that might be in a fashion magazine. Or at least he assumed such things were in fashion magazines. He had never so much as glanced through one of those things. "Which of these dress designs do you like the best?"

What was he supposed to say? They both had long skirts, tight tops, and lots of lace. "I think I'd look real silly in either one of them."

"Oh, you! Be serious."

"Which do *you* like best?" A surefire winner to all fashion questions.

"I can't decide. The lines of this one are absolutely stunning." She held one up. "But I'm afraid the neckline will make my neck look stubby. On the other hand, this one"—the other drawing came to the fore— "is very elegant, but the cut of the sleeves . . ."

"I can modify the details," the señora said. "But you must decide on the basic style."

Joey chimed in. "The narrower skirt gives you more height, Alicia."

"I thought that was what platform shoes did." Ben couldn't resist.

Alicia ignored him. Joey shushed him. "Oh, be quiet."

Quite forgetting they had consulted him in the first place, the three women launched a spirited discussion of lines, length, necklines, darts, tucks, and lace placement, with Tess a fascinated onlooker.

Ben studied the contrast of Alicia and Joey together, wondering at the unlikeliness of these two being friends. Alicia worked at pleasing everyone. She was all soft, girlish, refined enthusiasm, gay laughter, gentle suggestions. Joey, on the other hand, seemed to possess an abundance of sharp edges. She obviously was accustomed to taking charge, ordering details, expecting perfection, and arranging all things to run smoothly in defiance of the universal trend toward chaos. Beside Alicia, she was strong-looking and angular, no less attractive for looking more like an athlete than a Barbie doll. Ben speculated that every penny Joey DeMato possessed was earned by considerable sweat on her part, and that every penny that left her hand served a practical purpose. There was absolutely nothing about the woman that even hinted at frivolity.

What could Alicia and Joey have in common to provide the basis for friendship? Did contrasts sometimes enhance rather than obstruct a relationship? Ben hoped so, or he and Alicia were doomed to a stormy marriage.

Looking delighted as a child with a brand new toy, Alicia held up the drawing she had labeled as "elegant" and waved it in Ben's direction. "Do you like this one?"

"I love it." It wasn't precisely a lie. A dress was a dress, and Alicia would be a knockout in anything, even a rag fished out of a dumpster.

"This one, then," she told the señora, her tone carrying the gravity of a general deciding battle strategy. "And now . . ."

They shifted to the subject of fabric, and Ben's attention moved to his daughter, who stood near Joey looking distracted. At first she had shown close interest in the fashion frenzy, but how long could such things hold a nine-year-old's attention, even a female nine-year-old? Probably the fashion gene didn't kick in until they were at least twelve. But Joey made a point of including her in the discussion, and Tess seemed to like being a part of it. At least she wasn't sitting on the sofa playing with the fairies in her head. Tess had a rich fantasy life, to put it mildly. She would probably grow up to become a romance novelist.

"No, no, Miss Somers," Dolores chided, bringing Ben's attention back to the business at hand. "On such short notice you cannot expect me to do the attendants' gowns as well. I must squeeze time from a full schedule to make your dress, and I do it only because Josephine is such a good friend and she asks me this favor. The bridesmaids' dresses—no!"

"I don't get a dress?" Tess asked rather plaintively. Perhaps the fashion gene had kicked in.

"Of course you get a dress!" Alicia promised. "You're the junior bridesmaid. We can shop for it today, just you and I, and when you find something that's you, we'll plan all the bridesmaids' dresses to match. Would you like that?"

"I get to decide?"

"Well—sure. And everyone else will just have to fall in line."

Tess's smile was radiant, but it faded quickly when Alicia exclaimed, "Oh, no! I forgot. I have a dentist appointment this afternoon. Ben, you must take Tess shopping for a dress. I'll show you the colors I've decided upon."

Shopping wasn't Ben's forte, but he wouldn't have complained about any plan that let him spend a private afternoon with his daughter, so he regretted saying no. "Sorry. I have to go to work at two. Tess will be staying with a neighbor."

"Oh, Daddy!" Tess said, obviously disappointed.

"Sorry, kiddo. I have a meeting."

"On Saturday?"

"A Parks and Recreation thing."

Alicia's narrowed eyes silently reminded him that he wouldn't be working at all if he were sensible, but she turned to Tess with a tight smile. "We'll make it some other day, Tess. I'll just have to look at my schedule to see when I can fit it in."

"I could take her," Joey offered. She looked surprised, as if the words had popped out of her mouth without her meaning to say them.

"*You'll* take Tess shopping?" Ben's tone was dubious.

"We need to get the dress thing settled. Alterations take time, and we're on a short fuse here."

Tess jumped up and down in anticipation, her pigtails bouncing and her face split by a grin.

"Joey's right, Ben," Alicia said. "We should really get this done this afternoon."

"Bravo," Dolores agreed. "Josephine has excellent taste in clothing style. Selecting clothing is a woman's job, not a man's."

"I'll give you the colors," Alicia said, "and maybe show you what I had in mind."

"I thought I got to decide," Tess objected.

Ben was immediately out of the equation, pushed from all consideration. "Wait a minute!" he threw into the mix of chatter. "I'm not sure—"

"Not sure about what?" Alicia demanded. At once all eyes turned upon him. It was amazing how intimidating females could be when they ran in a pack.

"Uh . . . well . . . not sure that I want Tess buzzing around the city without me."

"Oh, Ben! It's not as if we're sending her off with just anyone!"

"Are you going to drive?" he asked Joey suspiciously.

"No. I thought we'd walk from here to the mall. Of course we're going to drive."

He remembered the Triumph doing eighty on the turnpike, and he didn't want his daughter in it.

"I'll drive really, really slow," she drawled. "A snail would beat me there."

Sarcastic, Ben noted. No man liked a sarcastic woman. So why did he like her sass? "You'll make her wear her seat belt?"

"Daddy!" Tess chimed in. "She's not a moron!"

There were worse things than being a moron, like driving even a half mile per hour over the speed limit with Tess Ramsay in the passenger seat. His eyes sent Joey the message. She smiled and patted his arm.

"I'll treat her like Waterford crystal. Pick her up at my place at five."

Joey and Tess ended up at Westminster Mall, a place with somewhat more reasonable prices than Cherry

Creek, which Alicia had suggested. Alicia blithely assumed she would pay for Tess's dress, but Joey somehow sensed that Ben wouldn't stand for that, and a cop's salary would hardly get a person through the door of Cherry Creek, much less allow for buying something there.

After going through the children's section of two department stores, Joey was discouraged. Tess's colors were old ivory and forest green. Manufacturers of dresses for nine-year-olds didn't produce much in forest green. Pink—yes. Yellow, orange, red—yes. Even royal blue. No forest green.

"Can we go in there?" In the Cinnabon shop a fan blew sweet aromas into the mall, trolling for hungry shoppers. Like a fish on a hook, Tess was reeled in. "I'm hungry."

"Shopping is a hungry job," Joey agreed. Who cared if one bite of cinnamon roll contained a week's worth of fat? They were on an outing of sorts. That deserved celebration.

They brought their shared treasure to a small plastic table outside the shop. Only with difficulty had Joey convinced Tess to split a roll with her.

"I could've eaten a whole one," Tess boasted.

"If you're still hungry after eating your half, I'll get you another."

"It's a deal."

"Just don't make yourself sick."

"I never get sick from eating cinnamon rolls."

"When I was about your age, I did just that. And I was taller than you and had a bigger stomach."

"Really?"

"Really."

"Well, maybe I'll just start with the half."

Joey hadn't had much experience with children. She liked them fine from a distance, when they weren't throwing tantrums, whining, smarting off, or doing any of the annoying things that came naturally to kids. She suspected Tess was as capable of those things as any other youngster, but she might still be likable in spite of it.

"I don't think we're going to find a dress," Tess said around a bite of bun. "Alicia won't be pleased." In spite of the pastry in her mouth, she sounded very grown up for a nine-year-old.

"We'll find one. Though it is looking like Mission Impossible."

"I hope it's today. Alicia doesn't have a lot of patience."

Very grown up, Joey thought.

"My dad won't care, though. He says fancy weddings are just another excuse for a party."

"Doesn't your dad like parties?"

"Yeah. He does. We do pizza parties, and movie parties with popcorn, and he always gives me a birthday party. My dad's cool."

Joey grinned. Now Tess was sounding more like a kid.

"But he gets mad real easy."

"Really?"

"Yeah. All the time. Not at me. My dad doesn't ever yell at me. But he says he doesn't buffer fools lightly—"

"Suffer fools?"

"Yeah. Suffer fools, and the world's full of them. So

he gets mad and sometimes gets in trouble, like with Captain Case. But it will blow over."

This was a scary kid, Joey decided. Cute, likable, but scary.

"I don't think Alicia's good for him," Tess said, considering the last of her part of the bun.

"What?"

"I don't think my dad is going to marry Alicia."

"Don't you think maybe your dad knows what he's doing?"

"No," Tess said with certainty.

"Don't you like Alicia?"

"I like her okay. She's nice. She's real pretty, and rich, and I guess she likes my dad a lot."

"Yes, she does."

"She has a really cool cat, too. His name is Puddin, and he doesn't scratch. Much. And Alicia said she'd get me my own horse after my dad marries her."

"Then why don't you think your dad should marry her?"

Tess shrugged. "I don't think they're going to get married, that's all. Will I get to keep the dress?"

"Tess, they're going to get married. Trust me."

"I don't think so."

Joey told herself not to be nosy. Nosiness had already gotten her into trouble once today, and she was talking to a nine-year-old kid, a kid who was probably leading her down the garden path just to get a reaction.

"If we're going to find you a dress, we'd better get cracking."

"Can I have the rest of your bun?"

"Be my guest."

They finally found a dress in a specialty shop that catered to children. It was forest green velvet with ivory lace. Off-white buckle slippers completed the ensemble. If Alicia had trouble matching the fabric for the bridesmaids, tough, Joey thought. She'd done her best. Tess herself had spotted the dress, and she looked like a little angel in it—an angel with a hint of the devil in her eyes. But she hadn't wanted to buy it until Joey assured her she wouldn't have to give it back when her dad gave Alicia the old heave-ho.

They were in the fitting room, and Joey was unbuttoning the two million buttons down the back of the forest green dress when Tess bit her lip and looked at Joey in the mirror. "Can I tell you something?"

Joey undid the last button and shimmied the dress down Tess's narrow shoulders. "Sure. What?"

"You won't get mad?"

"Why would I get mad?" A premonition sent a little chill down Joey's spine.

"Daddy said my 'magination runs away with me, but I know when things are real and aren't real. I do."

"And . . ." Joey prompted.

"And . . ." Tess bit her lip, gave Joey a narrow look, and sighed. "My mom told me that Alicia isn't right for Daddy. So they can't really get married, because my mom says it won't work. And that's the truth."

Ben knocked on Joey's front door at five sharp. He, unlike Alicia, was apparently never late. The surprise of his arrival was the pizza box he carried.

"It's a peace offering," he explained. "And a thank-you for taking Tess this afternoon. I know pizza isn't exactly what you're used to, you being a sort of a chef and all, but hey! Here it is. Pepperoni, mushroom, onion, olive, and Canadian bacon."

"How can you beat that?" Joey said. "And you're wrong. I have pizza all the time. I only cook when I have company."

"Really? I pictured you whiping up appetizers and sauces and exotic recipes every day."

Joey felt his eyes sweep over her blue jeans and CSU sweatshirt. His quick appraisal was a bit disconcerting.

"I was beginning to think those tailored suits were a permanent growth. Kind of like Businesswoman Barbie."

"You spend too much time with a nine-year-old."

"Not enough time, in fact. Speaking of nine-year-olds, is mine still alive after driving around town with you?"

Joey shot him a look.

"Sorry. Let's start over."

"No more speeding cracks."

"Promise."

"And admit you were rude and crude when you gave me that ticket."

"You *were* speeding."

She narrowed her eyes.

"Okay, I wasn't on my best behavior that day. I was in a bad mood, and I took it out on you."

"Best behavior?" She encouraged him with a lifted brow.

"You're right. I was an asshole."

"It was harassment, wasn't it? Just because you were in a funk about being on traffic duty."

He shrugged and smiled. "You and your smart mouth were natural targets. You're very harassable."

For that he got the look.

"Okay. You're right. It was all my fault."

Joey smiled. "Good. Now we've cleared that up, let's eat pizza before it gets cold." She took the box from him and led him into the kitchen.

"You *were* speeding," he muttered almost inaudibly, but she chose to ignore it.

The pizza was no sooner on the kitchen table, giving forth the magic aroma of pepperoni and Canadian bacon, than Tess burst through the kitchen door followed by the two corgis. Drover bounded about her feet, trailing dirt from the garden, and Piggy followed at a more sedate pace. Dogs and kid immediately focused attention on the pizza.

"Pizza pie!" Tess exclaimed.

The dogs' expression mirrored her approval.

"Dinner is served." Ben gestured expansively at the pizza.

Joey watched Ben with his daughter, thinking that a man who was obviously such a friend to his child was hard not to like. A man not afraid to admit that he was an asshole, as he had so descriptively put it, was also hard not to like. He wasn't really an asshole, she decided, and perhaps Alicia had found herself a good man after all. Alicia was a sharp lady, despite her disguise as a fluffhead. And she might have found herself a winner.

"You should see the cool dress we bought," Tess

told her father. "It took forever to find it. And Joey said if I didn't stop inhaling cinnamon buns she'd have to let out the seams."

"Joey doesn't know how much energy a nine-year-old burns up," Ben said.

"I'm beginning to get an idea. Tess, if you keep waving your pizza around like that, Drover is going to jump up and steal it."

Tess laughed. Joey wondered uneasily if she should tell Ben about his daughter's conversations with her deceased mother. She was reluctant. It wasn't her business. Then again, someone should tell him.

The idea nagged at Joey until they were taking their leave and Tess made a last visit to the bathroom.

"Uh . . . Ben?"

"That tone of voice says I'm in trouble."

"No. Not this time."

"A welcome change."

Joey smiled briefly. "The thing is . . . Tess told me something today. And normally I don't tell tales . . ."

"You females stick together," he said with a grin. "I know."

"Be serious. The truth is, Tess told me she talks to her mom. Not ordinary kid pretend conversation. She really thinks her mom says things to her."

Ben's grin faded. "I know. This isn't new. It started about a year after Annie died. I guess I'm hoping that having Alicia as a stepmom will help Tess put her real mother to rest."

Joey's heart went out to him. How could a man so ostensibly tough look so sad?

"I'm so sorry, Ben." Before thinking about what she

did, Joey placed a sympathetic hand on his arm. The warmth of hard muscle beneath her fingers made her realize her mistake. Hastily, she drew back. He gave her a startled glance, then a crooked smile.

"Tess is a great kid. She'll be okay. I'm going to make sure she's okay."

It occurred to Joey suddenly that Tess, the great kid, was lucky to have such a great father. And Alicia was lucky to get such a good man, even if he was a bit crusty around the edges.

And was that twinge in her stomach from the pizza? Or did she just suffer a pang of envy? She hoped that getting involved in this wedding wasn't an awful mistake.

CHAPTER 6

◆

WELL NOW, WASN'T this just too cozy? The solution to poor Alicia's problem was so obvious at this point that I can hardly take credit for the idea. But I will. Working for Stanley, I have to grab all the credit I can get, if only because the officious little twerp is so hard to please.

So I put on my thinking cap. That was harder than it sounds, because there was pizza in the house. Pizza is a distraction to any dog, and even though I'm not a genuine dog, I'm saddled with a lot of dog quirks, and topping that list of quirks is an overdeveloped focus on food. Especially pizza. The tantalizing aroma. The mouthwatering sight of all those darling little pepperonis, mushrooms, peppers. The lovely, lovely strings of gooey cheese as pieces are lifted from the plate to the mouth. The riveting possibility that someone might drop a crisp crumb of crust, or even a fat, round pepperoni.

See. Even talking about it sends my mind off on a tangent. Very embarrassing. I'm pursued by the curse of my doggishness at every turn. But back to my brilliant plan—here was Alicia's lamb chop cuddling up to Alicia's bosom buddy. It called to mind what happened with me and Amy's one-time hubby.

Well, maybe not quite. Ben and Joey weren't truly on the make—yet. And Joey wasn't nearly the hot item I was back in the good old days. I cut a swath through the male population—both available and unavailable—that rivaled Sherman's march through Georgia. Since then I've seen the error of my ways, sort of, but you have to admit that an accomplishment like that takes talent. Joey had a few things going for her, but no way was she in my class.

But I'm getting distracted again. The point is, I saw potential between Ben—the long, dull arm of the law—and Miss Never-Give-a-Dog-a-Pizza Joey. And what better way for Alicia to realize that Ben was Mr. Wrong than to catch him putting the moves on her best friend?

But wait! Was that a gobbet of cheese flying through the air, headed for a landing at Drover's feet? I gauged the possibility of reaching it before Drover could scoop it up. A curled lip from Drover told me the chances of getting a nip for my trouble were greater than getting a taste of cheese. Drover isn't the brightest bulb in the corgi chandelier, but when it comes to food, he admits no equals.

Expectant taste buds disappointed, I tried to concentrate on business. How could I maneuver our friend the cop into a position where he might be tempted by Joey's charms? In my experience, men were easily maneuvered by someone who understood male priorities. Someone like me. I might create a situation where—oh man! Look at that cheese!

The most likely food chump here was the kid. Any dog knows that kids are natural pushovers for the starving-dog look, something I had down pat. I'd already seen Tess sneak a couple of tidbits to Drover while Ben and Joey were engrossed in conversation, and I knew the kid liked me better than she liked Drover. All the time in the yard she'd followed me around trying to pet me, in spite of Drover fawning on her as if he had no dignity at all—which he doesn't, by the way. I'd given her a cold shoulder. Kids and I don't mix well. Even back in my predog days I didn't like them much—snotty-nosed, whining, irksome little carpet rats. But if this one was prepared to share her dinner, I could lower myself to accept it. The truth is, in true corgi fashion, I was willing to do somer-saults and dance on my hind legs if a nice juicy piece of pizza was the reward.

I misjudged my mark, however. What I got from the kid wasn't a dollop of cheese or a slice of meat but one of those eerily penetrating looks she'd been giving me since she walked through the front door. Those looks gave me a creepy feeling that she could see right past my foxy face and perky ears to the real me, Lydia Keane, a formerly hot number waddling through the afterlife looking like a stubby-legged sausage.

Of course, it was impossible for the kid to know any of that, but she still gave me the creeps. It got worse when she lec-tured me on my eating habits.

"You don't really want to eat this," she had the nerve to tell me as I tried my best pathetic-dog-starving-in-an-alley look. "Think of your figure."

Even her dad thought the remark strange. He gave Tess a puzzled look. "Since when do dogs worry about figures, kiddo?"

Tess shrugged. "Piggy does."

Is that weird or what? Okay, I'll admit it was a stretch to think it meant anything. The kid couldn't possibly sense my former obsession with maintaining a 115-pound package of attractive curves. Could she? The very thought gave me the creeps. If you ask me, that goody-two-shoes little voice of hers just masked the real smart-ass beneath.

The rest of the evening I ignored the little twit as best I could. Once the food was removed, I could truly concentrate on business. I decided to start things cooking right away, since Ben was there and so was Joey. It wouldn't be hard. I didn't need the two of them to fall in love; I just needed to generate a little interest here, a little chemistry there, enough to communicate itself to Alicia and make her see that she'd won herself a bozo rather than a hero.

Sucking them into my scheme was easy. They didn't suspect a thing when I pulled the cute poochie act and dragged my leash into the living room. It was a nice evening. How much cozier can a couple get than to take a walk in the park with a cute, frolicking dog? And what sane person can resist a corgi when she's acting cute? For the cause I could lower myself to be downright adorable, though it did turn my stomach. I hoped Stanley was taking note of my devotion to duty.

Tess was the one who actually persuaded them to don jackets and take a walk around Sloan Lake, which was only a short block from Joey's house. All five of us went. Drover larked about like an idiot, as usual. Tess threw the ball for him, effectively taking them both out of the equation. I hung back with Ben and Joey, prancing about in typical dog fashion but sternly squashing my four-legged instinct to chase after that ball. In all my prancing, I managed to wrap the leash around their legs—something that comes so naturally to corgis that my victims couldn't possibly have suspected ulterior motives. Not that they would have in any case. One of the few advantages of being a dog is that no one ever suspects you of conniving. Humans think that dogs aren't smart enough to connive. They are so wrong!

In all my frolicking and prancing I managed to get Ben and Joey into such a tangle they nearly went down one on top of the other. They didn't fall only because the cop managed to keep his balance and grabbed on to Joey. They were close as two people can be without being welded, and I didn't miss the spark that flew between them. If the voltage had been any higher, their hair would have stood on end. Am I good or am I good!

By the time the two potential lovebirds managed to get untangled, both were flustered and red-faced. Joey shot me a poisonous look, but Ben just laughed and commented that I could certainly zip here and there on such short little legs. I supposed he was a "man's man," which required that he like dogs, probably the bigger and smellier the better. Chump. A classy lady like Alicia really did deserve better.

During the rest of the walk, my two victims maintained a discreet distance, but a certain tension lingered between them that was clear to my perceptive observation. The tension not only lingered, but grew, until Tess and Drover gamboled up to our little group and somehow dissipated the charged atmosphere. I knew the kid was trouble. It was all I could do to keep from nipping her bony little ankle to make her go away again. Tess looked at her father and at Joey with eyes much too understanding for a knobby-kneed, pigtailed twit of nine. Then she looked at me and smiled, almost as if she knew what I was doing. It made the hair stand up along my back, let me tell you.

Stanley had hinted at some danger in his usual vague, unhelpful way, and I wondered now if Tess wasn't a part of that. Maybe old Stan hadn't implied real danger so much as annoying trouble. One should never understimate the troublemaking potential of a kid. I haven't had much experience with the creatures, at least not since I was one myself, but I know they're experts at mayhem. I'd bet my next bowl of kibble—

and that's saying a lot—that mayhem was Tess Ramsay's middle name.

The Boston Half Shell in downtown Denver was a wonderful place to have lunch, but the ambiance and good food couldn't be expected to compensate for the annoying company. The polite smile on Joey's face felt riveted at the corners with hot steel. Another minute and her cheeks were going to spasm. If Alicia's grandmother Irene let loose one more supercilious smirk—just one more!—Joey was going to empty her glass of ice water over the woman's bouffant do of blue-gray hair and watch it drip down her hatchet face.

She wouldn't really, of course. Joey was too much the professional to lose her cool with an irritating old woman. In her business she learned to deal with nuptial busybodies—parents, grandmothers (grandfathers generally tried to stay out of things, she had discovered), sisters, and cousins. Families frequently wanted a say in how a couple tied the knot, or whether they should tie the knot at all, and they seldom agreed with the bride and groom about how things should proceed. Mothers were the worst, usually, but since grandmother Irene had been the maternal stand-in for almost all of Alicia's life, it stood to reason that Granny was maternal stand-in for being a royal pain-in-the-tush about Alicia's wedding.

D-day was only six days away. That was how Joey had come to think of the day they were all supposed to depart for Bear Run ski resort. She had a million things to do and couldn't afford to be idling away time in a

posh restaurant, but Irene had invited both Alicia and
Joey to luncheon—or rather she had commanded their
presence—at the Boston Half Shell. Alicia had come
because obedience to her granny was ingrained. Joey
had come because Alicia was both a client and a friend,
and she didn't want to get Alicia in hot water with her
family.

Granny's ploy of the moment was to make Alicia
uncomfortable by her appraisal of the wedding guest
list.

"The Allens haven't RSVPed." Irene tapped a disapproving fork on her salad plate.

"I invited them," Alicia said, sounding a bit guilty.

"Well, I suppose I shouldn't be surprised." She gave
Joey a condescending look. "They're a very established
family, you know. Mrs. Allen has done such wonderful
fund-raising for the symphony."

"I know who the Allens are." Joey strained to be
polite.

"I doubt they consider this sort of thing an affair
they'd want to attend."

A twinkle surfaced in Alicia's eyes. "I don't know. I
can just see Agnes Allen on skis."

Irene gave her a look that quelled the twinkle. "The
Rockwells aren't coming either, I see."

"They're in their eighties," Alicia reminded her.

"And she's still very influential in Denver society,
dear."

Alicia grimaced meaningfully.

"I suppose we should have expected this," Irene said
with a sigh. "If you have an affair at a ski lodge, you attract the kind of people who enjoy that sort of place."

"Nana! Daddy thinks it's going to be great fun. He's invited some of the investors who are looking at the Big Thompson golf development."

If anything, Irene's face became even more pinched.

"And all my friends are wild to get up there. Five free days of spring skiing, partying, and playing in the snow."

"Hm . . . yes, well, who are these people? I don't recognize them. Riley, Gonzales, Cresiak, Krokosz."

"They're Ben's friends."

"Ah." Irene, like Señora Ramon, could manage a very speaking "ah."

The mention of Ben sent Joey's mind racing along an unwelcome tangent. Ben. Ben in the park, walking beside her. Ben laughing at Piggy. Ben catching Joey when the double-damned dog wound them in a Chinese puzzle of tangled leash. Ben holding her upright. The feel of him close against her, her mashed into him like butter on toast. Melting butter.

Admit it, Joey chided herself. You did melt all over him. There had been enough heat generated between the two of them to warm Denver for a solid week. What the hell was wrong with her?

And was it just her, or were Ben's fires stoked also? Imagination, Joey told herself. Strictly imagination. And it certainly wouldn't happen again.

"Joey! Tell her!"

"Huh?" With a jerk, Joey came back to the present. "Sorry. What?"

"Tell my grandmother that Ben can invite whomever he wants."

Joey sighed.

Alicia huffed in frustration. "Well, it is tradition for the groom to be able to invite his friends and family."

"I never meant to imply that he couldn't, dear. The Ramsays will be coming, I assume."

"Well . . ." Alicia stirred the lettuce on her plate. "Ben's mother might come. She's the Mrs. Cresiak. His parents are divorced. His dad lives up in Alaska. He can't come. But his brother Tom is best man."

Irene merely sighed.

Joey decided to intervene. "Mrs. Somers, I think you'll like the ceremony Ben and Alicia have planned. It's very traditional. The music is going to be beautiful. We've engaged a string quartet from the Colorado Symphony to play."

"How nice," Irene said frostily.

Alicia joined in gamely. "The lodge has tons of amenities for people who don't enjoy outdoor sports. There's a spa, a heated pool, a wonderful chef, and the rooms in the lodge are beautiful. A friend of mine just bought the resort, and he sent me pictures. The greatest thing is, from Wednesday on he's shutting it down so we'll have the whole place to ourselves."

The waiter came with their entrées—a crab bisque for Irene, which Joey thought very appropriate, and club sandwiches for Joey and Alicia.

"Have you heard, Alicia dear?" Irene said. "Dorothy Gilbert is getting a divorce."

"Dorothy? Oh no! She seemed so happy."

"When was the last time you saw her?"

"At her wedding. When was it? Three years ago?"

"Two and a half, actually. She's being taken to the

cleaners, poor dear, but I suppose she asked for it, marrying that construction worker."

"He wasn't a construction worker. He had his own remodeling business."

"There isn't much difference."

"Besides, there's absolutely nothing wrong with being a construction worker. It's an honest profession."

"Well, honest profession or not, this one isn't going to have to support himself anymore. He's getting half of Dorothy's assets, at least the assets not tied up in her trust fund."

Irene raised her eyes from her crab and gave her granddaughter a meaningful look. Alicia toasted her with a glare, wadded up her linen napkin, and slammed it onto the table. "I'm going to the powder room. Joey, would you like me to show you where it is?"

Joey declined. She relished a few moments alone with Granny Somers.

Irene frowned as Alicia stalked off, then she turned her sharp eyes to Joey. "You seem to be a very sensible young woman, Miss DeMato."

"I think so," Joey replied.

"What do you think of Alicia tying herself to a man like Ben Ramsay?"

"Ben seems to be an honest, capable man who thinks the world of Alicia." Ben again. Ben in the park. Ben's arms wrapping around her, making her heart race. No. She wouldn't think about it. That had been days ago. Soon she would forget it.

"I'm sure he does think the world of Alicia. She's going to be his meal ticket for the rest of his life."

"Mrs. Somers, I honestly don't believe Ben Ramsay gives a fig for Alicia's money. If anything, it makes him uncomfortable."

"Ah. That is the other problem. Even if Sergeant Ramsay is as honest and honorable as you say he is, he will never fit into Alicia's world."

That might be true, Joey admitted, but it wasn't her business. Nor was it really Irene's.

"I fear my granddaughter is making a grave mistake. She doesn't know the difference between infatuation and love. And this farce of a wedding is . . . well . . . it's so tacky. A wedding is a sacred ceremony, not a ski party." She pointed her spoon at Joey. "Alicia says you two were friends in college, Miss DeMato. Since you went to Mills, I assume you know something of the circles that Alicia moves in. If you said something—urged her to think a bit—she might come to her senses before making a terrible mistake. Obviously she won't listen to an old woman who has over twice her years and experience."

Joey sighed. "If I may be frank . . ."

"Please do."

"I have been in the wedding business for six years, and in that time I've consulted for many, many weddings. A wedding is a very stressful time in any family. It's a time when family relationships can be welded or shattered, and the effects are long lasting."

"What are you trying to say, Miss DeMato?"

"What I'm saying is this. If you value your relationship with Alicia, then accept with good grace that her idea of a suitable husband and a suitable wedding differ from yours. It's her wedding and her life. Neither you nor I nor anyone else has the right to tell her how to run either."

Irene's brows drew together in an unflattering scowl. "Family and friends are supposed to watch out for each other."

"Mrs. Somers, you've given Alicia your opinion. She knows very well how you feel, and she still chooses to marry Ben Ramsay in just under two weeks at Bear Run Lodge. Your harping at her is not going to change her mind, it is simply going to diminish her happiness on the day that should be the happiest in her life."

With a narrow, astute look, Irene asked, "And what do you think are Alicia's chances for a stable, happy marriage with Sergeant Ramsay?"

"My job is organizing a wedding, not making predictions. Trying to second-guess whether or not a couple will make it isn't part of the job."

Irene leaned back and regarded Joey with penetrating eyes. "My guess is that you're quite good at your job, Miss DeMato. You are a very forceful young woman. Do you often have to defend your brides from their families?"

The smile Joey gave her was half apologetic. "Almost every wedding." The apology part of the smile reflected Joey's own uncertainty about Alicia's future happiness with Ben Ramsay. She wasn't at all sure that Irene Somers wasn't right about some things.

The rest of the week gave Joey little time to think about anything but the business at hand. The days and hours before going to the mountains passed too quickly. Joey always expected last-minute details to go wrong, so she wasn't surprised when the usual crop of problems sprouted.

Bridesmaids, in Joey's experience, were always troublesome. Perhaps it was because no woman liked to play second fiddle while another woman took center stage, so bridesmaids, out of secret envy, created every difficulty they could. At least Joey was often led to speculate such things when dealing with them. Alicia's attendants were no exception. Sue Smythe couldn't find the correct shoes in her size—12D. Sue was another Mills girl. Joey had known her slightly, and she remembered that she'd always complained of having to special order shoes. Brides should be forbidden, Joey decided, from having any bridesmaid who didn't wear a dress size from eight to fourteen or a shoe size from six to ten. Anything else inevitably caused problems.

Teri Schaefer, the maid of honor who was flying in from North Carolina, had ordered her dress and then promptly gained seven pounds. She spent a half hour wailing through the phone into Joey's ear about how her new birth control pills made her retain water and gave her cravings as well. Joey suggested alterations instead of a crash diet; from what Alicia had told her about Teri's dating habits, she didn't dare suggest giving up the pill for a couple of weeks.

Carrie Meyer's problem was the easiest to handle. She wanted to bring a date to the resort. Joey had to hear all about the terrific hunk she'd met at a club a week ago—a real outdoor enthusiast who would absolutely love Bear Run, a super guy whom everyone would like. Joey listened politely, made appropriate noises of appreciation and envy for Carrie's find, and referred her directly to Alicia.

Then there was Alicia's father, who called at least three times to make sure his business investors would be given appropriately impressive rooms in the lodge and that the champagne she was planning to serve was of a vintage that met with his approval. Pat Haines, owner of Bear Run, pressed her for exact numbers, arrival times, special requirements, and to confirm she was inviting the press to the event. Publicity-wise, he was milking the wedding for all it was worth, and Joey didn't blame him. He was shutting down the resort for several days so that Alicia and her crowd could have the privacy to party. Besides the hefty fee Alicia was paying him, she'd promised Bear Run would be splashed all over the society page when the wedding took place. Pat needed the promotion, Alicia had confided to Joey. An old friend, he had bought the ski area on a shoestring budget, and he was having trouble getting the resort off the ground. That was one of the reasons she was so determined to have the wedding there.

Slowly, Joey managed to bring order out of chaos. The last alterations to the bridal and bridesmaids' dresses were finished. Catering arrangements fell into place. Transportation, guest lists, seating arrangements—Joey juggled them all.

As if things weren't frantic enough, Amy called almost daily from Hawaii to check on the welfare of her dogs, who as far as Joey could tell would be perfectly content anywhere they got fed. They had moved into her house, taken over her bed, and rearranged her schedule to suit them. When they were gone, Joey would definitely not miss the cold wet nose in her ear at five in the morning, a reminder that corgi bellies were empty and wanted breakfast. She had needed to smooth Amy's feathers on the subject of taking the dogs to the resort, however. Joey didn't really understand why Amy worried so about it. Drover was a very well-behaved boy—not exactly the sort to run off searching for the call of the wild. And only for food would Piggy bother to get off the couch. Of course there had been her one wild romp in the park the night Ben had brought pizza. She'd behaved as if a thousand butterflies had suddenly taken flight in her brain. So had Joey. She told herself not to think about it.

"They'll be fine," she assured Amy every day that she called. "You can call me at the resort. The cabin we're staying in has a phone. They'll be fine. Really. Stop worrying and enjoy Hawaii."

The dogs would be a good deal happier in the mountains than Joey would be. She looked forward to Bear Run with a nervous twitter in her stomach. Why? Alicia was ecstatic. Everything was in good order. It just might be Ben giving her stomach the flutters, Joey admitted. She'd seen him twice since he'd brought pizza to her house. Both times he'd been with Alicia. Both times he'd been reserved—almost as if that stupid incident in the park had meant something. It hadn't, of course. The sudden sizzle of their bodies banging unexpectedly together—that was just a natural hormonal thing. Didn't mean a thing. Nothing. No reason to think about Ben, Joey told herself. No reason to be on edge. This was going to be a truly perfect wedding.

She kept telling herself the same thing as the days marched on—until Monday rolled around on the calendar and couldn't be put off any longer.

The morning dawned cold and blustery, reminding Joey that while spring might be just around the corner, it wasn't quite here yet. She threw her warmest gloves into her suitcase, pulled a wool sweater over her head, and shooed the dogs from the bed, where they had insisted on investigating everything that went into the suitcase.

"Don't worry," she told the dogs. "You're going. But you're not going to be bridesmaids like you were in Amy's wedding. So forget grabbing center stage."

She looked out her bedroom window to see Ben's Taurus pull up in front of the house. They planned to caravan. Tess would ride with Joey and the dogs so Ben and Alicia could have some private time. Poor Alicia, Joey thought, arriving at her posh resort for her spectacular wedding in a beat-up, ten-year-old Ford. She did so love her little Mercedes, but it just wasn't designed to carry two people and a week's worth of luggage. Joey herself would have liked to take the Triumph. Zipping around the mountain curves would have been a hoot, but she also had luggage, and dogs, and some of the chafing trays, serving dishes, and cookware she would need for the engagement party and, later, the wedding reception. So she would be plodding along in her minivan.

Alicia was radiant as usual, cheeks flushed, blue eyes

sparkling. And why wouldn't she be? She was marrying a good man. And this morning he looked extremely handsome—or perhaps that lived-in face and crooked smile of his had grown on Joey. There was a strength about him that had nothing to do with his athletic build. As Dolores Ramon had commented, he was a man comfortable in his own skin, and it showed.

"Your cheeks are positively pink with excitement," she teased Alicia when she greeted them in the front yard.

Alicia laughed. "Red with cold, you mean. Ben's heater doesn't work very well." She took his arm possessively. "He's just going to have to work harder at keeping me warm."

Tess bounced up, carrying a Barbie overnight case and wearing a big grin. "Daddy says I get to ride with you. Where are the dogs?"

"They're still inside, probably trying to break into the closet where the dog food is kept."

"Can I go play with them?"

"Be my guest, sweetie. Try to wear them out, please. The trip will be easier."

Ben frowned as his daughter disappeared into the house. "You are going to drive like a little old lady from Pasadena, aren't you?"

"Ben!" Alicia chided with a laugh.

"Don't worry, Alicia," Joey said. "If I had a kid, I'd be protective, too. And Ben has the added disadvantage of being a cop. So he just naturally thinks everybody but him is a moron on the highway."

"Some people I *know* are morons on the highway," he muttered.

"Ben!" Alicia punched his arm.

"I'll let you lead the way—unless of course I end up towing that old clunker of yours up the mountain." She grinned tauntingly.

He glowered.

"And I'll strap Tess in so tight she won't be able to move, with the seat well back so she won't be too close to the air bag."

Mention of the air bag didn't make him look any happier.

"Not that the air bag is going to go off, mind you. Lighten up, Sergeant sir. You're headed to the mountains for a week of fun and frolic, and you're about to marry the prettiest woman in Denver. And I'm going to drive like I have nitro in the car, so don't worry."

He attempted a smile, but in Joey's opinion, Ben Ramsay didn't look anywhere near as happy as he should have.

They loaded Tess's suitcase and the last of Joey's luggage, then called for Tess to bring out the dogs. Two corgi-sized airline-style traveling kennels sat in the minivan among the baggage. Joey didn't worry about letting the dogs out front unleashed, because they always made a beeline for the kennels. Car rides were right below food on the corgi priority list.

This morning, however, Drover possessed an excess of energy—probably from the frantic game of chase-the-ball he'd been playing with Tess. He ran circuits around the front yard, barking his glee, leaping at fantasy butterflies or some other figment of his corgi imagination. Tess giggled at his idiotic antics. Piggy sat sedately and regarded him with disdain.

"Oops," Joey said, heading back into the house. "I forgot our lunch. I packed a picnic basket. If it's not too cold and dreary, we can stop at Dillon Reservoir for lunch. Won't be but a minute."

While they waited, Ben affectionately tugged Tess's ear. "You okay with riding with Joey?"

"Sure, Daddy. We'll have fun. Besides, her heater works."

Alicia gave Ben a poke in the ribs. "Tess honey, this is the last time we'll need to ride in your father's old jalopy. Once we're married, I'll see that he gets you a decent car to ride in."

Drover skidded to a stop in front of Tess and looked up at her adoringly. She bent down to pet him, then said, "Hey! Where's Piggy?"

Piggy's tailless little butt just then scooted beneath Ben's car.

Joey came out the front door just in time to see the dog's disappearing act. "Piggy, come out of there!"

"Why'd she go under the car?" Alicia asked.

Ben chuckled. "I'd guess that she doesn't want to go to Bear Run. Probably not a very good skier with those little legs of hers."

"Very funny." Joey peered beneath the car. "Come out of there, you little pointy-eared troublemaker."

Meanwhile, Drover had hopped into his kennel and looked out at the scene with a big canine grin on his face. One would almost think he enjoyed seeing Piggy get into trouble.

"I'll get her out," Tess volunteered, and before anyone could say yea or nay, she shimmied under the car with the agility of a chipmunk.

"Oh my!" Alicia knelt beside Joey, but they couldn't see what was happening. "Tess, be careful! You're going to get all dirty."

"You'd better get used to kids getting dirty," Ben warned her with a chuckle. "She's washable."

"Hi, Piggy," came Tess's voice from beneath the car. "What are you doing under here?" A few moments of silence was broken by a surprised "Oh! Uh-oh. You'd better come out."

They emerged with Piggy looking daggers at Tess, whose face and arms were smudged with grime. Tess smiled somewhat mysteriously, Joey thought.

"See," the girl said proudly. "I told you I could get her to come out."

"What was the 'uh-oh' for?" Joey asked.

The kid shrugged. "Nothing."

"You got dirtier than the dog," Alicia told Tess.

"The dog is made for low places," Joey said. "Let's get on the road. Samantha's driving up this afternoon with the kitchen crew, and I want to get things organized before she gets there."

"And I want to get there before the gang. Sue, Teri, and Carrie are going up today, too."

It was not to be. Everyone and everything was loaded, strapped in, tied down, or kenneled—and Ben's car wouldn't start. Joey momentarily entertained suspicions about Piggy, but that was simply too ridiculous to believe.

"Why do these things always happen when you're in a hurry?" she complained.

"Otherwise it wouldn't be as much fun," Alicia said with a laugh. "We could rent a car."

"That would take at least a couple of hours."

"Well, I really want to get up there before the girls. I need to talk to Pat Haines about where everybody's going to be staying."

As one, they all turned to look at Joey's minivan, which did have room for two more—just. "I guess we'll all ride together," Joey said with a sigh.

They started transferring baggage, and no one noticed when Tess gave Piggy a knowing wink.

CHAPTER 7

◆

THEY STARTED THE trip with Joey driving, Tess in the front passenger seat, and Ben and Alicia in the back seat, away from Tess's chattering observations about school, which was on spring break, the scenery, the prospects for her learning to ski, and the likelihood of her getting a horse of her own after the wedding. The arrangement didn't give the almost newlyweds the privacy they would have had in the Ford, but it was the best that Joey could do under the circumstances.

The almost newlyweds didn't seem prone to conversation, however. Ben seemed more interested in Joey's driving than settling back to enjoy the ride. For a while he said nothing, but Joey felt him looking over her shoulder at the road, the speedometer, and the traffic, which was heavy. Morning rush hour still clogged Interstate 70 through Denver and the western suburbs. Not until they were west of Golden did the flow thin out so that they could pick up speed—or what passed for speed. Joey didn't dare let the speedometer creep upwards with Ben's hawklike attention focused on her.

He was an almost physical pressure from behind, a swell of words almost but not quite uttered. Finally he said something. Joey had seen it coming from the moment they pulled out of the driveway.

"Uh . . . Joey?"

She sighed. "Yes, Ben?"

"The speed limit here is sixty-five."

"I'm not speeding, Ben."

"You're doing ten miles per hour under the speed limit. That's as dangerous as ten over."

"Ben!" Alicia scolded. "Leave Joey alone. She's a good driver. And besides, you drive like a maniac."

"Does he really?" Joey chortled.

"He does, really."

"I do not!"

"He does," Alicia repeated blithely.

"Well, at this rate, it's going to take all day to get there."

Joey bit her lip to keep from saying anything. She accelerated to sixty-five. "Better?" she asked.

"You know, you really shouldn't drive in the left lane so much. Especially if you're doing just the speed limit."

Joey couldn't bite down any harder without making her lip bleed. An inarticulate sound of frustration escaped her throat as she pulled onto the freeway shoulder and twisted around to glare at Ben. "Do you want to drive?" she asked sarcastically.

He immediately brightened. "Good idea."

She turned off the ignition and unfastened her seat belt. "Be my guest." As he came around to take her place, she gave him a tart, knowing smile. "Just can't stand to have a woman in the driver's seat, can you?"

His mouth twitched into a half smile. "It's a guy thing."

"Neanderthal," she muttered.

"What's a Neanderthal?" Tess asked.

"A guy that women find very annoying," her father told her.

"Are all guys Neanderthals?" the girl persisted.

Joey and Alicia looked at each other, and between them flashed a moment of the old college camaraderie. "Most of them," they answered in unison.

Ben shook a finger at his daughter. "Don't listen to them, kiddo. They don't know anything."

The driver switch resulted in musical chairs, with Tess moving to the back seat (she wanted to talk to the dogs, she claimed) and Joey moving to the front passenger seat. When Joey offered to switch with Alicia so that Alicia and Ben could be together, Alicia declined, saying she wanted to get better acquainted with Tess. So off they went. Tess and Alicia chatted quietly, with Tess frequently addressing comments to Piggy and Drover in their kennels behind the seat and Alicia genially falling in with the little girl's fantasy. Joey tried to be genial as well, in spite of Ben being a Neanderthal. She had to smile at how well he'd taken being ganged up on.

"What's the smile for?" he queried.

"I was feeling sorry for you."

"Really? Why?"

"You're going to spend a whole week with bride,

bridesmaids, bride's family—including a grandmother who could make a SWAT team tremble—the bride's high-toned friends, and two wedding consultants. Your friends aren't coming up until when?"

"My brother's coming up tomorrow in time for the engagement party. But knowing Tom, he'll be so busy pursuing snow bunnies that he won't have time for anything else. The ushers are coming Friday. Maybe Thursday if they can make it. Most of the others on my short guest list will be up Friday."

"So you're all alone, a lamb amongst the wolves."

"I thought I was a Neanderthal."

"Okay, one helpless caveman surrounded by saber-toothed tigers."

"That sounds about right from my point of view. But aren't you the one who's supposed to think wedding extravaganzas are fun?"

"They're fun for the bride, fun for the guests, and great business for me, but most grooms would rather walk on hot coals than endure more than a thirty-minute ceremony and a few hours sitting around the reception. You've let yourself in for a whole week, and we didn't even have to hog-tie you and throw you in the back with the dogs."

Ben chuckled. "Joey, it's a good thing you work mostly with brides. You shouldn't be allowed to talk to prospective grooms."

"Well, maybe I exaggerate just a bit," she admitted with a smile. "What I'm trying to say is that you're a curious mix of Neanderthal and Mr. Nice Guy."

He gave her a quick, enigmatic look. "Alicia's a special lady. She deserves to have whatever she wants."

"Right answer, Mr. Nice Guy," Alicia said from the back. "See how well trained he is, Joey?"

Joey laughed, but something about the look on Ben's face made her uneasy. Not for any real reason. Just gut instinct. Joey was a cynic when it came to the odds on marriage, but she wanted Ben and Alicia to live happily ever after. They were good people, and they deserved the fairy-tale ending.

"Why the look?" Ben asked.

"What?"

"The look on your face. You look as though you just bit into a lemon."

"Really?" She gave him a superior smile. "Must be because you're speeding, Officer."

He glanced at the speedometer. "So I am."

"The state troopers on this stretch are wicked. Some jackass might pull you over and give you a ticket and an asinine lecture."

"And you would laugh."

"I really, really would."

Ben flashed her a complacent grin. "Don't get your hopes up. Cops don't give other cops tickets."

They stopped at Georgetown at a gas station/food mart just off the freeway. Incongruous as it seemed in this picturesque Colorado mountain town, the food mart sold fresh egg rolls with hot mustard and sweet-and-sour sauce. They bought five—two for Ben and one apiece for everyone else—and filled the minivan with fuel. Then they waited, leaning against the van, while Tess walked Piggy, whom she insisted had to go.

"She has an eerie sort of communication with that dog," Joey observed.

"Tess herself can be kind of eerie at times, as you've already noticed." The look he gave her was enigmatic. "She's really warmed up to you, though."

"Ben, you shouldn't worry about Tess," Alicia assured him blithely. "She's just going through a phase. When I was growing up, everyone told my father I was spoiled and flighty and didn't have the sense of a chipmunk, and look how well I turned out." She posed grandly, and her companions laughed.

"You're still spoiled and flighty," Ben said indulgently.

"Says you!" As if to prove his point, she turned in a dizzying circle, her arms outstretched. "God! Don't you just love the mountains? I came here in January to go ice boating on Lake George. That is such a kick!" She looked winsomely at her husband-to-be. "We should buy a condo in Georgetown. Or a house—better! A big log house with huge windows and a deck looking up the valley to the high peaks. Wouldn't you love to live far away from anyone telling you what you should do with your day, your week, your life, here in the fresh clean air and pines where you can listen to the birds sing and catch snowflakes on your tongue?"

Ben put an arm around her shoulders and gave her a hug. "Birds sing and snow falls in the city."

"But in the city you're dealing with lowlifes and slime all day long."

"That's true, I guess. I met Joey in the line of duty."

Alicia pushed him away. "Oh, you are awful! Punch him, Joey!"

"And for that matter, I met you in the line of duty," Ben added.

"That was just a stroke of luck on your part," Alicia insisted.

"That's what I tell myself every day."

Her pout melted into a smile. "You're sweet, Ben Ramsay. A Neanderthal, but sweet. Isn't he sweet, Joey? Just lucky for him I'm tolerant."

The weather continued gray and damp; a low overcast spit snow, and a sharp, cold wind gusted around the valleys and mountains. But across the Continental Divide, the fickle mountains played one of their famous tricks. When the travelers entered the east portal of the Eisenhower Tunnel, snow had begun to accumulate on the highway, and low, scudding clouds obscured the peaks. But when they emerged from the west portal, the sun beamed at them. The shadows of a few low clouds scudded across mountain snowfields glittering with sunlight, and the sky was so brilliant it almost made their eyes ache.

"Sunshine!" Tess declared happily. "Now we can have our picnic!"

They pulled over at Dillon Reservoir. The margins of the lake were still frozen, but acres and acres of water were open to reflect the blue of the sky. On this side of the Divide, the temperature was pleasantly warm for a March day, and even on the lake's frozen margins puddles of meltwater announced that spring was just around the corner.

"We're probably the first people to picnic here," Tess said as she helped Joey clear snow from a picnic table.

"The first this season, at least," Joey agreed.

Released from his kennel, Drover found the nearest snowbank to tunnel through, then did his otter imitation by running at a deep patch and sliding through it like a furry torpedo. Piggy stayed by the table as food was laid out, her ears alert, her nose twitching with the scents coming from the picnic basket.

"She's always hungry," Tess noted. "How come?"

"How come you're always wanting to know how come?" Ben countered.

Tess shrugged and grinned, "It's just the way I am."

"Well, it's just the way Piggy is. I guess that's why her name is Piggy."

With their jackets firmly zipped to ward off a biting breeze, the four of them efficiently tackled lunch. The egg rolls disappeared first, because they'd all been smelling them since Georgetown, but the group did justice to the three-bean salad and the sandwiches made with homemade mozzarella and three different kinds of salami that Joey had packed. The whole was topped off with Oreo cookies and hot cider kept warm in a big Thermos jug.

Joey wasn't surprised when Tess and Alicia both slipped the dogs their sandwich crusts, but she was bemused when Ben surreptitiously did the same.

"Sucker," she accused.

His brows shot up in a pretense of innocence, but Joey just shook her head and smiled.

After lunch, with their stomachs full and the sun shining down from a burnished blue sky, everyone decided they weren't in such a hurry after all. Tess wanted to skip rocks at a spot where the open water reached the shore, and Joey volunteered to stay with her while Ben and Alicia took a short walk.

"I guess two people about to be married deserve a

little time to themselves," Joey told them. "Go on. Tess and I will have a rock-skipping contest."

Piggy trailed after Alicia and Ben.

"Can she come with us?" Alicia asked over her shoulder.

"Don't let her run off," Joey warned.

"I don't think she's inclined to run anywhere," Ben noted. "Amble is more like it."

"That's all right," Alicia told him with a happy smile. "After eating all that food, I'm only up for an amble myself."

As they walked off together, Tess watched them go and shook her head. "It's too bad they won't really get married," she told Joey very seriously. "Alicia's cool. And I really would like to have that horse."

I ask you, why do the people of Colorado insist upon including a "mountain interlude" in their romances? Back when I was a woman, I was very hot romantic property, yet I never, ever found it necessary to hike, fish, canoe, bird-watch, or even picnic in the forest, and any guy who suggested such a lame activity immediately found himself out the door. Skiing—now that's something else. Skiing is somewhat classy, as long as you don't insist on actually sliding down the mountain on skis. Skiing entails big cozy fireplaces, bars that serve warm Bailey's Irish Cream, spas where you can luxuriate in hot bubbly water, drink a hot toddy, and watch snow sizzle as it lands on the heated deck around you. Now that's skiing! But the rest of this Colorado "Rocky Mountain High" stuff is really over-rated—a fantasy foisted on a gullible public by the late John Denver if you ask me, which no one has, especially lately.

Anyone who read the story of my last adventure is already acquainted with my attitude toward the woods. I don't like them. The forest has bugs, mud, sadistic squirrels, dive-bombing birds, strange smells, sharp rocks, and raging torrents that no sensible creature would ever try to cross. The woods are also dirty. Dirt everywhere, along with rotting leaves and other stuff you really don't want to identify—bad enough if you're walking on two legs, but infinitely worse if, like me, you're a stumpy-legged dog who is so much closer to the ground.

Given these facts, I really don't understand why it's obligatory for Colorado couples to perform this stupid ritual commune with Mother Nature. Jeff and Amy did it big time, crossing rivers, prancing up mountains, sliding down snowfields, skipping across streams on skinny little logs, and expecting their long-suffering dogs to do the same. Most dogs are stupid enough to enjoy it. Most dogs think that mud, bugs, and squirrels are fun. I, however, do not.

Now Alicia and Ben indulged in the same silliness. Worse, because it wasn't even summer. Not only did we have to endure mud and dead slimy leaves, but snow and puddles of meltwater—make that ice water. Really! How enjoyable and romantic does that sound to you? Not very, if you have a brain in your head.

So why did I go with them, you ask? Because I had a job to do, and the sooner I got things settled between these people, the sooner Stanley would get off my back and let me relax. My excellent start getting Ben paired off with Joey had gone nowhere. The sparks had flown, but those two were both such wet blankets that the fire had only smoldered. That plan could still work. I hadn't given up. But letting Alicia wander in the woods with Ben while she was in such a giddy prenuptial mood was like throwing a lit cigarette onto a puddle of gaso-

line and expecting not to get toasted. Women who are about to get married float around in a state of near shock, something close to a happy hypnotic trance where reason is suspended and some fairy-tale fantasy moves in to take its place. I know. I had two weddings of my own, and my reason didn't return until weeks after the ceremony, when it was too late. Poor Alicia needed a real shock—like seeing Ben and Joey getting it on—to snap her back to reality. She's a smart cookie, is Alicia. When it came to Ben, though, she seemed dumb as a cork.

So, trying to look like a typical corgi eager for a walk in mud and muck, I heaved a martyred sigh and followed when the bridal-couple-to-be took off. Alicia and Sergeant Loser didn't suspect a thing. Humans look for ulterior motives only in other humans. When you're a dog you can be sneaky without anyone suspecting that you're up to no good. I didn't know what exactly I was going to do, but I was sure something would pop into my mind.

For a while we walked in silence—understandable considering the mud, sticks, rocks, downed branches, and veritable glaciers of snow and ice that made our journey difficult. Supposedly there was a path. I didn't see one, and I was about as close to the ground as a creature could get. My tummy feathers were soaked, my legs were coated in mud, my feet were freezing, and my ears were cold. I was certainly in no mood to cavort, but I made an effort for appearances' sake, prancing here and there (actually, I was trying to keep my feet out of the snow) and scampering over a log that proved too much for me. No more scampering for this corgi, if you please. I landed on the other side nose first. Alicia gushed about how cute I was, but gooey-eyed as Alicia was, she would have gushed about just about anything. In fact, she did. Slipping her arm through Ben's in a chummy, possessive manner, she prattled, "I just *can't believe we're really on our way to Bear Run to be married. Just a few months ago we didn't even know each other, and look at us now."*

She should have listened to her own words. Just months ago she didn't even know this guy existed, and she had been living a very happy life. Now she can't live without him? She gushed on.

"I'm just so excited! This week is going to be perfect. And then Jamaica for a honeymoon. I've been there twice already, but this time will be so much better. Jamaica is just so romantic. It really has to be experienced with someone you love. You're going to like it so much! And Tess is going to have great fun staying with Daddy and Nana. She's going to sleep in my room and keep Puddin company. And Daddy says he'll take her to see the house we want to buy."

I noticed that Ben didn't say much, but that didn't discourage Alicia, who took off down the trail in happy pirouettes, her arms stretched wide, her face sporting a silly grin. Anyone else pulling a stunt like that would have ended up on their butt in the snow, but she has the sort of athletic grace that comes with class. I woofed in admiration, and she laughed her giddy laugh. Ben grinned at her antics.

"Tell me you're having a good time," she practically begged.

"I'm having a good time," he conceded.

"Aren't these mountains wonderful?"

"They are."

"And look at that lake. There's a lake at Bear Run, you know. Well, more of a large pond, really. But it's the perfect size for skating. It's so beautiful, just like this. I'm so glad we decided to have the wedding there."

"We?" Ben chuckled.

She laughed again, then grew serious and dragged him to a

big flat rock and made him sit down. "I want to tell you something important," *she told him.*

"What?"

"How much I love you. How crazy I am about you."

The silly girl. Someone should have taught her long ago that a woman never, ever hands a guy that kind of advantage. Ben just smiled. Sometimes he gives Alicia the same indulgent sort of smile he gives his daughter.

"I just wanted to make sure I said it loud and clear and in a way that you would remember. If I pester you about things and tease, it doesn't mean anything. Whatever you want to do with your life and your talents is fine with me. I've waited my whole life for someone like you, Ben, and I do love you. You're my anchor, my strength."

"Sweet Alicia." *He touched her cheek, just as if he deserved to have a classy little fox like Alicia drooling all over him. Typical man, taking advantage of her vulnerability, her overly romantic nature, her recent trauma. He should have been ashamed of himself, but of course he wasn't. It was a good thing that Stanley put me on this job. Well, not really a good thing. I would have preferred to spend my time lying in the sun that streams through Joey's front window and heats her living room sofa, or better yet, sashaying around Hawaii in my original two-legged body.*

But since I was there, I figured I might as well save Alicia from herself, especially since Stanley was probably watching and keeping score.

They kissed, of course. The situation certainly called for it, and Ben wasn't so slow that he didn't know it. I sat for a few seconds and watched. Not that I'm a voyeur, but it had been a long time since I'd been kissed. Ben looked as if he might actually have some talent at it. He didn't turn the kiss into a

precoital slobberfest like some guys do. In fact, though I'm reluctant to admit it, he seemed sweet and gentle, almost as if
the girl were made of fine china. Maybe there was some passion there as well. Since I didn't experience the kiss firsthand,
it was hard to tell. You'd think a big hunky cop would show at
least some raw animal passion to the woman he loved,
wouldn't you?

Or maybe I just didn't give him time to work up a good
head of steam. What I said earlier about the lit cigarette and
the puddle of gasoline? Well, the ciggie was on the fly, and it
was my job, as I saw it, to make sure it didn't land on that
puddle. So I took steps to make sure it didn't—steps toward a
bank of slushy snow, to be exact. I was already wet, dirty, cold,
and uncomfortable, so a little roll in the slush was no big sacri-
fice, especially if getting a bit wetter and a little colder let me
put a damper on our lovebirds.

A spray of ice water from my muddy coat effectively put an
end to the kissing. Alicia sputtered. Lover boy cursed. I simply
stood there with a big corgi grin on my face and looked happily
innocent. I was prepared to flee if they got really angry, but
Alicia's sputtering turned to laughter, and even Mr. Mump
smiled. All's well that ends well, I thought smugly—until the
first icy snowball smacked into my ear. Turned out Alicia was
the vengeful type.

The situation deteriorated into chaos as Ben joined Alicia's
fun. They teamed up to pelt the poor innocent dog with snowballs and then began to plaster each other. They chased and
shrieked like children while I bounced about and barked like
an idiot. The bounding and barking weren't deliberate on my
part, mind you. A sudden attack of doggishness sort of carried
me away. Definitely uncool! Before you know it I'll be rolling
over begging for tummy scratches.

Then an idea shot into my fertile brain, jolting me back into focus. The idea involved risk to myself, but hey, I'd already proved I was a heroine. I could only hope that Stan was keeping track of what he owed me.

So I moved closer to the cavorting lovebirds, nipping at their feet, dancing around their legs, and enduring a barrage of snow missiles. Then we chased. Alicia dropped out, gasping and laughing, and I led Ben just where I wanted him, where an unexpected little crease in the landscape carried a runnel of snowmelt. He would have leaped it with ease if I hadn't turned and hit his ankles. Down he went in the snow and mud, the Three Stooges revisited. Ridiculous, and very unromantic. Can you imagine getting hot over Larry, Moe, or Curly?

"Goddamn dog!" was his reaction. The mud made an ugly sucking sound as he tried to pick himself up. Oops! He slipped again, landing on his butt as I jumped against his legs. This time he took a swipe at me when I came into range. Poor sport.

Alicia laughed so hard I thought she was going to pee. "Don't blame the poor dog!"

I knew I liked her.

"Ben! You are such a klutz! I never suspected! Straight out of Keystone Cops."

He muttered under his breath about hanging me from my ears, and I curled a lip just to let him know that I heard his rude comment.

"Really, Ben. Don't just sit there. Do you need me to help you up?" Alicia still laughed around every other word, but she didn't look as put off as I'd hoped.

Back in my dating days, if I'd seen a guy get tangled up in his own feet and take a nosedive into a pool of mud, I would have smiled politely and looked elsewhere for male company. I spent a lot of time making sure I was a true ornament on a date's arm, and I wasn't about to decorate some arm that wasn't worthy. And nothing says loser like showing yourself to be a geeky klutz.

Finally, Ben took Alicia's hand and allowed himself to be pulled up. She kissed him sweetly, saying, "That's all right, darling. I love you anyway."

I just about barfed. The woman really was beyond reason. And this job just might be harder than I thought.

CHAPTER 8

◆

THEY PULLED UP in front of Bear Run Lodge in the early afternoon after fighting the traffic in Glenwood Springs, enduring the narrow, winding road leading to the town of Aspen, and then taking off on an even narrower, windier road snaking through the ten miles of mountains between Aspen and Bear Run. Alicia bounced out of the minivan as soon as it stopped. With her arms stretched wide to encompass everything within sight, she crowed in a delighted voice.

"Isn't it wonderful? Isn't it positively the most beautiful place you've ever seen?"

Emerging from the van with a bit more restraint, Ben considered the picturesque log buildings, the hovering mountains with their manicured ski runs, the great chairlift supports marching like huge steel trees up the slopes. The mountain air smelled of burgers and fries rather than pine, and the majestic mountain silence lost out to the hum of machinery and buzz of conversation.

The place wasn't nearly as busy as the few ski resorts

Ben had seen—perhaps because spring was coming, or because the resort was closing midweek so that Alicia's wedding party would have privacy. Still, the runs were thick with skiers, tiny dark dots weaving back and forth down the ribbons of white. The wide deck that wrapped around the lodge boasted skiers munching sandwiches at outdoor tables, skiers swapping tales of the moguls on the upper slopes of "Comet's Tail," skiers clumping precariously here and there in rigid, cumbersome ski boots and bulky skiwear that looked as though someone had taken an air pump and blown up their clothing.

Ben couldn't agree with Alicia that it was the most beautiful place he'd seen. For real beauty, the skiers, chairlifts, and the smell of hamburger grease would have to go. But it was entertaining. Unable to resist the glow on her face, he gave her a warm smile. "It's great. Perfect."

"I knew you'd love it! Can you think of a more perfect place for a wedding?"

A church came to mind, or a nice quiet chapel, but he wasn't going to burst Alicia's bubble.

Joey got out of the passenger side of the van and surveyed the scene with an assessing air. Ben was willing to bet that instead of seeing the green and white mountain splendor and the sweep of blue Colorado sky, she wondered about the seating capacity of the lodge's Grizzly Room, where the wedding was slated, and the size of its kitchen. He could almost see her mental checklist of things that needed to be inspected, modified, organized, or rearranged in the days left before the ceremony. Always nose to the grindstone, eyes on the mark. He had to admire Joey's focus and energy. It reminded him of Tess's mother, his sweet, loving Annie, who had been just as absorbed in her work— the horses and the stable. Still, Joey almost seemed to hide behind her dedication. Did the woman ever relax? he wondered.

"Ben, are you listening to me at all?"

Alicia's somewhat tart inquiry cut through Ben's reflections.

"Huh? Did you say something?"

"Men!" She snorted. "Joey, would you tell me why we put up with them?"

"What? Oh. It's a biological imperative, I suppose."

"Don't you think a wedding consultant should pander a bit more to romance?" Ben asked.

Joey flashed him a smile. "For romance I charge extra."

Ben didn't get a chance to reply, for Alicia started bouncing up and down and waving, calling out to the man who advanced upon them from the direction of the ski rental hut. "Pat! Pat Haines! There you are!" She welcomed him with an enthusiastic hug and a kiss on both perfectly bronzed cheeks. "Come meet the group! Joey, this is Pat Haines. He's the nicest guy you'll ever meet. And he has his very own ski area to play in!"

Joey actually blushed when Pat took her hand. For a moment Ben feared the man was actually going to bow over it like some mustachioed slick from a forties movie, but he simply shook it and gave her a smile full of dazzling white teeth. The man was smooth, Ben decided. Anyone who could make Joey DeMato, sharp-tongued man-slicer extraordinaire, blush and stammer like a teenybopper had to be a practiced charmer of women.

Pat's next victim was Tess, who giggled when he took her hand and asked her when she was going to get married. Ben he greeted with a proper manly handshake backed up by an affable smile.

"So this is the lucky man, eh, Allie? The hero of the week?"

"That's the lucky man," Alicia confirmed, then laughed. "I warned you I wouldn't be available forever. I used to take ski lessons from Pat," she told the group. "He was once a carefree ski bum, but look at him now—master of his very own resort. Isn't that great?"

The man could have been Hollywood's idea of the macho ski instructor, the star of a winterized version of *Baywatch*. He was as tall as Ben, with broad shoulders made even broader by the thick wool sweater he wore. Black ski pants—the stretchy kind that the really good skiers wear—showcased sculpted legs. Stylishly trimmed blue-black hair framed a bronze face that would make a Coppertone model turn green with envy. Eyes blue as Colorado's sky positively twinkled with charm. If his nose was just a bit crooked and one eyebrow creased by a tiny scar, the defects saved the face from boring perfection.

Ben knew he wasn't going to like this guy. Pat Haines was too affable to be real. Too good-looking. Too . . . too something that Ben couldn't quite put his finger upon. Guys who looked like Pat Haines spent more time in front of a mirror than women did. Most of them relied on looks rather than hard work to make their way in life, and all that charm and sociability could hide dark habits. The dark habit of choice was frequently drugs, doing or dealing or both. Easy money. High living. Short lifespan.

Then again, he'd known the guy all of two minutes. Maybe he'd been a cop too long—or perhaps he was just envious of Pat's upper-crust looks and manners. "You own this place, eh?" was the only thing Ben could think of to say. Pretty lame. "Nice."

Again with the charming smile. "Sometimes I think it owns me. The life of a ski bum was easier in a lot of ways."

"Oh pooh!" Alicia scoffed. "You're going to make a huge success of this resort. I just know it. It's absolutely beautiful."

Pat's smile had just the right touch of humility. "We try to keep it that way. Uh . . . Ben, right? Did Alicia make you run beside the car on the way up?"

Ben looked down at his clothes. His shirt and jacket were—compliments of a certain demon-possessed dog—hopelessly spattered with mud.

Alicia laughed. "He challenged Joey's dog to a snowball fight, and the dog won."

"Looks like you were tossing mud, not snow. If you'd like to change, I'll show you right up to the Big Cabin."

"Oh no!" Alicia said. "We want the full tour, Pat. I'm dying to see this place you've told me so much about. Ben is too, aren't you, Ben?"

"Uh . . . sure. What's a little mud?"

Alicia gave Ben an air kiss—he was too dirty for the real thing—and turned to Pat to take his arm. "See how tough the Denver cops are?"

"Dirty, too," Joey commented from the side of her mouth as the group migrated toward the lodge. "I'd heard that about the Denver police."

He just smiled. "Literally or figuratively?"

"Both. I think I'll just stay here, take the dogs out, and start getting organized while you guys look over the place."

"Not a chance." Ben grabbed her arm, then hastily released her. Whenever he touched Joey—an accidental brush, a casual, meaningless little collision, a full-body weld while tangled in a crazy dog's leash—he felt unfaithful to Alicia. Not that he had the least desire to be unfaithful to Alicia. Not with Joey DeMato. Not with anyone.

Still, he needed to keep his hands away from Joey, because for some strange reason, they frequently strayed in her direction.

"Listen," he told her, "the dogs will be fine for a while, and you're not sending me alone on this tour with Bobby Unser and Picabo Street up there."

"I think Bobby Unser was a race car driver, not a skier."

"Whatever."

"And you have Tess to keep you company."

"Tess has already fallen under the man's spell."

Joey gave him a raised brow, but she fell in beside him as he followed the group toward the lodge. Ben wasn't quite sure why he so wanted her along, but he did. He didn't really feel slighted by Alicia's attention to

Pat Haines. Alicia was in her social butterfly mode, and Ben didn't object in the least to someone else handling all that bubbly energy for a change. Perhaps he felt a bit out of place surrounded by the winter playground and toys of the well-to-do, and Joey's down-to-earth, sometimes cutting perspective kept things more real.

"I think Pat Haines is charming," she said, blowing that theory as they walked through the big double doors of the main lodge.

"You would, being a woman."

"Don't tell me you're jealous."

"Not at all."

"Well, you shouldn't be. If Alicia wanted someone handsome and suave, she could have had her choice for the past ten years."

"Somehow I think I've just been zinged."

"Goodness no, I'm way above that sort of thing." She grinned. "But I did warn you that grooms were an entirely superfluous part of the wedding party, didn't I?"

They had halted in front of a big illustrated map of Bear Run Ski Resort. The map hung beside the stone fireplace of the Grizzly Room, which was the great hall of the lodge. The room was huge, and the fireplace was large enough to roast a whole cow if one were so inclined. Soaring up to rafters fashioned of hefty pine logs, the hall combined abundant space with an atmosphere of homey warmth. Near the entrance a wide staircase climbed to the railed balcony, which fronted a row of guest rooms. Facing the balcony was the fireplace, and above it, an authentic, snarling bearskin. The third wall of the room boasted floor-to-ceiling windows overlooking the deck, the chairlift, and the lower ski runs.

"Oh, Pat!" Alicia sighed. "This is exquisite."

"This is going to be a beautiful setting for a wedding," Joey said.

"I'm glad you like it," Pat said. "It's the biggest room in the lodge except for the restaurant dining room over there. The bearskin may be a bit over the top for the wedding. We can take it down if you like."

"Oh no!" Alicia exclaimed. "It looks so . . . so . . ."

"Dead?" Ben offered.

"No, silly! Well, it *is* dead, of course. But it looks so authentic Rocky Mountain, you know? I love it."

"You don't still have things like that around here, do you?"

Alicia and Pat ignored him, but Joey sent Ben a warning glance. "You're going to be trouble, aren't you? I can tell already."

Ben just smiled.

"Downstairs is the cocktail lounge, snack bar, and pool," Pat was telling Alicia. "Here we are on the map." He pointed to a cartoon illustration of the lodge on the wall directory, then pointed out the rental shop, chairlift, rental cabins, first aid station, ski patrol hut, and the various warming huts scattered along the runs. And at the top of the chairlift was a restaurant called Top of the World.

Alicia was struck with an idea. "Oh, Joey! Wouldn't it be fine to have the engagement party up there tomorrow night?"

"Uh . . . what about the guests that don't ski?"

"We could shuttle them up and down in the chair,"

Pat offered. "And we can take up your food by snow-mobile sleds."

"You'd have to take me up by sled as well," Joey said with a sheepish laugh. "The one time I tried to get on a chairlift I did a face plant in the snow."

"Oh, by the end of today you'll be a pro, won't she, Pat? After the tour we're all going to go out for lessons."

"Lessons?" Ben asked dubiously.

"Lessons!" Alicia confirmed emphatically. "Ben Ramsay! You don't think you're going to spend a whole week up here and not ski, do you?"

Ben grimaced. He had hoped.

The tour stopped next at the rental shop, where Alicia, with Pat's help, fitted them all with ski boots and skis. Tess was ecstatic about the prospect of sliding down an icy hill on two narrow, nearly uncontrollable slats, but then, nine-year-olds weren't known for their good judgment.

"I'll bet I could do the big runs, don't you think, Mr. Haines?"

"Well, sure," Pretty Boy said diplomatically. "Just as soon as you learn to do the little ones. And you are really in luck, because we have a great teacher to show you the ropes. Just for you. One on one. In a couple of days you'll be skiing circles around your dad."

"That won't take much," Ben commented ruefully. Pat gave him a glance that looked almost sympathetic, but Alicia just laughed.

"Mr. Negative. You'll do great. I've seen you in action, remember?"

Running gun battles and fisticuffs with the bad guys

was hardly the same thing as schussing around moguls on a hill that pointed straight down toward the first aid station, but Alicia didn't seem to comprehend the difference. "If I break both my legs," he warned her, "it's not going to be much of a honeymoon."

"Don't be silly," Alicia said. "You're invulnerable."

If only that were true.

Next they saw the first aid station, which Ben thought was appropriate under the circumstances. Then the rental cabins, which looked like luxury hotel rooms and cost even more. Last they trekked back to the lodge, where Pat served them hot spiced cider in the snack bar and showed off the heated pool and outdoor spas where guests could soak sore bodies in hot bubbly water while snowflakes melted on the deck around them. It was in the spa area that the little people's ski instructor met them. Her name was Marta Stein, and she was one of the best kids' instructors around, Pat told them proudly when he introduced her.

She was also one of the prettiest ski instructors around, children's or otherwise. Lustrous blonde hair fell smoothly to her shoulders, framing a face of sensual perfection. She was tall and statuesque, a perfect costar for *Baywatch*-in-the-snow. They could call it *Ski Patrol,* Ben thought wryly. Surround these two with weekly romance and crisis and it would be an instant hit.

The newcomer had an impact all around. Pat gave her a swift once-over with eyes that instantly lit in male appreciation, something that any man with blood in his veins would do, even if he saw the woman ten times a day. Ben felt himself do the same thing. It wasn't blatant rudeness, just instinct. Alicia's eyes narrowed just slightly as Pat introduced the woman.

"I'm so happy to finally meet you," Marta told Alicia in a melodic, slightly accented voice. "Pat has told me so much about you. You have been friends for so long, eh?"

"Yes, we have," Alicia said smoothly. "You sound German, Miss Stein. Am I right?"

"Please call me Marta. And yes, you are right. I have been here for ten years and still sound like a foreigner. I knew no English when I first came." Not giving Alicia a chance to comment, Marta turned to Tess. "And this must be Tess Ramsay? Pat told me I would have a very special student this week, and that I was to make her into an Olympic star. Is that not right?"

Tess giggled. "I want to ski."

"And you shall certainly ski. This afternoon, perhaps? I think you and I will have a very good time together, Tess."

"I like her," Tess declared after Marta had left. "She's really pretty."

"Yes," Alicia said in a somewhat chilly voice. "She is, isn't she? Is she your partner in this enterprise, Pat?" She gave the word "partner" more meaning than just business.

The implication didn't go over Pat's head. He seemed to enjoy Alicia's slight pique. "Partner? Marta? Not exactly." He chuckled. "Marta sort of came with the resort. She was here when I bought the place. Has a little house over in Basalt and a fiancé in Glenwood Springs. She's good people. The best."

The look on Alicia's face gave Ben pause. Usually

she wasn't competitive with other women. With her looks and money, why would she be? But Marta had set her off, that was for sure.

Finally Pat took them to the Big Cabin, where they would be staying. The place wasn't a cabin so much as a sizeable log house. Back in the seventies, one of Denver's oil barons had built the place as a "fishing cabin," Pat told them. When the resort had been built in the early nineties, the developers had bought the house as a place for important guests—investors, politicos, or any others who rated special attention.

"Now it's all yours," he said to Alicia. "At least for this week. Leonardo DiCaprio has it next week."

Alicia's eyes grew wide. "Really? Oh, Pat! Is *he* coming up here to ski?"

Pat laughed, and there was a sparkle in his eye. "Don't I wish! I'm kidding, Allie."

"I knew that," she said hastily.

"Of course you did. Actually, I've been living in the place since I bought the resort, so you'll have to put up with me banging around. But I'm not there much except late at night. I'm afraid I'm head maintenance man and manager as well as owner up here. I've even doubled as busboy in the restaurant a time or two."

It was hard to totally dislike a man who refused to take himself seriously, Ben acknowledged. Pretty Boy might not be entirely bad after all.

Ben volunteered to fetch the minivan, the dogs, and the luggage while the others settled into their rooms. Actually, he didn't so much volunteer as jump at the chance for a small piece of privacy, away from Alicia's ebullience, Pat Haines's suave charm, Tess's youthful delight, and Joey's constant watch-checking. Prewedding jitters, he told himself as he started the engine. He looked back toward the dog crates, where two sets of brown eyes regarded him questioningly.

"You're going to love it here," he told the corgis. "It's total frivolity. Right up your alley."

When Ben pulled the car up to the cabin, he saw that Marta had joined them. She and Tess were engaged in a running snowball battle on the front porch and in the snowdrifts next to the house. The woman did seem to have a way with kids. Dogs, too, for when Ben let the little brown monsters out of the car, Drover immediately joined the battle, barking and chasing the snow missiles until both combatants formed an alliance and pelted him with their entire store of armament. Poor Drover surfaced from the barrage looking like a short-legged snow sculpture, but his face wore a big corgi grin. Piggy took refuge on the front porch, where she assumed the sphinx position and watched the battle with diplomatic caution.

"What odd-looking dogs," Marta observed as she took mercy on Drover and brushed the snow from his coat.

"They aren't real dogs," Tess told her. "They're corgis. Supersmart."

"Really?" Marta cast a dubious eye upon Drover, who had decided to bulldoze a tunnel in the snow.

"Well, Drover's not so smart," Tess admitted. "But Piggy is special. I looked up corgis on the Internet. They're touched by the fairies."

Ben laughed. "Touched by leprechauns is more like it. Tess, quit spinning tales to Marta and come in the house. It looks like you need some dry clothes."

"But Marta's going to take me to get a snow bib."

"A what?"

Marta spoke up. "The nylon bib coveralls that will keep her dry when she skis."

"Alicia said I have to have one."

"Maybe Marta has something better to do than take you shopping," Ben chided.

"Actually, I don't, Mr. Ramsay."

"Call me Ben."

She smiled. It was certainly a lovely smile. "Pat asked me to entertain Tess so that you and Alicia can have some private time. But I think Tess will end up entertaining me. Right, Tess?"

"Can we take the dogs?" Tess begged.

Ben visualized Joey's corgis loose on the ski slopes, two moving furry moguls who would no doubt fill the first aid station to overflowing. "No, you can't."

"Why?" Tess whined.

"Because corgis don't ski, and they don't need snow bibs. You mind your manners and do what Marta tells you to do."

Inside, Ben found Joey organizing their living space. He wasn't surprised, somehow. She'd already made a list of needed groceries and taped it to the refrigerator door. Now she seemed to be cataloguing cooking utensils. The corgis promptly set about helping her. They probably thought that somewhere in the vicinity of pots and pans there had to be food.

"Where's Alicia?" Ben asked her.

"She went somewhere with Pat."

So much for private time with his fiancée. He felt guilty at a tiny hint of relief.

"Some digs, eh?"

"It's nice," Joey agreed mildly.

Nice was an understatement. The guy who built this "fishing cabin" certainly hadn't roughed it while he fished. A big living room with a stone fireplace and exposed log rafters offered every comfort of home—overstuffed chairs and chaise lounges, knotty pine tables, bookcases full of books, and a couple of shelves of board games. The rear of the house was a large country kitchen with all modern appliances, including a dishwasher and microwave oven. The rectangular kitchen table could easily seat eight or more along its benches. Off the kitchen were two bedrooms and a bathroom, and a staircase along one wall led to the sleeping loft.

"Pat Haines has the master bedroom," Joey told him. "He said you and Alicia can have the other. The rest of us will sleep upstairs in the loft. It's really nice up there. Divided into cute little cubicles, each with a full-sized bed."

"Uh . . ." Just how did he tactfully explain to Joey that he and Alicia weren't sleeping together? Not until the wedding. "Alicia and I can bunk in the loft."

She gave him a curious look. "No one is going to mind you taking the bedroom. After all, we're here for your wedding."

"We're waiting until after the wedding."

She looked surprised, then a bit flustered. "I'm sorry. I shouldn't have assumed . . ."

"That's okay. It's only natural."

"A lot of people who come to me to plan weddings are already living together."

"Yeah, well, we didn't want to set a bad example for Tess. And really, Alicia deserves someone who's willing to wait, don't you think?"

Her eyes softened. "That's a very nice thing to say."

"And you certainly wouldn't have expected me to say it, right?"

She laughed. "I'm taking the Fifth on that one. Do you want to look upstairs? I'm assigning beds."

"Of course you are," he said with a grin.

The sleeping loft was huge. Railed in knotty pine, it covered the area over both bedrooms, the downstairs bathroom, and half the kitchen. In one corner was a water closet, truly closet-sized. A small sitting area overlooked the living room, and the rest of the area was divided by knotty pine paneling into sleeping cubicles, each with a small dresser and a double bed. In all, the loft slept four very comfortably or eight somewhat more intimately.

"You should take the downstairs bedroom," Ben said to Joey. "Since Alicia and I don't want it."

"Not a chance. I'm the hired help, remember?"

"Like that makes a difference?"

"Appearances count. Maybe Alicia would like the downstairs bedroom to herself," Joey offered.

"I don't think she would," Ben said.

"Tess?"

"That's an idea. But I doubt she'd want to be alone in a strange place."

"She could have the dogs in with her."

"That should be entertaining. Two vigilant dogs should keep the monsters from coming out of the closet."

Joey smiled. "With Drover and Piggy in the room, I'm sure any monsters will stay behind a firmly closed door. Okay." She took a paper flower from her jacket pocket and twisted the stem around the doorknob of the first cubicle. "This can be Alicia's place. She's the bride, so she gets the flower." She smiled at his puzzled look. "I found it downstairs. So everyone knows where they belong, everybody gets an ID of sorts on their door."

"You're compulsive, aren't you?"

"Not at all. I'm merely organized. It's a requirement in my line of work." She hung a toy sheriff's star from the next doorknob. "This can be yours. The groom should be next to the bride."

"Good grief! Where did you get that?"

"The badge?"

"The badge."

"At a toy store in Denver. Where else?"

"You bought it to bring up here and pin on my door."

She gave him a Cheshire cat grin. "That's better than some places I could pin it."

"And what does your door get? An Indy 500 race car hanging from the knob?"

"No," she said with exaggerated patience. "My doorknob will make do with a mere rubber band." She held the item up for him to see, then slipped it over the knob. "This is so if we're coming in weary and befuddled late at night, we don't have to wake everyone by turning on a light to find our room. Samantha's room can have this 'Do Not Disturb' door hanger from the Holiday Inn."

He grinned. "You're a thief as well as a maniac on the road."

She looked down her nose at him. "It's torn. See? They didn't want it."

"You think of everything, don't you?"

"It's my job."

"Amazing." He shook his head. "And you're anticipating us coming in late most nights? Weary and befuddled?"

"It's likely."

"Well, I must admit, the very thought of skiing this afternoon has me wearier than I want to be."

She gave him a sympathetic smile.

"Don't look so smug," he said. "I suppose you're an ace skier?"

"Far from it, I'm afraid. But I have sense enough to stay off the slopes."

"Oh no you don't! I'm not going to be the only one in this bunch looking foolish. Besides, Alicia would be very disappointed. She wants one and all to have fun, even if it kills them. Including you."

"I couldn't possibly. The bridesmaids are getting here sometime this afternoon, and I have to make sure they're happy with their sleeping arrangements. And some of my kitchen staff will be coming as well, with Samantha. I have to work out some details for the engagement party tomorrow. Alicia didn't tell me she wanted to have it on top of a blasted mountain."

"You make me tired just talking about it. I'm glad to

have nothing to do but kick back and relax for a change." He sat down on his bed and bounced experimentally. "Yessiree. Nothing to do but entertain myself."

"Liar." She leaned against the doorframe and regarded him with a superior smile.

He stopped mid-bounce. "Huh?"

"Liar, I said. You'd like nothing better than to have something pressing that would keep you running. You are definitely not a man who takes to lounging around."

"Oh, really?"

"Yes, really."

Ben was taken aback. It was unnerving to be transparent, especially since he'd always prided himself on showing the world an unreadable face. "So what else do you think you know about me?" He was asking for trouble. Something told him he shouldn't invite those astute green eyes to probe too deeply into what he really thought and felt. But a stubborn streak of imprudence had him in its grip.

Joey, however, was more cautious than he. She considered him with mixed regret and mischief. "Sorry. I never get personally involved with clients. If you want analysis, you should go to a shrink."

"You're an infuriating woman, do you know that?"

She smiled. "I work at it."

Joey stood with her back to the breeze, wishing she were just about anyplace else. She had really hoped to get out of this little impromptu skiing lesson that Alicia had put together, but all her excuses had fallen by the wayside, one by one. The bridesmaids had arrived in plenty of time to join the group, and they were enthused by the prospect of hitting the slopes. Samantha had called to tell her that she and the kitchen staff would not arrive until later that night. And since Pat was with the group skiing, he wasn't available to discuss the logistics of carting hors d'oeuvres and guests up the mountain for Tuesday evening's engagement party.

Joey had run out of excuses, and when Alicia had pleaded, she'd caved. Alicia wanted everyone to have fun. That included Joey. And Alicia, having skied all her life, couldn't imagine why anyone wouldn't think that risking life and limb in such a manner wasn't a good time.

So here Joey stood in a group of bundled-up merrymakers freezing their tushes off while Pat explained the dos and don'ts of a chairlift for the benefit of the amateurs. The sky, bright blue when they had arrived at the lodge, was now overcast and spitting snow in their faces. Joey had to wonder about the sanity of anyone who would be out in a cold wind with snow getting in their eyes and sifting down their collars, especially when they could be sitting by a cheerful fire and guzzling hot cider. Even Tess didn't have the good sense to stay in. She was off with Marta in the Playpen, the children's ski hill, and they'd taken both dogs with them, since the area was securely fenced and there weren't any other kids skiing just then. Joey didn't even want to think about the havoc two corgis could wreak among energetic kids tottering on skis, but it probably wasn't much worse than the havoc that would ensue when she tried to ski down this blasted mountain.

The lifts were closed for the day, even though plenty of daylight remained, so everyone waiting in line was of the wedding party. Individuals were nearly unrecognizable in their insulated snow bibs, scarves, hats, and gloves—except Pat Haines and Alicia, who wore the stretchy, form-fitting ski pants and colorful sweaters that marked them as experts. Unlike run-of-the-mill skiers, experts don't regularly plow up the snow with their faces, so they don't need the protection of bulky clothes.

The rest of them were armored against the snow with nylon and wool. Sue Smythe of the size-twelve feet and her husband George looked eager to go. Teri kept talking about skiing in North Carolina, but where one would ski there was beyond Joey's comprehension. Carrie Meyer looked as uncertain on her skis as Joey felt, but her date Edward looked as though he belonged on the slopes. He teased Carrie about moving like a duck whose feet had suddenly grown too long. Joey totally related to poor Carrie.

And then there was Ben Ramsay. The man might have been a macho detective, but he looked like a penguin on skis—a penguin who hadn't yet learned to walk. He was the lever that Alicia had used to pry Joey off her backside and into a pair of ski boots. "You wouldn't want him to be the only real beginner out there, would you?" she cajoled. "He'd feel like the odd man out, and I really want him to have a good time."

So they were two odd men out, a man odd in more ways that just skiing, and a woman—was she odd? Joey wondered. Was Ben right when he labeled her bossy and compulsive? Of course, he'd been teasing, sort of. But it was true that her thoughts were generally tied up with the job at hand. And there was always a job at hand, it seemed. Maybe she should lighten up a bit, try to have fun at this little skiing adventure. Lots of people loved the sport, and really, how hard could it be once one got the knack?

She was about to find out. Pat was assigning them chairlift partners, matching them by experience level. He cast his former student Alicia in the role of perfect model of chairlift etiquette. Her job was to demonstrate how to get on the moving chair without looking like a blockhead. With her was Edward, who claimed to be experienced.

The two of them made the process look easy. Ski out to a line painted on the ground—or rather on the snow and ice—look over the shoulder to watch the chair whip around the turnstile, grasp both ski poles in one hand, grab the center pole of the chair with the other hand, then sit at just the right moment as the chair comes up behind. Easy as pie, Joey thought. An idiot could do it.

Beside her, Ben smiled darkly. "What do you think are the chances that we're going to land tail over topside?"

"Roughly a hundred percent," she replied with a sigh.

"Yeah, that's about how I figure it."

Sue and George, the next pair, didn't do badly, but they had obviously had some experience. The tip of Sue's right ski threatened to dig into a snowbank before the chair lifted them high, but she pulled it away just in time.

"Keep your tips up!" Pat called after her in warning.

Ben chortled. "Did he just say what I think he said?"

"No." Joey stifled a smile. "He said 'keep your *tips* up.' "

"Too bad," he sighed, returning Joey's grin.

"You are totally childish."

"Then you'll be glad to hear that I'm probably going to kill myself on this chairlift thing."

The next victims were Carrie and Teri. Teri giggled nervously, though she glided to the line competently. Carrie claimed to be a skier, but as her date Edward had so unkindly pointed out, she did move like a duck with unwieldy feet. She had the disadvantage of being short, so when the chair came around, it hit the small of her back instead of the bottom of her backside.

"Jump!" Teri advised her as the chair threatened to mow her down.

Carrie merely screeched, and Pat stepped in to give her a boost with a hand well placed under her buttocks. She landed safely in the chair and laughed as it carried her toward the top.

"Do you see what he did?" Ben asked Joey.

"So?"

"So if he does that to me I'm going to have to shoot him."

She laughed. "Sergeant Ramsay, your streak of police brutality is showing."

"Lord! What a man has to go through to get married these days."

Joey didn't have time to laugh, for they were suddenly at the front of the line. Suddenly it seemed a very long way to the red mark painted in the snow, and the chair seemed to move as fast as a locomotive. Ben shuffled his skis forward, and so did Joey, telling her stomach to stop doing flip-flops. Really, how hard could this be?

CHAPTER 9

◆

JOEY KEPT UP the mantra as she shuffle-slid forward. How hard could this be? How hard could this be? How hard . . . ?

Hard, it turned out. To begin with, there was the problem with skiing up to the red line—paint or blood? she wondered dismally—before the moving chair could round the corner and knock her aside. Next was the problem of stopping at the line. Skis didn't have brakes, and once they got moving over an icy surface, they wanted to continue moving without consulting Joey's wishes in the matter. She slid over the line, finally managed to stop, then had to shuffle backwards to be in the correct position to meet the chair.

Rattled by that little adventure, she purely forgot to look over her shoulder to check the progress of the chair. Pat's reminder came in the nick of time. Actually, not quite in the nick of time, because the minute she glanced behind her, the chair knocked her in the back-side, and not gently, either. Unbalanced, she started to tip forward as the inexorably moving juggernaut pushed her along.

"Oh nooooo . . . !" she moaned. "Help!"

Pat grabbed her on one side and Ben, safely seated in the chair, grabbed her on the other. Together they managed to get her half on the chair, and as the ground fell away and the chair began its climb, Ben dragged her flailing and kicking the rest of the way on board.

"Keep your tips up!" Pat called after her.

Ben gave her an impudent grin.

Half lying across his lap, clutching any part of him that offered an anchor, Joey groaned in embarrassment and frustration.

"Don't look down," Ben warned.

The warning, of course, made her look down. She shouldn't have. "Oh God! From the ground, these things don't look so high!"

"You're not going to fall."

She suddenly became aware of the hardness of his thighs beneath her and the loud thump of his heart, audible because her face was smashed against his chest. She didn't want to let go, but if she continued to crawl over Ben like a drowning woman crawling onto a life raft, he was going to suspect her motives. Keeping her eyes on Ben instead of the snowy terrain far below them, she pushed herself into some semblance of a sitting position.

"If we lower the foot bar," he suggested, "we can rest our skis on it, and our legs won't be dangling in empty space."

Her stomach sank. Empty space, all that empty space. "You didn't have to mention the empty space part."

Ben brought down the bar from over their heads. Once in place, it provided them not only with a ski rest but a metal bar that curved in front of them. Joey clutched it so hard she felt the weave of her mittens dig into her palms.

"That's better, isn't it?" Ben sounded as if he were talking to a scared child. With reason, Joey admitted.

"I lost my poles when I got on."

"Pat will probably pick them up."

She grinned feebly. "It doesn't make any difference. I don't really know how to use them."

"Join the club."

"At least you managed to get onto the blasted chair."

"We haven't gotten off yet."

Joey's stomach sank even lower. "You had to mention that. Something about what goes up . . ."

"Must come down. I remember vaguely Pat said something about how to get off without getting plastered into the snow."

"I think we were occupied cracking smart remarks in the back of the class."

"My high school teachers used to warn me that was a habit that would come back to haunt me."

She laughed. "I can imagine."

"And I suppose you never sat in the back of the classroom mouthing off?"

"It's a character flaw that's afflicted me only recently."

The end of the line was in sight—a steep up-ramp of snow leading to a platform where skiers got off the chair before it whipped around the turnstile and headed back down the hill. After exiting the chair they were supposed to ski down another steep ramp and turn sharply left to the beginning of the runs. A sign warned them to lift their security bar, which made Joey feel very insecure.

"Pat said to keep sitting and let the chair push you down the ramp?" she asked desperately.

"No, I think he said to stand up and lean forward."

They watched Carrie and Teri get off. Teri literally dove off the chair and sped down the exit ramp with admirable flair. Her chair partner, Carrie, didn't stand quite soon enough, or didn't lean forward aggressively enough, Joey couldn't tell which. The result was she lost her balance, the chair whopped her on its way around, and she slid down the ramp on her backside, landing in an ungraceful heap of tangled legs and skis at the bottom. The chair attendant matter-of-factly dragged her off the ramp before the next chair—Ben and Joey's chair— crested the hill to discharge its passengers.

"Oh, that looks fun!" Joey commented dryly.

"Be adventurous."

"I'm going to remind you of your adventurous attitude when you take off for your honeymoon with two broken legs. Oh shit!"

Joey generally didn't use foul language. But the suddenness with which the chair crested the steep ramp and pushed them onto the icy platform really did call for cussing. She tried to stand up as instructed. But her legs were long, and the seat of the chair was so close to the platform that her knees were practically around her ears.

"Stand up!" Ben advised. His strong legs successfully pushed him out of the chair.

Joey's legs were not as strong. "I can't!"

He took her hand and yanked. She shot forward—too late. The chair slapped against her knees and she went sprawling. Her slide down the ramp made Carrie's exit look graceful. At least Carrie slid down on her back. Joey plowed down the ramp with her face.

Ben pulled her out of the way before the attendant could reach her.

"Nice trip?" he inquired as she wiped snow from her face and eyes.

"That is so old. Can't you think of something original?"

"You're very cranky this afternoon."

"I hope you become intimate with a tree on your way to the bottom of the mountain. Very intimate."

Ben was pulling Joey ungracefully to her feet when Alicia skied up to them and stopped in a spray of snow. "Joey! What happened to you?"

Pat slid up beside her. "She took a header off the chair." He'd been on the chair behind them, and of course he'd seen the whole humiliating thing. Joey hoped he wouldn't feel compelled to go into detail. He didn't, just smiled, brushed a clump of snow from the collar of her jacket, and handed her the ski poles she'd dropped getting onto the chair. "You'll get the knack of it," he said brightly. "Everybody looks like a klutz the first time out."

"Tell me the hard part is over," Joey pleaded.

"It is. Getting to the top is the most difficult. Really. This run here, the one marked with the green circles, is easy as pie. Just remember to ski across the slope instead of straight down the fall line."

"What's a fall line?" Carrie asked. The whole group had gathered in a little knot.

"The fall line is straight down the mountain," Alicia told them.

Ben snorted. "No wonder they call it the fall line."

The group laughed. Joey didn't think the remark was that funny.

"Don't worry," Pat reassured them. "I'll help you get down in one piece. These runs are so gentle you'll be moving slow as molasses."

Alicia pouted comically. "Aren't you coming with us over to Comet's Tail? We want to ski the advanced runs." By "we," she meant everyone but Ben, Joey, and Carrie.

Pat looked torn between duty and desire.

Alicia laughed. "Don't worry about our newbies, Pat. Ben will take care of them. He's the next thing to invincible."

Pat gave Ben a questioning look. Ben glanced ruefully at Alicia, then shrugged. "Go ahead with the A team, Pat. We'll manage."

"You looked good coming up here, buddy." Pat clapped Ben on the shoulder. "Show these ladies the ropes on the way down. This run to the left is so easy that you won't have anything to worry about. Follow the green signs to Blitzen's Trail. Just remember—ski across the slope, weight on the downhill ski, then lift your body, shift your weight, and let the skis do all the work in turning. Easy as pie."

"Oh yeah, easy as pie," Joey groaned as Pat skied away to catch up with the others.

Alicia blew Ben a kiss and shouted, "See you at the bottom! Have fun!"

"Did anyone have the foggiest idea what Pat was talking about?" Joey blew out a frosty breath and looked apprehensively down the hill.

"Well . . ." Ben made a wry face. "I did take skiing lessons when I was in college. I wasn't exactly the star pupil, though."

"This'll be fun!" Carrie said with determined brightness. But her eyes were glued in the direction her boyfriend Edward had taken.

They all three slid carefully to where Blitzen's Trail started to slope downward. It seemed a gentle enough descent, but Joey had already learned that the skis on her feet had a mind of their own. Beside her, Ben and Carrie looked down the hill cautiously.

"Where's the lodge?" Carrie asked.

"Somewhere down there beyond the trees?" Ben speculated. "I guess the trail winds around a lot."

"Do you wish you were back in Denver working?" Joey asked him. "A shoot-out at Five Points might be more fun than this."

He grinned. "I'd have a better chance of getting out of it in one piece."

"Oh dear," Carrie sighed. "My skis keep wanting to cross."

"It's a long way down," Ben said grimly.

"Goodbye, sweet world," Joey said with a resigned shake of her head. "I'm never going to make it to the bottom."

All three of them did make it to the bottom, though.

They didn't have much choice, really, once they pointed themselves downhill. Gravity ruled. Halfway down the first little slope, Ben remembered how to stop. He tried to instruct Joey in the process, but she could stop only one way—by piling into him, which she did in a spectacular fashion. They both went down, skis, arms, and legs tangled, then surfaced, spitting snow. Carrie whizzed past them, totally out of control. She stopped by merely falling down.

Spread-eagled in the snow, Carrie tilted her head back to look at the tangled two. "You guys are just a disgrace," she said with a giddy smile. "Shame on you, Ben, an engaged man about to be married, groping another woman."

They *were* groping, much to Joey's flaming embarrassment. But they had to grope in order to right themselves. Righting yourself with skis on your feet isn't an easy task. So she tried not to notice when Ben's arm accidentally brushed her breast. It wasn't as though that breast wasn't covered by five layers of clothing. And it wasn't as though she couldn't find a perfectly good excuse for the breath leaving her body and a rush of blood heating her face. Joey also tried not to notice Ben's knee plunking down between her thighs, or the hard, broad chest that at one point pressed intimately against her cheek. With her skis pointed in opposite directions, she couldn't move, so she had to endure Ben's contortions while he righted himself.

Except that the ordeal wasn't so much endurable as enjoyable.

Finally, he was off of her. Ben rearranged Joey's skis so they were pointing the same direction and then gave her a hand up. When she was upright he slid down to Carrie and performed the same service for her—without the groping.

"Well," Joey said cheerfully. "That was a good start."

"Maybe we should review how to stop," Ben suggested.

"They really ought to put brakes on these things," Carrie complained.

It was a long trip down. Ben tried to teach them how to snowplow—pigeon-toeing their skis to keep down their speed—and how to dig their edges into the snow to slow the skis. These methods required just a tiny bit of skill, however, which neither Joey nor Carrie seemed to possess. The ladies continued to stop themselves by grabbing at trees, at Ben, at each other, and plowing up the snow with their backsides. Once it became clear that the worst consequence was getting snow up their backs—and up just about everything else as well—their sometimes spectacular crashes became a joke. Ben, far from an expert on the slopes, had his share of tumbles as well. When the three finally reached the lodge, they looked like a human avalanche. They took off their skis and proceeded straight to the fireplace to warm their backsides, which had seen much more contact with the snow than their skis had. There they ordered hot toddies and exchanged vows never to reveal the farcical nature of their descent, especially to Alicia, who might take exception to the fact that her husband-to-be was apparently not a hero on the ski slopes.

That night, Joey stumbled into her little loft cubicle and sank gratefully into her bed, nursing sore muscles

from her neck down to her toes. The day was over—
thank God! All were settled, the bridesmaids happy
with their rooms in the lodge, the dogs content to keep
Tess company in the downstairs bedroom, and the Big
Cabin was finally quiet. Sleep couldn't come soon
enough as far as Joey was concerned.

Her stomach was full of the excellent dinner served
in the lodge dining room—the chef was a whiz with
halibut. She'd have to pry the recipe out of him before
she left. And the company had been very entertaining.
Alicia's bridesmaids were a hoot, every one of them.
Sue's husband George was quite a talented classical gui-
tarist, it turned out, and he entertained them for a bit
after dinner. Teri Schaefer was an undiscovered come-
dienne who had kept them howling with accounts of
the "advanced" skiers' adventures on the moguls that
afternoon—it turned out that some of them weren't so
advanced after all. And Carrie's pleasant good nature
added a mellow note to the company.

Carrie's date Edward was nice enough, and certainly
charming, though he did seem a bit invested in his
own image. But that might just be her reaction, Joey
admitted. She too often leaped to judgment where
men were concerned. Look at the hard time she'd
given poor Ben.

Joey smiled when she thought of her friend's fiancé,
but it wasn't an entirely happy smile. Ben Ramsay
could certainly grow on a woman. Joey had had her
doubts at first, but Alicia had really struck gold with
Ben. The man had a sharp wit, a sense of humor, and a
sensible perspective on life. He didn't mind laughing at

himself, which was something many men had yet to learn. His daughter was a darling, and Ben obviously doted on her. It was hard for any woman to resist a man who could so adore a child. Not to mention that he was a hunk. What had seemed fairly ordinary packaging at first became more and more attractive as Joey noticed the details.

Joey was happy that Alicia had found someone so exceptional. And she was determined not to eavesdrop on the intimate conversation going on in the next cubicle, to which Ben and Alicia had retired. Soft murmurs were punctuated by cheerful laughter. Joey could picture them sitting together on Ben's bed, chatting about the life they expected to have together, maybe kissing, maybe caressing . . .

She hastily reined in her wandering imagination. What Ben and Alicia were doing in the next cubicle was none of her business. Just because Ben had said they weren't sleeping together didn't mean they couldn't enjoy a little interlude of affection before retiring to their separate beds. In less than a week they would be man and wife. They were in love. Committed. And Joey certainly had no business listening in on their private doings or imagining the details of their relationship. No indeed.

It was just that she was feeling a bit down. She didn't know why. Maybe she was worried about getting everyone and everything to the top of the mountain for the next evening's engagement party. Maybe she was overstressed after a very hectic day. Maybe she was getting her period. There were always a dozen reasons for getting the glooms. A day without a bit of depression was a day . . . well, a day she hadn't seen in a while.

And why was that? Joey wondered.

She didn't want to think about it.

The next morning brought aches and pains the like of which Joey had never experienced. Dragging herself out of bed was torture, creakily forcing her body into an upright position a near impossibility. The torture was made worse by the sight at the breakfast table of Pat and Alicia moving around with lithe unconcern, obviously untouched by the exertions of the day before. One would expect that from Pat Haines. He was a former ski instructor, after all. But Alicia at least could have the courtesy to be a bit sore.

"Ooooh, Joey," Alicia exclaimed with an impish little smile. "You look very stiff."

"Stiff is scarcely an adequate description," Joey groaned.

Pat handed her a cup of hot coffee. "What you need is a soak in one of the whirlpools."

"Outside in the snow, aren't they?" Joey said, wrinkling her nose. "I've had enough snow and cold—"

"Oh no!" Alicia laughed. "Being outside in the snow only makes the whirlpools seem warmer and more luxurious, doesn't it, Pat? It's not only relaxing, it's sensuous, all warm and tingly, with the jets of water nibbling at your toes."

Joey had to smile at the picture Alicia painted. "I'll have to remember to come back here and try it, if I ever have someone to be sensuous with."

"Don't worry about that," Alicia said blithely. "When I get back from my honeymoon, I'm going to reform you, my friend. Make a romantic out of you. I'm going to fix you up with someone who'll make you wonder why you've waited all this time to get married."

"Ouch! I thought we were friends."

"You're going to fix who up with who?" Ben asked as he gingerly came down the steps from the loft. At least he had the grace to look almost as sore as Joey felt.

"We're going to find a good man for Joey," Alicia informed him.

His smile looked dubious.

"He's thinking there's not a man anywhere who would put up with me," Joey speculated aloud.

"Or a man I would be willing to wish such a fate upon," Ben said with a chuckle.

Alicia smiled brightly. "See, you two are teasing. I knew you would learn to like each other. What did I tell you?"

Ben's response was a noncommittal "Mm." Then he stretched and groaned, working the kinks from his broad shoulders in a way that drew Joey's appreciative eye. When she noticed Alicia watching her, she blushed, but Alicia merely winked impishly.

"Where are the dogs?" Ben asked. "I thought I'd take them jogging with me."

"You're going to jog?" Joey asked, amazed.

"Best way to work out the kinks. Want to join me? I know Alicia won't."

Alicia seconded that with a grimace. "Not me!"

Joey laughed feebly. "Me either. I'm lucky I can

walk. But I'm sure Piggy and Drover would be glad of
the exercise."

At the mention of their names, the dogs scratched
furiously at the door that shut them into Tess's bedroom. Ben opened it a corgi width and peeked inside.
"Tess is still out like a light."

The dogs shot out like brown cannonballs, barking
furiously at the prospect of breakfast.

"Come on, corgis," Ben said. "We can eat when we
get back."

Drover bounced with excitement when Ben
snapped a leash to his collar. Piggy wasn't as enthused.
She retreated to the small space under the antique
Hoosier that stood against the kitchen wall and peered
out at the man with a look of incredulity on her face.

"I don't think she wants to go," Alicia concluded
with a giggle.

"She's an unnatural dog," Ben said in disgust.
"Come on, Drover. I guess this is a stag party. Alicia,
will you keep an eye out for Tess?"

"My soon-to-be-stepdaughter? Sure."

They watched out the window as Ben jogged somewhat stiffly down the road, Drover bouncing at his
side, occasionally straying from the road and sinking
into snow higher than his ears. Pat's expression was
very neutral as he said to Alicia, "He's a good man,
Allie. You've found yourself a good man."

"He *is* a good man," Alicia agreed with a little more
force than necessary.

Alicia sounded almost as if she was trying to convince herself, Joey reflected. She buttoned her lip,
though. The relationship between Alicia and Ben was

not her business. She contented herself with seconding the motion. "Ben is a good man. In a lot of ways, Alicia, you're lucky."

Further praise of Ben's goodness was interrupted by an electronic tweedling.

"My cell phone!" Joey snatched at the little holster that kept the phone continually at her side. Samantha's number appeared in the caller identification screen. "Samantha? Where the heck are you? You were supposed to be here last night!"

"I know," Samantha said, her voice tinny through a poor cell connection. "I'm really sorry. There was just too much to do."

"I was worried. You weren't answering your phone when I called."

"The battery was dead, and I didn't realize it. I should have called you, but I got so busy, and then it was so late. . . . So I figured I'd just call this morning and explain. A Leticia Downs from Arvada was very insistent on wanting to talk to someone this week, so I scheduled her for today. I couldn't blow it off, because it sounds like a very big job. I'll be up there later on today, hopefully before the engagement party starts."

"The party's going to be at the top of the mountain."

After a telling silence, Sam chuckled. "Don't tell me—Alicia, right?"

"Right." Joey couldn't say what she truly wanted to because Alicia and Pat were standing right there in the kitchen with her.

"Well, don't worry about the kitchen staff. They're on their way. I know they were supposed to be there last night, but Charlie's kid was sick. But they're headed your way, finally. So is the van with the food and chafing dishes and all the other stuff. I personally loaded up and sent them on their way before dawn."

"Great. Thank you."

"And I'll be along later. Is it snowing there? It's snowing here."

Joey glanced out the window. "It looks like it might snow later. Be careful driving up."

Alicia shouted at the phone, "Samantha. Bring your skis. We're having a great time."

Fortunately, only Joey heard Samantha's response. "Take care," she told her assistant. "Call when you get on the road."

Alicia poured them all another cup of coffee and then rattled around in the cupboards. "You want some eggs?" she asked the others. "I'm going to fry up some eggs."

"Fine by me," Pat said, and Joey nodded also, just as her phone tweedled again.

This time it was the driver of the catering van. "We're goddamned broken down," he said in no uncertain terms.

"Where?" Joey asked, visualizing a ritzy engagement party without food.

"Georgetown," was the reply. Georgetown was at least a four-hour drive, one way. Her heart sank.

"What's wrong?" Pat asked when she snapped her phone shut with a disgusted click.

She explained. "The catering van decided that it had to have new cylinders, or some such thing. It's stranded at Georgetown."

"That's bad," Pat confirmed. "They won't get that fixed today."

"I didn't think so. I don't suppose there's a good grocery store up here?" she asked hopefully.

"In Aspen. All the gourmet food you want."

Joey checked her watch, mentally ran over her schedule, and sighed.

"Alicia and I will go," Pat offered suddenly. "Just give us a list."

"Sure!" Alicia seconded. "We can go."

"Maybe Ben would like to go as well," Joey suggested.

"Oh no," Alicia said blithely. "Who knows when he'll get back from jogging. He gets in a zone, you know, and loses track. Pat and I will go. It's no trouble."

"No trouble at all," Pat confirmed cheerfully. "We could get brunch before coming back."

"Oh! That sounds fun. Joey, will you keep an eye on Tess? I think Marta's taking her up the bunny hill at ten or so."

"Sure," Joey said with a sigh.

Joey hastily wrote up a list and handed it to Pat. "Be sure you get heavy whipping cream. Not the light stuff. And the balsamic vinegar has to be at least ten years old."

"Don't frown," Pat chided her as he headed out with Alicia. "We'll be back in plenty of time, and I have the snowmobiles and sleds all lined up. Tonight will go smooth as silk."

◆

Who knew grocery shopping could be so much fun? Alicia slanted a smile up at Pat as he bagged Italian tomatoes. She was blatantly flirting, but it was harmless flirting, because both of them realized it wasn't headed anywhere. One could flirt for old times' sake. That kind of flirting made no promises for the future.

"Are you going to buy that zucchini, or just play with it?" Pat asked with theatrical huskiness.

Startled by the sudden image—only Pat Haines would consider an innocent vegetable a green phallus!—Alicia dropped the squash as if it burned her fingers. "Don't do that!" she objected with a little laugh.

"Do what?"

"Embarrass me. As long as I've known you, you've always taken great delight in embarrassing me."

He grinned unrepentantly. "That's because you're so easy to embarrass. Most women these days wouldn't blush if they walked into the middle of a porn festival. You get embarrassed looking at a zucchini. Alicia, you truly are a delight."

Her face heated, much to her disgust. Joey would not have been so easy a target. Joey would have simply given Pat that self-possessed "I don't have time for this" smile of hers and then sent him off to get a bag of onions. Not that Alicia truly minded Pat's teasing. To tell the truth, she'd invited it with her smiles and attention. Perhaps she was doing the nervous bride bit, taking one last gallop around the paddock before a husband snubbed her down to his own private hitching post.

Talk about images! Alicia didn't like that one. She didn't like it at all, and it wasn't the way it was. She had proposed to Ben Ramsay, not the other way around, and she was sublimely happy with her chosen man. Marriage would mean greater freedom, not less, and Ben was the ideal husband for her. She was supremely content at the prospect of her marriage, but being committed to Ben didn't mean she couldn't be chummy with her old friends.

"Trying to choke the artichoke?" Pat asked dryly.

"Oops!" Distracted again, Alicia thought. At least there was nothing the least suggestive about an artichoke. Or was there? "I was just trying to find a good one. Joey is a very picky chef, you know. She says the finished dish can't be better than the raw stuff that goes into it."

"Does she, now?"

"Don't use that tone. Joey's one of the nicest people in the world."

"I'm sure she is. I wasn't using a tone. She does seem a bit uptight, though."

Alicia laughed as she bagged the tortured artichoke. "That sounds like the ski bum talking, not the new nose-to-the-grindstone business entrepreneur."

"If the coming summer season isn't better than this winter season has been, I may be doing the ski bum bit again."

"Oh pooh! Bear Run has got all the ingredients to be a great success. You worry too much."

He laughed. "What I'm really worried about is finding this exotic cheese that Joey wants. Good old City Market isn't going to have this high-octane stuff, I'm afraid. I do know a gourmet deli close to Boogie's Diner, though."

Alicia smiled hugely. "Boogie's! I love that place, and I haven't been there since . . . well, since the last time we went there."

"That can be remedied. We'll do the gourmet thing, then get lunch at the diner."

"What could be finer?" Alicia rhymed with a giggle. She just knew that coming up here for the wedding was a great idea.

An hour later they sat in a booth at Boogie's Diner, a fifties-style "happening" diner above Boogie's emporium of haute couture jeans. Only in Aspen could such a combination be so successful. The place had been in business since 1987, the project of the very "Boogie" made famous by the 1982 Barry Levinson film *Diner*.

Alicia munched on the sesame chicken pasta salad and eyed a gigantic chocolate malt a waiter carried to another table. "I'm going to get me one of those," she declared. "I think I deserve a chocolate malted." She smiled nostalgically. "I do love this place. Coming here with you used to be such fun."

"You mean back in the days when I would play hooky from work after your ski lesson and we came here for hamburgers?"

"Yes. You were a very bad boy back then."

"I'm still a bad boy every once in a while."

"That's one of the things that makes you interesting to women. Good girls are always fascinated by bad boys."

"And if I remember correctly, you were a very good girl."

"Very good. So good I bored myself silly. I still do."

"I don't think you're in the least boring, Allie. I never did."

"Not as interesting as Marta, I'll bet." She immediately wished the words back into her mouth. Pat and Marta were certainly not her affair.

Pat didn't seem annoyed, however. "Marta?"

"I just assumed that you two . . ." She let her words trail off into obvious territory.

"Go on! Marta's a sweetheart, but . . ."

"Not to mention a knockout."

"Well, that too. But she's got a fiancé in Glenwood Springs, and even if she didn't, we're just friends. The spark isn't there. You know what I mean? No chemistry."

"The spark isn't there," Alicia said, stirring her salad pensively.

"We had sort of a spark at one time," Pat reminded her, a searching look in his eyes.

"I guess we did."

More than a spark, Alicia acknowledged privately. She had thought Pat was The One. She'd thought herself ready to follow him to the ends of the earth.

But she shouldn't think of that now. She was engaged to a wonderful man, and even if Nana thought he was plebeian, her father thought she'd done herself proud in choosing a husband like Ben. And she had, Alicia reminded herself.

Pat chuckled, letting go of his intensity. "Of course, that was back when I was a ski bum with no ambition."

Alicia was surprised at his self-deprecating tone. "That never bothered me."

"If it didn't, it should have. It bothered me."

"And just look where you are now."

"Not much better," he said ruefully. "I'm still a ski bum, only now I have ambition. That and a host of cranky investors who think they know how to run a ski resort better than I do."

"You're luckier than you know." Alicia heard the pride in his voice despite a note of discouragement. In a way she envied him. With a business to build, challenges filled every moment of his day. His life certainly couldn't be boring. If he succeeded, he'd have something to point to that he built with his own ambition and know-how. If he didn't succeed, at least he would have the knowledge that he'd tried. And he would have learned what he needed to be successful on the next try. Not boring at all.

"You're a fine one to talk about being lucky," Pat reminded her with a wry smile.

She flashed him a guilty grin. "Yes. Sometimes I forget. There's the money thing. If you've always had it, I guess you don't appreciate what a difference it makes."

"Uh-huh."

"And there's Ben."

"Ah yes. Wonderful Ben."

She frowned at his tone. "Don't you like him?"

"I do like him," he admitted grudgingly. "He's a solid sort of no-nonsense guy."

"He saved my life."

"Then I'm in his debt."

She studied him, wondering at the meaning behind his words, then decided that perhaps it was best not to probe. "Daddy got him as sort of my personal body-guard when that creep Jason Denny was sending me letters and threatening all those awful things. There was this charity ball I just had to go to, and Ben's boss, a Captain Case, didn't want to offend the hoity-toity . . ."

"Of which you are a member," Pat reminded her.

"Well, yes. But anyway, he didn't want to put cops in the ballroom at the Brown Palace, even though Ben asked him to. Ben didn't care much about how it would look—he's that way."

"So I gather."

"But Case won. He thought Jason wouldn't dare show up in such a public place. But he did. Bold as brass. Dragged me out of there with a knife at my throat. I swear to you, Pat, he was going to slice me from one end to the other. I could see it in his eyes. I've never been so sick scared in my entire life."

"I can imagine. But Ben saved the day."

"He faced him down. Told Jason if he hurt me that he'd personally . . . well, I won't go into detail about what he said. He was upset. Jason didn't care. He'd really lost it by then. Total wacko. Told Ben that if he didn't back down, he'd slit my throat."

"And . . . ?"

"And Jason stuffed me into his car and we drove off. Ben commandeered someone's car—a Caddy. He got in trouble for that. Anyway, he chased us. We must have been doing over a hundred. Way over. Jason was so wacko, but he knew if he stopped to carve on me like he wanted to do, Ben would get him. So he drove the car right into Cherry Creek Reservoir. He screamed something about being together forever, and then he just sent the car right off the dam. The water came in so fast, I was trapped, but Ben dove in and got me out."

"I'm impressed."

"Jason drowned."

"Couldn't happen to a more deserving fellow, sounds like."

She smiled brightly, trying to banish the nightmare shadows she had called from her memory. "And Ben's a hero."

"Is that why you're marrying him? A reward?"

"No! I'm marrying him because I love him. He's the first man I've ever known who truly doesn't care anything about my money."

Pat gave her a long, deep look, and Alicia instantly realized her gaffe. "You didn't care about my money, Pat, but you didn't care that much about me, either."

"That's where you're wrong," he said, quite serious.

Her stomach flip-flopped. "About which?"

He raised a brow. "Doesn't matter now, does it?"

It didn't, Alicia told herself. It really didn't matter. All the same, when her gigantic chocolate malted came, she'd lost her appetite.

CHAPTER 10

◆

TUESDAY EVENING'S ENGAGEMENT party, in spite of being on top of a snowy mountain, came off without a hitch.

"You always worry," Samantha reminded Joey. "But things always go okay."

"Because I work the details."

"You should learn to work the details without turning yourself into a basket case."

"I'm not a basket case," Joey said indignantly.

Samantha wore a knowing smirk. "Is that why you fell all over yourself in relief when I got here in time to help supervise the kitchen?"

"I had other things to do," Joey said primly. "Like make sure the guys operating the chairlift knew that they had to stop every chair for the guests to get on and get off. That chairlift can be a killer. Believe me, I know!"

"And did anyone have trouble?"

"No. But Granny Irene is still complaining about getting snow in her silk pumps."

"Anyone who would wear silk pumps at a place like this deserves to get snow in them."

"Don't say that in Irene's hearing."

They sat nursing flutes of champagne at one of the little tables surrounding the area cleared for dancing. The Top of the World restaurant had been transformed into a ballroom, thanks to Pat Haines and his crew. The small kitchen was adequate for her staff to prepare the hot hors d'oeuvres—tiny Swedish meatballs and crab-stuffed shrimp. The cold food had been prepared in the lodge kitchen and brought up by snowmobile sled. The cold shrimp, crisp cut veggies, and artichoke dip arrived at the buffet table with the perfect chill imparted by a journey through freezing mountain air.

When Alicia had first proposed moving the party up the mountain, Joey had imagined disaster. But everything was working just fine. The string quartet from the symphony had arrived in plenty of time and had been only a little fazed by the task of hauling their instruments up a mountain. They were staying to play at the wedding and reception. Joey hoped they remained such good sports for the rest of the week. Many of the wedding guests had arrived that day, eager to spend the rest of the week enjoying Bear Run as the wedding couple's guests. While some were apprehensive about getting to the party via chairlift, most managed it without difficulty. Their experiences on the lift provided conversation fodder if nothing else. Irene had complained, but Irene, Joey had concluded, would complain about anything that had to do with this wedding. She continued to make it quite clear, through innuendo and not-so-subtle hints, that she did not approve of her granddaughter's choice of a life partner.

"I think it's time to formally introduce the happy pair," Joey said. "Then we'll see if this party can really get off the ground."

At the close of the next number, she spoke to the musicians, then nodded to Alicia's father, who had rehearsed a nice little introduction of his daughter and soon-to-be son-in-law. His emotional speech thanking Ben for saving his daughter's life and congratulating Alicia for recognizing a good man when she saw one brought smiles to the guests' faces, and the solo dance by the engaged couple had everyone murmuring sentimental comments. Joey eavesdropped shamelessly.

"They're really a striking couple, aren't they?"

Pat Haines had come up behind her and commented quietly. He followed Ben's and Alicia's progress on the dance floor with eyes that suddenly looked more black than blue. Joey wondered exactly what he was thinking.

"They are striking," Joey agreed. "Ben's a very good dancer, isn't he? Big men aren't often that light on their feet. By the way, Pat, thanks so much for your help in seeing that everything moved so smoothly up here. You have a very professional staff."

"Thank you. They're a good crew. And it's my pleasure to help. Alicia's a good friend, and I'd like her wedding to be perfect."

The solo dance ended and other couples moved onto the dance floor as the musicians swung into as close as they could come to an old Creedence Clearwater hit from the sixties. Somehow Joey ended up in Ben's arms, giving her a chance to judge his dancing firsthand. He was fun to dance with, she decided. And dressed in sharply tailored brown slacks and a soft brown sweater, he was downright handsome. His eyes were dark as pitch, shadowy whirlpools where a woman could easily drown. The soft yarn of his sweater drew Joey's fingers, and her cheek, like a magnet. The urge to lean against his broad shoulder was almost irresistible. *Hands off!* she chided herself silently. He was Alicia's fiancé. Strictly forbidden fruit.

Not that she was truly attracted to Ben. He was a hunk. And nice—even though the nice took a while to show. And then there was that electric spark that jump-started her hormones every time they touched.

But she was truly not interested. Of course not. Interested would be just too disastrous to contemplate.

Ben broke in on her mental meandering. "This is more fun than I thought it would be. You did a great job on this party."

He sounded so grudging that Joey had to laugh. "The party was Alicia's idea, not mine."

"Alicia's idea. Your work."

"That's my job."

"Well, thanks for doing a great job. It's made Alicia really happy."

Their eyes went to Alicia, who was dancing nearby with Ben's brother Tom, who had arrived just an hour before the party began. She was radiant as any bride should be, laughing and chatting with her partner.

The two couples drifted together, and Tom gave his brother a ribald wink. "Who's the fox, bro?"

Ben grinned at Joey. "Ignore him. He's best man only because he's a blood relative, but usually I don't claim him."

"Oh, come on, Ben," Alicia chortled. "Tom's cute."

"Now here's a woman with taste," Tom gloated.

"She has wonderful taste," Ben parried. "She's marrying me."

"A momentary lapse, I'm sure. But it's true. Alicia's taken, and I'm still available, so I should be dancing with the fox. Tallyho!"

Tom twirled Alicia neatly into Ben's arms and at the same time pulled Joey into his own. Everyone laughed, and several other couples on the floor paused to applaud. Tom looked down at Joey with a triumphant grin. He was handsomer than Ben as far as classic looks went, but he lacked the warm spray of laugh lines around the eyes and the sometimes troublesome twinkle in the eye. Joey stepped hard on her mental brakes. She didn't need to be thinking of Ben as warm and twinkly.

"I'm Tom Ramsay—Ben's brother."

"So I gathered."

"And you are?"

"Joey DeMato, wedding consultant."

"Ah, the great Joey. Alicia raves about you, you know. Very unusual for one beautiful woman to rave about another beautiful woman in such a positive way. You are a knockout."

"And you are full of bull," Joey told him, laughing. "Where did you get your pick-up line? From an old sixties movie?"

"You mean it's not working?"

"Hardly. I know all about you, Tom. Boulder cop. Twice divorced. A new lady every month."

"Who ratted? My big brother?"

"I'm afraid he warned every woman here, including Alicia's granny."

Tom grinned ruefully. "Busted!"

In spite of his on-the-make mentality, Tom was entertaining, but Joey's eyes kept drifting to Ben, who now danced with Irene. Both Irene and Ben looked stiffly polite. If Irene's smile became any chillier, Joey mused, her cheeks would freeze and crack.

"Excuse me, guy." Edward, Carrie's boyfriend, tapped Tom on the shoulder. "You can't monopolize this one all night. There's a shortage of beautiful women in the room."

So suddenly Joey was dancing with Edward, and a glance toward Ben showed him with Teri Schaefer in his arms. The dance was turning into an old-fashioned snowball.

Edward was what Joey called a "fancy dancer." Tall, blond, lean, and good-looking, he had obviously taken professional dancing lessons.

"You're too advanced for me," she said, laughing as he bent her over his arm in an ostentatious dip.

"I'm sure you have a lot of your own good moves." His smile was flirtatious. She ignored it. Tom and now Edward—why did weddings always bring out the wolves?

"Carrie looks very nice tonight." A reminder to Don Juan that he had a date was in order, Joey decided. "I know she's glad you decided to come."

"I try never to miss a good party."

"Are you from Denver?"

"Golden," he told her. "The home of good beer. My family has major stock in Coors."

"Oh. How nice."

"The bride's beautiful, don't you think?"

"She is," Joey agreed. "She's also a very nice person. None nicer."

"Ben Ramsay really nabbed himself a prize. He surely did."

Joey didn't have time to answer before she found herself dancing once more with Ben.

"I forgot to thank you," he said, "for finding someone to watch Tess tonight."

"Tess is probably running rings around the poor girl. The dogs will be helping her."

He grinned. "I don't think so. Marta wore her out on Playpen Hill today. Says she's a quick study. Already schussing down the slope like a little pro. Takes after her mother in athletic ability."

"Well, obviously she doesn't take after you."

"Ouch! Though I'll admit I'm not exactly Brian Boitano on the slopes."

"Brian Boitano is an ice skater, Ben."

"Well, close. Ice, snow, they're both cold. Tess does take after her mother, in both looks and talent. Annie could do just about everything, and did."

"She must have been special."

After a moment of pensive silence, Ben gave her a tentative smile. "Did I ever apologize for being such an ass that day on the turnpike?"

"I think you tried once."

"But didn't do a very good job, huh? I *was* an ass. I'm sorry. It was a bad day, and I wasn't pleased to be on the traffic beat." His smile became lopsided. "Of course, you were quite a pistol yourself."

She tsked and shook her head. "And you were doing so well. Don't ruin a good apology."

"You're right. And I'm sure you'll apologize for your attitude as soon as you think of the right words."

She laughed and thought of several comebacks but chose not to use them.

"You're a nice person, Joey DeMato." All teasing left his voice.

Before she could think of a reply, Alicia's father cut in and took her away.

"Wanted to tell you what a wunnerful job your doing for m'baby." A miasma of alcohol accompanied the words. Mr. Somers had been hard at the champagne. "She d'serves the best, y'know? Sweet li'l girl. Raised her without her mother, y'know? Never a bit of trouble with my Alicia. Always a good girl. Best heart in th' universe."

"That's true, Mr. Somers. Alicia has the best heart in the world."

"An' m'baby found herself a good man. Good man! Damned good man. Salt of the earth. I keep tellin' 'er that."

"Yes, sir."

He gave either a laugh or a gurgle. It was hard to tell. "Little solid blood from the lower classes'll improve the family, y'know?"

That remark dumbfounded Joey, for all her practice in the art of keeping a conversation going. But Irene, who happened to be dancing close by with Pat Haines, had heard.

"Shame on you, Richard! Such a thing to say!"

Mr. Somers tittered weakly. "Jus' kidding, Mother."

Joey wondered wickedly if Irene was chiding him for calling Ben "lower class" or implying that Ben might add something to their family. She decided that she'd rather not know. The less she had to deal with Irene, the better she liked it. But ten minutes later when the musicians took a break, the older woman approached her as she checked the buffet table for items that needed replenishing.

"Miss DeMato!"

"Mrs. Somers." Joey tried to sound happy to see her.

"You are to be complimented on a lovely party. Working under such a disadvantage, too. On top of a mountain, of all things. So . . . so very 'with it.' Unusual. And you just got here yesterday, didn't you? How organized you are."

"Everyone seems to be having a good time."

"Yes. You young people do certainly have original ideas for social affairs, don't you? But it's a lovely party, dear. Alicia seems very pleased."

"I hope you and Mr. Somers like your rooms in the lodge."

"They're very . . . uh . . . quaint. All that knotty pine . . . But I meant to ask: The pillows on my bed are feather pillows, dear, and I absolutely cannot sleep on feathers. Do you suppose you could find me something orthopedic? I would be so very much more comfortable."

"I'll see what I can do."

"And I assumed my room would have a phone. This truly is a rustic place, isn't it? Primitive. But I suppose a ski lodge is supposed to be that way."

"There's a phone in the office and pay phones in both the snack bar and cocktail lounge."

Irene's brows inched upward. "Pay phones?"

And on it went. Joey began to count the hours and minutes until the guests, including Irene, would tire and start going down the mountain to their beds.

Boring. Boring, boring, boring. Dogs miss all the fun stuff in life, and never had it been more evident than that Tuesday night, when most everyone was partying up on the mountain and I, the onetime party queen of Denver, was stuck in a stupid log cabin with a pesky kid and a member of the housekeeping staff who was snoring on the sofa. Drover lay on the sofa watching her, fascinated by the sounds coming from her open mouth. She'd be lucky if he didn't start nosing around in her bridgework trying to figure out where all that rumbling came from.

I must admit, foolish me, that when we headed up to the ski resort I entertained some small hope of a good time. Skiing isn't my thing, though in my former life I did look stunning in stretch pants and a ski sweater. But even though I wasn't a ski buff, I thought ski resorts were very cool. Lots of ambiance. Cozy fireplaces, bubbling spas, sexy ski instructors. You get the picture. Of course, I knew most of the fun stuff would be off-

limits to a dog. But Joey and her pals could have been more considerate. Letting the kid drag me onto the bunny slope was just cruel. Tess expected me to act like a clueless dog, chasing snowballs, tunneling through the snow, yipping and yapping. Drover did all those things and looked like a furry idiot. Drover is a furry idiot. But Lydia Keane, even if forced to live as a dumpy-looking dog, is not an idiot. I still have some dignity.

Well, most of the time I have dignity. I'll admit to some minor snowball chasing and yapping on the slopes. I really have to battle the urge to do stupid things like chase squirrels and roll over on my back for tummy rubs. Very embarrassing! Not to mention scary.

I'll bet Stanley just splits his sides every time I go into dog mode. Every time I eye a fuzzy dog toy, contemplating the potential satisfaction of a good chomp to make it squeak; every time my little feet ache to dig a hole; every time my train of thought gets diverted by someone dropping a crumb on the floor; every time I hear the siren call of a mud hole that needs to be run through or rolled in—every time one of these things happens, I can almost hear old Stanley snickering, reveling in how low I've sunk. The heavenly boss may say that revenge is His, but a good deal of it apparently trickles down to his bureaucrats.

But back to the point, up to now this jaunt had been long periods of boredom punctuated by intervals of enforced physical activity. Only a real dog would find that entertaining. Other people partied, chugged the drinks in the lounge, ate the gourmet food coming out of the kitchen, and shopped the ski fashions in the ski shop. It wasn't fair.

Don't get me wrong. I'm not a whiner. Not me. I only catalog my woes to make clear just why I was so fed up babysitting *the kid while everyone else was out having a great time. I was bored. I ached from the day's "frolicking." And I was making absolutely no progress on my mission, thanks to being shut up most of the time. So when Tess fixed me with a canny eye and asked me to play checkers with her, I almost growled.*

"Oh, come on!" the kid pleaded. "It'll be fun. I'll even let you win, if you want."

As if I couldn't outthink and outmaneuver a nine-year-old with one paw tied behind my back.

"I'll give you a cookie," she cajoled devilishly.

That got my attention. I was, after all, a corgi.

With a happy grin, she plunked herself cross-legged onto the floor and set the checkerboard in front of me. She got the black pieces; I got the red—appropriate for an ex–scarlet woman, I suppose.

"You can move the checkers with your nose," the kid suggested, as if I couldn't figure out that one for myself.

But I wasn't dumb enough to give myself away. Tess knew more about me than she should have. I don't know how she knew. Kids are scary that way. I've always avoided them for that reason. The conventional wisdom that women indiscriminately gush over babies and children is a bunch of bunk. The same is true of dogs. Many of us just don't like the little crumb-snatchers. Still, there was that promise of a cookie. . . .

Treats are the downfall of most dogs. Corgis especially. As I've explained before, when the scent of anything edible— which includes almost everything vegetable, animal, or mineral—reaches a dog nose, the appetite completely takes over the brain. All reasonable thought shuts down, and we will do anything—fight, bark, whine, do tricks, stand on our heads if necessary—to snarf down a morsel. Embarrassing, but true.

So I gave in, corrupted by a vanilla wafer. What was one

game of checkers, after all? Stanley was probably looking down from wherever he looks down from, beetling his ugly brow about my breach of security, but it was his fault, not mine. He's the one who sent me to Earth as a stomach on four legs. He should have known better.

Anyway, it wasn't as if the kid didn't already have a good idea that I wasn't an ordinary pooch. No one would believe her if she squealed, so what harm could she do? What harm besides beating me soundly at checkers, that is, which she did promptly. Cleaned my clock. Had kinged men wreaking havoc all over the board while I was still trying to get my surviving red guys to the other side. It's hard to think about checkers strategy when you have to push around your pieces with your nose.

The next game was mine, though. My mind started to click again, reveling in the luxury of someone—even a nine-year-old—treating me as if I had a full set of brain cells. Not that I've ever been the brainy type, and I've been guilty a time or two of playing dumb to impress a date. But pretending to be dumb and being constantly dismissed as dumb—a dumb animal—are entirely different things.

Tess won the third game, but it was a close thing. I could have won if I'd tried harder. By the fourth the kid was getting bored, and she started to look for trouble to get into. Just as I forced her to king my second man, she looked into my eyes with a gaze that was much older than her years. Her big brown eyes were very much like her father's. They looked past the face, in my case a furry face with a wet nose and pointy ears, straight to the truth of the soul. If I were a perpetrator of evil, I would not want to have Sergeant Detective Ben Ramsay's knife-keen eyes holding my soul ransom when I tried to concoct an alibi, and sitting there over the checkerboard with my wet nose print on the checkers, I didn't fancy the scrutiny of his daughter, either. Neither did I like the knowing slant of her smile.

"I know what you are," she said, bold as brass. Very unattractive in a child. "Everyone thinks you're just a dog, but I can see who you really are."

I hoped not, because my real self was sort of X-rated, which is one of the reasons I ended up as a dog.

"My mother sent you to me, didn't she?"

At least the smart-ass kid wasn't a hundred percent right. I didn't know her mother. The lady had my sympathies for being dead, but I had my own problems in that regard.

"I know my mother sent you here to help. She doesn't want my dad to marry Alicia. That's what she told me. 'Cause Alicia won't be good for him, and he won't be good for her. My mom is really smart. She knows everything, so she must be right."

I guess at nine years old most kids still think their mothers walk on water. The innocence of childhood and all that. But it ticked me off to be relegated to mere messenger when I'd already proven myself an angelic heroine. So I gave the kid a look right back—just to show her that I wasn't intimidated—then wedged my nose beneath the checkerboard and upended it. So much for game four.

"Oh! You're bad, Piggy! You're just mad because I know your secret identity, and people with secret identities don't like to have other people know. Like Superman. Or Batman. Or Wonder Woman. But I'm one of the good guys. I just want to help."

Help? The kid was a menace.

"Don't you look at me like that! You can't bite me, 'cause you'll get in big trouble."

She was right. I couldn't bite her. Stanley had lectured me in painful detail about what happens to dogs who bite people. It went double for dogs who bite kids.

"Besides, Piggy . . ."

Her tone was wheedling, and that made me suspicious.

"I have something you might need," she said with an impudent grin.

I sniffed and turned away, demonstrating my disdain, but the little monster caught me by the collar.

"You know what I have that will help?" she whispered, as if our jailer weren't fast asleep on the sofa. "I've got hands."

Tess grinned, stretched all her fingers apart, and wiggled them. And just then, a really, really wicked idea popped into my head.

The hour was past two A.M. when Joey stumbled out of the lodge and headed for the Big Cabin. She was generally the last person to leave one of her parties. She had never felt right about leaving the final mopping-up to the staff—not literal mopping, thank goodness, but a cleaning away of the last-minute details. In this case the Top of the World had to be cleared out, cleaned, and the restaurant tables restored. The food had to be hauled down the mountain to the lodge and stored in the appropriate place, and last-minute problems with the guests, such as Irene's blasted orthopedic pillow, had to be solved. Not to mention that one of the string quartet members had disappeared. He was found in the men's public restroom, where he had passed out—from an overindulgence of liquor, Joey hoped, and not from anything that would bring the drug squad for a visit.

One would expect a classical musician to have more moderate habits.

But finally, every guest was settled peacefully in his or her bed, the last load from the mountaintop had been unloaded and dealt with, everything was clean and put away, and even faithful Samantha, who hung in until the very last, had gone to find her bed. And Joey was free to find hers.

The Big Cabin was only a few hundred feet from the lodge, but the walk felt long. Seldom in her life had Joey been so tired. It was the altitude as well as a couple of days of too much activity, too many new people, too many problems to solve and things to organize. And the wedding was still four days away. Four long days. Four days of making sure everyone had a great time. Four days of making sure Mr. Somers's investor friends were suitably impressed by the accommodations, food, and amenities. They were arriving the next day—no, Joey realized ruefully, this very day. Midnight was well behind her, and Wednesday had begun. Sheesh! Wednesday, Thursday, Friday, wedding day. She had all that time of keeping the little orchestra happy, of being polite to Irene, of being close to Ben Ramsay—now where did that come from? Joey thought fretfully. She really had to get some rest or she was going to be imagining all sorts of wild things.

Someone had left the light shining on the front porch, but the inside of the cabin was dark. Unwilling to flip on the lights and risk waking someone, Joey felt her way to the kitchen. The consideration was only partly good manners. The truth was that she didn't have the energy to so much as say hi, much less talk about the party, the music, the food, or the beautiful starlit view they'd had from the restaurant. All she wanted was to feel her head hit the pillow.

One short detour was necessary, though. She found the door of Tess's room and opened it only far enough to peek in. She had to be sure the dogs were settled. They were her responsibility, even though Tess and Ben had somehow taken over watching them, entertaining them, and feeding them.

Moonlight poured through the window and painted milky squares on the bed. Tess slept on her back amid a jumble of sheets and blankets. On the far side of her, Drover raised his head and gave Joey a corgi smile, as if to say everything was fine. On the near side, Piggy curled in a tight ball, her chin pillowed on one paw. Her only acknowledgment of Joey was one eye popping open. The eye caught the moonlight, and for a moment Joey imagined it gleamed with an otherworldly light.

She really was tired, Joey mused, backing away and silently shutting the door.

With only a misstep or two she climbed the stairs to the loft. It was very dark, and for a moment she stood, disoriented. Inching forward, she found a doorknob. Hanging from it was a toy sheriff's badge. How smart she'd been to mark the doors. All she had to do was find the knob with the rubber band. And there it was, right next door.

She went in, quickly stripped down to her panties and camisole, and climbed into bed, breathing a tired, grateful sigh when her head hit the pillow.

A grunt on the other side of the bed halted her drift

into sleep. She rose on one elbow, frowning, then collapsed again. The dogs were on the bed. In Denver they'd almost crowded her off the queen-size mattress. How two smallish dogs could hog so much room was beyond reason, but it seemed to be their peculiar talent. Again she drifted, drifted, drifted . . . then her eyes opened wide.

The dogs were on Tess's bed, not hers. Who was in her bed? Before she could shoot up to investigate, a long arm snaked around her and pinned her down. "C'mere, you," growled a sleepy masculine voice.

Ben had been wrung-out tired when he'd finally turned in that night. This whole week was supposed to be nothing but fun. At least that was Alicia's plan. One wouldn't expect fun to be so stressful, but somehow it was. Not that he had any right to feel stressed. He was about to marry a wonderful woman, the woman of every man's dreams—not only beautiful, but good-natured, sexy, smart, fun-loving, and rich. Wasn't that what every man in America wanted?

But he was tired. Bone tired. Maybe the engagement-party champagne was getting to him. Maybe the altitude was getting to him. Maybe he was too old to take up skiing. Whatever, he was dog damned tired.

Which was probably why he was plagued by erotic dreams from the minute his eyes closed. Not that "plagued" was really the right word. "Pleasured" was a better description. There wasn't a man alive who didn't appreciate a good X-rated dream now and then, and these dreams worked up to one so real he could feel the soft flesh in his grip, smell the light, sweet scent of a woman, and hear the excitement of her indrawn breath.

And then her shriek rudely woke him up. "What the . . . Shit!" Jerked from sleep, Ben's natural defensive instincts engaged. Blind and confused in the dark, he pulled the shrieker against him, shielding her with his body. But no mayhem followed. Nothing followed other than a determined struggle from the woman beneath him.

Slowly coming fully awake, Ben remembered where he was—not in the middle of zinging bullets and murderous mayhem, but in a peaceful loft at a swank mountain resort. At least the loft had been peaceful up until a few moments ago. He reached out to switch on the bedside lamp, easing his weight from the woman beneath him and looking down into Joey DeMato's wide brown eyes.

"Oh damn," she quavered.

"Shit," he said at the same time, and somehow forgot to move off her.

"Get your carcass off of me!" she hissed in an intense whisper.

"Huh?" He was still confused between dream and reality, Ben thought. At least that was Ben's excuse. Something in Joey's eyes didn't echo the rejection in her words. Fire lurked close below the surface, barely controlled, reaching up to him in flashes of desire that locked with his, making moving from his position atop her body a near impossibility.

For a near eternity they looked at each other, bathed in each other's heat, welded, it seemed, in immobility.

She was the magnet; he was the iron. She was the flame; he was the suicidal moth. Ben could feel himself lowering his head toward hers, targeting that inviting, irresistible mouth. He had no control over his actions. The kiss was inevitable.

Then Joey's face crumpled. The fire in her eyes flickered, doused by shame.

"Please."

Her soft plea broke Ben's trance. Almost painfully he withdrew, knowing that giving up her touch and her heat shouldn't have been such a chore. But it was.

As they tried to untangle themselves and the bed-covers, Alicia walked through the door.

CHAPTER 11

◆

WHEN THE OVERHEAD light flipped on, they all froze still as statues. Alicia's jaw dropped, but it was the only movement she made. With her tousled blonde curls and startled blue eyes, she could have modeled for Wronged Woman Barbie. "I . . . I just came in to say good night," she stammered. The statement seemed woefully inadequate to the situation.

Caught beneath Ben, Joey didn't even breathe. The only sign she was alive was the rapid flow of blood to her face. If her cheeks got any redder, Ben reflected with a strange calm, they were going to burst into flame. As for himself, he was trying to control the part of him that every man despairs of controlling once it goes on the rampage. And that part was truly on the rampage. The moment he moved, Joey was going to know exactly how upstanding he was, and Alicia also. Not that he wasn't in a heap of trouble without that little detail, but his condition would certainly put the icing on top of the devil's food cake.

Abruptly, Alicia laughed. It was not a cynical laugh,

or disillusioned, or hysterical. The laugh was genuine and unalarmed.

Irritated somehow by Alicia's equanimity, Ben snapped back to life. "Just what is so funny?"

"You! Oh dear, you both look as if the world is coming to an end."

Joey made a strangled sound. Alicia chuckled. "Joey, sweetie, you're as red as a beet. I wish I had a camera. All the time I've known you, I've never seen you looking like you were going to explode with embarrassment."

"Alicia," Ben choked out, "this isn't what it—"

"—looks like," she finished for him. "I know."

"What?"

"I know," she assured him with a smile. "Joey probably lost her way in the dark and climbed into your bed. I'll bet that was a surprise for both of you!"

Joey sputtered and struggled free of their entanglement. When she brushed against the unmistakable evidence that Ben had reacted to their encounter with much more than surprise, her eyes widened and she jumped away from him as if he'd poked her with a hot brand. Then she squawked, remembering her lack of decent clothing.

"Aaaack! Close your eyes, Ben Ramsay! I don't believe this is happening. Close your eyes, I say!"

He had no intention of doing so, not out of perverse desire, but from the simple knowledge that it wouldn't do any good. The image of long legs and high, perky breasts attractively set off by lacy panties and camisole was burned on his retina. Who would have thought that anything about businesslike Joey DeMato was actually perky?

And then there was that part of him that was still perking along quite nicely. As Joey hastily snatched her clothes from the floor and wrapped her jacket about her, Ben took advantage of the distraction, arranging the blankets to disguise his little problem.

"I didn't lose my way," Joey insisted. "Ben did. He's in my bed."

"Oh no," he replied. "This is my bed. Look around."

She did, taking in his luggage, the clothes hanging in the little closet, the shaving kit on the dresser. "But . . . but my rubber band was on the door!" She did a quick check and came up with the rubber band. "And your badge was next door. I put a flower on Alicia's doorknob, a toy badge on Ben's, and a rubber band on my doorknob just so something like this wouldn't happen."

Alicia looked quizzically at the evidence. "That's strange."

Ben's eyes narrowed as he saw a flicker of furtive action behind Alicia. He knew exactly who was being furtive.

"Tess! Get in here!"

Moments later, a meek little girl slipped through the door. Trailing her were the two corgis. Ben knew with paternal certainty, an extrasensory perception granted with fatherhood, that somehow Tess was involved in this situation.

"Tess, what are you doing awake, out of bed, and in the loft where you don't belong?"

Tess bit her lip. He could almost see the wheels of creativity turning in the little head. "Noises woke me up," she finally declared.

"So you came all the way up here to investigate?"

"Yes. I did."

"And instead of coming in and asking what was going on, you ducked behind the chairs out there and listened?"

"Uh . . . I didn't want to bother anyone."

"Think of a better one, Tess."

Her face screwed up as she thought, but Ben didn't give her a chance. If he let her, Tess could stand here all night and recite fairy-tale excuses.

"Did you switch the doorknob decorations so that we would be confused?"

Now she started to squirm, a sure sign that he'd hit on the correct scenario.

"Why would she do a thing like that?" Alicia asked incredulously.

Alicia was in for a rude shock when she became a stepmother, Ben mused. "Why do kids do anything? Tess?"

With a heavy sigh, Tess confessed. "I did it."

"When did you do it?" Ben could have sworn his little toy badge was on his door when he'd come in.

"We sneaked up here after I heard you go to bed."

"You were waiting up all night?"

"Uh . . . yes."

"And why did you wait until *after* I went to bed?"

Tess just looked at the floor. The obvious answer was that she wanted Joey to mistake his door for hers and they would both end up in the same room. But such a motive, involving double-dealing with sexual innuendo and the premeditated intent to destroy a relationship, was most certainly beyond Tess, who was much more into mischief than malice. "It was Piggy's idea," she finally squeaked out.

Joey laughed. "Piggy's idea?"

"Yes, ma'am," the little miscreant said softly.

Piggy showed no interest in the proceedings, even though she stood accused. She had jumped on the rumpled bed, and there she lay, yawning, totally unconcerned.

Ben glowered. "Piggy told you to do this?"

"Yessir. She needed help 'cause she doesn't have hands."

He was way too tired to deal with a daughter who thought she talked to Machiavellian dogs as well as the ghost of her dead mother. Obviously Tess had some issues with this marriage that she was expressing in a very peculiar way, but he couldn't deal with that tonight. "Go to bed, Tess. Take the dogs with you. No more plotting with Piggy. You and I are going to have a talk in the morning."

"Yessir," she said meekly. But Ben had better sense than to believe that pretense at meekness.

When she was gone, the adults all looked at each other and laughed somewhat awkwardly.

"Guess I'm lucky you're the understanding, sensible sort," Ben told Alicia.

Joey clutched her jacket about her and wouldn't quite meet his eyes, and Ben was still careful to keep the blankets over his lap. Joey gave Alicia a half smile. "Shouldn't you be just a little bit jealous?"

Alicia laughed. "Jealous of you, Joey? Don't be absurd!"

Joey looked hurt.

"I didn't mean it that way!" Alicia said. "Not like you're not worth being jealous of! It's just that you're a good friend, and you wouldn't . . . you know. And Ben's the most honorable guy I know. He wouldn't either."

Joey grimaced. "Yeah, right. Dull, dull, dull. We'd never make it on the daytime soaps, would we?" She didn't seem pleased by that insight.

"That's a good thing—right?" Ben tried to clarify.

Joey shrugged, and Alicia just smiled. Ben reflected not for the first time on the confusing labyrinths of the female mind.

But once all were settled in their own rooms and the dark of night once against descended, Ben found himself sleepless. The bedsheets smelled of Joey. His pillow smelled of Joey. Dammit! *He* smelled of Joey. She seemed to be in every pore, and the bad thing was, he liked it.

Worse still, Ben knew that before he'd awakened with Joey in his arms, he hadn't been dreaming of Alicia. Joey had been the one making his subconscious hot and sweaty. Not Alicia, his bride, but Joey. Joey, with her mocking smiles, smart-ass mouth, and damned perky breasts. Joey.

And just what was he going to do about it?

Pat and Alicia were right about one thing at least, Joey mused. Lounging in a hot Jacuzzi watching snow fall around you was the height of hedonistic luxury, and it felt good, too. She lay back indolently, up to her neck in warm bubbles, her head resting on the rim of the whirlpool bath and her eyes half closed. She would have closed them completely, blocking out the whole world, but she liked to watch the snow sift lazily down from the sky and sizzle on the deck. Tension flowed out of her, demons of worry exorcised by the gentle, comforting swirl of warm water. She could easily sleep here. She hadn't slept a wink the night before. How could she when her mind continually chewed on embarrassment, mortification, and anger? Exactly where her anger was directed Joey didn't know. Not at Tess for playing her tricks. Being nine years old in a crowd of adults was tough on a kid. Not at Ben, poor fellow. Ben of the sinewy arms and smoldering eyes. Joey suffered a flush of heat that had nothing to do with the whirlpool, but she wouldn't let her mind drift in that direction. What about Alicia? Good-natured, always-laughing Alicia, whose trust in friends and lovers was boundless. Joey wasn't mad at her, either.

Nope, Joey was mad at Joey. Joey was a fool. A stupid fool. A really stupid fool. And that was why six in the morning found her lying in a whirlpool, preferring to watch the cold dawn of a snowy day rather than face the group in the Big Cabin. The only person who had missed the night's debacle was Pat, who had still been at the lodge, but Joey was sure he would hear the story at breakfast. She would prefer not to be there to relive the experience. Living it once had been enough.

Joey sank deeper into the warm water, seeking comfort. She didn't want to think about the midnight fiasco, but there was no escape. It was certainly the low point of her life up to now. She didn't think anything could get much lower.

Except that it could have been worse if Alicia hadn't been such a sport. Dear, sweet Alicia, refusing to be jealous. How did one stay so trusting with the world the way it was, ripe with passions running amuck and ruining people's best intentions? If sweet Alicia only knew. Joey desperately hoped she never found out that she had every right to be jealous. Flaming jealous, and mad as hell. Because when Joey had looked up at Ben looming so large and solid above her, she'd been ambushed by a desire the likes of which she'd never before experienced. Worse, she'd seen the mirror of that desire in Ben's eyes. And he hadn't imagined she was Alicia in the confusion of waking. Joey was sure of it in her very soul. He'd known exactly who was spread out beneath him.

Joey would never act on that desire. Never in a million years. Neither would Ben. He wasn't the type of guy to betray a woman who trusted him. But how had this happened? How? Joey wasn't on the prowl for a man—even subconsciously. No way. And Ben couldn't be trolling for a woman. He had a woman, a great one. And even if they did seem mismatched at times, Ben obviously loved Alicia.

So what Joey imagined couldn't have happened. She had to be mistaken about the fire in Ben's eyes, the melting in the pit of her own stomach. Maybe the whole thing had been a nightmare. She'd had too much champagne. It hadn't happened at all.

"Don't I wish," she muttered to herself, then came nearly out of her skin when a voice behind her answered.

"Talking to yourself?"

Joey whirled about, lost her balance, went under in a cloud of bubbles, and came up sputtering. Bundled in down jacket, gloves, and wool hat, Ben stood on the textured concrete deck looking down at her. "Ben Ramsay! You are always sneaking up on me. Stop it!"

"Sorry. Comes with being a cop."

"Well, stop it."

"Your hair's going to freeze. It's only fifteen degrees out here."

"Well, it's about a hundred plus in here. Besides," she said peevishly, "my hair wasn't supposed to get wet."

"Then don't be so jumpy. Here . . ." He gestured her closer. "Come here."

"Why?" she asked suspiciously.

"Just come here." When she was close enough, he took off his hat and stuck it over her wet hair. "That should keep it from freezing."

"It wouldn't freeze anyway. Not with all this steam." She softened her expression. "But thanks. What're you doing up so early?"

"Looking for you."

His eyes sought and held hers. She saw a host of questions and a lot of confusion. Ben was as unsettled as she was.

"I couldn't sleep," he admitted with a rueful smile. "And I saw the note you left on your door. Only Joey

DeMato would run away and leave a note behind about where she ran to. Conscientious of you."

"That was so Samantha could find me."

"No rest for the social director, eh?"

"That's about it. I didn't leave the note for you."

"I didn't figure you did, but I read it anyway."

"You don't look as though you're dressed for sitting in the whirlpool."

"No. I figured we needed to have a talk without other ears listening in."

She pulled her eyes away.

"Joey? Do we have a problem?"

Damn the man for being so direct. Whatever happened to the civilized notion of polite pretense?

"Not answering isn't going to make it go away."

She sank into the water to her chin. "Last night was an accident. We were both exhausted. I was in the wrong place at the wrong time—which I wouldn't have been if Tess and her alleged corgi accomplice hadn't been playing tricks."

Ben grinned ruefully at mention of Tess's part in the fiasco, but the grin faded fast. "It isn't just last night, Joey, and you know it. We've got sort of a . . . a thing going. Like a connection that neither one of us wants to happen. But it has happened. I thought we should talk about it."

Joey didn't bother to deny it. Ben's eyes were keen inquisitors that saw right through her. She felt sorry for any perps that came under his scrutiny. "Okay. It's a chemistry thing that we can't help. But it doesn't mean anything. It's just chemistry."

He lowered himself to the deck, unmindful of the

accumulating snow, and sat with his arms looped about his knees.

"You're getting your butt wet," Joey warned with a half smile.

"I figure my ass is pretty much grass already. A little snow isn't going to hurt." For what seemed like a long time he regarded her as a scientist might study some exotic bug under his magnifier. She squirmed.

"I thought you came here to talk."

He shook his head slowly. "I guess when it comes right down to it, I don't know what to say."

"Ben, you're making a big deal out of nothing. Why is it that guys are so stupid about relationships?"

"Huh?"

"Really! Think about it. You love Alicia." It was a statement, not a question.

He thought a moment. "I do love Alicia."

For a moment, Joey's heart sank, but she pressed on. "Right. You love Alicia. You deserve Alicia. You're going to marry her."

He was silent.

"This . . . this connection between you and me is nothing, a blip of chemistry." *Was it?* "Are you going to let a blip of chemistry ruin your life? Think about it. Are you?" She was babbling. Desperately babbling. Maybe if she said often enough that their collision in bed was nothing, she would come to believe it herself.

He regarded her during the moments of silence, then shook his head. "No, I'm not going let mere chemistry change the course of my life."

"Right." She chewed her lip. What had she expected? "Of course you're not."

"Just because a man is in love doesn't mean he won't occasionally look at another woman."

"Right."

"It's only natural."

"Very true. This is just a passing thing between us." His eyes drilled through the lie.

"It doesn't mean anything. We're adults. In control of ourselves."

The corner of his mouth quirked upward. "Except for last night."

She glared. "Forget last night." She wished he wouldn't look at her the way he was looking at her—like she was the cheese and he was the rat. "Don't worry about it. We'll just go on like before and be careful about whose bed we stumble into." *Ouch!* That certainly wasn't the thing to say.

But he didn't whack her with a comeback, which meant he really was upset. He got up, dusted the snow from his backside, and leveled a long, disconcerting look at her. Finally he broke the silence. "You're right, Joey. We're adult. In control. Everything will work out, one way or another. I'll see you at breakfast."

"Maybe."

"You can't hide forever, kiddo. Be brave. Come to breakfast. Act natural. It's not a problem, remember?"

Be brave, indeed! Joey ripped the wool cap from her head and threw it at his retreating figure. It hit his butt with a splat. Scooping up the hat before it could hit the ground, he grinned over his shoulder at her.

"Just acting natural," she said airily.

He didn't answer, just chuckled and walked on in the falling snow. Something about his farewell salute told Joey she hadn't convinced him any more than she had herself.

Breakfast went unexpectedly well. The awkwardness Joey anticipated didn't happen. Pat hadn't been in on the experience, and the others had apparently given him a very low-key account of events, because he let it go with one casually teasing jab at Joey about finding her way in the dark. Alicia, incredibly enough, didn't mention the fiasco at all. She was her usual bubbly self, self-assured and cheerful. Joey was almost vexed that Alicia attached so little importance to finding Joey in her fiancé's bed. Were the words "can't attract a man" stamped on her forehead? She should be grateful, Joey told herself. But still, it rankled.

The only one who showed any effects of the night's shenanigans was Tess, who came to the breakfast table considerably chastened. Apparently her father had given her the promised talk and the full weight of fatherly disapproval had come down upon Tess's head. Responding to Tess's mood, Drover was subdued as well. But Tess's scapegoat, Piggy, seemed the same as ever. Of course, Piggy was never exactly cheerful, so it was hard to say.

For Joey, the day got worse from that point on, starting with Alicia's announcement that they were going cross-country skiing. Joey greeted the announcement with a chuckle and a shake of her head.

"Don't get wet-blanketish on me now," Alicia warned her. "You're going to have a good time here if it kills you."

How could she convince the well-intentioned Alicia that another skiing jaunt might do just that? "I have so much work to do," Joey threw out as a first try.

"No, you don't. The next official functions are the rehearsal and rehearsal dinner, and they aren't until Friday night. Today is Wednesday. Time to relax. Your nose is to the grindstone so much that you're going to grind it right off."

"Alicia, I am such a bad skier! I scarcely made it down the bunny slope on Monday."

"But this is cross-country skiing! It's easy. Really. Different skis, and no ski boots. Just things that look like real shoes. Tell her, Pat."

"It's easy," Pat said obediently. Of course, for him it *was* easy.

"Ben is going," Alicia told her.

"I am?" Ben sounded surprised.

"And he's as bad as you are."

Ben gave her a dry "Thank you," but he apparently was going to cave. Joey was stripped of excuses, and she couldn't insist too adamantly. Everyone would think she was begging off because of embarrassment over the night before. So she was stuck.

At least Joey wasn't the only one who didn't know what she was doing. The group that drove to the trailhead was a large one. Besides Pat, Alicia, Ben, and Joey, the bridesmaids were there along with Ben's brother Tom and several of the guests who had arrived the day before. Noticeably absent was Edward, who had pleaded a pulled muscle left over from Monday's ski jaunt.

"He has a whopping hangover," Sue whispered in

an aside to Joey. "That guy puts away beer like no one I've ever seen."

Joey envied the guy, hangover or not. At least he'd gotten out of skiing.

Several others besides Joey were novices at the sport. Ben had cross-country skied once, Carrie and Teri not at all. A girl by the name of Danielle, a society friend of Alicia's, hadn't skied since she was ten, so she joined the novice group as Pat gave patient instructions.

Pat Haines was probably an excellent ski instructor, Joey reflected. But a certain lack of enthusiasm on her part joined with her native lack of talent. The very skinny cross-country skis were almost impossible to control—much more difficult than the downhill skis. Connected to her foot only at the toe of her shoe, they lacked the sharp metal edges that give downhill skis control in a turn. At least, Joey had been told the edges give control. She herself had experienced very little of that in her downhill descent two days before. To turn on cross-country skis required one to assume a very awkward position that looked like a supplication to the gods, one knee almost to the ground and the other balancing precariously in a more upright angle. Ridiculous but appropriate, Joey thought. If she ever tried to turn these silly skis, she'd better be begging the angels to preserve her hide.

The group started onto a trail that was easy enough. The terrain was flat, winding gently through majestic pines, spruce, and aspen groves. It took only about a tenth of a mile, however, for Joey's legs to turn to rubber, and when that happened, her traitorous skis took any excuse to dump her, almost as if the skinny little fiberglass boards possessed a malignant consciousness. Joey tried conscientiously to perform the slide forward, bend knee, heel up, slide forward that Pat had demonstrated, but no matter what she did, the skis dumped her. Even standing still they dumped her. Every five step-glides they dumped her. She collected more snow in her clothing than Frosty the Snowman.

After a half hour of this uncomfortable humiliation, Joey gave up. "I think I'll just crawl back to the van and wait for you guys," she moaned.

Ben, Carrie, and Danielle eagerly volunteered to join her. Ahead, the group had strung out into smaller groups. Tom and Teri concentrated more on flirting than skiing, but they were still doing better than Joey. Sue and her husband George were skiing very well indeed and seemed to be having a grand time, as were, of course, Alicia and Pat, who skied back to the end of the line to investigate the holdup, making the process look as easy as walking.

"I'm the troublemaker," Joey confessed without shame. "I'm going back to the van."

Ben spoke up. "I'll go back with her. I'll drive her to the lodge and send the van back to pick you all up."

"I'm going too," Danielle and Carrie both said at the same time.

Alicia's face fell. She did so want them all to have a terrific time. Joey felt a stab of guilt. "It's okay, Alicia. Go ahead and ski. We'll be relaxing and drinking hot toddies at the lodge—my idea of heaven. Ben, you can stay here with Alicia. You don't have to take us back. We can manage, can't we, ladies?"

Carrie and Danielle vociferously agreed.

"No," Ben said. "A hot toddy sounds good to me, too. Go on and ski, Alicia. I'll see you back at the lodge."

Alicia looked torn. "Are you sure?"

Ben scowled. "I don't need a babysitter."

Now she looked hurt. "I didn't mean it that way. I just want you to have a good time. I don't mind going back to the lodge with you."

In spite of Alicia's effort, though, she wasn't very convincing. Ben gestured her aside, where they engaged in an animated discussion. Pat tactfully skied back toward the head of the line. The others labored politely not to hear what the bridal couple were saying. Ben wore a poker face, and Alicia looked unhappy. They parted with a lukewarm kiss, and Alicia glided back toward Pat and those who were eager to go on. Ben came back toward the quitters. "Back we go," he told them.

Joey had fallen on her backside yet again. Even standing on the silly skis for more than a few minutes was an unlikely feat. Ben gave her a hand up, and she started to slog back the way they had come. "Heck," she said, "I'm so slow that by the time I get to the van, Alicia and her group will have gotten enough of skiing for the day."

Ben gave her a rueful look. "No chance of that, I think."

Tess reached the top of little Playpen Hill, dragging her reinforced inner tube behind her. Her enthusiasm wasn't dimmed by previous slides down the slope that had covered her from head to foot with snow. But then, her enthusiasm for almost everything in life—except zucchini—could withstand the assault of most things the world threw at her, and during her short nine years of life, the world had lobbed a few good ones her way.

She hauled the tube over the crest of the kids' beginner slope and sat down a moment to rest. Drover, close on her heels and equally covered with snow, bounced around her in a surplus of energy. She laughed and smacked him with a snowball. The second snow missile he caught in his mouth, chewed, then shook his head in surprise as his snack turned out to be insubstantial as water.

"Silly!" Tess said. "You can't eat snowballs."

By that time Piggy had slogged up the hill to join them. She looked more disgusted with every step she took. For her effort she got a snowball in the face.

Tess laughed merrily as Piggy gave her the hairy eyeball. "Don't be such an old poop, Piggy! Piggy's a poop! Piggy's a poop!"

Piggy pointedly turned her back and plopped down in the snow. Her status as a very un-ordinary dog earned her no respect from Tess. Fortunately for her, Tess's attention was diverted by Alicia's father and grandmother seating themselves at a table on the lodge deck, cups of something hot in their hands.

"Hello!" Tess waved to them.

At the bottom of the kids' hill, Marta looked up and waved. She was waiting for Tess to make her next run down the hill before she started up, but Tess wanted Richard's and Irene's attention also.

"Hello!" Tess called again. "Mr. and Mrs. Somers!"

Irene looked in her direction, and even from the top of the hill Tess could tell that she was annoyed. Alicia's granny was frequently annoyed. It didn't bother Tess. Mr. Somers looked up also.

"Watch me!" Tess called. "I'm going to go faster than ever!" She jumped on the tube and gave it a shove downhill. Drover barked madly and chased after her as she bounced over little hillocks and sped in dizzy circles. All the way down she laughed, then shrieked when the safety net at the bottom of the hill caught her. It wasn't a pretty landing. Her rear ended up in the air and her head in the snow, but she popped up with a big smile and watched Marta climb the hill. At the top, Piggy still waited glumly.

Tess called up to the sour-looking corgi, "Piggy's a poop! Piggy's a poop!"

Piggy *was* a poop. Tess's mom could have chosen a more cheerful creature to help Tess down here on Earth, but maybe Piggy was the only thing that came to hand. That was sad, Tess felt. Heaven should give Annie Ramsay an army of angels if she needed them. But she got only Piggy.

Still, Tess would certainly help her mom all she could, and she would make sure Piggy did her part. If her mom thought her dad shouldn't marry Alicia, then he shouldn't. Not that Alicia wasn't nice, and pretty. She had cool clothes and she said Tess could have a horse. But Annie knew best. Tess never doubted it.

And if her mom thought Piggy could help, then Tess didn't doubt that either. She sort of liked it that Piggy was a dog, to tell the truth. Piggy was as cranky as Tess's schoolteacher, Mrs. Bigley, but Tess being a person and Piggy being a dog, even a dog with some grown-up lady's soul beneath the fur, gave Tess the upper hand. She liked that. She wished, in fact, that Mrs. Bigley might turn into a dog.

Marta had reached the top of the hill and was scratching Piggy's ears. Piggy still didn't look happy. She didn't ever look happy unless food was somehow involved.

"You can't come down as fast as I did!" Tess called up to Marta. Marta was cool. She did things kids did and enjoyed them almost as much. Her being a grown-up put her at a disadvantage, though. Tess had to feel a little bit sorry for her.

Marta shoved her tube down the hill and came down lickety-split. Surprisingly, Piggy jumped up and gave chase, barking wildly, her little feet spewing snow in all directions. She couldn't catch the tube, however, and mid-chase she stopped, shook herself, sneezed, gave the world what looked like a very embarrassed look, and stalked back up the hill.

"Wait for me!" Tess called as she grabbed her tube and ran up the hill. Drover galloped to and fro in front of her. Maybe, Tess thought, she could get Piggy to chase her!

But when she reached the top, Piggy didn't seem ready to play. She stood erect, or at least as erect as a dog with such short legs could stand. Her pointy ears alert, the corgi stared toward the Big Cabin. Tess squinted in that direction. Someone had just furtively come from the back of the cabin, walking in sneak mode. Tess knew the mode well. She used it whenever she stole into the kitchen to snack on the refrigerated cookie dough that her dad said she shouldn't eat. The figure ducked behind a thicket, but Tess could still see he was there, frozen in place as if he couldn't move.

"That's weird," she told Piggy seriously. "Maybe he stole something. We'd better go see."

Piggy seemed to agree. The little dog dashed down the slope. But just as Tess started to follow, her father's voice came out of nowhere to halt her mid-step.

CHAPTER 12

◆

JOEY'S MUSCLES COMPLAINED when she climbed out of the van. One wouldn't think that skiing such a short distance would result in sore legs and arms, but the mere sight of skis made her body ache. Her exit from the van was more of a lurch than a graceful descent. But since Carrie and Danielle had the same problem, Joey at least didn't feel alone.

"Bring on the hot toddies," Danielle groaned as she tried to straighten her legs.

"Ditto," Carrie agreed. "Joey, are you still alive?"

"Just barely."

Ben caught the speculative looks the ladies cast his way. "Forget it!" he said. "I'm not carrying any of you up those steps. I'm as sore as you are."

"Chivalry really is dead," Carrie moaned.

At that moment a whirlwind combination of Tess and Drover barreled around the corner of the lodge and smacked into Ben. Tess wrapped her arms around his legs while Drover bounced about happily and noisily. For a small dog he had a very loud bark. Following at a more sedate pace were Marta and Piggy.

"Daddy! Guess what Piggy and me saw over by the cabin? There was—"

Ben picked her up for a big hug. "There was what?"

"There was—"

"A great tubing contest," Marta supplied as she walked up. Her clothes were covered with snow and a smile warmed her face. "It's almost as much fun as skiing."

"And skiing is so much fun," Danielle commented with a grimace. "Excuse me, folks. I hear a Bailey's Irish Cream calling."

Joey was about to join Carrie and Danielle as they limped toward the lodge door, but Tess demanded, "Do you know how to tube, Joey? Do you want to learn?"

Joey groaned. "Does it involve skis?"

"No. You get on this rubber tire thingie and slide really, really fast down the hill. And the net at the bottom stops you before you crash."

"Cool."

"Cool," Ben agreed with a laugh, and set Tess back on the ground. "Well, Marta. Has my daughter worn you down yet?"

"Not yet," she said, her accent turning the reply into something exotic. "Your Tess is a very special little girl."

Irene and Richard Somers joined the group.

"Where's Alicia?" Richard asked.

"Still skiing," Ben said.

The older man's brows rose a bit, but he said nothing.

"What is that dog making such a racket about?" Irene complained.

It was Piggy making noise now. She jumped on Tess and barked in the direction of the Big Cabin.

"Piggy, stop that!" Joey reached down to grab the dog's collar and clamp a hand around her overactive jaws. Piggy gave her a wounded look and grumbled through clamped teeth. "What's wrong with you, you little devil?"

The corgi squirmed and cast a pleading look toward Tess, as if the little girl might save her, but Tess's attention had been effectively diverted. She had taken her father's hand and grinned up at him in her best wheedling fashion. "Marta says people ice-skate on the lake. Can we go ice-skating, Daddy? Please?"

Marta sent Ben an apologetic look, and Irene spoke sharply. "Your father is tired, Tess. Don't bother him."

Ben sided with his daughter. "I'm never too tired for my Tess, am I, kiddo? We can go skating as soon as I go up to the cabin and put on some dry clothes. I spent as much time plowing into the snow this morning as I did skiing on it."

"Skating sounds like a wonderful idea," Richard said heartily. "I'll join you, since my business associates haven't yet arrived. I used to skate when I was a kid. You should come and watch, Mother. Enjoy yourself for a change."

Ben turned a look on Joey. "Want to come?"

She had sore muscles, a nose close to being frostbitten, and a desire to do nothing more energetic than sink into a chair by a fireplace with a warm drink in her hands. But she found herself saying yes. There were so many reasons she should have said no, but she still said yes.

Joey got her fireplace to collapse beside, and the warm drink as well. A maintenance worker at the lodge offered to build them a fire beside the lake. A fire ring surrounded by benches of planed-off logs was already in place, and cozy bonfires beside the skating area were a regular service offered by the lodge. Suspended over the fire was a graniteware coffeepot full of hot cider.

Tess did not let Joey sit and enjoy the warmth. The little girl badgered her to don her rented skates and join her on the ice.

"Where do kids get all this energy?" Joey asked Irene, who at her son's urging had joined the party. Not all of Richard's teasing had persuaded the older woman to rent skates, however.

"It's beyond me." Irene cuddled into a blanket and sipped hot cider. Joey gave her an envious look while lacing her skates.

"I only had one child," Irene continued, "though since I raised Alicia, I suppose you could say I had two. Richard was always very well behaved, and Alicia was a model child, always wanting to please, always doing what she was expected to do. But little Tess is of a different stamp, isn't she?"

Joey felt the need to defend Ben's daughter. "She's a sweet kid. Full of energy and imagination."

"I suppose." Irene sounded skeptical. "I understand she caused a commotion last night?" A stylishly plucked gray brow raised in an invitation for Joey to fill in the details.

Joey wasn't about to tell Irene anything. It was bad enough that the story of her embarrassment had gone beyond the cabin. She just smiled. "Like I said, Tess has energy and imagination."

"Joey!" Tess hailed from the ice. "Come on!"

Tess's ankles were wobbly and her balance on the skates was precarious, but she didn't lack enthusiasm. She demanded enthusiasm from Joey as well, taking her hand and pulling her along over the gleaming cold surface of the ice. "Do you know how to skate, Joey? It's cool, isn't it? I've never had lessons. Have you? I betcha couldn't tell that I haven't had lessons."

Joey had taken figure-skating lessons when she was growing up, and the knack hadn't left her, despite sore muscles. She smiled at Tess, marveling at how adeptly the little girl could change from a child of the Twilight Zone to a normal kid. "You're doing really well, Tess. Try pushing the skates out to the side instead of just moving them back and forth."

"Hey!" Tess's face lit up when she took Joey's advice. "That works! Look at me!"

They skated circles around each other, Joey with a fair amount of her old grace on the blades and Tess a good deal more awkwardly.

"You're really good!" Tess told her with a grin. "My dad's good too. He likes to skate."

Ben and Richard had returned from gathering wood for the fire, and Ben was helping his future

father-in-law lace his skates. Richard had rented skates
along with the rest of them, saying that it was his last
chance to act the fool, because his investors were arriving later in the afternoon and he would have to buckle
down to work. Joey wondered briefly about a father
who turned his daughter's wedding into an opportunity to impress business associates. But then, didn't she
herself dedicate all her time to building her business,
telling herself she didn't have time for romance or dating, didn't have time for vacations? Her best and just
about only close friend was Samantha, her assistant.
Perhaps the only difference between Joey and Richard
Somers was that Richard was very rich and Joey very
definitely wasn't.

"Your dad's a good skater, is he?" She smiled down
at her little partner.

"He's really good. Just like you. And he hates to ski,
just like you. You know, Joey? You're a lot like my dad.
Maybe you should marry him. I don't think my mom
would mind if my dad married you."

Joey chuckled, not entirely comfortably. One
minute Tess acted like a normal nine-year-old, and the
next she was talking about her dead mother's agenda.
"Tess, sweetie, sometime soon you and I need to have
a long, serious talk."

"Okay. But if it's about my mom, we better talk to
Piggy, too. I think she knows her."

Joey sighed. They were skating uncomfortably close
to the Twilight Zone. But Ben rescued her. He skated
up to them with a big grin on his face.

"I see you're not nearly as inept on skates as on skis."

"Thank you for that very flattering observation,"

Joey replied tartly. "As I recall, you're not exactly an Olympian on skis either."

"She really is good, Daddy."

"I can see that," Ben agreed with his daughter. "Can I cut in on your dance, Tess? I'll take this lady farther out on the ice and have her show me what she can do."

Joey was sure the double entendre was unintentional. She kept a virtuous smile on her face. "Maybe you should show me what you can do."

"With pleasure."

They escaped just as Mr. Somers wobbled up to join them. Tess grabbed that gentleman's hand and questioned him on did he believe that she hadn't had lessons and didn't she skate really well?

Ben took Joey's hand and pulled her along beside him as they skated for the center of the pond. "Thank you for being so nice to Tess," he said. "When you're around, she seems like her old self. No long, mysterious looks. No ghosts."

Joey wondered if she should tell Ben that Tess's fantasies had expanded to include Piggy, but she decided against it. Soon Piggy would be out of the little girl's life, and Ben had enough troubles to deal with. And when he grabbed her hand and wrapped it in his, thoughts of Tess flew right out of Joey's mind. A ridiculous warmth emanated from his touch and produced a glow in her entire body. It *was* ridiculous, because their hand-holding was entirely innocent, something skaters had done since the first skaters strapped wooden blades onto their boots. Only their gloves touched. No naked skin was involved, but that made no difference. Joey decided she was probably losing her mind, and she certainly had lost every ounce of common sense that she'd ever possessed.

"You skate well," Ben told her as they circled the lake. "Just like Monica Seles."

"Make that Michelle Kwan and I'll be flattered. Monica Seles is a tennis player."

"Whatever. Be picky. Michelle Kwan."

Joey laughed. "Not nearly Michelle Kwan. But I did take lessons for a lot of years. I even entered a competition when I was in high school. I think I came in last." She spun away from him in a couple of turns, then skated backwards as they sped together along the perimeter of the ice. "And what can you do? Tess was bragging most outrageously."

"I can go like hell and stop on a dime. I played hockey in college."

"You're kidding! Really?"

"Why is that hard to believe?"

"You have all your teeth."

"I was better at dodging pucks than hitting them."

"How much time did you spend in the penalty box?"

He grinned. "Enough. Compared to my teammates, though, I was a very even-tempered guy. A real saint."

"Right." She doubted that.

Richard and Tess wobbled out from shore with every appearance of having a grand time. Tess chattered away and her soon-to-be stepgrandpa listened raptly. Joey and Ben whizzed past them, now skating side by side in the traditional couples' position. Having a truly good time, Joey ducked beneath Ben's arm in a quick spin, then skated a loop and came up on the other side. They sped by the fire, where Irene sat primly, watching.

"You should smile like that more often," Ben said.

Joey laughed at him. "You're a fine one to talk, Mr. Stern-as-Steel Policeman."

Ben acknowledged her point with a wry grin. "Maybe we should both smile more often."

Tess waved at them to slow down so she could join them. Moving in concert, Ben and Joey skated up behind her, slowed, parted, and each grabbed one of Tess's hands. She squealed in laughter and wobbled between them as they skated in a threesome into the center of the ice.

As the van pulled up in front of the lodge, Alicia pondered how much better tired felt when the tired resulted from fun and physical activity rather than social tension and frustration. Her everyday life was filled with Junior League meetings, symphony fund-raisers, and charity balls, all of which positively hummed with social tension and frustration. Even on vacations her father frequently entertained business associates, and she was expected to be the perfect hostess and model daughter, smiling at the right people, dishing out witty, inoffensive conversation, and making sure everyone was suitably impressed with her father's credentials.

A day's skiing trip where she could put her energy into negotiating the trail instead of negotiating social intricacies was as refreshing as a cool shower in a heat wave. For the most part, her life was busy but boring. She needed to get a life.

Ben was going to give her that life, she reminded herself. He had saved her life and now would give it back to her better than before. Romance did that for a person. At least, that was the message of so many movies and romance novels. Alicia would not allow herself to think that life with Ben might be boring as well. He needed to loosen up a bit—true. He needed to remove his proverbial nose from the proverbial grindstone. But that would happen. She wouldn't think about the possibility that it might not happen.

"Are you going to get out, or are you just going to sit there and stare into space?" Pat had opened the side door for her. Teri and Tom had already piled out, and Sue and George couldn't get out until Alicia did.

"Oops! Daydreaming," Alicia admitted.

Pat helped her alight. "You look tired."

"Tsk! You're never supposed to make a negative comment on a girl's appearance."

He shrugged. "I flunked chivalry school."

"Could have fooled me."

"Or maybe I'm just ready to graduate to something more lasting than charming the ladies."

"Who's charming the ladies?" Teri asked, coming up behind them to get her skis from the rack.

"I thought I was," Tom said with a leer. "Haven't I charmed you yet?"

"Absolutely," she giggled. "It's a good thing for you I live in North Carolina, or I'd be throwing out the net and hauling you in. Don't you know that weddings make married women cry and single women plot?"

Tom crossed his two index fingers in an X to ward her off.

"Look!" Sue alerted the group. "Everybody's ice-skating! And they have a bonfire."

"Service of the resort," Pat said with a grin. "We aim to please."

"Oh, that looks fun," Teri said. "But I'm too tired to even climb the steps to the lodge. I'd end up ice-skating on my butt, anyway."

Tom patted the relevant part of her anatomy. "And such a sweet little butt it is, too. Would you like me to carry it into the cocktail lounge?"

"You are such a jackass!" Teri declared, but didn't object when he picked her up, skis and all, and headed for the steps.

Alicia laughed and slanted a look at Pat. "Now there's someone who didn't flunk chivalry school!"

"Do you want to go down to the lake?" Pat asked. "It looks like Ben is there."

She should, Alicia told herself, even though a hot spiced cider in front of the fireplace called to her. But Ben might have been piqued by her staying on the mountain to ski instead of returning to the lodge with him, even though he'd told her to stay. She'd made the offer to come back with him. What had he expected her to do? Pleasing Ben, pleasing her guests—and yes, she wanted to please Pat also—was no easy task.

But if Ben was miffed, Alicia told herself, the sooner she got back into his good graces, the sooner she could stop worrying about it.

"I have about enough energy left to watch," she said. "You?"

"That sounds good."

Alicia admitted to relief. She'd been afraid Pat would take off for a relaxing drink in the lodge, and she did enjoy his company—especially when she expected a rather frosty reception from Ben.

Richard and Irene sat on one of the log benches by the bonfire. Alicia's father struggled to unlace his skates while Irene looked on. "I did warn you, Richard, that when a man your age indulges in acting like a youngster, he soon discovers how much youth he doesn't have left."

Richard groaned as he pulled off one boot. "Who would guess a person could get so stiff so fast?"

Alicia laughed as she and Pat sat down. "What's wrong, Dad?"

"My old bones can't take this sort of thing anymore."

"You're only as old as you feel."

"Whoever made up that cliché was obviously under thirty."

"Is that Joey out on the ice with Ben and Tess?" Alicia squinted to see through the afternoon glare. "Goodness, I had no idea she was such a good skater. And Ben too."

"They seem to have that in common," Irene said crisply.

"They look as if they're having fun," Pat remarked.

"Indeed," Irene agreed. "Ben and Joey have been making themselves quite a couple on the ice. And young Tess is doing very well between them, don't you think?"

Alicia caught Irene's smirk and knew exactly what it

meant. Irene never gave up. "I want Ben and Joey to be friends. I have few enough real friends, and I want those friends I have to like each other so we can spend time together."

"They're spending plenty of time together, as far as I can see."

Pat had adopted a very neutral face, and Alicia's father eyed Irene as if she were about to give away state secrets.

The skating trio spotted Alicia and waved, but they didn't come in. Now they were in a conga line of sorts, carving figure eights with Joey in front, Tess in the middle, and Ben in back. They did look like they were having a barrelful of fun. In fact, they looked like carefree kids. Alicia wouldn't have expected such bubbly laughter from Joey. She was always so serious. Work, work, work—never getting her mind off work. And Ben had seemed disturbingly unenthusiastic about all the activities Alicia loved. But even sitting beside the fire, she could see the grin on his face.

Her eyes narrowed as she pondered her grandmother's not-so-subtle intimations. Ben and Joey did seem to fit very nicely together out there on the ice, with Ben's daughter laughing and giggling between them. They seemed comfortable, relaxed, and was that just a bit of electricity sparking between the two of them, or was she imagining things that weren't there?

And if there was a certain charge between her friend and her husband-to-be, shouldn't she be more upset about it?

♦

As far as Ben was concerned, nothing quite matched sinking into a cushy chair in front of a fireplace after playing out in the cold. The heat thawed face, nose, ears, and fingers, and relaxation soothed tired muscles. Absolute heaven. Ben had forgotten how good it felt. Back when he was a kid he'd been one of those gung ho idiots who would stay on the sledding hill until he was soaked through to the bone and his clothes were freezing to his skin. His mother would scold until his ears burned, but she would heat a can of soup and wrap him in a big fuzzy towel while she was scolding.

Funny how becoming an adult sometimes sucked all the fun out of a person. Then one insignificant event brought it all back. Skating with Tess and Joey had done that. He couldn't remember having such fun since he was Tess's age.

"You guys were really good out there," Alicia declared. "I halfway expected you to start doing throws and side-by-side jumps."

"I think that's a bit beyond me." Ben reached down and ruffled his daughter's hair. " 'Course, I guess I could have thrown Tess. Think you would have landed on your feet, kiddo?"

"Sure thing."

They were gathered in the Big Cabin in front of the fireplace—Ben, Pat, Alicia, Joey, and Tess. The adults sprawled in easy chairs and Tess sat on the floor beside Ben, playing solitaire with an old deck of cards. Drover was trying to play with her, much to Tess's frustration, for at least half the playing cards ended up beneath his paws or in his mouth. He didn't understand the principles of the game, but he was obviously determined to win. Piggy had taken herself into Tess's bedroom and enthroned herself on the bed, sulking in isolation. Just what she sulked about no one quite knew.

The odor of a beef roast drifted in from the kitchen. Alicia had volunteered to cook dinner, and a beef roast, she had declared, was one of the few pieces of meat she had a chance of cooking correctly. She'd said often enough that cooking wasn't one of her skills, but tonight she seemed anxious to cook.

Since they'd gotten to the cabin and shed their jackets, Alicia had been falling all over herself to be sweet, witty, accommodating, and thoughtful. The reason was no mystery to Ben. His wife-to-be was suffering a few pangs of guilt for leaving her intended to his own devices while she spent the day skiing. He'd told her to do exactly that, of course. Maybe he should have insisted she spend the day with him, even if it ruined her fun. Maybe he should be jealous of her friendship with Haines. He didn't quite understand why he wasn't.

Alicia was in hostess mode. "Ben, can I bring you a hot cider? Or maybe a beer? Hot chocolate?"

"Beats a warmed-up can of soup."

"You want soup? I guess I could find some soup in the pantry."

Ben waved the notion aside. "An old memory," he explained. "My mother used to pour hot soup down me when I came in from sledding."

"How sweet."

"Cider would taste good."

Joey joined in. "Me too."

"Me three," Tess piped up.

"I'll help," Pat offered.

"Oh no," Alicia said too quickly. Was there a reason, Ben mused, why Alicia didn't want to be alone with Pat? "I'll just bring a whole tray. How's that? Chips and dip too."

Pat sank back into his seat. He'd been eager to go.

Ben sighed. "I'll eat anything I don't have to fetch myself. If I could eat dinner here in this chair, I'd do it." And just why, he wondered, didn't Alicia want to be alone with Pat?

Alicia's attempts to get back in Ben's good graces were blatant. He wasn't really mad, though, so much as frustrated. Alicia constantly flitted away from him, pulled by activities and people that interested him not at all. Spending time with him and Tess didn't seem to be high on her priority list, though he had to admit that she did try. Ben couldn't help but wonder if he was going to be fighting this for their entire married life.

"Here's your cider," she said cheerily, offering him first choice of the tray. "And chips with nacho dip."

"Great. Thanks."

Her eyes probed his, obviously expecting more.

"Really great. Thanks, Alicia."

She gave him a hesitant smile and handed a cup of cider to Tess.

Several hours and an overdone beef roast later, Alicia managed to corner him. After playing endless hands of hearts with Tess, Joey had opted for sleep. Pat was at the lodge playing host. Ben had sent Tess to bed with the dogs for company. She had objected, of

course. Objecting to bedtime was some sort of law for
nine-year-olds, no matter how tired they were.

The exodus had left Ben and Alicia alone, and as
Ben had expected, Alicia took advantage of the situation to pull out every charm she possessed. He let her.
Alicia being charming was an experience that no man
would want to miss, and it never failed to entertain.
But he didn't love her for her charm. He loved her for
her heart, her courage, her somewhat bewildered
innocence that contrasted so brightly with a world
grown sour and nasty.

"I think I owe you an apology." She began her pitch
with a wry little smile. "I should have come back with
you today, even though you were noble and told me to
stay." She took his hand and played with his fingers,
darting looks at him from beneath long lashes. "But
you're going to have to forgive me."

"And why would that be?"

She grinned her sweet impish grin. "Because I
love you."

"You didn't act like it out on that trail." His tone
was more serious than he'd intended, but he realized
that he meant every word.

"I'm sorry." She sounded truly contrite. "I didn't
mean it to seem that way. You know I love you, Ben.
I'd rather be with you than anything, but I haven't
skied in so long. All winter. And Pat is . . . was . . . a
good friend. I admit it's been very nice seeing him
again, but I don't mean to ignore you."

Ben relented and touched her cheek. "Alicia, I don't
require that you live in my pocket."

"I know."

"And it's only natural that you want to keep up with old friends—"

"There aren't that many."

"—and things that you like to do, you should do. But do you realize that I hate skiing?"

"Well, yes. I'm beginning to realize that."

"And that I hate charity balls, society parties, and dressing up in anything fancier than jeans?"

"But—"

"That I'd rather take Tess to Disney World than vacation at Monte Carlo."

"I guess, but—"

"Don't you think we should work on finding some common ground here? It's Wednesday, Alicia, and we're going to be married on Saturday."

"Oh, Ben! You're making a big deal out of this, and it isn't. I was just plain rude. I'm such a spoiled brat that sometimes I'm intolerable. It's what comes of having a doting father who's very, very rich. I'll try to behave better. Really I will. Forgive me? Please?"

"Alicia, this isn't a matter of being mad, or of you behaving better, it's—"

"Pretty please?" She put on a face that was comically plaintive, the expression she'd once confided to him was her strategy of last resort. Knowing the ploy didn't make it any less effective.

He laughed. "You are a spoiled brat."

The face melted into a happy grin. "I know. But you love me."

"I do."

"You'll have to say that in all seriousness on Saturday."

"And so will you."

"No problem. And on that note, I'm going to bed. We skied about fifteen miles today, and it tuckered me out. Oops! There I go again, talking about skiing. Tomorrow I'm going to be a new woman. Maybe you and I should go into Aspen tomorrow and do brunch. Just you and me for a little romantic tryst." She raised a questioning brow.

"That would be good."

Ben sat back in his chair and watched her walk into the kitchen and climb the stairs to the loft. No other woman had a walk quite like Alicia's, sort of undulating and perky at the same time. It certainly did draw a man's eye.

When she disappeared up the stairs, Ben stared at the magazine in his lap, wondering if he also should go to bed. He was tired but also restless. Things would be more comfortable, he told himself, once this ridiculous spectacle of a wedding was over with.

Thoughts of the wedding brought with them thoughts of Joey DeMato, something he definitely didn't need at that moment. Early this morning he'd left her in the hot tub along with their confessions of mutual attraction and their protestations that those feelings didn't mean a thing. He'd turned his back on her in that pool and vowed to keep his distance, and that same afternoon had found them skating an ice duet and laughing together like lovers, which they most definitely were not. Ben wished that images of Joey wouldn't flash into his mind at odd moments to shake him off balance. He wished he weren't living in the same cabin with her, sleeping one cubicle away. He wished—

The wish hadn't yet solidified in his mind before the cabin suddenly echoed with Alicia's scream.

CHAPTER 13

◆

IF I COULD have talked, I would have had a blast with the I-told-you-so's. If those narrow-minded, arrogant morons had listened to me in the first place, all the commotion could have been avoided. But no—don't listen to the dog. The dog barks an alarm, and everyone thinks squirrel or bunny, not villainous skulker. Jerk the poor dog by the collar and tell her to shut up. Don't thank her for her courageous and diligent protection. Don't give her cookies for her virtuous attention to duty. And by all means don't trust in the noble dog's ability to spot trouble, even though dogs have better eyesight and better noses, and sometimes better brains, I swear, than people.

Technically you could say I'm not really a dog, and that's why I have more on the ball than your everyday pooch. But there are times when I think the average basset hound dragging its ears and lips on the ground can outthink your run-of-the-mill person any day of the week. I must admit, when I walked on two legs (two very shapely legs, I fondly remember), I probably wouldn't have listened to me, either, so I guess I have to cut the wedding weenies some slack, but that's hard to do when they act like such idiots.

I tried to warn them, you remember. But they didn't listen. So when Alicia went to her cubicle to turn in for the night, she discovered what the skulker had left for her, and the noise she made could have started an avalanche on the mountain above us. We're lucky it didn't. That girl has a set of lungs on her. Of course everyone rushed to see what was amiss. Ben got there first, of course, since he had a vested interest in keeping Alicia alive. Though that implication is unfair, I guess. He really did look concerned. I sometimes judge people by myself—my human self, that is. And when I was in a shape that could have married a man, my eagle eye was set for a rich one. Not that I found any. Twice I got derailed by sexy and smooth-talking. But I just naturally assume that a working slob like Ben marrying a rich babe like Alicia has ulterior motives that have nothing to do with love.

Never mind. Back to the story. Ben rushed up the stairs in a frenzy, and the others weren't far behind. What they found was a stunned-looking Alicia with a piece of fancy stationery in one hand and the other hand gripping the dresser for support. I saw the whole thing, because Tess had awakened and trundled up the stairs behind the adults, and of course Drover and I, with typical corgi curiosity about anything that looked like trouble, were right at her feet.

Alicia didn't say anything. She couldn't have said much, even if she'd wanted to, because air was pumping in and out of her lungs in frightened gasps. I'd thought she was made of sterner stuff, but I guess her experiences during the last few months would have made most people a bit jumpy. She melted into Ben's arms—very romantic, if her nose hadn't been running and her face splotched with tears. A few choked words tried to make it around the sobs, but nothing anyone could understand. So Ben took the piece of paper from her hands and read. As he read, his expression overall didn't change, but some infinitesimal alteration of lips, eyes, and brows hardened him into something that even the sleaziest evildoer wouldn't want to encounter in a dark alley. Where was Ben, I ask, when I was murdered in just such a dark alley?

Everyone echoed Ben's silence, intimidated by the frozen menace in his face. Finally, he read aloud, one arm still tightly holding Alicia.

> "Roses are red,
>　　Violets are blue.
>　　You won't like
>　　What's waiting for you."

Really bad poetry. Really, really bad. Obvious the villain had no literary bent.

Alicia sobbed anew and reached for the offending poem, her intention to destroy it written on her face. But Ben kept the paper for himself, folding it carefully and deliberately in a way that sent chills down my furry spine. It's always an unpleasant shock when someone you've considered an ordinary schmo turns out to be competently dangerous. How did I know? Let's just say at that moment I knew. Dog senses are one of the few advantages to being a dog. We not only see, smell, and hear better than people, but we have a sixth sense that penetrates through skin and bone and sees right into a person's soul. I won't claim this sixth sense has always worked for me. Those of you who read my first adventure know that I've been mistaken at least once. But then I was new to being a dog, not to mention overwhelmed by the villain's good looks and celebrity status. This time I was sure. Ben might be a schmo in lots of ways, but he wasn't a man to be messed with. As he folded *that stupid, threatening rhyme he was no longer a mump, a wet blanket from Dullsville. His eyes changed from plain, ordinary brown to a tawny promise of mayhem. I could see it, and so could everyone else. Anyone who threatened Alicia was in big trouble.*

The room got very quiet, with only Alicia's sniveling to break the palpable tension. Surprisingly, she drew away from Ben's embrace. If I were in her place, I think I would have tried to crawl inside him and draw him around me like a suit of armor.

Predictably, Joey was the one who tried to ease the tension. Like a general, she took charge, lowering a glare at Ben as if the situation was his fault. "I thought this stalker person was in jail."

"He isn't in jail. He's dead. This isn't Jason Denny. This is just some jerk who thinks he—or she—is being funny."

"You think it's a joke then?"

"Probably. But I never assume something like this isn't real."

How very policeman-like he sounded, but his obvious authority didn't seem to give Alicia the comfort she needed. She let loose another flood of tears, this time drenching Joey's shoulder instead of Ben's. "I d-d-don't want to be left alone. Please."

Joey looked cool and collected, but she positively emanated eau de fear. Dog noses are very good at picking up that particular odor, and the room was thick with it. But she plowed on, little organizer that she is.

"Of course you won't be left alone, Alicia. You can sleep with me in my bed, and Ben can sleep in your room just in case . . ." *She looked a challenge at our resident detective, but he just nodded.*

"What about me?" Tess piped up—as if Drover and I weren't security enough. Ungrateful kid.

Joey ended up marshalling all us females, and Drover as well, into Tess's big room downstairs. Ben was assigned the hot seat—Alicia's cubicle—and Pat slept in his own bed.

Mr. Hunky Haines—now there was a seething pile of frustration. The odd man out in this little group wanted nothing more than to grab Alicia, hug her to his manly chest, and tell her that he would protect her. Frustration is something else a dog is good at picking up, especially me, because I seem capable of inspiring it in so many people. The reason for poor Pat's frustration was obvious. It didn't take a dog's sharp senses to know he was head over heels for Alicia, but he was smart enough to know that he'd be treading on another stud's territory, so to speak. And he wasn't fooled by Ben Ramsay's mumpishness on skis, either. He knew the man wasn't someone to cross.

Unfortunately, the night wasn't yet over. Everyone was nearly settled down when who should show up at the door but Alicia's rich daddy and interfering granny. They'd heard the commotion clear down at the lodge. I told you Alicia had an Olympic-class set of lungs. So of course the hysteria had to be relived, and Granny added some more of her own, even casting dubious glances toward poor innocent Tess until Ben was forced to defend the kid against Irene's suspicious mind. Some old people grow to think kids are just naturally guilty of any hooliganism that occurs within a ten-mile radius of them, and I can't entirely blame her. As I said before, I'm not too fond of the little crumb-snatchers myself.

Daddy and Granny weren't going to settle down any time soon, I gathered, so I decided to take advantage of everyone's distraction and do something useful—a concept apparently far *from anyone else's mind, given all the futile hullabaloo going on in the cabin.*

It was easy to slip away, as everyone, including Tess, was engrossed by the current drama. The latch on the back door was conveniently accessible to an enterprising dog's nose. The night was dark, with the moon barely showing through a high layer of clouds, but dog eyes see great in the dark, and even if they didn't, I scarcely needed to see. My nose was a faithful guide, telling me where I was and who had passed this way within recent memory. Snow and damp make scent all that much more sharp, and we had snow and damp in spades.

For me, the most frustrating part of this whole incident was the fact that I had seen the culprit that afternoon and no one had paid me any mind when I pointed him or her out. These people were all buried in their own agendas. None of them could see past their noses. I was the only one thinking straight, so I was going to have to save them from their own incompetence. It wasn't enough that I had to rescue Alicia from a marriage she would regret and aid Joey in some manner yet undetermined—Stanley had specifically mentioned her, though I can't imagine why. The woman seemed perfectly content to be a frigid workaholic bore. Now on top of everything else I had to foil this villain who writes such ludicrous poetry. I hoped Stan was giving me lots of brownie points for this little job. Not only was I not getting the easy, fawned-upon life that a heroine deserves, but I was forced to work with a pack of bozos.

Oh well. Piggy to the rescue. I'd done it before, despite stubby legs and no hands, and I could do it again.

All this ran through my mind as I trotted about the area where I'd seen the mysterious stranger near the cabin. My nose was to the ground, expertly sifting through scents of squirrel, *bunny, porcupine, skunk—oops! That one made me sneeze, even though it was at least a week old. You'd be surprised at the number of forest beasties that brave the haunts of man. Birds, chipmunks, a maintenance man I recognized. Pat Haines—of course he'd left his scent everywhere. He lived there, after all. Ben, Alicia, Joey, Samantha, Marta, Tess— they'd all been out here. And another human scent that I recognized and couldn't quite place. Definitely male. Testosterone has its own peculiar odor; its own peculiar effects, too, if you ask me. The scent was fresh, and it was the only one I couldn't identify as having reason to be there. I filed it in my memory for future reference. There weren't that many people at Bear Run now that Pat had closed the resort to everyone but the wedding guests. The culprit shouldn't be hard to find, and I'd know him when I smelled him.*

It was that easy. Just call me Sherlock.

I was extremely proud of myself for maintaining focus through all those temptingly distracting squirrel, bunny, and chipmunk scents. Those sorts of things become more of a problem the longer I wear the dog suit.

I was happily visualizing the laurels I would receive when a pair of all too familiar feet planted themselves firmly in front of my nose. My jailer had noticed I was gone. "There you are, you rotten beast!"

Joey was not in a good mood. Understandable, considering that wedding consultants usually didn't have to deal with the things she was having to deal with. Still, she didn't have to take out her temper on a poor dog.

"I have been calling for five minutes. You nearly gave me a heart attack! I could just picture losing Amy Berenger's stupid corgi in the woods and having to call out the ski patrol, or whatever, to track you down. What are you doing out here?"

I felt like telling her off. That would have truly given her that heart attack she talked about. It's probably a good thing I couldn't talk.

"Why can't you be well behaved like Drover?" she complained, snapping a leash on my collar and tugging me rudely toward the house. "At least he has enough sense to stay in the cabin when the temperature's ninety below."

It was not ninety below—more like twenty above, and Drover didn't have enough sense to scratch when he itched. But all I could do was sigh and submit to being maligned.

It's tough being a dog.

The cocktail lounge was empty and dark, but Pat had given Ben the keys to both the door and the liquor. Alicia badly needed a drink, and Ben just as badly needed to say a thing or two. Alicia's perfect wedding was turning into a nightmare.

Alicia was still pale and shaken as Ben turned on the lights and ushered her to a booth. "What'll you have?" he said in his best bartender baritone.

She managed a small smile. "You mean you can fix something other than beer, wine, and straight whiskey?"

"Haven't I told you that I worked as a bartender after college?"

"You did?"

"Just name your drink."

She sighed. "Something strong. Long Island iced tea."

"Coming up."

In three minutes a Long Island iced tea was on the table in front of her, and Ben had his straight whiskey.

He didn't drink strong liquor very often, but tonight was definitely a straight whiskey kind of night. "Don't guzzle," he advised Alicia. "I don't want to end up carrying you to the cabin."

"I feel like getting dead drunk."

It was a poor choice of words and made the tears flow again. "I can't believe this is happening again. Jason Denny couldn't have gotten out of that car."

"He did get out of the car, but he was dead at the time. I know that for a fact because I'm the one who pulled him out. This is some practical joker with very poor taste."

"All these people up here are my friends, or yours."

Many more of hers than his. Besides his brother and two fellow cops he'd asked to be ushers, no one belonging on his side of the aisle would arrive until Friday. There were only a few of them—a sad commentary, he thought, on how much he'd closed down his life after Annie had died.

"Anyone here who you think might have a warped sense of humor?"

"More than one." She gave him a wry little grin. "They are my friends, after all. But no one this warped. Everyone knows what I just went through. No one would do this to me."

He asked gently, knowing there was no way to be tactful. "Any old lovers who might resent your getting married?"

"No! What are you implying?"

"I'm trying to get a handle on this, that's all."

She took another gulp of her potent drink. "I'm totally bummed. This week was supposed to be so perfect." Her eyes swam in tears. "Daddy's furious because his investors are going to see this chaos. . . ."

"Hang Daddy's investors!"

"But Daddy's always relied on me to make sure his business friends get only the very best. I feel like I'm letting him down. And poor Pat. The press is coming to the wedding, and if someone spills the beans about that stupid note, the reporters will blow it up to look like an assassination attempt. That's definitely not the sort of notoriety Bear Run needs."

"Hang Pat and Bear Run." How typical of Alicia, Ben thought, that she thought of everyone else's inconvenience while trying to ignore her own distress. It was one of the things he loved about her, and one of the things that drove him crazy as well.

"Can I have another drink?"

"I don't think so. Your pupils are dilated as it is."

"I'm not drunk."

"You will be if you drink another one of those." He nodded toward the empty glass in front of her.

She sighed morosely. "You're right. But I do feel better. More sensible."

"Good," he said brightly. "Because I have a sensible idea, and I want you to think sensibly about it. Why is it we came up here to Bear Run?"

She shot him an incredulous look. "Earth to Ben Ramsay. We're here to get married. Did you forget?"

"No. I didn't forget. We came here to get married. So let's dump all this trouble and get married. Tomorrow. Forget Daddy's investors. Forget the press and Pat Haines. Forget the rehearsal dinner and fancy wedding and reception. And especially forget the joker who put the note on your bed. We can go into Aspen and find a minister. We already have the license."

"But . . . but . . ." She looked alarmed. "My family."

"Can come along. And my brother and Joey."

"But the bridesmaids—"

"Got a free ski vacation, and so did the rest of the guests. Alicia, the important thing is that we're getting married. I don't like what's happening here." It wasn't just the note on Alicia's bed he didn't like. Everything was out of focus, what with Alicia spending most of her time having fun at things he found dull, Joey on his mind entirely too much, and now the déjà vu of Alicia being someone's target. It might be a joke, and then again it might not.

A mental warning light told him that a hasty elopement wasn't going to ease his doubts, get Joey out of his mind or the stalker off Alicia's back. But he had made a commitment to Alicia, and he could think of no better way to protect her.

Alicia reached out and took his hand, her fingers cool on his. "Ben, we can't. It's way overreacting. We can't just ditch our plans and leave."

"Why not?" He tried to ignore a sudden flood of relief.

"Because we can't. Everyone would be disappointed."

"Everyone didn't get a cute little poem on the pillow tonight."

She withdrew her hand from his and pulled a face. "Okay. I overreacted. I feel better now."

"That doesn't have anything to do with whether or not it was a genuine threat."

"Always the cop."

"Always concerned about you," he countered.

She fingered her empty glass and sent him a pleading look. "I really do need another drink."

"Fine." Feeling less and less like protecting Alicia from herself, he took the glass to the bar and mixed another Long Island iced tea—somewhat watered down. He could feel her eyes on him, assessing, gauging his mood. It wasn't good.

"Ben, it isn't like I wouldn't love to marry you right this minute. I'm the one who proposed, remember? But I just can't disappoint all these people. They came all the way up here to see a great wedding and have a great time. I owe it to them to stay. Besides, now that I can think about it more calmly, I'm sure the poem was just a joke."

He put the drink on the table in front of her.

"I was upset," she admitted. "But it was a stupid prank by someone who knew our history. They were trying to spice up the week with a little drama is all."

"Alicia, you can't assume that."

"What a stern face you have," she teased, tilting her head winsomely. "You've been a policeman too long, my love."

He refused to soften.

"Not that you're not an absolutely wonderful policeman. You are wonderful. The best there is, and don't I know it. But Ben, you don't have to be a cop here. This is our wedding."

"Yes. And I want my bride to be in one piece."

She threw up her hands. "Listen to yourself! One little prank and you're paranoid!"

"I'm not paranoid. I'm reasonably cautious." Frustration tightened a knot in his stomach. "Alicia, you're a high-profile person, and you're a natural target for crazies. You ought to know that by now."

"That was different!" she said stubbornly. "That was real."

"How do you know this isn't real? You're ignoring the risk. This is stupid. We would be just as married if we found a minister in Aspen tomorrow. And everyone here has had a load of fun. No one will think worse of you under the circumstances. Tess could go home with your dad and Irene, and we could go off to Jamaica. I doubt our lousy poet would follow. Meanwhile, I'm going to send the note down to Denver to have someone look at the handwriting."

"Just like that? No matter what I think or what I want?" Her eyes snapped with vexation and her jaw stiffened in complaint.

"Alicia . . ."

"Don't use that tone with me, Ben Ramsay. You talk to me as if I'm a child, and I'm not. You use that tone all the time, and it drives me up a wall. Every time we disagree, you make out like you're Mr. Sensible and I'm a flake."

"That's not true."

"Yes it is. I love you, Ben, and I'll marry you—on Saturday, as we'd planned. And when absolutely nothing scary happens between now and then, I'll expect an apology. A good one. So start thinking of a very contrite little speech." She downed half the glass in front of her with one swallow and slammed it down on the table, tossing him a defiant look. "I'm going to bed. And tomorrow I'm damned well going to have fun."

"I'll walk with you."

"Don't bother."

"Alicia, I don't want you going anywhere alone."

She stood rather unsteadily and attempted a pugnacious scowl. It simply made her look like a confused and rather frightened little girl. "I hope you don't think you can get away with being this bossy for the rest of our lives. I'll go where I want. Nothing is going to happen. And stop treating me like a child!" This last was nearly shouted. Ben winced. Alicia nodded in satisfaction and stomped off.

Alicia woke up the next morning with a miserable hangover. The last time she had drunk Long Island iced tea had been her graduation party at Mills College, and she'd been sorry then, also. She just barely remembered stumbling into the cabin and finding her way to the kitchen, where Joey had been waiting up for her, bless her. Faithful Joey. Such a good friend. How could she have gone off to get married in Aspen when Joey had spent so much time on the wedding plans for Bear Run? How rude that would be.

Alicia couldn't quite remember what she'd said to Ben, but she was sure every word had been a stinger. She felt ashamed for being sharp with him. He'd meant well when he suggested they elope. She shouldn't have puffed up like an irate adder. No doubt he was angry and disappointed at her show of temper. Briefly she wondered if she should apologize, but only briefly. He would take an apology to be consent to his ridiculous plan. No idiot jokester was going to spoil her perfect wedding and get away with it.

Alicia was in Tess's bed, where she and Joey had spent the night safe from practical jokers. Tess had slept on a mattress on the floor with the dogs. Samantha, brave soul, had tried the floor but finally retired to her own cubicle to sleep. But right now Alicia was alone in the little room. Voices from the kitchen told her everyone else was having breakfast, something that certainly didn't tickle her fancy with her stomach feeling on the edge of a heave. But huddling beneath the covers would make the others think she was upset and frightened. She couldn't allow that. One had to maintain appearances. That was something Irene had taught her early in life.

Even apart from her uneasy stomach and aching head, though, breakfast was a miserable affair. Ben was flawlessly polite, but his quiet demeanor bore witness that he was not pleased with her. The others were jumpy, as if a boogeyman might jump out at them from any corner of the house. Joey, always the social tactician, made a valiant attempt to smooth things over, but it didn't work. Samantha announced her intention of driving to Denver and back that day to take care of some business at Joey's office. From the surreptitious look she gave Ben, Alicia suspected that she was delivering the offending ditty to Ben's cronies at the police department. Pat tried to be jovial and teasing, but she could tell that even he was worried.

The only person at the breakfast table who seemed cheerful and unaffected by the events of the night before was Tess, whose chair was predictably flanked by the two corgis—not out of any canine devotion or urge to protect, Alicia was sure. They'd quickly come to learn that the kid was the person most likely to slip them food. Tess gobbled down a stack of three pancakes and asked for eggs as well, and her only worry seemed to be if Marta would let her try the "big people's" chairlift today. Briefly Alicia considered the possibility of Tess having left that awful note. The poem was certainly childish enough, and there had been that earlier trick she'd played. Kids could be unpredictable little demons. Not that she'd ever been that way herself. She'd always been boringly well behaved, eager to please everyone. It would be just desserts, Alicia supposed, if she ended up being stepmother to a nine-year-old with an itch for trouble. Justice, but she wasn't sure she was up to it.

She was glad to escape the breakfast table to seek a bit of comfortable solitude. Ben gave her a steely-eyed look when she announced her intention to take a walk, but she stuck out her chin to let him know she wasn't a child to be told she shouldn't go out of sight. Alicia supposed she should be grateful he cared so much for her, but in this case his attitude was very annoying.

Just the same, she didn't leave the resort grounds. Just beside the bunny hill were piles of snow that just ached to be fashioned into a snowman, and Alicia obliged them.

She hadn't made a snowman since she was a kid, but Alicia discovered that once the art is learned, it doesn't fade. Before a half hour had passed she had built herself the perfect man with a cheerful pebble smile and bright blue eyes improvised from the spare buttons on her jacket.

"I'll bet *you* wouldn't be such a killjoy," she told her frosty companion. "You would always say, 'Yes, Alicia dear. You're very right, Alicia my love. Whatever you want, honeybunch.' As it should be, of course, because between the two of us, I'm certainly the one with all the brains."

The snowman agreed with an idiot grin. Alicia grinned back. "Let's see." She regarded her creation critically. "You need arms. We definitely don't want you to go without." Arms were easy to come by in the pile of firewood beneath the deck of the lodge. Two forked aspen sticks even provided rudimentary hands.

"Everything you need," Alicia said, "I can provide. You wouldn't be one to think I'm childish and helpless just because I have money and I've never had to do a thing for myself. I could do anything if I put my mind to it. Don't you think?"

Even to herself her words sounded petulant, and what was she doing having a conversation with a snowman, anyway? Suddenly she was flooded with a great longing to do something that would let her hold her head high. Something she could point to and say "I created this!" or "I built this!" She was more than financially independent. She was downright filthy rich. But she had been infected lately with the oddest urge to be like the heroine of a novel she'd read a few months back. That women was destitute, betrayed, and deserted, yet she'd managed to pull herself up by her bootstraps and create an independent life that was her own and no one else's. Not that Alicia wanted to be destitute. Or betrayed. Or even deserted. But she wanted *something*. Something like Joey had—her own little company that was the product of her own innovation and hard work. Something like Pat had—a resort that he'd sunk all his hopes and dreams into, not to mention his money, and would grow or flounder according to his dedication and know-how.

Maybe there was something she, Alicia Somers, was supposed to be doing in life, something that she was missing because she simply did what she was told to do—pleased the right people, went to the right parties, donated to the right charities, married the right man. . . .

And that thought led her to ponder uncomfortably her refusal to elope to Aspen with Ben. Ben did have a point. Taking a painful, honest look at the situation, Alicia could admit that. Was her refusal just because she was too invested in her plans for a spectacular wedding, or was she reluctant to rush to the irrevocable commitment? And did Pat Haines have anything to do with her hesitation? Was she fooling herself that all she felt for Pat was fond friendship?

Before she could reflect further on that sticky point, a familiar voice interrupted her solitude.

"You haven't made a snowman since you were ten years old," Irene said in a strangely wistful voice.

"Geez, Nana, you remember?"

The old woman chuckled. "Probably better than you. Who do you think taught you to make a snowman? It's an art, you know."

Alicia laughed. "What do you think of Frosty here?"

"I think Frosty is a very plebeian name."

"What do you think he should be named?"

"That, my dear, is up to you."

"Ah. You don't like the name I chose—"

"There's nothing wrong with it. It's just a bit common."

"But you can't offer any other suggestions?"

"I'd be glad to pass judgment on any ideas you have."

"I'm sure," Alicia said in a droll voice, well aware that it wasn't snowman names they discussed. "Did Ben send you down here?" she asked suspiciously.

"Yes," Irene admitted. "He said you shouldn't be alone, and for some reason he didn't believe you wanted his company right at the moment. I take it you two had a spat."

Alicia pulled a face. "Not exactly a spat. Well . . . maybe a spat. He wants to lock me up somewhere and throw away the key, just because some jerk is playing a practical joke."

"My dear girl, in this case I think you should listen to Mr. Ramsay. The man is a police officer, after all, and I've never said that he didn't know his business. Now, why are you looking so miserable, Alicia? You've told me many, many times that this is the man you want and that you're deliriously happy. You don't look happy, dear."

Beyond Alicia's control, tears rushed to her eyes and slipped down her cold cheeks. "I just have prewedding jitters. It's nothing." It was nothing, Alicia told herself firmly, but just the same, she had an overwhelming need to talk to someone older and wiser. And while she'd never really been close to her rather intimidating grandmother, Irene was definitely older, and probably wiser.

They sat beneath the deck on uncut fireplace logs. Hesitantly at first, then in a flow of words that became a flood, Alicia spilled her doubts, Ben's idea that they should cancel the big wedding, and her own nebulous feelings that she needed to be doing something that she wasn't doing. Irene listened intently, nodded now and then, smiled a time or two, and then offered surprising sympathy. In the back of her mind, Alicia had expected either a lecture or a stinging dismissal of Ben Ramsay.

"You do have a case of prewedding jitters. But my dear, that's just natural. There's nothing wrong with examining your motivations before you take such a huge step in your life. If you weren't doing that, I'd say you weren't taking this nearly seriously enough."

"How did you feel before marrying Grandpa?"

"Scared. Scared about a lot of things. Back in those days we weren't nearly as sophisticated as you young people today. I scarcely even knew what marriage was. And of course, young women didn't have nearly the opportunities you have today. Still, I had second thoughts. And third ones as well," she remembered with a little smile.

"But you married him."

"I loved him. Do you love your Ben Ramsay?"

Alicia's first instinct was to declare "Of course!" in a loud voice, but she didn't. Her very hesitation scared her. Ben was the solidest, bravest, best man she'd ever met. Even her father thought he was a gem. Of course she loved him . . . didn't she?

"I see you have to think about that," Irene said softly. "Remember, dear, that you don't have to do anything you don't want to, just because people expect you to do it. And that includes your old nana," she offered with a faint smile. "If you need time to think, then take time to think."

Alicia was feeling more and more confused. When had life gotten so confusing? She looked at her snowman, who stood stalwartly with his unchanging smile and outstretched arms. "It's too bad perfect men aren't as easy to come by as perfect snowmen," she said wistfully.

Irene patted her hand. "If they were, dear, the world wouldn't be nearly as interesting. Trust me."

CHAPTER 14

◆

KEEPING THE BRIDE calm and in good spirits is traditionally the maid of honor's job, and Teri Schaefer took her duties seriously. So Thursday, when she perceived that Alicia was a bit down in the dumps—and who could blame her after finding that hideous note on her pillow?—Teri determined that the very thing to cheer up the bride was a bachelorette party in Aspen. All the women in the wedding were invited. Irene declined with a succinct opinion about the propriety of young women drinking and carrying on like men. Joey pleaded work as an excuse, along with her need to wait for Samantha, who was driving back from Denver that evening. But everyone else, including Marta, went along with the idea—over Ben's objection.

"We're going to the J-Bar at the Hotel Jerome," Alicia told him half-apologetically. "It's very upscale, and absolutely nothing can happen to me there. Besides, I'll be with a pack of women. No one in his right mind would mess with a pack of women." When he gave her a stern look, she pouted. "Ben, you can't put me in a glass jar and close the lid. I need more than air-holes to survive."

So Alicia and her pack of ladies ended up dining, drinking, and exchanging feminine confidences and laughter at the J-Bar in Aspen's very old, very classic, and very upscale Hotel Jerome. The food was a mere accessory to the freely flowing liquor. And the more freely the liquor flowed, the more lively the conversation grew. Of course, everyone's observations revolved around men, romance, and marriage. This was a group of young women, after all, most of them unmarried.

Sue, the only married woman in the party, enjoying razzing Alicia about the pitfalls of matrimony. "Prepare yourself," Sue warned. "The romance lasts about as long as the fizz in the champagne. There is nothing sexy or romantic about living together and dealing with everyday life. Not that it's not nice having the same man in your bed every night, but Lord! The little things can drive you crazy."

Teri Schaefer responded with a wicked chuckle. "George doesn't look to me like he has a little thing."

Sue grinned. "I'll never tell. And I'd better not catch any of you trying to find out, either!"

"Like George would ever look at anyone else," Teri said. "He's got eyes only for Sue. All of us should be so lucky to get a husband like him."

"George is great," Sue conceded. "But just be warned, Alicia. Like I said, the little things"—she sent a quelling glare toward Teri—"will get to you before any of the big issues will. Like with me, I have this fetish about toothpaste. Toothpaste blobs drive me crazy. The smell of the stuff someone else has spit in the sink makes me gag. And George brushes his teeth and spits in the shower!"

"That's disgusting," Carrie agreed.

"And he makes like a federal case when I object. Not to mention the stinky socks he doesn't unroll before tossing in the laundry, and his refusal to throw anything—anything at all!—away, whether or not it works. Our garage shelters so many appliances and lawnmowers, even an ancient refrigerator that hasn't worked since the beginning of time, that we have to park the cars outside. Sheesh!"

"That may be," Carrie said a bit enviously. "But marriage has to beat dating. Dating is a game that women are set up to lose before we begin. Take my date Edward." She rolled her eyes comically. "Please someone take my date Edward!"

"He's a hunk," Danielle declared. "I'd take him."

"Yeah! That's what I thought when I met him. And he seemed just so sweet and attentive. But he seems less interested since I got up here. Maybe it's because I'm such a dork on skis. At the engagement party he paid more attention to Alicia than to me, and Alicia's taken, for heaven's sake!"

"Well, at least *you* have a date!" Teri told her. "Since breaking up with my boyfriend three months ago, I haven't gone out once. I've just about memorized the television schedule, all seven days of it, because that's where I spend all my evenings, in front of the TV. A friend from work tried to set me up with her brother a couple of weeks ago, and the guy took me to a basketball game. Booooring! And he never called again, I guess because I didn't know who Jamaal Magloire was. Can you imagine?"

"Who's Jamaal Magloire?" Carrie asked.

"Some guy with the Charlotte Hornets. Like I should know that?"

"Bummer," Carrie agreed.

Alicia sighed. "Sue, did you have prewedding jitters?"

"Oh God yes! Still do."

"You've been married four years!" Teri reminded her.

"Yeah, and I still wonder what the hell I did to myself. Don't sweat the jitters, kid. Everyone gets them. What you need is another beer."

"That would be good." Alicia held her mug beneath the pitcher of Michelob while Sue poured. At least tonight she had sense enough to stay away from the Long Island iced tea. These were her friends, but she didn't want to get drunk and cry on their collective shoulder. Her uncertainities at this late date—two days before her wedding—were an embarrassment. A together sort of woman wouldn't be wavering and unsure. Wonderful Ben didn't deserve a bride who was wavering and unsure. And she didn't want to look like the fool she felt herself to be.

So instead of talking about her confusion, she turned her attention to Marta. Marta, who got to work day in and day out with Pat Haines. Marta, who seemed an integral part of Bear Run and had somehow won Pat's admiration and respect, and perhaps his affection, for all that he denied it. Lovely, mysterious Marta. At least that was what she seemed to Alicia.

"Marta, Pat tells me you have a fiancé in Glenwood Springs."

Marta smiled her quiet smile. "I suppose one could call Greg a fiancé, though we've not set a date of any kind."

"Ooooh," Carrie cooed. "Another single sister falls to matrimony."

"No time soon," Marta assured them. "Greg is an import, much more recent than myself. He is from Sarajevo and has much trouble speaking English, though he can read it. He has trouble holding a job, and he must work through some difficulties before we can be together."

"Oh my," Danielle said. "That's romantic."

"Not so much," Marta denied. "We are very practical people."

"You must be," Teri agreed. "Otherwise you would have fallen for that sexy Pat Haines."

Alicia was surprised by a bolt of pure jealousy. She quashed it, and in the most normal tone she could muster said, "That's right. You and Pat seem such good friends, and you have so much in common."

"God, what a beautiful couple they'd make," Carrie said, her words beginning to slur.

"It is not that way at all," Marta said. "Pat and I are very good friends. He is a wonderful man. Smart, patient, hardworking, clever, and always kind. But he is not romantic. I think his heart has been taken."

Marta didn't look at Alicia with anything besides

candid friendliness, and Alicia quelled the urge to ask just who had possession of Pat Haines's heart. She didn't want to know. She really, really didn't.

Instead she held up her mug for yet another beer.

"Drink up, bro," Tom advised Ben. "This is the only bachelor party you're going to get. It would be more fun if Todd and Gary hadn't turned in so early. Just because they drove up here after work and they're tired, poor babies, that's no excuse. I mean, it's the job of the best man and ushers to get the groom drunk. It would be better still if we had some great-looking honey jump out of a cake. But if we spend enough, maybe we can get the waitress to do a little kootchie dance for us."

"Tom," Ben said patiently, "it's amazing to me that some woman hasn't knocked you into the next county."

Tom grinned. "It's my charm. Gets 'em every time."

"Yeah, I'm sure."

"Want another whiskey?"

"Why not?"

Tom summoned the waitress, who along with the bartender was watching Denver Nuggets basketball on the bar TV. She sauntered to their table and gave them both a cozy smile. "Want another?"

"You bet we do, beautiful. Keep 'em coming. My brother here's the honored groom of the week, and he needs to get soused."

"I can't believe Pat Haines is keeping all this open just for the wedding guests," Ben commented.

The waitress shrugged. "I think it's great. The workload is light, and I get paid anyway."

Tom smirked. "Treat us right, and the tip will make it worthwhile."

She snorted dubiously. "Honey, I've heard that one before."

When she left, Ben shook his head at his brother. "You are such a sleaze."

"And you are such a Captain America. But I love you anyway, bro." He raised his almost empty shot glass to his brother in toast. "Seriously, big brother. I'm really glad to see you getting such a great girl. Alicia's a fox. She's rich, and she's sweet. And what a figure! Mmmm!"

"Sleaze."

Tom ignored him. "Annie was terrific, too. I have to admit, you've had great luck in women. But seriously, I thought you were going to crater after Annie died. That's why I'm so glad to see you back in the saddle."

"Tom, I think Alicia's too good to be your sister-in-law."

"Well, at least it will protect her from my advances. Even I wouldn't put a move on my brother's wife."

Pat Haines came through the door of the lounge and waved to them.

"Come join us!" Tom invited. "This is Ben's bachelor party, such as it is."

Pat grinned, flashing perfect teeth. "You should have told me. I would have brought up a good bottle of champagne."

"We're doing fine on whiskey," Ben said.

Pat sat down. "That sounds good. Think I'll have one myself. Hope the ladies are having fun in Aspen. The J-Bar's a nice place. Alicia and I went there a time or two a few years ago."

Ben stabbed a look his way, but Pat's face was bland.

"You're getting a great girl, Ben. There aren't many like her around. Usually a woman with that kind of looks and money is a real pain in the ass. I get enough of them up here to say that from experience. But Alicia isn't that way. She's a good sport. Smart. Has a great sense of humor, and she's always going out of her way to please."

Tom nodded agreement. "Ben's got all the luck."

Ben couldn't very well snap Pat's head off when he was praising Ben's choice of a wife, but it still didn't sit right to hear about how well acquainted they were. There were limits to geniality.

"I remember a time a few years back," Pat went on. "I was working at Vail as an instructor. Allie came up for a lesson. I was real down on my luck at the time. Renting a dump in Avon, living off Vienna sausages." He grinned. "Ski instructors don't get paid all that much, and certainly not well enough to live decently in a town like Vail. I don't know how Alicia knew it, but she did. She had a fanny pack of the best French bread, cheese, wine, and brownies that were the closest thing to heaven I've ever tasted. We spent more of the day eating than skiing. And she made out that the picnic was for her. I knew better. She's a special lady."

Ben was actually grateful when Edward showed up, though Carrie's date wasn't really someone he would choose to hang out with. The man smiled too much, as far as Ben was concerned. But at least his arrival changed the subject, and Ben wasn't all that comfortable hearing about Pat's picnic past with Alicia.

Edward greeted the group with a jovial, "Hey there. I wondered if the guys would get together and take advantage of the girls running out on them for the evening."

"Here we are," Tom said.

"Drinking whiskey, I see." Edward signaled the waitress to bring him the same. "Mind if I join you?"

"Sit down," Ben invited.

"Ben, old man. You don't look very happy for a man about to marry a rich, beautiful woman."

Tom laughed and twisted his hands around an imaginary rope. "No man looks happy when he feels the noose begin to tighten. Even when a gorgeous piece like Alicia is doing the tightening."

"Alicia's not tightening any damned noose," Ben growled.

"Of course she's not," Edward agreed. "She's an independent soul, isn't she? I'm surprised you let her out of your sight after that little incident last night."

Ben managed to be minimally polite. "Alicia's hard to tie down."

"She thinks the whole thing is a joke," Pat said.

Ben's eyes flashed with irritation. "Is that what she told you?"

"Yes."

"Sometimes she can't see past the end of her nose. Especially if it's something she doesn't really want to see."

"I agree with Ben," Edward chimed in. "It sounds

to me like this person, whoever he is, might pose some real danger. Alicia should watch herself. She really should. This fellow might be someone to deal with."

Joey and Samantha sat at the kitchen table drinking hot tea and going over the menus for Friday's rehearsal dinner and the last-minute details of the wedding ceremony itself. The hour was late, and they were both tired. Samantha had driven to Denver and back that day, and Joey had told her she should be in bed, but Samantha wasn't one to rest when there was work to be done. The wedding was approaching fast, and they had to have their ducks in a row.

"I'm glad the van is finally fixed," Joey said.

Samantha grumbled, "Too bad all that food had to be dumped. If that dolt had thought to keep the refrigeration unit on, most of the stuff could have been saved."

Instead, the driver had caught a ride back to Denver and left the catering van in the hands of the mechanic, who was concerned about the engine, not the food in the back, at least not until he started smelling it.

"I plan to have a word with Ron about that," Joey said. "Oh well. Now the menu is once and for all finalized—and if Alicia makes one more change I'm going to personally throttle her—we can pick up the groceries we need. I'll drive over to Aspen tomorrow to go shopping, and the wedding cake should be ready. Plus we need a few more chafing dishes. I'm going to end up spending most of the day there."

"And leave me here to manage this pack of loonies?" Samantha gasped theatrically. "I don't think so.

"What do you mean?"

Samantha snorted. "You've got a bride mooning over a hunky former boyfriend. You've got a father who's trying to turn the affair into a business meeting. You've got a practical joker, or worse, scaring the bejesus out of everyone. You've got a grandmother who makes a dill pickle look sweet. You've got a couple of zany dogs who make every meal a game of keep-away. And to top it off, the groom is packing heat, I'm sure, and looks ready to shoot the next thing that makes a wrong move."

Joey sighed. It was just as well Samantha didn't know about the wedding consultant mooning over the groom, and the groom—was he mooning for the wedding consultant? Joey didn't want to think about it, because the whole situation was ludicrous. If any of them got through this wedding with their sanity intact, it would be a miracle.

"And worst of all," Samantha concluded, "I think the wedding consultant is lusting after the groom."

"Samantha!"

Samantha spread her hands in a fatalistic gesture.

"I am not lusting after the groom!"

"You're a terrible liar."

Joey huffed indignantly.

"Don't puff up like an angry peahen. I don't mean to say you're doing anything improper. There's nothing wrong with harboring a little lust in your heart. Joey, sweetie, you know this marriage is doomed before the bride and groom say 'I do.' Why don't you talk some sense into these two nice people?"

"Sam, I have a hard-and-fast rule. Never interfere. Trying to run someone else's life can end in disaster. Cripes! Sometimes running my own life is a disaster. I'm in no position to tell Alicia and Ben what they should do."

"It's on your head then."

"Nothing is on my head! And I am harboring nothing, not lust, not anything else, in my frigging heart!"

Samantha smiled. "I suppose that's why you're touchy as a cat in heat."

Joey groaned.

"And it's only natural you'd want to escape for a while, but there's just no way you are spending a pleasant day in Aspen while I stay here with this crew." Samantha was emphatic. "I'll go to Aspen. I'm not the one to be here in case anything or anyone blows up. In my life I've managed to dump three husbands and offend most of my relatives. No one can accuse me of being diplomatic." Samantha grinned wickedly. "Just remember, dear, that rules were made to be broken."

"Oh, be quiet."

Tess stuck her head into the kitchen and regarded them with serious eyes. "Are you guys arguing?"

"No, Tess," Joey said. "We're discussing. That's all."

"Oh. Well, Piggy and I want you to come play Truth or Dare with us."

"You do, do you?"

"I've got to warn you, though. Piggy cheats."

"Doesn't Drover get to play?" Samantha asked.

Tess snorted. "Drover's just a dog. He's not smart enough to play."

Joey and Sam exchanged a glance, both in agreement that this subject was something best not pursued. "Okay," Joey said. "Truth or Dare it is."

For the next hour the four of them played—Joey, Samantha, Tess, and Piggy. Piggy wasn't much competition, as she simply sat in place regarding the other players through bored eyes.

When Samantha had to fess up a truth, she wimped out by stating that she had a secret crush on Mel Gibson.

"There's nothing juicy about that," Joey complained. "Every woman in America has a crush on Mel Gibson."

Joey could have sworn that Piggy rolled her eyes. Coincidence. It had to be.

"Who's Mel Gibson?" Tess asked, nose wrinkled.

Samantha chuckled. "Definite generation gap."

When Joey was put on the spot, she confessed that her worst secret was she had no juicy secrets to reveal. "That's a pretty sad thing for a woman my age to say."

"So," Samantha advised slyly, "go do something wild and abandoned, and you won't have that problem anymore."

"I don't understand." Tess's nose wrinkled even more.

When Piggy's turn came, the dog just continued to look bored. "How's she supposed to tell a secret?" Samantha asked.

"She has a secret," Tess said impishly. "But she can't talk."

The dog glared at Tess, almost as if she knew what the girl was saying.

"Maybe Piggy has a secret hankering for Mel Gibson, too," Joey speculated with a grin.

"I don't think so," Tess said. "I don't think Piggy likes anybody very much."

"Maybe she's more of a Harrison Ford type," Samantha suggested.

"Who's Harrison Ford?"

"*Star Wars*," Samantha informed the child. "Indiana Jones, *Patriot Games,* and lots of others."

"I know *Star Wars,*" Tess said. "It had Ewan McGregor in it. And some old guy named Liam Neeson. No one named Harrison Ford."

"This is scary in more ways than one," Joey said. "You have just impressed me with just how young you are, Miss Tess, or how old I am. And I think it's past your bedtime. Way past."

The traditional objections followed.

"Wait a minute!" Samantha said with a smile. "We still don't know Piggy's secret."

"She used to be a lady," Tess revealed solemnly.

Joey chuckled. "Well, she's certainly no lady now. Not with her manners."

Samantha laughed. "I could swear that dog is absolutely frying you with her eyes."

"That's her normal expression," Joey said. "Come on, Tess. It's bed for you."

Joey wasn't accustomed to having a kid around, and she'd always told herself that she couldn't communicate with children. But putting Tess to bed, getting her into flannel Winnie-the-Pooh pajamas, making sure she brushed her teeth, and tucking her into bed seemed uncannily natural.

"My dad always kisses me good night."

"Do you want me to kiss you?" Joey asked dubiously.

Tess pointed to the middle of her forehead. "Right here."

Doing the honors gave Joey a fluttery feeling in her heart. She hoped she wasn't developing motherly instincts. Motherhood had never been in her career plan.

"Thank you, Joey. I'm sorry you're having to go to all this trouble when my dad isn't really going to marry Alicia."

Better to go with the flow, Joey thought. "We'll just see what happens."

The dogs settled themselves firmly around Tess's body, Drover sharing the big feather pillow and Piggy, still glaring, curled at a distance that afforded her a bit more privacy. Joey wiggled two fingers in a little good-night wave as she eased the door shut.

Scary things were happening at Bear Run Resort, scary enough to keep me from curling comfortably into a warm little coil of dog fur and settling down for a pleasant night's sleep.

Right at the top of my worries was the kid. Not only did Tess see right through me, the little toadlet was a blabbermouth to boot. Fortunately, the adults around here were sensible enough, or narrow-minded enough, depending on your point of view, to dismiss her prattling. Frustrating for Tess, but lucky for me. Good thing the kid had blown her credibility with all that talk of chatting up the ghost of her mother. Who was going to listen to anything she said? Her insistence that I was a "lady" in a dog suit wasn't any more believable than her other claims. Normal, sensible people don't fall for that kind of far-out stuff. You have to be dead, really, before you realize that a lot of weirdness really is true. Surprise.

Also on my scary list, of course, was the kook who was out to give Alicia nightmares, as if the poor girl didn't have enough problems as it was. I didn't figure this thing would end with just a bad poem. Stanley wouldn't be satisfied with throwing me into a situation fraught with mere annoyance. No indeed. He likes the big stuff. In my first adventure as a dog, he didn't warn me at all that mayhem would be involved. And look what happened there! Major mayhem. This time he'd mentioned—oh so casually—just a little peril. So I figured we could count on something that made a James Bond movie look tame. And here I was, relegated to keeping a kid company, ignored by all, locked up more often than not in this dull cabin that didn't even have a doggie door! And Stanley expected me to work in these circumstances?

Last but not least of my worries was a peculiar longing to be home curled on Amy's bed, or in my own fake fleece dog bed, with the familiar scents of Amy and the other dogs and, yes, even Dr. Doofus, Amy's husband, marching in familiar parade across my sensitive dog nose. Why was this bit of home-sickness worrisome, you ask? It was worrisome because I was longing for dog things in Piggy's dog life, not Lydia's big brass bed and Denver apartment with the retro Beatles posters and the closet full of knockout clothes. My dogness was winning, blast it! Really winning. And Stanley was no doubt laughing up his sleeve, the creep!

So I lay awake there on Tess's bed, listing all the scary things wrong at that moment and listening to Drover snore.

Drover snores hugely. A corgi's nose is ideally made for a good snore.

Then another noise intruded, not nearly as loud as Drover's symphony but with a certain out-of-placeness that made my ears come on line like finely tuned sonar. Something was afoot. I was sure of it. Double damn Stanley for getting me into this fix!

With Tess safely stashed in bed, Joey and Samantha got into a cutthroat game of Hearts. Joey was just about ready to score a victory when the phone rang.

"Uh-oh!" Samantha groaned.

"Why uh-oh?"

"That's got to mean trouble. Everything that's happened since Monday has meant trouble."

Samantha was right. On the other end of the line was Marta, who tried to be gentle about revealing the problem.

"It was very generous of you to let us drive your minivan to Aspen this evening," she began.

"Oh God!" Joey borrowed a bit of Samantha's pessimism. "Did you wreck it? Is anyone hurt?"

"We didn't wreck it, Joey. It's perfectly fine."

"What then?"

"Alicia isn't feeling well."

"Then bring her home."

"Uh . . ."

"Spit it out, Marta. What's wrong?"

"I'm afraid Alicia has had a very lot to drink."

"She never could hold her liquor."

"She *hasn't* held much, to tell the truth. Most of it

has come up, but it hasn't made her feel better. She seems very depressed."

Joey still didn't see the problem. "Bring her home, Marta."

Marta sighed. "We can't. She threw the car keys down the toilet."

"She what?"

"As I said—"

"I heard what you said. I'll kill her! My house key was on that chain."

"That is unfortunate. We were hoping you had a spare key to the car."

"Why did Alicia throw my keys down the toilet?" Joey prayed for patience.

"She says she can't come back to the resort. I'm not sure why. She *is* very drunk."

"Cripes! I am going to kill her. Yes, I have an extra key to the car. I'll drive over in the resort van and pick you up. Hold on to Alicia. Don't let her get away."

"Don't worry. She's in no condition to get away."

"And all of you are sworn to secrecy, you understand? No one hears about this. No one. Just ignore whatever it is Alicia is babbling."

Joey hung up the phone and gave Samantha a morose look. "You were right. Trouble."

Once Joey was on her way, Samantha breathed a short prayer of thanks that she was just the assistant, not the boss. The boss was the one who had to deal with such things as brides who got tanked and started having

second thoughts about getting married. She herself had
never had second thoughts about getting married until
sometime after the wedding. Her second thoughts always appeared when it was too late.

She browsed through the books on the bookshelves
that flanked the fireplace and selected a classic gothic
romance for appropriate bedtime reading. Then she
glanced around the room—the big, quiet, lonely room
with its great expanse of windows looking out into the
very dark, quiet, lonely night—and she put the gothic
romance back on the shelf. This was not the right time
or place to read dark and scary.

Then she jumped nearly out of her skin as an eerie
caterwauling filled the night. Her heart pumped so
hard in her chest that it was a full thirty seconds before
she realized that the sound wasn't a pack of wolves, it
was a dog. Two dogs, in fact. And they were in Tess's
room.

Samantha ran through the kitchen and yanked open
the door to Tess's bedroom. The dogs shot out, nearly
knocking her over. Tess was sitting up in her bed, rub-
bing her eyes. There was no threat in the room that
Samantha could see.

"Are you all right?" she asked Tess.

"Sure. What are Piggy and Drover barking at?"

"Those cursed dogs. Probably a squirrel on the roof.
Or worse, a skunk on the back porch."

"Eeeww!"

"Exactly."

Tess climbed out of bed and put on a pair of bunny
slippers. "But I don't think it's a skunk," she said

calmly. "Piggy's a wonder dog, you know. She's smarter than a lot of people, and she has supernatural powers. And she knows my mom."

"Oh, that's nice. Can you tell the wonder dog and her sidekick to be quiet before they wake up the whole mountain?"

Tess trundled out the door, throwing Samantha a glance that indicated she was likely one of those people that Piggy was smarter than. Then the girl fearlessly looked up the stairs to the loft, where the dogs had dashed after their escape from the bedroom. "Piggy? Is something wrong?"

The barking had become a sporadic grumble rather than an alarm. When Tess called, the dogs trooped down the stairs, Drover wagging his tailless fuzzy butt and grinning happily. But then, Drover always seemed happy. Bringing up the rear, Piggy muttered under her breath in ill-natured woofs, occasionally glancing over her shoulder at the dark loft.

This did not make Samantha feel good at all. "I'm sure it was a squirrel, or a branch hitting the roof, or something very innocent. Stupid dogs. But I suppose I'd better go up there and take a look around." She hated being the adult in a situation like this. If she'd been Tess's age, she would have had an excuse to dive under the bedcovers and cower until daylight made the world seem friendlier.

Tess, though, wasn't inclined to cower. "You'd better take the dogs with you for protection," she said seriously.

Samantha regarded the stubby little legs and sausage

bodies. "Yeah, they're really going to scare off the boogeyman."

"And I'll go with you, too."

"No you won't. You'll get back to your room, and take Rin Tin Tin with you."

"Who?" Tess's elfin little mouth pulled sideways in puzzlement.

"Never mind. Go back to your room."

"My dad always says people should stick together in a crisis."

"This isn't a crisis."

"Then why should I go back to my room?"

The kid was hopeless. "All right. I'll grab the griddle, and you take that little frying pan for protection."

As they climbed the stairs, Samantha wished she'd brought a carving knife instead of the griddle. But when she flipped on the loft light, nothing and no one needed carving. Everything was as it had been before. The doors to the cubicles were closed. The little sitting area was undisturbed. The tiny water closet was empty.

"We should look in each room," Tess said.

She *would* say that, Samantha thought sourly. But no danger lurked behind any of the doors. Samantha's clothes lay in a jumbled heap on her bed, just as she'd left them. Joey's room was neat as a pin. Ben's room was Spartan. Alicia's was somewhat jumbled, but Samantha understood that Alicia wasn't the neatest person in the world. Her cosmetics were scattered over the dresser. A wool sweater draped sloppily over the back of the chair. The teddy bear on her bed guarded the pillow.

Nothing seemed to be disturbed at all.

"Like I said," Samantha told Tess in some relief, "the dumb dog was barking at a squirrel."

She didn't really like the glower she got from Piggy, but then, her imagination seemed to be working overtime.

While Tess and her bunny slippers went back to bed, dragging the dogs with her, Samantha surveyed the sitting area once more, just to reassure herself. A cold draft led her to the window, cracked open despite an outdoor temperature in the twenties. Samantha's heart started racing again as she glanced out and downward. The night was dark, but nothing seemed amiss. Shutting the window, she thought to herself that rustic log cabins were very charming and all that, but they did provide many jutting protuberances as foot- and handholds for any sneaky villain wanting to climb through a window.

She was being silly, Samantha told herself. Nothing was out of place, and there was no one lurking anywhere. Her imagination really was working overtime.

CHAPTER 15

◆

WITH MARTA AND Carrie's help, Joey managed to pour Alicia into the front passenger seat of the minivan and buckle the seat belt about her. Fortunately for all of them, Alicia was no longer throwing up or raving hysterically as she'd done for the last hour. She sat placidly if a bit woozily in her seat and stared into the night.

Joey gave Marta the keys to the resort van. "You take the group back to Bear Run. Alicia and I need to have a little private chat."

"Good luck," Teri Schaefer said, rolling her eyes. "She's soused."

Joey blanketed the little group with a warning frown. "Put a freeze on the smart remarks, ladies. You all helped Alicia tie one on, so cut her some slack. She doesn't need people poking fun at her about this."

The few murmurs in response were apologetic.

"Marta, if Pat asks why you all came home in the resort van, just tell him Alicia couldn't find the keys to the minivan. And Ben, too, if you see him. Especially Ben."

Marta nodded. "Do not worry, Joey. My lips are sewn shut. I wouldn't worry about the men. They probably think we merely drink lemonade and talk about sex. Men think wild parties are strictly a male tradition."

"Not!" Carrie said with a giggle.

"Are you girls all right to drive home?"

"I am," Marta assured her. "I do drink lemonade."

Joey watched the resort van pull out of the parking lot. Then she climbed into the driver's seat and leaned her forehead against the cold steering wheel. The mother of all headaches throbbed inside her skull.

Alicia's quavery, tear-choked voice was not a comfort. "I'm really, really sorry, Joey."

In the dim glow of the minivan's dome light, Alicia gave her a helpless, apologetic look, and most of Joey's desire to scold evaporated.

"Are you okay?" she asked the miserable-looking bride.

"No," was the tearful answer.

"I didn't think so."

"I don't know what came over me."

Joey shook her head and grimaced. "In the toilet, Alicia?"

A tear slid down Alicia's cheek, following in the tracks of the outpouring that had come before.

"Oh damn. Don't cry again."

More tears.

"Alicia, the keys aren't important. For cripes' sake, don't worry about the keys." Joey turned the ignition, wanting nothing more than to get back to the cabin, pour Alicia into bed, and somehow have everything be back to normal in the morning. Alicia's hand groped for hers where it rested on her keys—her spare set of keys—in the ignition.

"Please, no. I can't go back there. I just can't. When . . . when I thought about getting in the car and going back to the resort, I just got this really awful feeling. And before I knew it, I was dropping the keys . . . the keys . . ."

"Yeah. Okay."

"I am sooooo sorry."

"Why can't you go back to the resort, Alicia?"

Alicia merely sobbed.

Joey turned off the engine. It was inevitable. She was going to be sucked into the role of confidante. It was one of a wedding consultant's jobs. Brides sought her advice on wedding gowns, cakes, bands, interfering parents, potentially difficult in-laws, obstreperous fiancés—the whole gamut of problems that can attend a wedding. Joey had always filled the role with professional aplomb. But for some reason, she felt inadequate and nervous about Alicia using her shoulder to cry on. Perhaps because Alicia was a personal friend. Or perhaps because Joey was more emotionally involved in Alicia's situation, and with Alicia's fiancé, than she should have been. A knot tightened in her stomach as Alicia buried her face in her hands and cried.

"Alicia, the liquor is doing this to you. You'll feel a lot better once it's out of your system."

Alicia didn't raise her head from her hands. She just shook it in denial.

Joey drooped back against the car seat, staring into the dark, waiting for Alicia's flood of misery to ease. If

Alicia didn't dry up sometime soon, they were going to need life rafts.

"Alicia, tell me what's wrong. Are you worried about that stupid poem on your pillow?"

The miserable girl shook her head.

"Is Irene giving you grief about something?"

"No," came the broken response.

"Your dad?"

Another negative shake of the head, but the tears had slowed from a fountain to a trickle. Joey reached over and massaged the tight muscles in Alicia's neck.

"It's Ben," Alicia choked out.

"What did he do?"

"Nothing. He's wonderful."

Joey sighed. "Yeah, that's worth crying about all right. You're about to marry Ben, and he's wonderful."

"But so is Pat," Alicia wailed.

Pat. Joey sighed, even though the dilemma didn't take her by surprise. She had hoped that Alicia's attention to Pat didn't mean what Joey thought it meant. But it did. She didn't know what to say.

"I love Ben," Alicia sobbed. "I really, really do. He's the anchor of my life. He makes me feel safe and loved. But Pat . . . Pat makes me feel . . . all melty inside, you know? He doesn't make me feel safe. In fact, he needs someone to save him. He doesn't know how to deal with investors, or how to promote, or anything, you know? But he's such a sweetie, and he's got guts, you know?"

Joey didn't know. "Alicia . . . you've got a bad case of the bridal jitters. Maybe you should just postpone the wedding until you get this straight in your mind."

"And disappoint everybody? No! What would I say

to Ben? What would I say to Pat? What would I say to Daddy and Nana? I'm acting like a twelve-year-old. One minute I think I'm making a mistake, and then I'm certain that I'm doing the right thing. And now some joker is trying to play games with my mind. Oh, Joey!" She gave Joey a pleading, teary-eyed look. "What should I do?"

Joey suffered a stab of panic. "Alicia, I can't tell you what to do."

"But you're always so calm, so together, so sensible. I'm not a bit sensible, and I never have been. Tell me how to be levelheaded and mature. Do you think I'm making a mistake marrying Ben? Do you think we're too different? Do you think it's possible to love two men at the same time, or do I just have an old-fashioned crush on Pat and it doesn't mean anything? Tell me!"

"Alicia! This is not a question of a dressmaker or florist, or how many tiers should be on the wedding cake! This is your life. I can't tell you what to do!"

"But Joey!" Alicia whimpered. "I can't see things clearly at all. And you're always so smart about things like this."

"Not so smart," Joey said. "You don't see me getting married to a nice man like Ben or even having a wonderful friend like Pat."

"Because you're busy building a business and doing things that are important."

"Catering parties and arranging other women's weddings! You think that's important? You think working twelve to fourteen hours a day, then coming home to an empty house is an exciting life?"

Alicia answered with an uncertain shrug.

Joey sighed. "Alicia, I'd been in business about a year when a casual friend of mine who was a Ph.D. candidate at Colorado University came to me for help with her wedding. She was marrying a construction worker whose highest level of education was a welder's certificate, or some such thing, from a community college. These people didn't seem to have anything in common. He liked football. She liked the opera. His friends were Jim Carrey fans. Her friends discussed Shakespeare. They were as mismatched as any couple could possibly be. Both sets of parents were against the marriage. The bride's mother asked me to talk some sense into the bride. Since I was the bride's friend, her mom thought maybe she would listen to me when she wouldn't listen to anyone else."

"Did you?"

"Sure. I was just like the parents and the friends. I thought I saw things more clearly than the bride and groom. I told her the marriage had less chance than a snowball in hell and that passion couldn't get them through the next forty years. Probably not even through a couple of years. She called me an interfering busybody and took her business elsewhere. Losing the business didn't hurt as much as losing a friend."

"But you were right."

"I was wrong. I was an interfering busybody, and an ignorant one at that. They're still very happily married, with a beautiful little daughter, and a baby on the way. He's going to college part-time. She's got a great job with a local publishing firm. She's still not speaking to me, but I get news from her mom every once in a while."

"Oh," Alicia said in a small voice.

"So you see, I butted into their lives with sensible advice, and if they'd taken it, they would have missed out on a wonderful marriage and family. So I don't give advice like that anymore. You never can tell if the sensible way is the right way. Only you know what's right for you. If you really love Ben, then marry him no matter how different you are. If you don't really love him, then don't marry him, no matter what people expect you to do. As for Pat, well, maybe you need to make up your mind about Ben before you think about Pat. You need to take some time to think. Explore your real feelings and needs. And you won't find any answers in a six-pack of beer, or whatever it was you were drinking in there. You need to step apart from all this wedding dither and do some serious thinking."

Alicia sank deeper into the passenger seat. "I don't feel so well."

"At this point, neither do I. Can we go back to the resort now?"

"You won't let me run off to Timbuktu?"

"I don't think we have enough gas to get there."

Alicia's weak laugh became a moan. "Wherever we're going we'd better hurry. And it better be someplace with a bathroom."

They made two roadside stops along the way, not an easy thing to do on a narrow mountain road in the dark of night. But it was stop or let Joey's minivan suffer the consequences of Alicia's queasy stomach. The miserable girl moaned apologies both times Joey had to help her lean out to toss the meager contents of her stomach onto the gravel shoulder.

Joey was almost glad she had Alicia's wretchedness
to deal with. It kept her from thinking about the stick-
ier problem——the problem that was really Alicia's, she
reminded herself, not hers. She was ashamed to admit
that in this case she longed to break her rule about not
giving personal advice. She could tell Alicia to consider
the great differences between Ben and herself, differences that seemed to have become more pronounced
by the day, but would she reacting in Alicia's best interest, or because she herself had an eye for the groom?
Joey didn't want to think she could be so self-serving,
but who knew what really lay in the heart? No doubt
she could easily convince herself that self-interest was
the furthest thing from her mind. Would it be true?

She just needed to keep her mouth shut and her
eyes off Ben Ramsay. Likely Alicia would end up marrying him, and that would be that.

When they arrived back at Bear Run, the hour was
well past midnight, but a light was on in the lodge. The
light seemed to be coming from the bar, and Joey
hoped it was the men still partying, safely out of the
way. Poor Alicia didn't need to cope with either Ben
or Pat in her current state of woozy misery.

In the dark cabin she roused Samantha from sleep.
Together they managed to get Alicia into the bathroom, washed, undressed, and dressed again in the
T-shirt and long underwear she'd been using as night-
wear. Somewhat revived by the cold water Joey had
splashed on her face, Alicia climbed the stairs to the loft
with just a little assistance. Joey preceded the others
through the door to Alicia's cubicle and, leery of
another unpleasant gift in Alicia's room, turned on

the light. Nothing more than normal clutter waited for her.

"Come on in," she told Alicia. "Everything's fine. Do you want a couple of aspirin or maybe some Alka-Seltzer?"

"I just want to go to sleep," Alicia groaned as she came through the door.

Samantha followed. "If I were you, I'd put an ice pack on your eyes. Look how swollen they are. They're only going to get worse when you lie down to go to sleep."

Alicia didn't answer. She was transfixed by something on the bed, though Joey could see nothing out of the ordinary. The bed was neatly made. The extra blanket lay folded at the foot, and Alicia's teddy bear sat against the pillow. But Alicia's eyes stared, wide and fearful. Her mouth became a thin, tight line in an ashy gray face.

"Alicia . . ."

The tight mouth opened to let a quavering wail escape, and the wail became a horrified scream.

A few hours in a bar with the guys could go a long way toward making a man feel better about the world. Sometimes. On this evening, the magic of manly bonding over a table littered with empty beer bottles didn't work. Or at least it hadn't worked yet. At one A.M., the evening was still young, Ben told himself. He had made some progress. He was learning to look past Pat Haines's sterling looks and too-perfect smile and recognize that an okay guy lurked behind the dazzling teeth. He'd caught up on news with his brother Tom, whom he saw only once or twice a year despite the fact that they lived only forty miles apart. And he'd managed to convince himself that he and Alicia were going to be reasonably happy together once they settled down to a normal life away from Pat Haines, Joey DeMato, vicious pranksters, and this damned ritzy ski resort that made him feel like a square peg in a world of round holes. They were adults who loved each other, and they could compromise. Alicia would stop hinting that he should quit work and be a rich woman's gigolo, and he could make an attempt to enjoy some of the things she enjoyed. He could get used to vacations in Europe and a ski trip here and there, and Alicia might learn to enjoy the Denver Broncos. After all, she had season tickets. How hard could it be for her to use them?

Conversation with Tom and Pat had slowed to a near stop. They were just as lost as Ben in their ruminations. As usual, Tom was in a blue funk about a female—Teri Schaefer this time. If there were such a thing as a Woman-of-the-Month Club, Tom would have been a charter member. Pat was likewise distracted. If the three of them had been talking instead of staring into their beers and pondering, Ben might not have heard the hint of sound that was little more than a very thin wail. His head was the first to come up, then Pat's. Ben pushed out of his chair so fast it fell backwards. Pat was right behind him as he headed out the door. Tom's confused "Huh? Where're you guys goin'?" trailed after them.

Ben was the first up the loft stairs. He found Alicia

with her head buried in Joey's shoulder, sobbing. Samantha looked on helplessly, obviously distressed. He suffered an eerie flash of déjà vu—it was the night before all over again. Yet everything seemed in order.

"What happened?"

Joey gave him a helpless look. "I don't know. She came in here and shrieked. Since then she hasn't said anything comprehensible."

Without raising her face, Alicia waved an arm in the general direction of the bed, then she went back to flooding Joey's shoulder. Ben looked at the bed—the neat counterpane, the plump pillow, the teddy bear. His eyes fastened on the teddy bear. He didn't remember Alicia bringing the stuffed animal with her.

"The bear?"

Alicia's sobs rose to a new level of distress, and for one traitorous moment, Ben found himself wishing she wasn't quite so histrionic in her reactions.

"Alicia, pull yourself together and tell me what has you so upset. There's nothing here that can't be dealt with."

It wasn't fair to compare Alicia's wild swings from hysteria to denial and back to hysteria with Joey's steady strength. After all, Joey didn't have a nutcase making her life miserable. All the same, Ben couldn't help but wish that some of Joey's composure might rub off on his fiancée.

"That's . . . that's my . . . my bear! I won it at a . . . a raffle." Alicia sobbed.

"Yes?"

"I gave it . . . gave it to . . . Jason Denny! B-before I . . . decided he was w-weird."

Ben's jaw clamped down hard. Things had suddenly gotten serious. Jason Denny, the stalker who'd obsessed on Alicia to the point of trying to kill her, was dead, drowned in the car from which Ben had pulled Alicia. Ben had seen him drown when he dove down to the car a second time to get the man out. The guy had croaked right before his eyes. He'd seen the body carted away and read accounts of the funeral. Jason Denny hadn't put that bear on Alicia's bed, but someone who was connected with Denny had.

"There's got to be more than one bear like this in the world," Ben said, picking up the stuffed toy—and things immediately got worse. Protruding from the bear's back was a pocket knife. He took it out and quickly palmed it, but not before an alert Joey saw. His eyes locked with hers, and she said nothing. Joey was a smart lady; she caught on fast. There was no sense in upsetting Alicia more than she already was.

Alicia once again flapped her hand toward the stuffed bear. "Jason's ghost! I'm being haunted. Jason's ghost put it there!"

"Not unless ghosts need to open windows to get in," Samantha said. "About an hour ago the dogs barked."

"Piggy knew there was someone here!" Tess and the corgis had joined the crowd in the loft. "I told you that she wasn't barking at a squirrel! Piggy's smart, and she knows what she's barking about!"

Samantha winced at the I-told-you-so look she got from Tess. "That's just about right. The dogs were making a racket and ran up to the loft. I checked it out and nothing seemed wrong. I did see the bear, but I just thought that Alicia had brought it with her. The window over there was open a bit. When I looked out, I didn't see anyone."

Ben went to the window, slid it open, and looked out. It would have been easy enough for someone to climb the protruding logs at the corner of the cabin. A flood of anger made him clench his jaw. This was no mere prankster. Someone wanted revenge on Alicia for her part in Jason Denny's death, someone who had been close enough to Denny to know that Alicia had given him that damned bear. A close friend? Relative? Lover? How far were they willing to go? Just an unpleasant scare or two? Or did they want an eye for an eye?

With guilty surprise he realized that he relished the challenge of solving this puzzle. In this situation he knew exactly what he was doing and had the confidence of long experience. The doubts and quandaries of the last week were shoved aside. He would protect Alicia. He would nab the lowlife responsible for this new threat. And then he could deal with the twists and turns of romance and marriage, a labyrinth that made detective work look like a straightforward walk in the park.

Up until a few months ago, Alicia had led a very ordinary life, if one could consider top billing in the society page, vacations in Europe, and a wardrobe full of designer clothing ordinary. Now she lay awake with her wedding just over a day away, and was she dreaming of romance and a rosy future? No. For the second time in just a few months she was trying to figure out who was out to get her, toying with her like a cat amusing itself with a mouse. As if that weren't trouble enough, her heart was confusing her with mixed messages about the man she was set to marry, and feelings for someone from her past were intruding on plans for her future.

Alicia didn't know if she was coming or going, frightened or angry. Her current state between drunk and hungover didn't help the situation. Emotions burned like raw nerve endings, reacting to every word, every silence, every thought that passed through her head. Not long ago she'd thought her life boring and humdrum. It had been her daily complaint. Now she wished for boring with all her heart. Being the romantic heroine of a drama wasn't all it was cracked up to be.

Tonight she slept in Joey's cubicle, in Joey's bed, with Joey's even breathing and warm presence to comfort her in the dark. Ben slept in his own bed, and Alicia's room was empty. No one would have thought it strange if Alicia had sought the comfort of sleeping with Ben tonight. Even Ben would have welcomed it, Alicia suspected.

A week ago she would have taken full advantage. Inexperienced though she was in sexual matters, she had itched to make love to Ben since the day they met. But not now. Now she had too many things to think about, too many doubts clouding her mind. Nothing was clear except a burning need to bring order to confusion and clarity to her tangled emotions. She had only one day to do that—one day before she made vows that meant forever. Many brides and grooms thought forever stretched only as far as convenient. But Alicia wanted more than that. She'd been so sure that Ben was the perfect choice for a husband. The Denver media had positively swooned at the romance of society's darling marrying the hero who had saved her life. Even her uncompromising father was so proud that Alicia had snagged what he termed a "real man." And Ben *was* the perfect choice for her. He was her life's anchor, her rock in an uncertain world. Even now, filled with doubts, she wasn't truly afraid of this vicious prankster who was seeking to frighten her. She had Ben to protect her, and no villain could get past Ben.

As her mind woozily revolved around her problems, a portion of the clarity Alicia sought clicked into place. Ben was a wonderful, courageous, unselfish man, and Alicia going into their marriage with uncertainties wasn't fair to him. Not fair at all. Therefore it was Alicia's duty to resolve her doubts before the wedding ceremony on Saturday. She owed it to Ben to be very, very certain, no matter what it took. And she owed it to herself as well.

Alicia knew just how she could explore her doubts and put them to rest. Ben might be a bit angry at first, but he would realize, when she explained, that she was being reasonable and cautious. She would attack an adult problem in an adult way, with Ben's best interests at heart. Instead of fleeing her problems, she would confront them, putting herself to the test in the most stringent manner she could think of. Hadn't Joey herself advised Alicia to get away from the confusion and meditate on her choices? And Joey's advice was always sensible.

With plans turning in her mind, Alicia finally drifted into sleep.

"She what?" Ben roared at Joey over the breakfast table.

Joey flinched at the sheer volume of Ben's indignation, not to mention the thunderous look on his face. "You heard me," she said somewhat pugnaciously.

"Of all the harebrained, idiotic, childish things to do. Why the hell did you let her go?"

"Why did *I* let her go? I'm not her jailer. Besides, she was very quiet. I didn't wake up. Neither, I remind you, did you, Sherlock Holmes!"

"I wasn't in the same bed with her!"

"Well, maybe you should have been!"

"What's that supposed to mean?"

At their feet beneath the kitchen table, Piggy growled and glared.

"You're upsetting the dog," Joey scolded.

"To hell with the damned dog. I'm pretty upset myself! What the hell was that remark supposed to mean?"

Joey took a sip of her coffee and tried to stay cool, but chilling out was tough. This week had been rough on the nerves, and she did feel a bit guilty about Alicia leaving without her knowing it. "What that means," she said with controlled calm, "is that for a man in love with a woman, you're not acting very loverlike. Last night you give poor Alicia a couple of perfunctory comforting squeezes and send her to bed with me, of all things."

"She's the one who insisted on sleeping in your room."

"Maybe if you'd made your room a little more inviting, she would have been in your bed, and then you could have stopped her. Alicia is going through some tough times. Maybe she needs your arms around her."

"Last night she didn't act as if she wanted my arms around her, Dear Abby. Not that our love life is your business."

"It's my business when you start stomping all over me because *you* weren't doing your job."

"My goddamned *job* was supposed to be over when Jason Denny died!"

Joey rocked back as the volume battered her ears. His voice literally roared with frustration as he half came out of his chair. Piggy barked and eyed the door.

"Sorry." He sat back down with an obvious effort at control, but he crumpled Alicia's note in his fist until Joey thought it might turn to powder. "This is getting to me. I can't believe she was stupid enough to do this. The morning after someone stabs a stuffed bear and puts it on her pillow—"

"You didn't show her the knife. She thought it was just the teddy bear, Ben."

"She was hysterical. I didn't want her to know how twisted this person really is. So she doesn't realize quite how serious it is. That's still no excuse to take off for a full-day back-country ski trip with Pat Haines."

Joey knew exactly why Alicia had taken off with Pat

Haines, and it was partly her fault. She was the idiot who had advised her to go off somewhere to explore her doubts and feelings. She wasn't going to tell Ben about her part in this, though, not in his present mood. She'd just as soon stick her head in a lion's cage.

"She's probably safer in the back country with Pat than she would be here at the resort," she said hopefully. "No one knows where they headed, and it's snowing, so even if he wanted to, the bad guy would have trouble tracking them. They'll be back in time for the rehearsal tonight, and tomorrow after the wedding you can cart Alicia off to somewhere the teddy bear ripper can't follow. It'll all be over."

Ben snorted unhappily. "It won't be over until this creep is found."

Joey's temper strained at its leash. She was incredibly irritated by the whole situation. Or perhaps she was simply upset by the thought that Ben would marry Alicia tomorrow. Whatever moronic fantasies were hatching in her subconscious would be squashed flatter than bugs on a windshield. The man who marched through her dreams every night would officially be someone else's husband. His smile would belong to Alicia. The lines that crinkled the corners of his eyes would crinkle only for Alicia. The mysterious little scar on his chin would be Alicia's property. The bad-tempered growl that was really a cover for worry and frustration, the short bark of a laugh when something funny caught him off guard, the sturdy, square hands, the glint that sometimes came into his dark brown eyes, the way he had of looking into instead of through a person—all that would belong to Alicia, who was off cavorting with another man she was silly enough to compare to Ben Ramsay. That really lit the burner under her temper.

So there was a definite edge to Joey's tone when she snapped, "Don't rag on me about letting Alicia go. And if you're going to find the creep, Sherlock, then find him today. Tomorrow you're getting married and you'll be too busy."

He smiled halfheartedly. "Sherlock?"

"You're a detective, aren't you? Go solve the mystery."

He shook his head ruefully. "When Alicia gets back, I'm going to throttle her."

Joey smiled sympathetically. "They can't have planned to go far. Drover's with them. He has four-inch legs."

"Maybe they took him along as a guard dog."

Joey laughed, but the laugh was feeble.

It was going to be a very long day.

CHAPTER 16

◆

"THIS IS HEAVEN! Absolute heaven!" Alicia tilted her face toward the white sky, reveling as big, puffy snowflakes landed on her face. "I love this!" she declared. "I love it all. The snow is beautiful. The mountains are majestic. The trees are stately. Even the cold—it makes you feel alive. I even love the burn in my arms and legs."

Pat twisted on his skis and gave her one of his devastating smiles. When she'd first met him she thought that knockout smile of his was a cultivated thing designed to charm women, but she'd been wrong. People could be put off by his good looks. Men thought he must be stuck on himself. Women suspected he was a professional heartbreaker. He was neither. Pat Haines was a genuine guy—down to earth, hardworking, smart, and fun-loving. A good friend.

"Do you need a rest?" he asked.

"No! The way I feel I could go on all day! The snow is great, and this time I got the wax on my skis just right. They stick when I want them to stick and slide when I want them to slide. And Drover hasn't tripped me once. He's really good at bounding through the snow. Just like a weasel! Who would have guessed that such a funny-looking dog could be so agile? He's really very entertaining. I'm glad he insisted on coming."

"Come on, then. We take the fork to the right. The one on the left goes into a valley where the avalanche danger is too great."

"Do you know I've never seen an avalanche?"

"Well, you don't want to see one here, not if you want to get back to the lodge in time for the rehearsal tonight."

They hit a good stride, Drover bounding along beside them. The air was fresh and cold and clean as Alicia sucked it into her lungs. Perfect. The day was perfect, and she refused to let disturbing thoughts darken such a perfect day. They started to climb, and the effort felt good.

"So there's no avalanches in this valley?"

"Not likely. The slopes aren't steep enough."

"Do you ever go with the avalanche patrol to set off slides above the ski area?"

"All the time. First light of day we look at the basins and set off anything that looks unstable. Especially this time of year when the snow has a lot of moisture and gets heavy."

"What fun. I'd love to go up with the patrol sometime."

"If you ever come back here, we'll do that."

That was a reminder that her life was somewhere else and with someone else. Alicia had been so engrossed in the day—the snow, the mountains, the wonderful effort of gliding along the trail—that she'd almost forgotten reality. It wasn't all that unusual a feat for her, Alicia admitted. Not that reality was a tough pill to swallow. In a couple of days she would be honeymooning in Jamaica, sunning herself on a beach with Ben Ramsay at her side. Then it would be back to Denver—or Evergreen, if she could persuade Ben to live in the house she wanted. Evergreen wasn't exactly in the high country, but it would be better than living in the city. Ben would go back to work beating the streets, or whatever cops did on a daily basis. And she would go back to her charity fund-raising and Junior League functions, and they would settle down to a life of married bliss. Maybe.

On their left the valley sloped gradually toward a half-frozen creek, and for a while they skied beside dancing little waterfalls that burst from pristine snowbanks, ice sculptures carved by the current, bubbling water that rushed below a veneer of translucent ice. The wind smelled of wet snow and fresh pine. Other than the quiet plash of the creek and sigh of the wind, the mountains were silent with a silence that was a presence rather than an absence. It filled the valley, settled around the trees, and filled Alicia's soul as well. She stopped, planted her poles in the snow, and looked around her in awe. "How could anyone not love this?"

"To each his own, I guess."

She ignored Pat's pragmatism. "You are so lucky to live up here and have all this day in and day out. How could anyone prefer to live in the dirty, noisy, crowded city instead of spending time here, where nature is clean and peaceful?"

Pat chuckled. "Making a living might have something to do with it."

"You're making a living. Not only that, you're building something you can be proud of."

"Maybe," he equivocated.

"Besides, Ben doesn't have to tie himself down to the drudgery of a day-to-day job. I don't know why he won't just quit the police force and leave Denver. I swear, sometimes he acts as if my money is poison."

Pat gave her an irritated look. "Alicia, you really don't understand men, do you?"

"What do you mean?"

"I think your experience with the real world is sort of limited."

"Oh?" Her tone was tart. Pat was beginning to sound just like Ben.

"Most men, good men—and I think Ben is a good man—don't like to sponge off a woman, even if the woman is a wife."

"Well, that's just silly. Married people share."

"Yes, but most time the sharing goes both ways. Besides, even up here in the mountains, surrounded by all this scenery and nature you're so wild about, most of us have to work our butts off to make a living."

"Is this going to be the standard lecture on how lucky I am, how spoiled I am, and how I can't understand anything because I just have way too much money?"

He grinned, then motioned with one arm. "Come

on, you lucky, spoiled, poor little rich girl. If you don't get moving, your muscles are going to stiffen up. And if that stupid dog doesn't stop chasing snowflakes, he's going to be so tired we'll have to carry him home."

They went on. The trail left the stream and climbed a long, gentle ridge. On either side of them the land fell away to valleys filled with dark evergreens. Tracks of rabbit, deer, elk, and the tiny footprints of squirrel dented the fresh snow, but they were quickly disappearing, obliterated by cottony white. Drover sniffed at all of them, eyes bright and face split in a huge corgi grin.

"To him all these scents must be like a menu," Pat observed with a smile. "A forest-sized menu."

"Joey says that corgis think the whole world is a menu. Though I'd like to see that little guy take down an elk."

"Maybe a squirrel."

"Uck. What a disgusting thought."

The snow was changing in quality, and Alicia's wax wasn't working as well as it had before. She had to work harder, but that was good, because hard exercise always cleared her mind. Coming up here had been an excellent idea, she mused. The little trek took her far away from whoever was playing dirty tricks on her, far away from the source of her confusion, far, far away where she could see the world clearly. Not that she had found the answer to her dilemma, but she did feel a lot better about it.

"You know, Pat," she said. "Bear Run could be a real moneymaker for you. You've got the good slopes, nice facilities, Aspen really close by, and the coziness of a smaller resort."

"You make it sound very easy," was his amused reply.

"Well, I didn't mean to imply it was easy, but how hard could it be?"

"I've got Aspen for competition, for one thing. A lot of people, especially well-heeled people, prefer flashy and famous to cozy. Then there's labor problems, maintenance problems, state inspections of everything from the kitchens to the chairlifts, weather problems, and a set of backers who really don't understand the ski industry and expect huge profits from day one."

"So it's a challenge," she asserted with a small pout. "Challenges are stimulating, aren't they?"

"Oh sure. Stimulating. Here's a good place to have lunch. That thicket over there is pretty sheltered. I'm hungry."

They were both hungry, and they ate the sandwiches Pat had prepared in silence, each saving a big crust for Drover, who looked downright scary with droolcicles hanging from his lips. But Alicia's mind continued to work.

"What you need," she pronounced with the air of mountaintop guru, "is a backer who understands the ski business and wants to hang in with the venture for the long run."

Pat laughed cynically. "While you're at it, find me the pot at the end of the rainbow."

"Don't talk as if it's impossible."

"Anything is possible. Bill Gates could discover a

sudden interest in skiing and decide to sink a ton of
money into an obscure little resort on Aspen's coat-
tails."

"You don't need someone with pockets as deep as
Gates's."

"Ted Turner would do, I suppose," Pat said face-
tiously.

"You are such an idiot. The answer to your problem
is obvious."

"Really?"

"Sure it is. Me. I have the money, the interest, and I
trust you. Of course, you'd have to let me have some say
in developing the resort. Otherwise it wouldn't be any
fun. I need some purpose to my life, you know? And I'd
love to be involved in making Bear Run a success."

A slow smile spread across his face, but then he
shook his head and pinched the bridge of his nose. "It's
a nice thought, Allie, but I don't think your dad would
ever go for it."

"Daddy doesn't have to go for it. I have plenty of
my own money from Mom's estate. It's just been sitting
in investments, growing and growing."

He shook his head. "Allie, last I heard you were getting married tomorrow."

"So?"

"So what would Ben think of you sinking a bunch
of money and time into Bear Run?"

She shrugged. "I don't know. Does it matter,
really?"

"Don't you think he should have some say?"

"This isn't the nineteenth century," she reminded
him tartly. "My husband doesn't control my money."

"No, but usually married people make major decisions like this one together. You'd just be asking for trouble, Allie."

"Don't be ridiculous. Ben isn't interested in my money."

His eyes narrowed. "And you don't think he would be interested in your pouring money into a joint venture with a former boyfriend?"

"You really are an idiot! I try to help you build your dream, and you make it sound as if I'm proposing something sleazy!"

"I don't know what exactly you're proposing. Do you?"

"You are *sooo* out in left field!" With a disgusted snort, she stuffed her trash into her fanny pack and got to her feet. "I came out here to ski! Are you coming?"

"Hold on, Allie. I know it's early, but I think we should head back. The snow is getting heavy and the wind is picking up."

"I'm not going back until I'm ready. And I'm not ready. You can go back if you want." Snapping the toes of her boots into the ski bindings, Alicia glided onto the trail without a backward glance. Drover shook off his coating of snow and bounded after her.

Muttering a curse under his breath, Pat followed. "Allie, wait up, dammit!"

She didn't, and he had a time catching up to her, because the steam of indignation fueled her every glide-step. When he did catch her, breaking new trail to come up beside her, Pat had a fair head of steam going himself.

"You might at least have mercy on the poor dog."

"He's doing okay."

"He's panting like a locomotive."

She stopped and made a face at him. "Drover's a good boy. I'll bet he never nipped at the hand that offered him a dog biscuit."

"Is that what you did back there? Hand me a nice little treat? What would I have to do to earn it?"

"I ought to slap your face, Pat Haines."

He backtracked. "Allie, you're acting crazy. What is this really about—this private little ski trip the day before your wedding? You leave your guests and groom behind so you and I can have this little tête-à-tête, then you make me a major business proposition, and you totally don't care what your husband thinks about it. What the hell is going on with you?"

Alicia didn't know how to answer, because she wasn't sure herself what was going on with her. Her idea about going off alone with Pat to explore her feelings just wasn't working out. He wasn't reacting as he was supposed to, and neither was she. Making decisions had never been Alicia's strong suit. She tried to make Pat understand, but the right words were hard to come by.

"I'm not married yet, Pat. Quit treating me as if I were someone else's property."

His answer brought little comfort. "Allie, it's only a few hours until tomorrow. If you're really going to marry the guy, then stop acting as though you're a single woman. Because you're not."

This was not going at all as Alicia had planned. She looked down her nose at him—a difficult feat with her nose mostly coated in melting snowflakes—and moved on. But the painful composure she had wrapped about herself disintegrated when she realized that she couldn't see the trail either ahead or behind. While they were arguing the sky had truly opened up and the wind had increased to a near gale. Pat touched her on the arm to get her attention. "I think we're going to get whacked by the weather."

Alicia suffered instant remorse. She'd let her thoughtlessness lead her into trouble. Worse, she had taken Pat Haines with her. Her emotions already on edge, she gave in to tears. "Oh, Pat, I'm sorry. I should have listened to you earlier. I can be such a brat."

He smiled. Now that he had to deal with the snow and the mountains instead of her tangled behavior, he seemed happier. "I should have dragged you out by the collar. You have always been able to make me leave my better judgment behind, Allie."

Not entirely, Alicia thought sourly. But her offer of money and whatever else went with it—she herself didn't honestly know—was neither here nor there. The problem of Ben and marriage and what to do with her future would be purely academic if she didn't have a future. Snowstorms had claimed the lives of more than one party of foolish skiers, hikers, and hunters in the Colorado mountains. Alicia had never considered herself foolish, at least as far as winter sports went, but she was apparently a fool in other arenas. Why not this one as well?

Pat took a length of rope from his pack and fastened them together, along with Drover, so they wouldn't be separated by the poor visibility. Then he shouted into

Alicia's ear to make himself heard above the wind. "I know a place we can shelter. It shouldn't be too far."

"But we can't see!"

He held up an object in his gloved hand. "I have a compass. I know where it is."

If she lived through this, Alicia thought, she was never going to forgive herself for putting Pat in danger. "I'm sorry," she said again, as if repeated apologies might wipe away the feeling of guilt.

He touched her cheek with a woolly thumb, and for a moment she thought he was going to say something. He didn't though, and in silence they labored forward through the rapidly accumulating snow, Drover plodding along behind them.

"Anything?" Ben asked his brother.

Tom made a rude noise.

"Nothing here either." Ben went over his notes while he and Tom drank hot coffee in the cabin kitchen. He had interrogated Samantha to pin down the exact time that the dogs had raised a ruckus and run to the loft. Then he had questioned every guest to ascertain where they had been at that time of night and who could vouch for them. Tom had done the same with the staff. After several hours' work, they weren't much closer to finding the person who was harassing Alicia.

"Too many people with no alibi," Tom complained.

"Yeah, well, that's to be expected that time of night—people in rooms sleeping alone, or sleeping beside someone else who was sleeping. But alibis aside, it's hard to imagine what kind of motive most of the guests would have. This has to do with Jason Denny. It has to be someone connected to him."

"Two of the maintenance staff—Harry Kramer and Joe Leeds—hired on just a couple of weeks ago. That makes them suspect. Joe claims he was in Basalt drinking, but he can't name anyone specific who can vouch for him. Harry lives alone over in Carbondale. He was watching TV, alone."

"As for the guests, I figure we can trust Todd and Gary."

Tom grinned. "If you can't trust a fellow cop, who can you trust?"

Ben answered with a dubious snort. "I suppose Richard and Irene are possible . . ."

"Alicia's own relatives?"

"They would have known about the teddy bear, and Irene, at least, would love to see Alicia scared out of marrying me."

"That harmless old lady?"

"Never underestimate the capabilities of a woman, young or old. Sue, Carrie, Marta, Teri, and Danielle were with Alicia, and Joey was on her way to pick them up. I couldn't pry out of her just exactly why."

"Now there's a woman whose capabilities I would never underestimate. Can't get her to even look my way, though."

Ben gave him the hairy eyeball. He didn't know quite why. Joey was a single, adult, available woman, and Tom had every right to be putting the moves on her. But Ben didn't like it.

Tom ignored him. Tom had been ignoring his big brother since they had learned to talk.

Ben looked down at his notes and continued. "Edward—he was at the bar with us, and I'm not quite sure when he left. Do you remember?"

"No."

"Well, we'll check him out along with your two maintenance guys. Unfortunately, we're not limited to people here at the lodge. There's more than one private cabin close enough that someone could get over here pretty easily on skis or snowshoes, even in the dark if they knew the country."

"Why don't these things ever work out cut and dried like they do in mystery novels?"

"Yeah. Sherlock Holmes." Ben smiled as he thought of Joey's gibes about old Sherlock, then he looked at the clock on the wall and sighed. He got up to pour himself another cup of coffee. "I sent that stupid poem to Denver with Samantha yesterday. She took it in to the PD. I'd appreciate it if you'd go back down the mountain and do a background check on our three unlikely suspects. Take the damned teddy bear with you and find out if you can get bears like that at any store in town or if this one's likely to be the very one Alicia gave Jason. You think it would be worthwhile to run prints on the pocketknife?"

"Doubt it. It's pretty damned small, isn't it?"

"Yeah. And I probably ruined anything getting it out of the bear. I was in such a hurry to hide it from Alicia that I wasn't thinking like a cop."

"You mean you're less than perfect?" Tom needled.

"Stow it, kid. I'm not in the mood."

"Okay, okay. There goes my ski vacation."

"It was going to be over tomorrow anyway."

"What'll you do for a best man?"

"Assuming my bride shows up, I think I can manage to get married without you."

"You think?"

"I think. And assuming I get married, while Alicia and I are in Jamaica, I'd feel better if I knew someone here was trying to find out who this joker is. I'm going to call the Pitkin County sheriff and talk to him about it, but I don't hold out a lot of hope that they're going to take a stupid poem and a stuffed bear very seriously."

"I'm on the case, bro."

"Then get going. If it keeps snowing like this, the road's going to be bad."

Joey tried to keep her mind on what she was doing as she checked the tables for the rehearsal dinner, but place settings, centerpieces, and sociable seating arrangements weren't sufficient to distract her from her worries. The bride was somewhere in the woods with an ex-boyfriend, doing heaven only knew what. The groom was harassing the guests, her staff, and the resort's staff trying to find the sicko poet teddy-bear slasher who had a grudge against Alicia. The staff was upset, the guests were confused, and she herself was halfway through a bottle of aspirin.

Joey moved Teri's place card next to Tom Ramsay's and separated Carrie from Edward by the distance of Sue and George—Carrie had not been getting along too well with Edward.

Why was she in such a tizzy, Joey asked herself? She'd survived problem weddings before. There was the one where the divorced parents had started throwing food at each another during the reception, and the one where the reception hall's sewer line broke an hour before the wedding party was scheduled to arrive. Then there was the wedding where three of the groom's former girlfriends had banded together to have a talk with the bride while she was in the church dressing room donning her wedding gown. That had turned out badly. Very badly indeed.

But Joey had survived it all with her composure intact, her mind in high gear, but her emotions not truly engaged. This time, she admitted, her emotions were wringing her out like a washrag. Ben was getting married in twenty-two hours and fourteen minutes. That was why she was upset. Ben Ramsay was getting married. And Joey DeMato was a fool. She and Ben had never so much as kissed. They rarely had a peaceable exchange. Trading insults and subtle digs was their specialty.

But some people were simply connected, Joey admitted. She and Ben had connected the minute she'd seen that rugged face in her car window, the first time she'd felt the impact of that off-center, sardonic smile. He'd felt the connection as well. Joey was convinced of it. Every time they were together—which had been way too often during the last week—they exerted a pull on each other as inevitable as gravity.

But tomorrow Ben Ramsay was getting married to the wrong woman, and every scruple and shred of good sense that Joey possessed forbade her from interposing her bossy, nosy self between Alicia and her intended. Those two needed to work out their lives for themselves.

"Damn!" She had unthinkingly damaged one of the flower arrangements with her clenched fist. Now she would have to hunt up another. Of course, this wouldn't be much of a rehearsal dinner—or a rehearsal, for that matter—if the bride didn't show up, so perhaps a missing flower arrangement wouldn't make all that much difference.

Just then her cell phone tweedled. A worried-sounding Samantha was calling from Aspen. "Hey, boss lady, have you heard the weather forecast?"

"I've been busy."

"Well, a major snowstorm is expected for the mountains this afternoon, tonight, and maybe forever, the way the weather people are talking."

"Forever?"

"Well, maybe not quite forever. But it's already snowing really hard here. Look out your window."

Joey did. The world outside was a virtual whiteout. "It *is* snowing! Damn!"

"Ditto. My feelings exactly. I still have the cake to pick up. It won't be ready until three. And I need to find some chafing dishes."

Joey sighed. "Sam, forget it. Hole up in a hotel tonight. I don't want you driving the road between Aspen and Bear Run in this storm. It's not worth it."

Samantha hesitated. "But . . . the groceries. The cake."

"Don't worry about the groceries. I'll improvise. It won't be the first time. You stay safe. Boss's orders."

"Well, okay. I'll admit I wasn't looking forward to turning the minivan into a snowplow."

Joey chuckled.

"Did Ben find out anything about the teddy bear ripper?" Samantha queried.

"That's the least of my problems. Alicia's off in the mountains cross-country skiing with Pat. I can only hope the storm doesn't catch them."

"Surely they can't have gone far, not with the rehearsal and dinner tonight."

"I don't think they intended to go far. They took Drover, and he isn't exactly a canine athlete."

"You know spring storms," Samantha said hopefully. "Sometimes they promise a lot of snow, then peter out in a couple of inches."

"Yes, and sometimes they promise two inches and deliver two feet," Joey said pessimistically.

She thanked Samantha for the warning and went in search of a television, which she found in the bar. Ben was in the bar also, and he looked as though he was having a bad day, too. On her way through the door she brushed by a barrel-shaped law officer on his way out.

"Consulting the local authorities?" she asked Ben.

"The sheriff's department. They're not real impressed by a guy who writes bad poetry and stabs teddy bears. They'll be glad to help when a real crime has been committed."

"You'd think they would consider Alicia's recent history."

"Around these parts they're used to high-profile celebs with entourages of stalkers and obnoxious fans.

Alicia isn't real high on their priority list. They think likely our man—or woman—is a prankster."

"We've got other problems. Samantha just called and said there's a major storm moving into this area. I came in here to find a weather forecast."

The Weather Channel confirmed Samantha's warning. Radar over the Colorado Rockies showed an ominous, solid green blanket of precipitation, and no one could make a firm prediction on just when the storm would move out.

"What else can go wrong?"

Ben sighed. "Don't ask."

Joey wished her bottle of aspirin weren't already half empty.

It's not easy playing Miss Marple when you have four legs and a wet nose. The image is all wrong. But I didn't let that stop me. I had a job to do, and by damn I was going to do it. When I discovered the evildoer and straightened out this tangled romantic mess, I intended to wave my success under Stanley's arrogant, pinched nose and tell him to leave me the hell alone. You'd think that when a person dies, the least she could expect is a little rest. I wasn't asking for a cushy cloud to lounge upon and a harp to play. A nice soft dog bed and a bottomless box of dog cookies would have done just fine at that point.

I was hot on the trail of success. If I could put my wet little nose on the victimized bear, then I could pin down the culprit for sure. The scents I'd detected the Night of the Pernicious Poem were fresh in my mind, and if I could suck in a good

*sniff of that teddy bear, I could do a comparison. I'm no
dummy. People used to think I was dumb because I was beautiful. Now they think I'm dumb because I'm a dog. They were
wrong in both cases.*

*So I searched for the poor stabbed bear. Tess and Marta
were out gallivanting in the snow and they'd left me locked in
the house. Really locked! I couldn't even open the latch on the
rear door—usually a snap. Actually, Tess had tried to seduce
me into going out with them. That kid is way too fond of exercise. I hid beneath the bed and eventually she gave up.*

*I started my search in the kitchen, which is the logical place
for a corgi to start any task. A kitchen is always the favorite
room in the house. Diligently I looked into every cupboard I
could get my nose into, which was basically everything below
counter level. There's hardly been a cupboard latch made that
can resist a determined corgi. I didn't find the bear, but I did
find graham crackers, saltines, Cheerios, a package of Oreos, a
loaf of cracked wheat bread, and some tasty granola. You can't
say the search wasn't at least a partial success. I thought of
how much Drover would have enjoyed this particular task.
The moron had gone off skiing with Alicia and Pat. He has
an obsession with going—just going. With Drover it doesn't
matter where as long as he goes. I think he would have enjoyed searching the kitchen much more than skiing, though.*

*Fortified by my little snack, I moved on to Pat's bedroom,
where I found nothing, and then Tess's. I knew I wouldn't find
anything in Tess's room, but I believe in being thorough. Next
I tackled the loft. Samantha had a Three Musketeers candy
bar in her suitcase. Tasty. But no bear. Joey's room was neat
enough to be a nun's. That woman really has to loosen up
and get a life. In Ben's room I struck gold. No bear, but I did
find the murder weapon, so to speak—the pocketknife that*

our villain had stuck into the poor bear's back. That was just as good.

Congratulating myself on being an ace detective, I took a good, long sniff of that knife. Ben's scent signature was there, and so was another, fainter scent that I recognized. It was one of the ones I'd detected the night of the poem, the one that I'd known hadn't belonged.

Bingo! I had the culprit. Or at least I had his smell, which to a dog is better than a set of fingerprints and a mug shot. Now I would just let my nose lead the way.

The afternoon was dismal, cold, and white as the wedding guests and the wedding party, without the bride, sat in the Grizzly Room, where the wedding itself was scheduled for the next afternoon. It was beginning to look as if there would be no rehearsal and no rehearsal dinner because there was no bride. They were a dejected, uneasy bunch. Even Piggy, who had been allowed in the lodge on the head housekeeper's reluctant probation, was quiet. The dog had greeted each guest in turn with a friendliness unusual for her. Joey thought she must be missing her buddy Drover. Now she sat staring, unmoving, and looking quite unhappy.

"I don't like the way that dog is staring at us," Edward complained. "She looks as though she wants a piece of someone."

"Piggy always looks disgruntled," Joey explained. "Don't pay her any mind."

"She doesn't look disgruntled," Edward said uneasily. "She looks downright hostile."

"I wouldn't worry about it," Ben said. "The highest she can reach is someone's shins. There are no vital organs there."

Edward shot him an impatient look. "Very funny."

"Who cares what the dog is up to?" Irene snapped. "My granddaughter should be back by now, and look outside! It's a blizzard! I think we should call out the ski patrol or whomever one calls in this situation."

"Search and Rescue won't go out until the snow abates," Marta told her.

"And no one knows when the snow's going to stop," Joey said disconsolately.

"Pat is very wise to the way of the mountains," Marta said. "When he realized the snow was going to be so heavy, he would have headed for the cabin that is about five miles from here. It is an abandoned cabin that the Forest Service maintains as an emergency shelter. Since so many of our guests ski in the area, we stock it with bedrolls and blankets."

"Food?" Ben said hopefully.

"A few canned goods. If the storm lasts more than a couple of days, not enough. We were about to restock it, but we haven't gotten around to it."

He sighed. "Can you show me on the map where the cabin is?"

Marta was able to pinpoint the cabin exactly on a topographic map she brought out from Pat's office.

"It looks like someone could take a snowmobile up this valley and get to the cabin pretty easily." Ben traced the route on the map with one finger.

"That someone would have to know how to handle a snowmobile," Teri said dubiously.

"I used to be a motorcycle cop," Ben said. "It's not that different. If I could haul food and first aid supplies to the cabin, enough to last for a few days, it might make all the difference."

"Assuming they're even at the cabin," Edward said thoughtfully.

Irene complained, "Alicia has never been so foolish. I don't know what's gotten into her."

"She's never done anything like this," Richard said.

Joey knew exactly what had gotten into Alicia, but she wasn't going to spill the beans, even if she could talk. Her throat positively clenched at the thought of Ben buzzing up a snow-clogged valley on a snowmobile.

"You should not go alone, Ben," Marta told him.

He should not go at all, Joey added silently.

Everyone looked expectantly in Marta's direction, as if her German accent and ski instructor status made her the maven of all winter sports. She gathered in their glances and shook her head. "I ski. Ski only. I have never learned the snowmobile. Best I stay here talking to Search and Rescue and try to organize that effort if it becomes necessary."

Suddenly, Joey jumped up. She glared over her shoulder at Piggy, whose cold, wet nose had poked insolently into the bare-skinned gap between her sweater and jeans.

"You know how to handle a snowmobile?" George asked her, obviously surprised.

Joey found every eye upon her. They all thought she had just volunteered herself. Piggy looked especially satisfied with what her cold nose had wrought.

For a moment Joey searched for a way out, then she realized that she didn't need out. "As a matter of fact," she told them, "I used to ride a snowmobile quite a lot when I was a teenager. We lived in Bailey, and sometimes we couldn't get to school any other way."

Ben didn't look happy. "I don't know . . ."

"I'll bet I can outride you, Mr. Ex–Motorcycle Cop."

"Ice-skating, snowmobiling—you're just a regular winter sportsman, aren't you?"

"That was before I had to work for a living. I'm not sure we can find that cabin with the snow coming down like it is, though."

Ben grinned. "I have a GPS. I'll just plug in the co-ordinates from the map."

Edward smiled dryly. "Ain't technology great."

An hour later, Joey straddled one of the resort's fleet of snowmobiles. Together she and Ben were packing food, first aid, a small propane stove, sleeping bags, a two-way radio, and a small arctic dome tent. The supplies were enough to last four people several days, and if the storm hadn't abated by then, they would try to make it out riding two to a machine. The snow was blinding, in spite of Joey's goggles, and the wind cut like a knife. As much as she wanted to aid Pat and Alicia, Joey wondered if this was a good idea.

"Ready?" Ben asked, glancing over from his machine. "You don't have to go, you know. In fact, I sort of wish you wouldn't." His face was covered by a mask, as was hers, but Joey could read everything in his eyes. Suddenly she was sure—absolutely rock-solid sure, in spite of the improbability—that Ben Ramsay loved her. The knowledge drove the cold from her bones.

"I wouldn't dream of letting you be the only hero," she told him. "We'd never hear the end of it."

He seemed to look straight into the deepest part of her. "We won't take any risks."

"Of course not."

He nodded, gave her a thumbs-up, and gunned his throttle. "Let's go."

Tess stood with Marta, watching the snowmobile lights reflect eerily from the falling flakes and listening to the whine of their engines. She looked up at the German woman who held her hand. "This is a good thing," she said confidently.

"I hope so," Marta said.

"Don't worry," Tess assured her. "Everything will be all right. My mom told me so."

CHAPTER 17

◆

ALICIA STARED OUT the window of the little cabin, even though she couldn't see a thing. Wet snow stuck to the dirty panes in a solid curtain. But perhaps if she stared hard enough, willed it strongly enough, the snow would stop and the sun would come out. Or perhaps it would be the moon. The solid white whirling about the cabin gave her little clue about the time of day, and to tell the truth, she didn't much care. She just wanted it to stop.

"Don't worry," Pat said from where he sat on a sleeping bag. "We'll be fine. It's not as if we're out in the elements."

"I know." Her answer was half sulky. This was certainly not how things were supposed to turn out. She had planned a pleasant day's outing to get her mind straight, to explore her feelings for Pat and her jitters about getting married. Now thoughts of her wedding, of Ben, of marriage itself seemed somehow irrelevant. She was scared right down to her bones. In spite of Pat's attempt at a cheerful tone, she knew very well that every year or two some fool wandered into the mountains at the wrong time and ended up a frozen corpse by the time Search and Rescue dug him out.

The old cabin to which Pat had led them wasn't much. One eight-foot-by-ten-foot room was the entire floor plan. The log walls were adequately chinked to keep out the snow, however. The floor was lumber, smoothed by years of use—first by the miner who built the structure years ago, and subsequently by hikers and skiers who'd made use of its shelter. Rough shelves held scant canned goods—and fortunately a can opener—that the resort kept here as well as six sleeping bags that any Cub Scout would have rejected. In the small, sooty fireplace, Pat had built a fire, welcome warmth indeed, but the badly designed chimney allowed as much smoke into the room as up the flue. A meager pile of dry wood was stacked beside the hearth, enough to provide heat—and smoke—for maybe half the night if they were very sparing. Then the only source of heat would be the old kerosene lantern that hung from a nail in one wall.

"You want some beans?" Pat asked.

Lovely, Alicia thought. She should be dining on the chicken marsala that Joey had planned for the rehearsal dinner, but now her dinner would be a can of beans—and she should be grateful to get it.

"I could let Drover have them," Pat suggested when she didn't answer.

"I'll share with Drover," she grudgingly conceded.

"I've already shared with Drover. Who could resist that face?"

"I wonder how roast corgi tastes."

"Poor Drover!"

Hearing his name in the conversation, Drover looked inquiringly from Alicia to Pat and then back to Alicia.

"Don't worry, little boy," she told him. "I can't see anyone being that desperate." She dropped down next to Pat on the sleeping bag and dipped a rusty tin spoon into beans heated over the fire. "This isn't so bad," she said, trying to match Pat's brave cheerfulness. "I could live on this. How many cans do we have?"

Pat looked up to the shelf. "Five."

"Oh. Well, I wanted to lose some weight, anyway."

Pat chuckled.

Alicia supposed that laughing in the face of danger was the manly thing to do. But she was not a man, and she wasn't feeling brave. In fact she was miserably afraid. And as if that weren't enough, guilt ate at her conscience. All her life she'd done as she pleased without giving a second thought to the possible consequences. Today was just another example. She had finagled Pat into taking her skiing when she should have been glued to Ben's side—the very day before her wedding, of all times! And when Pat had shown good sense and wanted to turn back, she'd stubbornly and petulantly insisted on continuing—all because she wanted what she wanted and to hell with listening to anybody else.

"You know, Pat, I'm really sorry about getting us into this mess."

His eyes smiled at her. "You didn't get us into this, Allie. It's my fault. I never should have let us leave this morning without calling the National Weather Service first, and when I realized the snow was getting heavy, I should have insisted we turn around."

"I was being a brat."

"And I was letting distractions get in the way of my judgment."

She flagellated herself for another moment, then wondered what he meant by distractions. "What distractions?"

He grinned. "Fishing for compliments?"

"No, really. What distractions?"

"Allie girl, don't tell me that you really don't know how you knock my feet clean out from under me."

For a moment she forgot their grim situation. "I do?"

"Don't be coy. You know that you do."

Her lips twitched in a flirty little smile. "Well, I suspected there was some interest there. You've been eager enough to cut me out of the crowd. But you never really said anything."

"Heaven help me, woman! You came up here to get married, and not, I might add, to me!"

She acknowledged his point with a little shrug. "That's true." Right then honesty seemed important. Playing games wasn't a good idea when the future might be narrowing down to a few precious days. "Do you know why I wanted to go skiing today?"

"You're trying to drive poor Ben crazy?"

"No! Way off. I would never want to hurt Ben."

Pat rolled his eyes, and Alicia realized she'd gone wrong there as well. Had she really thought that Ben wouldn't care anything about her prancing off with Pat? That very moment he was no doubt tearing his hair out with worry, poor man. She'd driven him crazy like this ever since they'd met. She really didn't deserve such a wonderful man.

"Okay," she conceded. "I've been rude to Ben. I confess that I'm childish, spoiled, selfish, and thoughtless."

"You're also bright, generous, and good-hearted."

"I am?"

"Absolutely."

She savored the compliment, and then confessed. "I wanted to ski with you today because I thought maybe that I loved you instead of Ben, and I had to find out for sure before I got married tomorrow."

Pat was silent for a moment. When he spoke, his words were cautious. "We didn't have to go skiing to talk about this, Allie."

She shrugged. "Well, I wanted to go skiing, too."

His lips twitched upward. "You *are* a brat. Did you make up your mind?" he asked in a seemingly offhand voice.

"Maybe," she teased, and then immediately regretted it. This wasn't the time for teasing. "No, I take the maybe back. I do love you, Pat Haines. My heart isn't shilly-shallying anymore. I know exactly where it is. This storm made it easy for me to decide, strangely enough. When you look death in the face, suddenly you know what's important in your life. I don't want to die lying to myself and playing games with you. I do love you. I've loved you since you worked at Vail."

A muscle twitched in his jaw. "You sure about this?"

"Oh yes. I'm very sure—for a change."

"I suppose you know that I've loved you a long time, Allie. You were an unattainable dream, the highest thing on my wish list." He grinned wryly. "Like winning the lottery. Nice to think about, but will never happen."

She touched his hand. "Too bad we're having this discussion too late. My fault again. I find my deepest feelings while assuring that we both end up human ice cubes."

He shook his head. "We'll be fine, Allie."

"I don't want false reassurance, Pat. I want honesty. What if this is one of those long, bad spring storms? What if no one finds us here? What if we die?

He just looked at her, his expression a mystery.

"Really, Pat. I can take it. You don't have to tiptoe around the truth."

His eyes were clear as blue diamonds, and they seemed to drill into her soul. "Listen to me, Allie. And listen well. You're not going to die in this storm, and neither am I. And when we don't die, when we have to face tomorrow and tomorrows after that, are you going to still know where your heart is?"

"Oh yes. Absolutely." Without a second thought Alicia moved into Pat's arms. "You are the right man for me."

Pat's arms closing about her filled Alicia with the most profound peace she'd ever felt in her life. She lifted her eyes to his and drank in the steady affection she saw there. This was a man, she realized, who would love her no matter what. He loved her now, when she'd been rude and foolish and careless. And he

would love her always. She didn't have to earn his
love. His devotion was hers whether she deserved it
or not.

"Do you know what I want?" she whispered softly.

"The same thing I want, I hope."

She smiled flirtatiously. "And what would that be?"

"You are such a brat," Pat said with a grin, but he
was busy with the fastenings of her jacket.

She helped him peel off her jacket, then helped him
again with her sweater, cotton turtleneck, and then her
thermal undershirt. The pile of discarded clothing
grew into a convenient mattress, and two sleeping bags
zipped together made a handy bed. Outside, the snow
continued to fall. The hidden sun sank toward the
horizon. Inside, the fire burned low. But Alicia and Pat
found inventive ways to create heat of their own.

Riding a snowmobile, unlike ice-skating, was apparently a skill that didn't survive the test of time. Or
maybe the problem was that Bear Run's snowmobiles
had much more horsepower than the machines Joey
had ridden as a teenager. The one she rode seemed eager to jump out from beneath her and plow through
the woods without its rider. Joey's goggles needed
windshield wipers, and the snow was a lot bumpier
than it looked. To make matters worse, Ben liked to go
fast. Keeping his lights in sight was all Joey could do,
though occasionally he did stop to make sure she was
keeping up. Next time he tweaked her about her
"speed demon" habits on the highway, she was going
to remind him of his burning tracks in the snow.

The third time Ben had to stop, he shouted back at her over the wind. "You okay?"

Joey wasn't about to admit that her snowbuzzing skills weren't all that she'd boasted they were. "I'm fine. Let's go."

"The GPS shows the cabin two miles in that direction." He pointed in a direction diagonal to the trail. "But the valley winds a bit. I'd estimate maybe three and a half more miles up the trail."

"As if we can see the trail," Joey muttered under her breath. She sent up a brief prayer that Pat and Alicia were at the cabin. If they weren't, no one would find them in this blizzard—not until the snow cleared, and who knew when that would be? Night was less than an hour away, and cold as it seemed now, the temperature would soon plummet.

"Let's go," she said.

"I'll try to take it easier."

He did, but Joey still had problems keeping up. She wanted to get off and kick her machine. It squirreled around on the snow, refusing to track a straight line—or maybe she just didn't have the knack of steering on a surface where all the holes and bumps were hidden by a cushy-looking foot of white. There were no shadows to show topography; everything was white, white, and more white. Sometimes she couldn't tell land from sky. When she gunned the throttle, the snowmobile jumped alarmingly. The brakes grabbed on the wet snow or sometimes didn't grab at all. Joey tried valiantly to keep up, afraid to lose sight of Ben's lights, but her luck ran out when she turned too quickly to avoid a nearly hidden stump. She landed upside down in a snowbank. The machine ended up becoming intimate with a tree.

Ben had been paying more attention to her situation than Joey thought, because he got to her while her backside still hung out of the snowdrift. "Are you hurt?" he demanded anxiously.

"No," she gasped. With his help, she managed to extricate herself. "With the number of layers I have covering me, I would have had to crash into concrete to do any damage."

Joey wasn't wearing enough layers, however, to protect her from the lightning bolt reaction that sizzled through her when Ben brushed the snow from her clothing. Such heat shouldn't have been possible standing in the middle of a blizzard.

"Uh . . . that's okay, Ben. Thanks. I'm fine."

He took her chin between thumb and index finger, tilting up her face for his scrutiny. "You scared the hell out of me," he told her.

"Me too," she admitted sheepishly. But what really scared her had nothing to do with the snowmobile and everything to do with a riot of feeling for Ben Ramsay. Love was a lot like a disease: At first it gave just a hint that you might be infected, a daydream here, a heart palpitation there. Then it hit you like a ton of bricks—fever, loss of reasoning power, and serious cramps of the heart. The infection had been building ever since Joey was stopped along the Boulder Turnpike by a smart-mouth cop, and now she was at the terminal stage. Someone, she thought desperately, should work on a vaccine.

"I'm afraid your machine is going on the injured re-serve list."

Joey wrenched her attention from Ben and focused on her poor, misbehaving steed. It was wrapped around a tree, and one ski dangled like a pathetically broken leg. If it had been a horse, someone would be getting out a gun. "What do we do now?" she asked.

"Double up. My machine can carry both of us plus the supplies, but it's going to be slow going."

Once they'd transferred the packs, only a very little space was left for Joey to straddle the seat behind Ben. Very glad that she wasn't driving, Joey scrunched as close to Ben as their heavy clothing allowed, arms clutching his waist and cheek plastered against the back of his jacket.

"Why aren't we moving?" she mumbled into nylon-covered goose down.

"I'm entering these coordinates into the GPS so we can find your snowmobile again."

On they went, slowly, the machine groaning under the twin burdens of too much weight and too much snow. Night crept in on them, making the snowfall seem even heavier. Oddly enough, Joey found herself perfectly happy to be exactly where she was, despite cold, snow, the oncoming darkness, and a certain degree of peril. She enjoyed the feel of Ben in the circle of her arms. In what other situation could she warm her cheek against his body and tuck her thighs so tightly against his?

Joey silently laughed at herself for turning a perfectly innocent snowmobile ride into high sensual drama, but she had to take what she could get. Once this crisis was over and life returned to normal, she might not see him again. And if she did encounter him, he would be protected from her mad advances by a gold band around his finger.

Wouldn't you know it? Joey grumped silently. She was the one who didn't want a man, didn't need a man, and proudly declared her independence to the world. Love and marriage were gambles not worth the risk, at least not for her. She was too smart, too savvy, too busy, and immune from such silliness as romance.

And look at her now, head over heels for an unavailable man, reduced to milking thrills from riding double with him on a snowmobile! If the situation weren't so stinking pathetic, it might be funny. From the moment Ben had first stuck his face in her car window, Joey had known he was big trouble. She'd traded tart rejoinders when what she really wanted were smiles, dueled with facile little insults when she longed to shut up and touch him, make love to him . . .

Enough of that! Joey warned herself. Even if Ben was torturing himself with similar feelings, nothing would come of it. They weren't the sort of people who could yank themselves off the established path of their lives to take such an unexpected detour. And neither of them would hurt Alicia for the world. Ben did love Alicia, Joey mused, wondering that she found no resentment in the thought. And Joey loved her, too.

"This seems farther than three and a half miles!" she shouted above the labored whine of the engine.

"Another half mile!" he bellowed back at her.

And then the world seemed to collapse. The machine dropped from beneath them as the unstable snow at the edge of the trail gave way. They rolled downhill—and rolled and rolled and rolled. They finally came to rest at the bottom of the little valley, Joey plastered into a snowbank, Ben sprawled on top of her, and the machine ten feet away.

For a moment Joey just lay there, waiting for the world to stop spinning. When it did, she croaked to the heap on top of her, "Are you alive?"

"I think so," Ben groaned. "Are you okay?"

"Nothing hurts, so I guess I survived."

They didn't move. He looked down at her, his eyes searching. She looked up at him, wondering that she could be so calm, so downright content to lie there with him pressing her down into the snow, stranded in the middle of a blizzard with their transportation lying dead ten feet away. Their precarious situation didn't make a dent in her illogical serenity.

"This is goddamned impossible," he growled.

"What's impossible?"

"Not kissing you."

He slanted his mouth across hers in a kiss that began in tentative exploration and ended in thorough occupation. Like a man feasting after a long famine, Ben devoured her with lips and tongue. His hand cupped her face, warmly caressing, cherishing as he held her, a willing captive. Their already intimate position became more intimate still as he shifted. The press of his thigh between her legs ignited an urgency in Joey that drowned her last shred of common sense. The world started to spin in a manner that had nothing to do with falling down the ravine and everything to do with the man blanketing her with his body.

"What are we doing?" Joey breathed when they paused for air.

"Kissing." Ben's lips moved against her neck. "I've wanted to kiss you ever since I watched you unfold yourself from that Triumph."

How could she feel so warm when she should be so cold? How could she be lying in the snow kissing this man when a blizzard raged around them and they were in truly desperate straits? Well, maybe not desperate, but certainly worrisome.

His mouth moved again to her lips, and Joey gave herself over to the pleasure of the kiss without searching for logic or good sense. Some things just hapened, and you had to let them. Some moments in life had nothing to do with the real world, but were simply to be accepted as a gift. Kissing Ben Ramsay was such a gift. He invaded her every sense. He bathed her in the warmth of his lips and the pleasant scrape of his cheek against hers. His heartbeat thundered in her ears even through the many layers of their clothing—or was it her heart so desperately drumming? She inhaled his scent—wet wool, warm male, and strong soap—a smell she decided instantly that she loved. Joey felt that nothing could make her happier than dissolving into Ben completely, like the snowflakes lighting on his cheeks and thawing slowly, absorbing his heat, melting to warm liquid and soaking into his skin until they were a part of him.

Except that the snowflakes weren't melting into

Ben, they were melting on him, turning into icy water and dripping down upon Joey—nothing very sensual about that! That icy dripping and other invaders from the real world—the wind, the dark, and the insidious creeping cold—finally brought them back from where they had gone. The chill of unwelcome reality was far colder than a mere Colorado blizzard. Ben's face hovered above hers as they looked at each other.

"Joey, you know . . ." he began, then faltered. "I . . . damn!"

"I know," she assured him, not sure exactly what she knew. But she knew, all the same. She knew much too much. Ben would never jilt Alicia. Alicia was too innocent, vulnerable, and downright sweet. And Joey didn't want Alicia hurt any more than Ben did.

Did Alicia really want Ben, though? Did even Alicia know the answer to that question?

It didn't matter. Ben and Joey had met at the wrong time. Worse things happened in the world. Far worse. They would be adult and learn to live with it.

He rolled off her, sat up, and sighed. "We've got to talk about this later."

They wouldn't, Joey knew, but she didn't contradict him.

Ben sighed, looked around to a view of nothing but snow, and seemed to gather himself together. Joey tried to do the same.

"I dropped the GPS on the roll down," he told her. "Got to find it."

After a bit of searching along the path they had scraped down the side of the ravine, they found the little handheld GPS. That was the good news. The bad news was that it no longer worked. Their guiding star had just winked out. The radio that had been topmost in the saddle pack on the snowmobile was also out of commission, not surprising after being rolled down a hill. Just as a matter of form, Ben righted the snowmobile and examined it for damage. For a few moments they entertained hope that it might yet carry them farther if they could get it back up to the trail, for though one ski was bent, nothing seemed broken. The snowmobile was having nothing further of their abuse, however; it refused to start.

Their situation was more inconvenient than desperate, however. They had food, a propane stove, and the arctic dome tent. They would be relatively safe and warm once they had erected their shelter—safer and warmer, no doubt, than poor Pat and Alicia, even if the pair had made it to the Forest Service cabin.

Staying close together for safety's sake, they searched out a place relatively sheltered from the wind. Ben was cursing the tent assembly instructions when a familiar yet very out-of-place sound carried to them on the wind.

"What the hell?" was Ben's comment.

"A dog barking! I'll bet it's Drover!"

The looked at each other and smiled.

"Not as good as GPS," Ben commented, "but it'll do." He grabbed the larger of the packs. "This way. Keep barking, dog. Keep barking."

Trust a corgi to have a voice that could carry above a shrieking storm.

◆

The night dragged slowly by for those gathered in the Big Cabin. Alicia's father morosely related stories of his little girl's childhood, acting like a man attending his daughter's wake. Irene kept silent, but her red eyes left no doubt that she'd been weeping in private. At about ten, Richard retired to the lodge bar and Irene to her bed with a sleeping pill.

"Poor Mr. Somers," Teri noted. "He's even ignored those investor friends of his today. The way he's acting, you'd think Alicia was dead for sure."

"It's not for sure," Carrie said.

"It's not for sure at all." Sue, sitting on the window seat with George, gave them all a stern look, then darted her eyes toward Tess, who was curled on the sofa with Piggy beside her. "Little ears," Sue reminded her friends.

"They're going to be fine," Teri said with a show of optimism. "I'll bet Pat knows these mountains like the back of his hand."

"Sure he does," Sue seconded.

George stared out the window. "I should have gone with Ben. I knew I should have gone."

His wife snorted. "George, you've never been on a snowmobile."

"Still, I should have gone."

"Just because you're a man doesn't automatically qualify you for Search and Rescue, dear. Besides, they're going to be fine."

Carrie and Edward sat by the fireplace, passing the time with a game of cutthroat Monopoly. After putting a hotel on Park Place, Edward glanced up. "Wasn't it just last fall that two hunters lost their way in a storm over by—where was it?—someplace near Fairplay? They were ice cubes by the time Search and Rescue found them. Grim. Really grim."

"Edward!" Carrie chided. "You are such a moron!"

"A moron who owns just about every asset on the board."

"Get real! And be a little more considerate!" She jerked her head toward Tess.

"Don't worry about me," Tess assured them in a serene voice. "I know everything is all right."

"I suppose your mother told you?" Edward said with a sneer.

Tess hadn't hesitated to tell all of them about her mom's ghostly interest. They could take comfort, she assured them, that someone in Heaven was looking in on the case.

"That kid is spooky," Edward said under his breath to Carrie. "And her dog is just as bad. I wish someone would lock up that mutt. It's got a weird look in its eye."

"Piggy isn't my dog," Tess said calmly. "She's her own dog."

"Sharp little ears," Carrie warned Edward. "So stop with the spooky business."

A knock on the cabin door interrupted the blossoming tiff. Teri opened the door to what looked like an Eskimo. When the newcomer walked in and shed parka and mukluks, he was revealed as the round-faced, red-cheeked minister who was to perform the wedding ceremony.

"Reverend Thomas!" Carrie greeted him. "We were so worried about you. You were supposed to be here by five! Did you drive up from Denver?"

"No, no. Lucky for me, my wife and I decided to spend a few days visiting Aspen before the ceremony tomorrow, so we were up here when the storm broke. Good thing. I had trouble getting here even from Aspen. I started right after lunch and it's taken me until now to get here. What time is it?" he asked, glancing down at his watch. "Almost eleven. Dear me. Good thing the wife stayed at the motel. She hates driving on icy roads. I always say if God's going to call you home, He's going to call you home no matter what. Anyway, the lady at the lodge—Miss Stein was her name, I think—said most everyone was up here. So here I am."

"Well, come in and get warm," Teri offered. "Hot coffee?"

"Don't mind if I do. Glad I got here. Wouldn't want to disappoint the bride and groom tomorrow. Sorry about not showing up for the scheduled rehearsal, but perhaps we can do that tomorrow morning. I'm so glad I managed to get here. I've known Alicia since she was five years old. Watched her grow up. Darling girl." He looked around. "Already in bed, is she?"

Edward snorted. "You might have saved yourself a trip, Reverend. It looks as if there's not going to be a wedding tomorrow."

"What?" the minister cried. "What happened?"

"Quit being such a pessimist," Carrie snapped. "Everything might well be fine by morning."

"What's this? Don't tell me Alicia and her beau have quarreled at this eleventh hour."

"Worse," Sue told him with a sigh.

They explained, and at the end of the story the

reverend looked very grim indeed. "Poor Alicia. Poor child. And the others as well. We must pray for them. Perhaps you good friends of the bride and groom would like me to pray with you."

"You don't have to worry," Tess piped up. "They're going to be okay."

The minister turned a compassionate eye upon her. "Of course they'll be all right, my dear. But it's never a bad idea to enlist God as a backup."

Just then the door opened and Marta blew into the room on a gust of snow and cold air. A smile split her face. "They're all just fine at the Forest Service cabin. I got a radio call."

"They waited long enough!" George complained.

"They just now got the radio fixed. It got zapped when Ben crashed his snowmobile. Or something like that—the transmission was really bad. But they're all fine, and whenever the snow lets up, we'll go in and get them."

"Heaven be praised!" Reverend Thomas cried.

"Told ya," Tess said.

Everyone talked at once: "Super!" "I knew it!" "Guess there'll be a wedding after all!"

Sue announced, "This calls for a celebration! Do you drink wine, Reverend Thomas? There's a great merlot in the fridge."

"Oh yes." He smiled expansively. "A good wine never did anyone any harm."

"Well, what do you know?" Edward finally spoke. "I really thought they'd be frozen stiff. But there's going to be a wedding after all."

"Wine, Edward?" Sue offered.

"Huh? Oh, no thanks. I'm tired. Think I'll head for bed. Good night, all." Making a marked detour around the sofa where Piggy lay draped across Tess's lap, he went out into the storm.

◆

CHAPTER 18

IF I WEREN'T stuck in a dog suit, my job would be just about done. At this point in the story, Sherlock Holmes would be strutting about and explaining who murdered whom. But not me. No. I'm just a dog, and no one listens to a mere dog. I knew who the murderer was—well, not the murderer. No one had been murdered except for me, and that was another story. Still, I knew who the mischief maker was, but could I point out the villain so that anyone would listen? No. Even Tess was too distracted to listen to me. She's pretty smart about a lot of things, but she is still just a kid.

Somehow I had to get through to someone. Anyone who can stab a cute little teddy bear is seriously sick, wacko, twisted, and deranged. And I suspected he would cause more mischief before he was done. He had to. The wedding was imminent, and this interlude in snowy hell was almost over. Alicia would soon be out of reach in Jamaica. He'd already scared the poor innocent girl to pieces, gotten Ben in a grim tizzy, worried all the guests, and gotten me yelled at for my efforts to put an end to his reign of terror. All right, maybe it wasn't quite a reign of terror, but close. Who could tell? He might actually murder someone for his next stunt. Then we'd be in a real mess.

I had to stop this, or Stanley would pin me up by my ears and demote me, though I don't see how I could get much lower than where I already am. Like most bosses, Stan's expectations aren't always realistic, and he tends to get cranky when they're not met. He sent me down here with no tools to do my job— no hands, no language, no status, and in a package that comes with bad habits that get me into trouble. (You should have seen the big deal Joey made about my search through the kitchen! You'd think a few raided cracker boxes and Oreos constituted a capital crime.) But in spite of all these disadvantages, the boss still expects miracles. Solve this problem! Mend this heart! Find the bad guy and don't let him hurt anyone. But do all this as a stumpy-legged, sausage-shaped, big-eared, stupid-looking dog!

Sorry. I get a bit carried away when I think about the injustice of it all. And speaking of Stanley—when the teddy bear ripper cashes in his chips, Stanley is going to take him apart limb by limb, figuratively speaking, of course. Look what the prissy little bureaucrat did to me, and all I did was sleep around a bit. Okay, okay—I did worse than that. I robbed my best friend of her husband. I admit that was rotten, but it doesn't even compare to what the villain du jour was doing. Stanley is going to blister his ears until the poor guy wishes there really were a hell, and then he's going to send him somewhere really unpleasant to learn the lessons he didn't learn in life. Knowing Stanley, our villain will probably end up back on Earth as a slug. Being bad might be fun at times, but trust me, it doesn't pay. Stanley can get very creative in making the punishment—or as he puts it, atonement—fit the crime.

But our sicko villain had more to worry about than

Stanley, because here on Earth, Ben Ramsay is on the case. Our Ben seems to share an attitude with Stan when it comes to mischief-makers. At least Stanley plans retribution to be educational; I'm not sure Ben is so noble.

But I digress. Pleasant as it is speculating about our villain's fate in either Stanley's or Ben's clutches, neither of those fellows was around. Stanley was no doubt looking over my shoulder, but he has a bad habit of not helping out. And as for Ben, he was off in the blizzard playing hero, leaving me to take care of things on the home front. As usual, it was up to the dog to save the day.

But I was up to the task. Early on Saturday, Alicia's supposed wedding day, I woke to a ray of sunshine in my eyes. Contrary to the weather forecast, the snow had ended and the sky was blue. That's the Colorado Rockies for you! Drives weathermen nuts. I knew immediately what I had to do, for I had a feeling deep in my gut—besides a sharp longing for breakfast—that our evildoer had performed more mischief either late the night before or in the wee hours of the morning. I myself had seen the intent upon his face when he left the Big Cabin the night before.

Tess was fast asleep, but I woke her with a well-placed nose in the ear. She was my ticket to track down potential problems, for with her at my side I could go almost anywhere. First, of course, we stopped by the kitchen. A corgi doesn't do anything without breakfast.

With food in my stomach I focused on my mission. I didn't waste time examining the cabin. If our villain was up to no good, he would concentrate on the lodge, where the wedding ceremony was to take place. We trotted through the front entrance with no problem. This time of morning almost everyone was sleeping. The scent of my prey tingled in my nose, for not many had passed this way since he'd come through the night before. His trail led through the front entrance, up the stairs, then to his room. We followed, Tess carefully tiptoeing behind me.

The scoundrel had gone straight to his room the night before. That much was clear. But he also came back out. It didn't take a bloodhound to figure this out. To me his path was so clear it might have been marked in neon paint. Really. You can't believe the abilities of a dog's nose until you've been a dog.

Anyway, we turned around and followed the track back down the stairs, to the bearskin on the wall, then to the big window overlooking the slopes, to the fireplace, the cupboard under the stairs, then back to the window. This guy was certainly a busy little bee. I couldn't imagine what he had been doing, but I knew he was up to no good.

I returned to the fireplace, Tess trundling faithfully behind me.

"What is it, Piggy? Something's wrong, isn't it?"

Like I could answer. Of course something was wrong. Would I have gotten out of bed this early if something weren't wrong?

The fireplace seemed a logical place to cause trouble. Proving myself more athletic than anyone gave me credit for, I jumped onto the raised stone hearth and cranked my neck so I could look up the flue. The grate was an obstacle, but I managed to push it aside so I could get a better view. The ashes were cold, by the way, in case you're wondering how stupid I really am. I'm not stupid at all, which wasn't the opinion of the head housekeeper, who came barreling in at that moment acting as if I'd just brought the place down around her ears.

"What is that . . . that dog doing in here?" she cried

melodramatically. "What are you doing in the fireplace, you stupid beast! Get out! Get out at once!"

Tess leaped faithfully to my defense. "You shouldn't talk to Piggy that way! She's on a mission!"

"I'll give her a mission out the nearest door! You don't bring that dog in here! Look at the mess!"

So I'd kicked a few ashes onto the floor. Big deal. But the woman had a broom in her hand and looked as if she knew how to use it—and I don't mean to sweep!

The mess that resulted was the housekeeper's fault, not mine. If she hadn't come after me with that blasted broom, I wouldn't have had to move so fast, upsetting the grate and spilling the larger part of last night's ashes onto the floor. The finer stuff poofed into the air and settled slowly on the furniture as gray, gritty dust. The black little footprints I left in the wake of my retreat didn't make the woman any happier.

"Someone will hear about this!" she shouted after us as we pelted for safety.

Someone would hear about it indeed! Probably the whole resort had heard about it. My ears rang from her bellowing. We left the lodge not much wiser than before. The only thing I knew for sure was that our villain had been prowling through the Grizzly Room the night before when decent people were sleeping, and there was nothing in the fireplace other than ashes. What could the scoundrel be planning? What had I missed?

Suddenly it came to me: the cupboard beneath the stairs. It was the only really good hiding place in the room. Could he have put something in the cupboard that might explode, or maybe leak noxious gas? Or had I seen too many grade D thrillers? Up until now the worst thing the jerk had done was stab a teddy bear.

I needed to get back into the lodge, but a glance over my shoulder showed the housekeeper guarding the entrance, glaring and shaking her broom. The old witch. What was I going to do now?

Alicia didn't think she had ever been so weary, exhausted in mind, spirit, and body as the little cavalcade of rescuers and rescued pulled up in front of the cabin on five snowmobiles, the castaways each riding double with one of the Bear Run staff and the damaged machines being towed behind the fifth. The only one of them who had an ounce of energy after the misadventure was Drover, who perched in front of Pat Haines and looked very pleased with himself.

The night had been long and unbelievably awkward. After the first amazed greetings when Ben and Joey had shown up, they'd all huddled in their separate bedrolls talking of inconsequentials, their minds buzzing with things left unsaid. Alicia had tried not to look Pat's way, for if she had, the feelings would have burned in her eyes for all to see, and how could she hurt Ben after he had risked his life once again for her safety? She could scarcely believe he had actually gone out into the storm to try to find her. A girl just didn't say, "Hey, I've decided not to marry you after all," to a man who had done something like that. As for Pat, Alicia could feel the heat of his gaze, the pressure of his silent questioning. What could she say to him after having expressed her love in such an intimate, joyful manner? She had betrayed Ben with Pat, and now she betrayed Pat because of what she owed to Ben.

Then there was Joey. Alicia couldn't even guess what Joey thought behind her calm smiles and quiet conversation. Joey couldn't possibly know what currents flowed beneath the blankness of Alicia's expression—could she? Why Joey accompanied Ben into the storm was something Alicia didn't understand.

"I had a bit of experience on a snowmobile," Joey had explained with a peculiar smile. "At least I thought I could ride a snowmobile. Turns out I can't."

Alicia had wondered at that strange smile and had given up before she figured out its meaning. Sensible, competent Joey was always on top of things. She had to think Alicia was a fool. She probably thought they were all fools. But Alicia was almost too tired to care.

Now they were safely back at the resort, and everyone rushed out to greet the returning prodigals. Even Piggy ran out of the cabin with uncharacteristic energy. She gave Drover an anxious once-over, bounded about with him in a typical corgi hello, then remembered herself and gave him a hard, irritable butt with her nose. Tess latched on to Ben, wrapping her arms around his legs and babbling some nonsense about her adventures with the stupid dog. Ben made an effort to listen to the child, but his attention dragged behind. Gently he shushed her chatter and promised that later he would listen. So gentle, he was. He was a man who gave himself up to his loved ones. Alicia was included in the circle of love, loyalty, gentleness, and courage. She told herself she should be thankful. A week ago she had been thankful. A week ago, Alicia realized, she'd been a different person. Perhaps a better person. Certainly a more innocent one.

It was over now. The great blizzard adventure was over. Her brief rebellion was over. It was all over. Embracing Joey, Alicia thanked her sincerely for riding to the rescue. Then she clutched at Ben and buried her face in the front of his jacket. "I'll have a whole lifetime to thank you. It'll take me that long."

He didn't say anything, just patted her back.

"I think we should go ahead with the wedding." She almost added, "Let's get this over with," but that was surely the wrong thing to say about one's wedding.

"Are you sure you're not too tired?" Ben said, sounding very tired himself.

"No. Let's get married. Hot showers and coffee first," she said with a weak smile. "Then a wedding." She ignored Pat's scalding stare and headed into the cabin.

Pat caught up with her in the kitchen, where he pulled her through the back door, onto the back deck, and down the steps into the knee-deep snow. "We need to take a walk."

Alicia suffered a flutter of panic. Her meager store of moral courage was just about depleted, and she didn't have the resources to face Pat Haines right now, even though she owed him an abject apology. "Pat, can't we do this later? I've had about as much snow as I can take for a while."

"Later will be too late," he growled. "And we have things to say that aren't meant for anyone else's ears."

Alicia sighed and allowed herself to be pulled toward the edge of the pines, where Pat spun her around to reluctantly face him.

"I can't believe you still intend to marry Ben

Ramsay!" His hand tightened almost painfully on her shoulders. "Allie, you love me, dammit! Yesterday we made love. We were a part of each other in a way that was a hell of a lot more than physical. You can lie with words, with promises, but you can't lie the way we communicated yesterday! You love me!"

"Yes, I do." There was no sense in denying it. Alicia didn't even want to deny it. "But I have to marry Ben."

"That doesn't make sense."

"Pat, he came out into that storm to save me, even though he was probably mad as hell at me for going out with you yesterday. That's twice now he's risked his own life to save mine."

"We weren't in that much danger."

"We could have been! Some spring storms last a long time and are really bad. He risked a lot in coming after us. You don't repay something like that by dumping a guy on his wedding day, Pat. You just don't. I may be a spoiled rich bitch, and I might never do anything more useful in my life than organize a fashion show for the Junior League, but I know right from wrong and kind from cruel."

Pat kicked a tree trunk and succeeded only in dislodging a clump of snow from an overhead branch. It narrowly missed him. So he kicked the tree again.

Alicia had never felt more miserable in her life. She suffered an overwhelming urge to leave it all behind— Pat, Ben, her father and grandmother, the wedding— flee to Evergreen, pack up her things, collect Puddin, and light out for somewhere that she could start over and be someone else. Someone who didn't let other people's expectations bog her down. But she couldn't do that. She had promises to keep and obligations to fulfill.

"Do you think it's right or kind to marry Ben when you don't love him? When you're going to be miserable with him?" Pat asked sadly.

"I do love Ben. Not the same way I love you, but I do care for him. I'll make him a good wife."

"You'll make him a terrible wife. He's a good man. Do you think he'll be happy with your gratitude instead of your passion? Do you think he wants a wife who merely cares for him instead of a wife who truly loves him?"

Alicia moved her toe back and forth in the snow, staring at the aimless patterns as an excuse not to look into Pat's accusing eyes. She would probably never again be able to look him in the eye. "Ben wants me," she whispered miserably. "Look what he's been willing to do to take care of me."

"Oh bull! He's a cop. Taking care of people is what he does. He's so used to leading the cavalry charge that he'd probably walk through fire to save a goddamned stray dog. You're using that as an excuse to be a good girl and do what you're supposed to do."

"What do you mean by that?" A spurt of anger was a welcome relief from misery.

"I mean that you'd turn yourself inside out to be a good little girl and please everyone but yourself. Please Ben. Please Daddy. Please Joey."

"That's not true. Ben was my choice, no one else's!"

"Oh yeah? I'll admit that Irene has given you a hard time about Ben, but how many times have I heard your father say what a good man you chose? 'Solid as oak, real hero material.' "

"Well—"

"And didn't all the society editors just drool over the story of the rich damsel in distress falling in love with the brave, everyday guy who saved her butt? The press would have been here in droves if the storm hadn't kept them away."

"That's not fair!"

"And isn't every little girl brought up on stories where the princess fair falls in love with the hero and they live happily ever after?"

"Oh! That is *so* out of the ballpark!"

"Allie! Listen to me! Marry your stalwart hero and you won't live happily ever after! Either one of you. Ben deserves a woman who loves him, and you love me. You've goddamn loved me since I was a penniless ski instructor in Vail, and don't tell me that you haven't. Because last night, when you thought the storm was going to do in both of us, you were a lot more honest than you are today."

Swamped by confusion, Alicia clung to her notion of what was noble and right. "Leave me alone. I can't . . . I can't . . ."

"Break out of the mold for once, Allie. Do something you're not supposed to do. Marry me."

She turned away, tears burning in her eyes. It was her wedding day, and somehow she had to find a way to look happy when she walked down the aisle to meet her groom. The wrong groom.

◆

Tess was beginning to think that grown-ups, for all that they got to drive and set their own bedtimes and didn't have to sit in school, weren't all that smart when it came to the important things. She'd always thought her dad was really smart, but lately he'd been just as bad as everyone else. He wouldn't listen, really listen, to anything she had to say. And he thought that Tess was just a kid.

Not that Tess wasn't. But kids sometimes knew things. And sometimes they had important stuff to do. But once grown-ups weren't kids anymore, they forgot that kids were people, too, with real minds and real thoughts. Mostly her dad wasn't like that. But lately he had been.

And of all the days Tess's dad needed to listen to her, today was the day. She'd been trying to get through to him ever since he came back from spending the night out in the forest. He still wouldn't listen. He smiled and nodded and said "uh-huh," but where there should have been understanding was a blank wall. And now that she had waited for him to get out of the shower and tagged along behind him to the loft, he was getting that look on his face—the same look he wore when she pestered him one too many times for an ice cream or a horse of her own. He looked tired and dejected. If her dad felt bad, then this probably wasn't a good time to bug him. But Tess just had to make him understand. Terrible things were going to happen if she didn't.

"Daddy!" She demanded his attention in a determined voice. "Don't you believe me?"

He sat on his bed, an old terry-cloth robe wrapped around him, and visibly summoned patience. "Tess, kiddo, it's been a big week for both of us. I think we're both kind of tired, and your imagination has been playing games with you."

"Daddy, you have to believe me!" How did a kid get through to a grown-up? Sometimes talking to her dad was like talking to a rock. "I'm not making things up! I was there, this morning, really! And Piggy found something bad in the big room in the lodge, only I don't know what it is. Something's really, really wrong. Can't you at least look for it?"

"Look for what, Tessie?"

"I don't know!"

"Honey, I don't have time for pretend games, and I don't have the energy, either. It's about time for you to get into that nice dress Joey found for you. . . ." When he said Joey's name, he looked funny. Not funny ha-ha, but funny peculiar, as if a dark cloud had appeared over his head and was dumping rain all over his brain. Tess didn't like the way he looked. "You get to go down the aisle in front of everyone," he said finally. "Won't you like that?"

"Daddy! You're not listening! Piggy knows who stabbed the teddy bear and left the awful poem. I just know she does! And she found something awful in the lodge!"

Her dad looked worried, but for the wrong reason. He looked at her the same way he looked whenever she told him about her conversations with her mom. "Did Piggy tell you that?"

"No! Piggy can't talk!" That was unfair in itself. For a moment Tess was angry with her mom for sending her an assistant who was a dog. Dogs were cute, and they were great friends, but no matter how clever and special Piggy was, no matter that Tess could look into those brown doggy eyes and see somebody else inside, Piggy couldn't talk. Convincing everyone of the problem was up to Tess. "Piggy can't talk, but she's not really a dog, Daddy. And she's really smart, and she knows Mom."

"Tess . . ."

"And you can't marry Alicia anyway!" To Tess's horror, tears welled into her eyes and her voice cracked. "You can't marry Alicia because Mom says you won't be happy, and neither will Alicia. That's what Piggy thinks too."

Her dad took a tissue from the bedside table and dabbed at the tears running down her cheeks. "It has been a hard time for you, hasn't it, kiddo?"

"Daddy . . . !" she quavered.

"Things are going to get better, honey. Really they are. You're just a little overwhelmed right now."

"I'm not!"

"Right now isn't a time for fantasies and pretending. Piggy is a very nice little dog, but she's not some kind of wonder dog. And your mom would be happy that I'm marrying a person like Alicia. She'd like Alicia."

"But there's something in the lodge!"

"That's enough now." His tone acquired an edge. "It's time for you to get cleaned up for the wedding. If you can't behave like the little lady I know you are, then you can stay in the cabin during the ceremony. But that would disappoint me a lot, because I want my sweet little kiddo there with me when I get married. And Alicia wants you there, too. Alicia likes you a lot."

Tess bit her lip. She was getting nowhere.

Her dad touched her hair gently, then smiled. "If your mom could see what a beautiful little girl you've become, and how smart and kind and caring you are, she would be very, very proud. Now go get dressed."

The rock was not going to budge, Tess realized. It was up to her and Piggy to save the day.

As tired as she was, Joey thought it should be an easy task to keep her mind blank as she worked. There were a host of details to be seen to. The guest seating for the reception in the dining room. The inventory with her catering staff of what was available in the kitchen, since they had not, obviously, been able to get the groceries for the menu she had planned. The photographer could not get here, of course, and someone had told her that Edward Reese had a camera. But Edward was nowhere to be found. Carrie told her that they'd had a quarrel and he'd left to go to Aspen. Carrie was hitching a ride back to Denver with Sue and George after the wedding. Edward was *sooo* history, Carrie had declared.

Edward's camera was also history, unfortunately. It had taken Joey an hour to find a guest who could loan her one that was suitable. She herself would have to take the photos, and heaven knew she was no photographer.

Added to those problems was the absence of a wedding cake, a sad shortage of champagne, and some clueless member of her catering staff who had put unpressed tablecloths on the tables, with creases going every which way. This final straw made her sink into a chair and try to fight down the tears. Joey DeMato, the wedding consultant who never lost her cool, who could deal with late photographers, wedding cakes that toppled over in delivery vans, tearful brides, quarreling bridesmaids, tipsy grooms, and any other difficulty a wedding could throw at her, wanted to weep over wrinkled tablecloths. She had come to this sad state. And this had been planned as the perfect wedding.

She was overtired, Joey knew. And the perfect wedding had turned into a shambles. But that wasn't the real trouble. The real trouble was that today Ben Ramsay was marrying the wrong woman. The woman Ben loved was sitting in a deserted dining room weeping over tablecloths while the woman Ben was going to marry was donning her wedding gown, and from what Joey had seen from her brief glimpse into Irene's room, which was serving as a dressing room, the bride didn't look any happier about all this than Joey did.

Why were they doing this? Joey asked herself incredulously. She would bet her last dollar that Alicia loved Pat, and she was almost as sure that Ben loved her. But Ben was stubborn as an oak rooted in rock. He had promised to marry Alicia, and unless Alicia cried off, marry Alicia he would. And who knew what Alicia was thinking? Joey should put an end to the travesty by shouting the truth for all to hear. But was it the truth? Could she be sure, when her own heart was involved? Or was she just seeing what she wanted to see? If neither Ben nor Alicia spoke up, could she in good conscience speak for them?

No, she couldn't, goddamn it! She could only sit alone and cry over wrinkled tablecloths.

"Miss DeMato! There you are!" The head house-keeper's face matched her tone, and neither was pleasant. More trouble, Joey thought. "I need to have a word with you, Miss DeMato."

"What is it, Mrs. Benitez?"

"You must do something about your dog! Not only did the creature traipse through the Grizzly Room this morning, sticking its nose into the fireplace and tracking soot on my clean floor, but now it is physically threatening your wedding guests as they gather for the ceremony."

"Really?" Joey couldn't imagine Drover offering even a total stranger anything other than a friendly lick, and after the previous day's adventure, he shouldn't have the energy to twitch an ear. And she doubted Piggy would lower herself to indulge in such undignified behavior. Of course, there had been that incident at Dillon Reservoir, when Piggy had toppled Ben into the mud and snow, or so Ben had claimed.

"Really, Miss DeMato! It is barking and leaping about like a mad dog. I shooed it out once with a mop from the kitchen, but it came right back. You must lock up your dog, Miss DeMato, before it attacks someone!"

"I'll take care of it, Mrs. Benitez." Joey sighed, mentally thanking the dog for adding yet another problem to her list, but at least this was a problem easily solved. She didn't care what was troubling the furry little fiend, whichever one it was. Piggy and Drover could complain about it shut in Tess's bedroom.

The culprit turned out to be Piggy, who was indeed wreaking havoc with the guests who were collecting in the Grizzly Room. The guests looked more annoyed than frightened, and Piggy wore an expression of almost human frustration. She stood in the doorway barking her fool head off. A guest or two tried to shoo her away, but she stood her ground.

"Piggy!" Joey marched over to the little miscreant and grabbed her by the collar before she could dodge away. "What's gotten into you?"

Piggy whined. Joey couldn't recall ever hearing this dog whine.

"Don't try to apologize, you scamp. It's back to the cabin for you."

Piggy locked all her joints and refused to move.

"You little devil!" Joey growled. "All right, have it your way." She scooped the dog into her arms and marched out the door, grumbling, "If I end up with dog hair all over this suit, then you're going to be on bread and water until Amy gets back. Cripes! What else can go wrong with this stupid wedding?"

CHAPTER 19

◆

FOILED! FOILED AT every turn! I'll just bet Miss Marple never got hoisted under somebody's arm and carted away from the scene of a potential crime! There I was, turning myself inside out to keep people out of the danger zone, and what thanks do I get? I get locked away in a stuffy bedroom with nobody but stupid Drover for company. Typical human attitude. The dog is having a little fun? Then lock up the dog. The dog in the way? Then lock up the dog. The dog trying to save the day? Then lock up the poor dog.

Not that Drover cared. He was a lump on the bed, nothing more. In fact, he hadn't moved since Joey so unjustly tossed me into the room. That little skiing adventure had been a bigger bite than he could chew.

For the first few minutes after the door closed behind an irate Joey, I fussed and fumed. As if I didn't have trouble enough doing my job, Miss Clueless Joey DeMato has to throw yet another obstacle in my path. At least when I was working with Amy and her boyfriend Dr. Dull, they had some idea of how to communicate with a dog. Or they thought they did. In most cases, they weren't nearly as perceptive as they *thought they were, but they tried to listen. Joey, however, might as well be deaf where I was concerned. Talking to Joey is like trying to communicate with a stump. She's got her mind so set on being the noble romantic martyr that she wouldn't see trouble if it came up and kicked her in the butt, which it was likely to do any minute.*

So I was bedeviled at every turn. Joey wouldn't listen to me, and Ben wouldn't listen to Tess. If he had, this story would have ended differently. But he didn't. And I couldn't really blame him. Ben Ramsay was distracted by woman problems. I could relate. When I was a woman, I was an expert at creating such distractions. I could be the mother of all woman problems when I wanted to be.

So why was I sympathetic to distracted Ben, you ask, and ragging on poor distraught Joey? I'll tell you why. Men are supposed to be distracted by women. Nature made them that way, thank heaven. But women are supposed to be the smart ones. We are the distracters, ladies, not the distractees. We are supposed to hold things together.

Regardless, I had to work with what I had. Joey and Ben were obviously more hindrance than help in this crisis, and I didn't know where little Tess had taken herself. Where was the kid when I needed her? The only thing I could think of to do was yell for help from Stanley. That's how desperate I was. Usually he is the last creature in the universe that I want to see.

Stanley rarely comes when he's called. In that regard he resembles a corgi. But this time he came. He must have sensed that I needed a steadying hand, because suddenly he appeared, leaning casually against the iron bedstead.

"Well, my girl, have I given you a problem beyond your abilities to solve?"

I wasn't about to let him get the upper hand. "Listen, Stan. Lip from you is not what I need right now."

"Lip? Really, Lydia. Beings in my position don't give 'lip.' "

"I need help! You know what's going on, don't you? You always claim to know everything."

"Well, not quite everything."

"Don't turn modest on me, Stan. You know this penny-ante terrorist. He's a sicko and a creep."

"He has a few lessons yet to learn."

"He's been leaving notes and teddy bears and scaring people. Now he's booby-trapped the wedding ceremony."

"Ah, the wedding ceremony. I'm a little disappointed in you this time around, Lydia. Or Piggy. You should be getting used to that name by now. I was pleased when you figured out most of what needed to be done—not all, but most. But I don't see much progress."

"Plug in your brain, Stan! We have serious trouble here! And I'm locked in a frigging bedroom."

"Lydia, heavenly agents do not use that kind of language."

"Stanley, get a life. Language is the least of our problems. Now, spring me from this bedroom, and then help me convince someone, preferably Ben Ramsay, that there's trouble waiting in the lodge."

"I'm not allowed to interfere in such a manner, Lydia. That's your job."

"You are so full of bull! You interfere in everything!"

With a superior smile on his face, Stan faded out without answering. His advice as he left was a lame "Carry on. And keep in mind that you can't win them all."

I was definitely going to have a few choice words for that

misbegotten excuse for a heavenly gatekeeper. I deserved a va-
cation. But right then I had work to do. Stanley obviously
thought I was going to fail, and he was getting ready to gloat.
But even with everything going against me, I had no intention
of failing. I would show that mealy-mouthed officious bureau-
crat what I was really made of. There was more gray matter be-
tween these pointy ears than he gave me credit for.

Things were getting down to the wire, and Joey desperately tried to not think about anything except the need for getting the bridesmaids ready and in their places for the procession. She didn't want to think about Ben donning his rented tux and preparing to make his vows. She didn't want to think about Alicia, getting dressed with Irene's help, looking less excited than any bride had a right to be. She especially didn't want to think about how empty her life suddenly seemed. What had happened to her peaceful satisfaction with a life of work, more work, and an occasional evening curled up alone on the sofa reading a good book?

"Joey, is this hem truly straight?" Teri posed in front of the mirror and frowned at her reflection.

Who cared if the stupid hem was straight when three people's futures were about to disintegrate and not one of them had the guts to stop it? "The hem is straight," Joey told her. "Shoulders back. If you slouch, you'll ruin the line of the dress." For years she'd been a matrimonial general, issuing orders and advice to an endless parade of bridesmaids, brides, grooms, ushers, photographers, chefs, dressmakers, and limo drivers, spending her life creating perfect weddings for other women. It seemed so unfair, suddenly. She wanted a wedding of her own.

"This color is really good for me." Teri smiled wickedly. "I wish Tom hadn't left. He'd like me in this dress."

Carrie snorted. "I'd steer clear of that one, sweetie. He'd like you better without the dress, but I don't see him settling down any time soon."

"Like you have such good judgment in men!" Teri tossed back.

Carrie didn't take offense. "True. What a loser I brought up here. I'm just as glad he took off. Edward's a good-looking guy, but looks aren't everything, I guess."

"Your hat is a bit crooked," Joey told her.

"I'll fix it for her," Sue volunteered, then in a quieter voice said, "I think Tess needs your help."

Indeed, little Tess did not look happy. Her usually sunny face was glum. After everything that had happened, the kid had a right. Joey came up behind her and fixed her perky straw hat so it sat correctly on her head. Sue had styled the little girl's hair—usually worn in two stubby pigtails—into a smooth French braid tied with a silk ribbon that matched her dress.

"You look absolutely lovely," Joey told her.

Tess's big brown eyes met hers in melting despair. "Joey?"

Joey squatted beside the girl. "Yes?"

"It's not supposed to happen this way, Joey. My dad isn't supposed to marry Alicia. My mom told me so."

Joey sighed and brushed the girl's cheek with one

finger. Tess's dead mother hadn't spoken a word to her, yet she thought the same thing. But she certainly couldn't say that to Ben's daughter.

"And Piggy told me there's something wrong in the wedding room. Maybe in the fireplace."

"Honey, there's a fire in the fireplace. There's nothing wrong there."

"Piggy thinks there is, and she's a—"

"I know. Piggy's a wonder dog. Tess, I'm sorry to disillusion you about Piggy, but she isn't a wonder dog. She's just a bad-mannered, spoiled little corgi, and she doesn't know about anything other than playing and eating and rolling in dirt. Corgis love to get dirty. That's why she was tromping around in the fireplace. Not because there's anything wrong there."

Tess regarded her gravely and with more than a little pity.

"And I think your mother would be very happy that your dad is marrying Alicia," she lied, "because Alicia's a wonderful person. Both your dad and Alicia love you a lot."

Tess shook her head, and her eyes had a very adult-looking sadness in them. "You don't really believe that. You're all making a big mistake."

I don't give up easily when it comes to something I really want, and I really wanted out of that bedroom. If I'd been human, the task would have been easy, but the dog suit was a real disadvantage. I had to be very creative. Very creative indeed.

The first thing I did was wake up Drover. He was just an

ordinary dog and a bit of a twit besides, but I needed his brawn. Beside the dresser sat a ladder-back chair; not a heavy piece of furniture, I'll grant you, but still difficult for a lone little corgi to move from one place to another. Drover woke up a bit grumpy. He actually snapped at me when I butted him sharply in the side to get him moving. I snapped right back. An impressive show of teeth convinced him that his nap was over. There's a reason female dogs are called bitches.

Laboriously we pushed the chair to the window, using our heads as if they were bulldozers. Once the chair was in position, I scrambled up to the seat, which put me within reach of the latch. Then came the really hard part, because paws don't work well on brass latches. In case you haven't noticed, dogs don't have thumbs. It's a built-in disadvantage. This latch was stiff. The window probably hadn't been opened all winter. I had to use my teeth, and even then the job wasn't an easy one.

Brass really doesn't taste great. It's sort of cold and green in your mouth and clanky against your teeth. Not to mention slippery. Getting a purchase on the thing was almost impossible. I had to clamp down very hard with my neck twisted all the way to the left, then, holding on so hard I thought my teeth would crack, I twisted my neck—bringing the latch with it—all the way to the right. It took me about twenty tries before I managed it. Ten wasted minutes, and who knew what was going down in the Grizzly Room. Nothing too grisly, I hoped.

I wasted another few minutes pushing the window open, wedging my head against the wooden frame, and pushing with all my might. Corgis are a lot stronger than we look. Finally the window slid to the side and I dashed out, Drover right behind me. Tired or not, that boy is always up for adventure.

◆

Ben had been in a few dangerous situations in his career as a police officer, but never had he felt quite so doomed as he did standing beside the Reverend Thomas in the Grizzly Room, facing all those people who'd come to see him get married. On one wall, the skin of a long-dead bear snarled silently at him in glassy-eyed rage, and Alicia's staring friends and relatives seemed no less intimidating than the bear. They were a high-class group. Diamonds winked at him, fur stoles abounded on the shoulders of the less politically correct ladies. The gentlemen sported hundred-dollar haircuts and custom-tailored suits, and they regarded him with eyes that seemed to wonder why Alicia had chosen this particular peasant to marry.

The room wasn't as full as it might have been, for the guests who hadn't arrived by Friday morning couldn't get into the mountains because of the storm. The press was also missing, a blessing for which Ben was duly grateful. He'd gotten his fill of the media after he'd pulled Alicia from that sinking car. If the newspapers and television crews had shown up, the room truly would have been overflowing. Joey would have been beside herself accommodating them all, but she would have managed. She always managed. Calm, cool, superorganized, always-in-control Joey.

He didn't want to think about Joey, Ben reminded himself. He shouldn't think about the taste of her mouth—a haven of warmth when the whole world was frozen. He shouldn't think about the feel of her beneath him, supple and surrendering, when they'd landed together in the snow. She'd been warm and yielding, her normally sharp green eyes soft with desire.

Damn! He definitely shouldn't think of Joey right then. Those thoughts were grossly unfair to Alicia.

Gary, taking Tom's place as best man, leaned a bit closer to him and said, "Buck up, man. You look as if you're headed for your own funeral."

Was it that bad? Ben wondered. The answer sounded like an alarm bell in his brain. His funeral would be a party compared to this. Conventional wisdom among bachelors held that any man reacted in a similar fashion on his wedding day, but Ben knew it shouldn't be this way. What the hell was he doing?

"You're a lucky man," Gary told him in an undertone. Next to Gary, Todd gave him an encouraging smile, and Pat—filling in as an usher—just looked blank. Pat was as tired as he was, Ben thought, and he looked just about as happy.

The string quartet launched into the obscure Mozart piece that Alicia had chosen for the procession. Starting down the aisle was Tess, looking so lovely that his chest swelled in paternal pride. The scamp who was the center of his life had changed into a demure young lady. In a way the change made Ben sad, even though he knew it wouldn't last past the wedding ceremony and reception. They would be lucky if it lasted that long.

Yet part of the change in Tess's demeanor had nothing to do with the ladylike hairstyle or dressy outfit. The usual sparkle in her eyes was missing, as was the characteristic bounce in her step. He thought of her frustration that he wouldn't play her fantasy games. At the time he'd thought her pique was due to not being the center of attention, but maybe her distress ran deeper. Was he doing something to genuinely hurt his daughter?

Behind Tess came Sue, her face appropriately solemn. But Carrie wore a big grin as she followed. Apparently she was weathering Edward's desertion quite well. Teri, the maid of honor, looked misty-eyed, and behind her was Alicia, his bride, standing quite still at the foot of the stairs. She was white and perfect as a statue of fine porcelain, beautiful as any man could hope for. Her eyes met his, then slid away uneasily. The smile on her face was no more than lip deep. Even from across the room Ben could read her. He knew her well enough, all her moods from ecstatic to mischievous to sulky, that he could recognize a false smile when he saw one. Whatever she was thinking, she wasn't happy about it.

With a sinking feeling that nearly stole his breath, the certainty that he and Alicia were making a mistake hit Ben like an avalanche of Rocky Mountain snow. This wedding was a big, huge, stupendous mistake. He had known it for days, Ben realized, but he'd been too pigheaded, too locked into the course they had set, to acknowledge that they just weren't made for each other. He should have called it quits when he first grasped that he and Alicia had very little in common beyond the shared excitement of danger. And his attraction to Joey should have put an end to the sham once and for all. Those feelings had been totally unexpected, and they had quickly erupted into something more than attraction, more than simple desire. He loved Joey DeMato.

Joey DeMato, whose smart mouth and brusque efficiency hid a tender and generous heart—Joey was the woman he loved. Alicia was someone he liked and admired, a vulnerable woman he'd needed to protect.

So what the hell was he going to do now? It was Joey he wanted to live with until both of them were tottering with old age—and beyond. But it was Alicia walking up the aisle on her father's arm, ready to say vows with him. The eleventh hour was ticking away its last seconds.

His mind clamored: *Do something, Ramsay! Do something!* No matter which way he jumped, the results were going to be ugly. But he and Alicia couldn't do this. They just couldn't.

Out of the corner of his eye, Ben caught Pat's hungry look directed at the bride. He'd seen that look before and hadn't been jealous so much as annoyed. That should have told him the score right there, but he'd been more dense than usual this last week. A man madly in love should have been jealous as hell. He looked at Joey, who stood on the sidelines with a camera. For once she didn't look like the cool professional. Her expression was rather dazed, and the camera in her hand all but ignored. How beautiful she was whenever she smiled, and how her eyes glowed when she put him firmly in his place with a zinger during their verbal sparring. Her eyes weren't glowing now.

Then Alicia was there, right in front of him. Her father smiled complacently and placed her hand in Ben's as Ben moved to his place facing the minister.

Suddenly he was calm. They would wade through this, he and Alicia. Probably no one would be happier than she when he told her they couldn't go through with it. With a small movement of his hand, Ben forestalled Reverend Thomas, who had taken a breath to begin the ceremony. He smiled at his bride and squeezed her hand. "Alicia, we have to—"

An explosion of noise cut off the words before Ben could say them. Two corgis blew into the room, twin furry torpedoes sailing in on a frenzied gale of barking. Shrieks and cries of surprise mingled with shouts of "Get away!" "Off! Off!" "Shoo!" and "Aaaack!" Chairs toppled as the guests tried to escape the devilish little duo. Amid the confusion, Ben actually breathed a sigh of relief.

The dogs raced around the room, faster and more agile on their short little legs than anyone could have imagined. They circled the guests as they might run the perimeter of a herd of sheep, squeezing them into a confused knot moving toward the door.

Tess jumped for joy, clapping her hands and shouting encouragement. "Go, girl! You go, Piggy! Git 'em, Drover!"

Joey had put down the camera and was making a futile attempt to corral the dogs, but they deftly eluded her. Ben almost laughed, but Alicia appeared to see no humor in the situation at all. She stared at the dogs and the confusion, looking like a person just awakened from a dream, not knowing where she was or what she was doing.

Piggy had turned the herd over to Drover, who had them well in hand—or in paw—and moving toward

door. He avoided one lady's swing with a Gucci handbag and a gentleman's annoyed but clumsy kick. Meanwhile, Piggy barked furiously at the cupboard beneath
the stairway. It was a seldom-used storage area for odds
and ends, old linen, table centerpieces, and a collection
of Pat's old skiing magazines.

"Crazy dog!" Pat scoffed. "Get them out of here!"

Tess dashed up to her father. "Please, Daddy!
There's something in there! Piggy knows! Believe her!
There's something wrong!"

Joey managed to hook her fingers through Piggy's
collar and pull her back with a sharp command to
shush. Piggy became even more frantic. Ben felt a familiar tingling running up his spine. Always before,
that eerie tingle had signaled danger, seen or unseen.
As if a sixth sense told him where to look, he turned
his eyes toward the entrance. He could see the front
deck through the big double door that had been
pushed open by the dogs. On the deck stood Edward
Reese, the same Edward Reese who had supposedly
left for Aspen. Strangely enough, Ben wasn't surprised.
His gut instincts had been alert to the signs, but he had
ignored them. Vague suspicions solidified. Conjecture
became certainty. Too late. In his hand Edward held
something that might have been a television remote or
a garage door opener, but it was neither. It was a remote trigger to a very nasty surprise that apparently
was stowed in the cupboard. They should have listened
to Piggy.

Edward saw Ben looking at him and smiled. He
held up the device in his hand and mouthed the words

"You're toast!" Then he waved and headed for the steps leading from the deck. Time stretched and took on that unreal nightmare quality where every second seems an hour. There wasn't enough time, but Ben had to try.

"Everyone out!" he commanded at the top of his voice. "Now! Move it!"

The authority in his voice made people obey without hesitation. They hurried toward the door. Some of them got out. Not all of them. Some were blown through the door when the bomb exploded, landing mostly unhurt on the deck outside. Those closer to the cupboard caught a blast that lifted them from their feet and tossed them toward the huge window overlooking the slopes. Glass shattered, tinkling musically as it rained around wedding party and guests. Most ended up on the rear deck outside the window, stunned, bruised, and picking shards of glass out of their clothing and hair. One lady found herself looking up into the snarling jaws of the grizzly bear skin, which had been ripped from the wall and had fallen on top of her.

At the same time the bomb had exploded, Ben had instinctively reached for Tess and Joey, tackling them both together and shielding them with his own body as the blast carried them through the window and onto the deck. Joey still had hold of Piggy, who struggled beneath them as Ben lay stunned, listening to the cries and shouts of people who had been tossed about like so much straw in a stiff wind. Tess struggled free of his embrace.

"Oh wow!" she cried. "Oh wow!"

In Ben's arms, Joey neither moved nor made a sound. A bolt of desperate fear shot through him as he shifted his weight off her. "Joey? Joey!"

His only answer was from Piggy, who barked indignantly and untangled herself from Joey's grip. The dog shook herself, looked around, then was off like a shot. As she dodged around upended furniture and dazed wedding guests, Drover joined her, barking furiously.

Joey came to her senses slowly. Spots danced in her vision as she tried and failed to remember how she came to be lying on the deck with Ben, cold air raising goose bumps on her skin, and her nose twitching with the odd odor of something akin to gunpowder.

Then the truth filtered through her dazed awareness. An explosion. Screams. Glass everywhere. And Ben grabbing her, going down with her as all hell seemed to break loose. Ben . . .

"Ben!" she croaked fearfully. "Ben, are you . . . ?"

"I'm fine, Joey. Are you hurt?"

Tess crouched beside them and clutched her father's arm.

"Tess, kiddo, are you all right?"

"Y-yes. Wow! This is just like TV."

"Are you sure you're all right?"

"I'm okay, Daddy."

"Joey? You okay? Tell me you're okay."

"I don't know. I . . . no, I'm okay. Really, I'm okay. Tess, are you sure you're all right?"

Tess sighed tolerantly. "I'm okay. See, Daddy. I told you so."

Joey croaked, "What happened?"

"Piggy was right," Tess declared.

All around them people were picking themselves up and dusting themselves off. Just through the shattered window stood Pat and Alicia. Alicia looked fairly composed, but Pat wasn't letting her out of arm's reach. Irene was scolding Alicia's father, who winced at every word. Near them were Sue and George, who seemed relatively composed and unhurt.

"Piggy *was* right!" Ben growled. "Edward Reese!" He scrambled up. "Damn if those crazy dogs don't have him on the run! Stay here with Tess!"

Of course Joey didn't do as he ordered. She left Tess with Sue and George and ran after Ben, who had disappeared out the front.

The chase that followed was one of the most extraordinary things Joey had ever seen. Edward had made the mistake of sticking around long enough to witness his triumph. But his little homemade bomb, wicked though it was, had neither killed, maimed, nor disabled, leaving his victims free to get revenge.

Edward pelted down the snow-packed road, but he couldn't outrun the two corgis, who in spite of their short legs pursued him like furry brown bullets. Behind the corgis came Ben, and behind Ben half a dozen irate husbands, fathers, and friends.

Piggy was the heroine who brought the villain down, launching at him as he stumbled on the uneven, slippery surface of the snow. Drover piled on for good measure. Edward tried to throw them off, but it was like trying to dislodge a couple of pointy-eared piranhas. By the time Ben got to them, the villain almost looked grateful to see him.

Content to turn the confrontation over to Ben, the dogs stood back and watched with tongues hanging as Ben pulled Edward up by the collar of his jacket and put him down again with a solid punch to the jaw.

"Why, you bastard? Tell me why!"

"Justice!" Edward declared harshly. "That rich bitch killed my brother."

"Damn!" Ben's fists clenched. "The brother! Jason Denny was your brother!" It was more accusation that question.

"Goddamned right he was my brother!" He got up and charged, head-butting Ben in the stomach. Ben took advantage by tucking Edward's head under his arm and holding it for another iron-fisted punch. By now, the others had caught up and stood around cheering as Edward went down once again.

Edward's eyes were wild as he scanned the crowd and shouted, "Did I get the teasing little bitch?"

Ben grabbed him and hauled him roughly to his feet. "You have the right to remain silent, but you'd damned well better not."

Edward swung, landing a blow to the side of Ben's head, which Ben ignored. He merely shook Edward like a terrier shaking a rat.

"You have the right to have an attorney present if you can find one willing to defend your sorry ass."

Edward swung wildly and missed. "I don't care! I loved my brother. I'll get back at that whore. She led him on! Led him to his damned death! If I didn't get her this time, I will next time."

In the crowd, Carrie gasped. Edward looked at her and laughed. "You don't think I really wanted you, did you? In your dreams, loser girl. You're just a name I found listed in the society column as a wedding hanger-on."

Ben hit him again. "I've changed my mind, jackass. Don't talk. Shut your filthy mouth."

Edward staggered back but ignored the advice. "It should have been a bigger bomb," he shouted to his audience. "You should have all been toast! I should have walked out of here with no one knowing." He focused his venom on Alicia. "You were never good enough for Jason Denny."

A solid fist to the jaw silenced the insults. "Some people just don't know when to shut up." Ben seldom got genuinely angry, but he was angry now. Not until Joey stepped up and grabbed his arm did he release his victim.

"Ben! Leave off! He's all done."

Piggy snorted. Obviously, she thought the perp hadn't got nearly the whipping he deserved.

Richard offered his necktie. "Hog-tie the bastard!"

Ben bound Edward's hands behind his back and pushed him back toward the lodge.

Miraculously, no one was seriously hurt. Minor scrapes, bruises, and cuts abounded, but the biggest thing any of the victims would take home was a story they would be telling for years to come.

So much for the perfect wedding, Joey thought as she collapsed onto the front steps of the lodge. Her head was swimming. She was very near the limit of what she could take, Joey mused, and if she lapsed into hysteria, no one could blame her. In fact, she probably owed herself a nervous breakdown. She and Alicia could share one.

Alicia, however, didn't look nearly as frazzled as Joey expected. She sat down beside her on the steps and actually smiled. "Are you all right, Joey?"

"Am *I* all right? What about you? This whole week has been one disaster after another, and now . . ."

"Don't worry about me. It's such a kick that your little dogs saved the day, or at least tried to. And they did catch the villain." She reached out to pet Piggy and Drover, who were sitting by Joey's feet. Drover gave her a delighted grin and slobbered on her hand. Piggy accepted the accolade as her due, looking quite indignant that someone hadn't mentioned her heroism earlier.

Joey smiled weakly. "They did, didn't they? And after the way I treated poor Piggy, locking her up when she was just trying to keep people from getting hurt. It's humiliating owing an apology to a dog."

Alicia giggled. "I'm sure she'll find a way for you to make it up to her."

Joey gave her friend a curious look. "You're weathering this awfully well, Alicia. Your chin is scraped, your beautiful wedding gown is dirty and torn, and your wedding just blew up in your face—literally! And you actually have the nerve to look cheerful."

Alicia's quick smile bore out Joey's observation. "Guilty as charged. It's an awful thing to say, but this may actually be one of the best things that ever happened to me. Talk about a lightning bolt from the sky!"

"More like a bomb in the cupboard." Ben joined them, Tess tucked in the circle of his arm. "Fortunately it wasn't a very big bomb, and Eddie boy didn't put it in the right place to do the most damage."

"Damage enough," Joey said with a sigh. "At least no one was badly hurt."

"And I'll see that Pat's lodge is put back together better than new," Alicia said. Her voice had a confidence and assurance that Joey had never heard before. "As for us, my wonderful Ben, my dear friend Ben, my hero Ben . . ."

Ben's jaw tensed as if someone were about to hit him.

"I think that the universe is telling us not to get married."

Ben's eyes widened. His mouth battled with a grin. A grin would not have been an acceptable reaction to being jilted, especially in front of the one doing the jilting.

But Alicia didn't even try to hide her relief. "Go ahead and smile," she told him. "I know your secret."

"What . . . ?"

"When the chips are really down, my friend, true feelings show through all the bull. When that bomb went off, you reached for Tess. That's as it should be. You also reached for Joey, not for me."

His mouth dropped open.

"Pat Haines reached for me. And it was mutual. I reached for him, too."

Alicia leaned over and kissed her ex-fiancé on the

cheek. "I love you, Ben, but not like a woman should love her husband. I mistook respect and security and high romance for true love. And you were so busy saving my butt that you thought for a while that you loved me, but you didn't really. Did you?"

His mouth stretched into a wry grimace of admission.

"You love Joey," Alicia pronounced. "Only a real dunderhead wouldn't see that."

Joey's face flooded with heat, and Alicia just grinned at her.

"Never fear, though," she continued cheerily, "today is going to be my wedding day, one way or another. It would be a shame to waste a wedding. The minister is still in one piece, and my bridesmaids may be a bit on the tattered side, but I imagine they'll still do." She clamped a steely-eyed look on Pat, who was talking to the chief of the fire crew who had made their way from Aspen. "Pat Haines!" She got up, gathered her soiled ten-thousand-dollar gown about her, and marched over to the resort owner. Her demeanor was brave, but Joey could sense the tension in her body. "Pat, you'd damned well better marry me before the minister gets away."

It was Pat's turn to drop his jaw.

"You're going to need my money even more, now that you have a new lodge to build."

"To hell with your money."

She ignored him. "You'd better take it, because I'm a high-maintenance woman. And you'll want to keep me happy. I'm also spoiled, and I can be a brat. You'll be expected to put up with that."

Pat's mouth twitched in the beginnings of a grin.

The sudden pressure of Ben's hand on her arm wrenched Joey's attention closer to home. "As long as there are proposals flying around . . ."

Another jaw dropped. This time it was Joey's. "You've got to be kidding!"

"Nope. Not kidding."

At this point Tess erupted with glee. She and the corgis danced around each other in celebration.

"Tess, would you take the dogs up to the cabin and clean them up, please?" Ben requested.

"Oh, Daddy . . ."

"Go."

"Okay." She complied reluctantly, looking over her shoulder at them every other step.

Joey looked at Ben. Ben looked back, his eyes unwavering.

"You hardly know me," Joey said. That nervous breakdown was just around the corner.

"I know you," he asserted. "You know me. For some people it happens fast. One minute I think you're a pain in the butt, and the next I'm thinking I want to spend my whole life with you. It's crazy, but take a chance on me, Joey."

Joey concentrated on breathing. Surely she was much too tired to make a decision of this magnitude. She knew any marriage was a long shot in today's complicated world. She knew a few weeks' acquaintance wasn't a basis for a serious relationship. An hour ago Ben had been about to take vows with another woman.

As if reading her mind, he told her, "When the

bomb exploded, I was about to tell Alicia we had to call it off. Eddie boy did it for us, though. I guess I should thank him for that, at least."

"You weren't going to marry Alicia?"

"Last-minute revelation. I love you, not her. I'd known it for days, but sometimes it takes things a while to get through my thick skull."

Joey had known it for days also—had known she wanted him, loved him, and couldn't have him. Now she could have him. It was time to put up or shut up. "We'd probably fight a lot."

"What I do best," he said with a grin.

"And I'd want children."

"Tess could put up with brothers and sisters."

Joey tried to breathe.

"Marry me," Ben prodded.

"You can't mean today."

"Hell no. That's rushing it. Next week would be fine." He grinned. "Marry me."

Sometime during the conversation a weight had lifted from Joey's heart. She no longer felt tired. Ben was there looking at her like she was a hot dog and he was one of those blasted corgis. Ben with his lived-in, rugged face that had come to seem so handsome, his brown eyes that saw through to a person's soul, his dear crooked smile that could be arrogant and at the same time wry. He was loyal to a fault. Honorable to the point of madness. Short-tempered at times. Irreverent, sometimes brazen, and often annoying. Dear, wonderful Ben. She loved him so.

"Marry me," he urged.

"You're a persistent cuss."

"That's so. Marry me."

She smiled back at him. "Fast worker, too. A month ago you were giving me a speeding ticket. Now you want me to marry you?"

His grin grew wider. He knew that he'd won, but in this game, Joey hoped, there wasn't going to be a loser.

"Hell, Joey. I'll do you a deal. Marry me, and I'll pay the damned ticket."

EPILOGUE

$\blacklozenge$

I HAD DONE it again—made sure the right guy got the right girl and foiled the villain in his nasty plot. Not that I got much credit for it. All the humans were too absorbed in their own little affairs.

Alicia did marry Pat that very afternoon. How they persuaded the Reverend Thomas to stick around until they could get to Aspen and back—they had to purchase a license—is beyond me. But when you're rich, people tend to do what you want them to. They even managed to get a license on a Saturday. I'd like to try it someday—be rich, that is. I suppose, though, that a fat bank account wouldn't do a dog much good. The bridal couple left for Denver right after the ceremony. The trip was going to be a slow one on the icy roads, and they had a flight to Jamaica early the next day.

Ben didn't seem to mind that Pat was taking his place on the honeymoon. He had his eyes full of Joey. They got married only a week later. I guess Ben wanted to strike while the iron was hot, so to speak, and he didn't want to give Joey a chance to change her mind. No fancy formal wedding for Joey, proprietor of A Perfect Wedding. Ironic, isn't it? She makes her living planning these big marital hooplas for everyone else, yet she had a minister, the minister's wife, one matron of honor, and one best man at her own wedding, set informally in her own house, in the sunroom overlooking the garden. Tess was there, smiling so widely that her face looked ready to split. The best man was Tom, who, by the way, did start a relationship with Teri Schaefer over e-mail. He eventually persuaded her to move to Colorado. Can I take credit for that one, too? The matron of honor was Samantha, of course. Oh yeah, Amy Berenger, my so-called owner, was there too. She got back from Hawaii just two days before the wedding. Dr. Dull came along as well. Unfortunately, wherever Amy goes, he's likely to be right there, and like a toothache, he's hard to ignore.

As for the rest of the cast, Eddie boy got a hefty term in the slammer. Carrie started choosing her dates more cautiously. Tess got her pony—a gift from Alicia that Ben and Joey didn't have the heart to decline, and much later the kid and her "pony" made the Olympic cross-country team. Tess was always good at communicating with animals. Richard Somers never did get those investors to buy into his new enterprise— some Internet deal that probably would have made them a cool million. That's what it made for Mr. Somers. Irene Somers, no longer having Alicia to boss around, married a prominent Denver politician and set about making the city council miserable. And Drover and I went back home with Amy and Jeff. Once again I had to share my space with cranky Miss Molly and Jeff's two brown-nosing border collies.

Stanley didn't make an appearance to comment on how well I'd handled my latest assignment. No doubt he was sulking behind some cloud—or wherever beings like him hang out. He was going to have to admit once again that I was smarter than he thought I was. Poor Stanley. He doesn't deal well with annoyance, and I hope he finds my continuing success very annoying. He owed me a reward and an apology, and he could take all the time he wanted to pay up. It just gave me that much more time to think over my demands.

In the meantime, I was content with two square meals of kibble a day, a soft bed, a mooch or two from the kitchen, and all the ear-scratches I could handle. For a dog, even a dog who isn't quite a dog, this was about as close to Heaven as I could get without a halo and wings.

ABOUT THE AUTHOR

Emily Carmichael, award-winning author of twenty-one novels and novellas, has won praise for both her historical and contemporary romances. She currently lives in her native state of Arizona with her husband and a houseful of dogs.

Look for
Emily Carmichael's
next sparkling romance,

THE REAL THING,

coming from Bantam Books in Fall 2003

With Marilyn Pappano
sometimes miracles do happen . . .

Some Enchanted Season
___57982-7 $5.99/$7.99 Canada

Father to Be
__57985-1 $5.99/$8.99

First Kiss
__58231-3 $5.99/$8.99

Getting Lucky
__58232-1 $6.50/$9.99